PRAISE FOR AMY CLIPSTON

"*The Heart of Splendid Lake* offers a welcome escape in the form of a sympathetic heroine and her struggling lakeside resort. Clipston proficiently explores love and loss, family and friendship in a touching, small-town romance that I devoured in a single day!"

—DENISE HUNTER, BESTSELLING AUTHOR OF THE BLUEBELL INN SERIES

"A touching story of grief, love, and life carrying on, *The Heart of Splendid Lake* engaged my heart from the very first page. Sometimes the feelings we run from lead us to the hope we can't escape, and that's a beautiful thing to see through the eyes of these winning characters. Amy Clipston deftly guides readers on an emotionally satisfying journey that will appeal to fans of Denise Hunter and Becky Wade."

— BETHANY TURNER, AWARD-WINNING AUTHOR OF *PLOT TWIST*

"[Clipston] gives us all we could possibly want from a talented storyteller."

—*RT BOOK REVIEWS*, 4 1/2 STARS, TOP PICK! ON *A SIMPLE PRAYER*

"Amy Clipston's characters are always so endearing and well-developed."

—SHELLEY SHEPARD GRAY, *NEW YORK TIMES* AND
USA TODAY BESTSELLING AUTHOR

"Revealing the underbelly of main characters, a trademark talent of Amy Clipston, makes them relatable and endearing."

—SUZANNE WOODS FISHER, BESTSELLING AUTHOR OF *THE DEVOTED*

"Clipston's heartfelt writing and engaging characters make her a fan favorite."

—*LIBRARY JOURNAL* ON *THE CHERISHED QUILT*

"Clipston delivers another enchanting series starter with a tasty premise, family secrets, and sweet-as-pie romance, offering assurance that true love can happen more than once and second chances are worth fighting for."

—*RT Book Reviews*, 4¹/₂ stars, TOP PICK! on *The Forgotten Recipe*

"[Clipston] will leave readers craving more."

—*RT Book Reviews*, 4¹/₂ stars, TOP PICK! on *A Mother's Secret*

THE HEART OF

Splendid Lake

THE HEART OF

Splendid Lake

AMY CLIPSTON

THOMAS NELSON

Published in Nashville, Tennessee, by Thomas Nelson. Thomas Nelson is a registered trademark of HarperCollins Christian Publishing, Inc.

Thomas Nelson titles may be purchased in bulk for educational, business, fundraising, or sales promotional use. For information, please email SpecialMarkets@ThomasNelson.com.

Library of Congress Cataloging-in-Publication Data

Names: Clipston, Amy, author.
Title: The heart of Splendid Lake / Amy Clipston.
Description: Nashville, Tennessee : Thomas Nelson, [2021] | Summary:
  "Bestselling author Amy Clipston transports readers to a picturesque lakeside
  town in this heartwarming contemporary romance"-- Provided by publisher.
Identifiers: LCCN 2021010577 (print) | LCCN 2021010578 (ebook) | ISBN
  9780785252900 (paperback) | ISBN 9780785252917 (ebook) | ISBN
  9780785252924 (downloadable audio)
Subjects: GSAFD: Christian fiction. | Love stories.
Classification: LCC PS3603.L58 H42 2021 (print) | LCC PS3603.L58 (ebook) |
  DDC 813/.6--dc23
LC record available at https://lccn.loc.gov/2021010577
LC ebook record available at https://lccn.loc.gov/2021010578

Printed in the United States of America

21 22 23 24 25 LSC 10 9 8 7 6 5 4 3 2 1

*In loving memory of my father, Ludwig "Bob" Goebelbecker,
and our wonderful family vacations at Schroon Lake
in New York, the inspiration for this story*

PROLOGUE

Brianna couldn't help but smile as she nosed her prized '93 Mustang into a parking spot right in front of Bookends, just one of the inviting shops lining Main Street. The quaint little bookstore was one of the many reasons she loved her hometown. Splendid Lake, North Carolina, was everything she could ever want—even if she usually had to park a block away from this central thoroughfare.

Still happily singing along with a favorite hard-rock song blasting through the speakers, she turned off the engine. But once she stepped into the cold January air, she shivered and quickly buttoned her sherpa-lined jean jacket, stopping only a second to pluck a long blond hair off one sleeve. Why hadn't she grabbed her heavier coat? At least the bookstore would be warm.

Waiting a few moments as people hustled along the sidewalk in front of her, Brianna took in some of the welcoming signs on that side of the street. The Christmas Shop was open year-round, and the Warner—Splendid Lake's single-screen movie theater, Morningside Bakery, and the Flower Shoppe all sat between its festive façade and Scoops, the local ice cream parlor. Like all the shops, they were owned and operated by local residents.

Glancing to the north, she took in the town hall, library, fire station, and police station rimming the town square. Less than a block away stood the town's hardware store, grocery store, and her fiancé's store, Reese Farm Supply. An only child, Taylor had taken over from his parents when they retired. He had a small apartment nearby and worked hard to serve the farming community. She was proud of him.

That was about it for the town of Splendid Lake, but then there was the lake itself, just a short walk away. She smiled again as she breathed in its familiar smell mixed with the delicious aromas coming from the town's longtime family restaurant, the Splendid Kitchen, and all the shops that served treats and beverages.

She turned to look at the Coffee Bean across the street. She was still so pleased that the shop her best friend, Ava, and Ava's younger sister, Brooklyn, owned and operated had become such a hit. She'd see them both soon. Her plan was to purchase a book for her mother and then pop into the Coffee Bean to pick up three special coffees to take home.

She didn't have time to waste, though. She was meeting Dad in their workshop to determine everything they needed to do to get their family's small marina and lakeside cabin resort ready for its annual opening on Memorial Day weekend. That was a mere four months away, and they always started with a thorough to-do list.

When she yanked open the bookstore's door, a blast of warm air greeted her. She nodded hello to a few acquaintances as she made a beeline for the romance section, where she quickly found the novel her mother was so eager to add to her collection. Pulling her cell phone from a pocket to check the time, she found it was almost ten thirty. She'd promised Dad she'd be home by eleven, so that left just twenty minutes to finish her errands and then make the ten-minute drive home, just around the south end of the lake.

Her phone pinged with a text from Taylor, and she began reading it as she moved through the mystery section on her way toward the cash register. Then she slammed right into someone, one of her purple western boots smashing down on a foot.

Gasping as she righted herself, she looked up at a tall man who stared down at her—with a pained expression. "I'm-I'm so sorry. That was totally my fault! I wasn't paying attention . . ."

Her cheeks burned, and she was surprised to see his face light up with a smile. "No worries. Lucky for me, I decided it was too cold to wear my flip-flops today."

After giving him a nervous laugh, she pocketed her phone. He didn't look familiar, which was also surprising since she'd grown up in Splendid Lake. She either knew or would recognize all the locals, and it was rare for tourists to detour to Splendid Lake in winter.

This guy was certainly handsome, though. His baby-blue eyes presented a striking contrast to his thick, light-brown hair cut short on the sides. Longer locks on top of his head were windblown, which, coupled with the stubble on his chin, gave him a rugged look. He was maybe two or three inches taller than Taylor's five eleven, making him a good eight or nine inches above her own height.

He nodded toward the paperback in her arms. "I'm looking for a good read. What have you got there?"

She held out the book. "This is the third novel in a series my mother is enjoying."

"What's it about?"

"Oh, you know, the typical romance. Boy meets girl, girl dislikes boy, then girl likes boy, and finally boy and girl fall in love, get married, and live happily ever after."

"Huh. You said it's a series. Should I start with the first book?" He grinned.

She returned the grin. "I suspect you'd like something in this section more." She pivoted and searched the shelves behind her, then spotted a familiar series and pulled out the first volume. "Here you go. My dad just finished this one last week and loved it."

He took the book from her, then briefly examined its cover front and back before once again meeting her gaze. "Thanks for the recommendation."

"You're welcome." She looked to her right and then to her left in conspirator fashion. "I'll even fill you in on a little secret my dad told me."

"Oh?" His eyes danced with interest.

"You might think the butler did it, but he didn't."

The man laughed at her dramatic whisper, the sound warm and contagious.

"Enjoy." She grinned again and gave him a wave before heading to the register, where only one customer was ahead of her, being waited on by a friend of her mother's.

"Hey, Mrs. Lang," she said when it was her turn.

"Good morning, *Miss Porter*!" Then she smiled. "Again, please call me Emma. If I remember correctly, you're about twenty-six years old now. You're allowed to call me by my first name."

"I'll try." Brianna smiled as she handed her the book.

"Oh, this is a good one."

"Great. Mom's eager to keep going with this series." She lifted her wallet from her purse.

After Emma handed Brianna's credit card back to her, she placed her purchase and a receipt in a bag. "Tell your mom hello, and have a great day."

"Thanks. You have a great one too."

As Brianna pushed open the front door to leave, she glanced to her right and spotted the same handsome man looking at her with an amused expression. He nodded, and she returned the gesture before exiting the store. He'd been fun to talk to, but she doubted she'd ever see him again.

A few snow flurries tickled her nose as she put the bag in her car's passenger seat, and she shivered again when she started toward a crosswalk on her way to the Coffee Bean. Thanks to her little mishap in Bookends, she'd really have to hurry now. But then her cell phone rang, and unwilling to step on anyone else's toes, she stepped aside to stand near a shop window. Pulling the phone from her pocket, she read *Mom* on the screen, then unlocked it and held the phone to her ear as she started down the sidewalk again.

"Hey, Mom. I got your book. I'm just running into the Coffee Bean and then—"

"Brianna." Mom's voice sounded strange. Throaty. "Come home. It's-it's your dad."

When her mother began to sob, Brianna froze in place, every plan forgotten.

CHAPTER 1

ONE WEEK LATER

*B*rianna leaned against a wall in the family room of the lake house she'd lived in her whole life, then shut her eyes and took a deep breath. If only she could stop her frayed nerves from practically vibrating. And the smell of strong coffee and multiple casseroles had overwhelmed her senses so much that she'd had to swallow bile back from her throat.

All the walls seemed to be closing in on her. Despite the murmur of their conversations, surely the crowd milling around could hear her heart hammering against her rib cage.

A warm hand caressed her shoulder, and a comforting voice sounded next to her ear. "Brie? Are you okay?"

She nodded as she opened her eyes and found Taylor staring right into her face. Leaning down like that, he was so close that the familiar musky aroma of his aftershave presented an unwelcome addition to her senses. But his deep-brown eyes were full of concern.

"I'm fine." She pushed a lock of her long straight hair behind one shoulder. "I'm just feeling a bit overwhelmed."

He opened a bottle of water and handed it to her. "Here. Take this. You need to stay hydrated."

"Thank you." She took a long drink, enjoying the cold liquid on her parched throat. But that did little to help her nerves. Everything felt so wrong, so off-kilter, and it was. Her life had shattered a week ago, and she craved some time alone so she could begin to comprehend what happened. Today she'd sat in church and stared at the coffin that held her precious father, then watched it being lowered into the cold, hard ground. She needed to catch her breath.

It all seemed so surreal, like a nightmare. Just a week ago she and Dad had been about to make plans for readying their resort for its opening in May. But now he was gone. Forever. How was she supposed to go on without him?

"Brianna."

She turned as Dr. Sabella approached. Splendid Lake's pediatrician always wore a kind smile. She nodded at him and cleared her throat.

"I'm so sorry about your father." He shook his head. "Such a good, hardworking man."

"Thank you." Her voice sounded hoarse, but she wasn't surprised given how hard she'd fought all day to hold back fresh sobs. She had to be strong for her mother.

Taylor slipped his arm around her waist. "I still can't believe he's gone. We had so many great times with him. It seems like just yesterday we were out in a boat fishing with him, and if we weren't fishing, we were swimming or roasting marshmallows on the beach."

"I'm sure you all have many wonderful memories of Martin," Dr. Sabella said.

Finished with her water, Brianna set the empty bottle on the end table beside her.

Mrs. Sabella sidled up to her husband. She was a petite woman with short-cropped hair dyed such a bright red that it always reminded Brianna of the Raggedy Ann doll she'd had as a child. "Oh, Brianna, you poor dear. We are all so sorry. I saw your father at the post office the day before it happened." She patted Brianna's hand. "Had he been ill?"

Brianna shook her head, and Taylor rubbed his hand over her back as if to tell her he would handle this. "No, this came as a complete shock. He never said anything about feeling bad, and he saw Dr. Weissman for his annual physical and routine tests just a couple of months ago. The family was told massive heart attacks can just happen without any detection or warning."

While Taylor said more, Brianna looked across the room to where her two sisters, both older, sat on either side of her mother on the sofa. A long line of people had made their way there to express their condolences.

Her stomach constricted as she took in the grief etched on her mother's face, resembling a porcelain doll's. Her skin was white, making her graying blond hair appear darker than usual. Her beautiful face was gaunt, as if she'd lost at least ten pounds, and the lines around her mouth and dark shadows taking residence under her powder-blue eyes made her look closer to seventy than her true age of sixty. The constant stream of tears flowing down her face had made her cheeks puffy and her eyes bloodshot.

Cassie, the middle daughter, nodded as one of their neighbors spoke to her, and Brianna found herself thinking about the differences between them. At twenty-eight, Cassie was two years older than Brianna, and while all three sisters had inherited their mother's golden-blond hair, somehow Cassie had received their maternal grandmother's piercing green eyes. Brianna had always secretly coveted those eyes over her and Jenna's brown ones, but now she was glad she had her father's eyes.

At the moment, though, Cassie's beautiful eyes were red, and her high cheekbones were splotchy, evidence that she'd spent most of the day crying. Also thinking about how she envied her sisters' identical five-seven height, Brianna noted how Cassie's simple black, short-sleeved dress showcased her trim, fit body. Her sculpted arms were evidence of the hours she spent in the gym when she wasn't working as an editor at a publishing house in Los Angeles. But at least Brianna had managed to stay trim as well. After all, she got plenty of exercise working around the resort, even in winter.

Jenna, her oldest sister, was holding Mom's hand as they both listened to Olivia Hernandez, who with her husband, Eddie, owned the Lakeview Inn next door. Jenna's hair was styled in a flawless french twist, and her makeup accentuated her own high cheekbones. Also wearing a classic black dress—although certainly more expensive than Cassie's—Jenna was beautiful and sophisticated. She definitely looked like the high-class, New York City corporate lawyer she was. She always reminded Brianna of a runway model, ready to strut her stuff down the catwalk, and Brianna often wondered if she secretly used the most expensive age-reversing skin care products she could find. At thirty-two she appeared ten years younger.

Both sisters had been in more than one relationship, but none had lasted. Still, they'd been happy for her when she and Taylor announced their engagement.

As Mr. Hernandez took his turn speaking to Mom, his wife moved on to the kitchen, where a buffet with dishes like homemade lasagna, green bean casserole, and an array of desserts prepared by friends and neighbors covered the table and counters. Brianna was tempted to go with her. The family room felt too small and too crowded, and for once she was glad both her parents had been only children like Taylor was. She had no aunts, uncles, or cousins to add to the confusion, and all four of her grandparents had died long ago.

She spotted George Wellington, the town's police chief, sitting in Dad's favorite recliner. That's where her father had watched the Motor Trend Network to enjoy his favorite car shows.

"Right, Brianna?" Taylor's voice crashed through her thoughts, slamming her back to the present. Taylor and the Sabellas were all staring at her with renewed concern in their eyes.

Heat crept up her neck. "I'm sorry. I didn't hear what you said."

"Dr. Sabella said your dad's absence will be a great loss when the resort opens this year." He gave her hand a gentle squeeze.

"Right."

Dr. Sabella raised his cup of coffee and took a sip, then said, "You and your dad ran this place together. How are you going to manage everything without him?"

Brianna opened her mouth to respond but then closed it. She was just trying to make it through this day, and she had no idea what she'd do tomorrow or the next week, let alone throughout the resort's season.

Taylor squeezed her hand again. "We'll take it one day at a time."

"Well, we're here if you need us," Mrs. Sabella said.

Dr. Sabella nodded. "That's right, Brianna. We all stick together in Splendid Lake."

"Thank you," she croaked as the couple stepped away to talk to her family. She turned to Taylor. "Would you please get me another bottle of water?"

"Of course." He kissed her cheek before turning toward the kitchen.

Brianna folded her arms as she watched him move through the crowd, then grasp her bottle of water while talking to Ava and her husband, Dylan Burns. When two more friends joined them, her pulse picked up speed. Now was her chance to get out of the house and breathe—*alone*.

She slipped away toward the hall, then once she'd made it past the laundry room, she took a right through the next doorway and sped past the large board where keys hung behind the desk where cabin guests checked in. Then she sprinted out the guest entrance door.

Met by a wall of chilly air, she breathed it in, allowing it to fill her lungs before she exhaled. Shivering, she rubbed her arms, wishing she'd thought to grab a coat to pull over her thin, long-sleeved blouse and skirt. At least she still wore the black sweater she'd put on before the service. Even as a child she'd learned the sanctuary was always cold no matter the time of year.

But the chill felt good as it seeped into her skin. It was a relief to feel *something* after spending the afternoon as a numb shell, listening to her mother and sisters sob first in a pew at the front of the church and then at the gravesite. She still didn't know how she'd kept her emotions in check, but she believed her father would want her to take care of the rest of his family. So she'd forced back her own sobs as tears streamed down her face. Taylor always said she needed no makeup, and today she was glad she'd worn none.

Brianna walked the length of the wraparound porch, past the row of rocking chairs and porch swing, until she came to the back steps of the large, two-story, cedar-shingled house she'd always loved. She loved everything about their property. Beautiful Splendid Lake glittered in the early evening light, and when she glanced to her right, she could see Paradise River and then Willard Mountain State Park in the distance.

When she felt a brush against her bare leg, she looked down to see her black-and-white tuxedo cat blinking up at her. Oh, how she loved Bucky's adorable black face with its permanent white "base-ball stitching" that stretched from his forehead to his little nose and complemented his "milk mustache" and white whiskers. She smiled. The cat's purr always reminded her of a car engine.

"Hey, Bucky." Brianna stroked the cat's head, and he closed his eyes as his purr grew louder. He was the resort's resident pet, a favorite among the regulars who enjoyed his visits to their cabins in search of treats and chin rubs. "Oh, sweetie. I need to fill your bowl." She glanced behind her and found both his food bowl and water dish half full. "Cassie must have already taken care of you. I'm sorry I forgot."

The cat gave Brianna's shin another rub and then trotted toward the front of the house. "See you later, buddy," Brianna called after him.

She began making her way down the porch steps, her uncomfortable four-inch wedges clomping on the wood. She'd always preferred jeans, T-shirts, and hoodies to dresses, and for sure western boots to heels, but she'd do anything to look good for Dad today.

A crisp breeze whipped over her, and Brianna hugged her arms to her chest as she tottered past the row of twelve cabins her family rented in summer and early fall, then toward the beach down the hill. Their little resort was the only one on Splendid Lake, and it was her grandfather's legacy, passed down to her father. Grandpa Porter purchased the land and built the resort while at the same time private homes popped up all around it. His dream was to offer cozy cabins for families to rent as an affordable and fun getaway. Now she thought about her father's dream: to keep the resort alive.

Dad, I'll work hard in your memory and make you proud. It was a promise she'd whispered even as his body was carried out of the house on a gurney.

The voices behind her faded away as she took in the whole of their property. To her left was the small convenience store and bait shop, which was next to the barn where Dad kept the lawn mower, ladder, and other large equipment and tools.

Once down the hill, she stopped to pull off her shoes, then held them by their straps as she continued. Gazing at the lake, she envisioned the floating raft they'd bring out for sunbathers when the water turned warm enough. Then her gaze moved to the marina and workshop, the latter next to a large pole barn where they kept their two dozen aluminum johnboats until it was time to put them in the water for guests and visitors to rent them. She and her father had spent hours working side by side there.

Tears stung her eyes, and her lower lip trembled. Dad had taught her everything he knew about fixing boats and small engine repair. He'd been her mentor, her business partner, her best friend, along with Ava. But now he was gone, and she would have to work in that shop alone without his guidance.

She picked up her pace as she approached the beach. The rocks at the edge of the water were cold and bit into the soles of her feet, but she ignored the pain and looked up at the cloudless, dark-blue sky. Without her father, how would she handle all the necessary work before opening the resort? Her mother would still help with things like cleaning, of course, but she and Dad had managed most of the business with minimal outside help.

Another crisp breeze drifted off the shoreline, bringing with it the smell of the lake. Up close, its scent wasn't quite as inviting and fresh in winter and spring as it was in the summer and fall, but she didn't mind. She loved the water all year long.

As the cold air seeped through her clothes, though, she shivered once more and headed toward the two Adirondack chairs where her parents had enjoyed watching the sunset nearly every night since she could remember, leaving her to tend to any needs their guests had. She hadn't minded. And somehow the guests knew the chairs weren't for them. They belonged to their hosts, Martin and Lois Porter.

A lump of sorrow swelled in her throat as she sank into the chair on the left—Dad's chair—and tried in vain to block the vision of her parents holding hands as beautiful colors spread across the western horizon.

The quiet lapping of the tiny waves on the shoreline filled the silence, and in the distance, a dog barked. The aroma of a wood-burning fire from a nearby chimney floated over her as she lost herself in memories of her father teaching her how to swim, barbecuing on the Fourth of July, helping her and her sisters find just the right Christmas tree . . .

Tears swam in her eyes and spilled down her cheeks as twilight formed.

When she heard a rustling beside her, she turned and gasped as a tall man approached her.

"I'm sorry." He held up his hands as a hesitant expression crossed his face in the waning light. He jammed his thumb toward a copse of maple trees behind him. "I tripped on a fallen branch over there and nearly fell on my face. I thought for sure you'd heard me."

She blinked up at him and shook her head. "No. I didn't."

He wasn't one of the locals, yet something about him seemed so familiar. She felt as if she'd spoken to him somewhere, shared a con-versation with him. Then it hit her. He was the man she'd smacked into at the bookstore the week before. They'd had a brief but delightful exchange about books, and now his warm laugh echoed in her mind. For a moment she considered asking him if he remembered her, but it would be awkward if he didn't, and she didn't have the energy to deal with that kind of embarrassment today. Clad in jeans and boots, he also looked as though he was just searching for a place to relax.

He gave her a sheepish smile. "I suppose I could have kept the embarrassing details of my clumsiness to myself, then."

"I guess so." She swiped her palms down her face to ensure all evidence of her despondency was gone, then pushed herself up from the chair. "I was just leaving."

"No. Wait. I was going to ask if I could join you, not run you off." He pointed toward the sky. "I think the sunsets here at Splendid Lake are the best in all of North Carolina."

Brianna glanced up toward the heavens, where the horizon seemed to mock her somber mood with its cheerful explosion of yellow, orange, and red hues, all chasing each other across the darkening sky.

"Don't you agree?" His expression seemed to plead with her. Why did this stranger care if she enjoyed the sunset?

"Sure." She shrugged, even though she did agree with him. Everything about Splendid Lake was the best of North Carolina, but now she'd have to try to enjoy it without her precious father. Another stab of grief pierced her heart.

The man pointed to the other chair. Mom's chair. "Would it be all right if I sat quietly beside you and enjoyed the view?"

"Suit yourself." She settled back as he folded his long torso into the seat beside her.

As they sat in silence for a few minutes, she again peered out over the lake. Her mind flashed with images of everything her father would miss, like walking her down the aisle someday—once she and Taylor got around to setting a date. And Dad would never meet his grandchildren or teach them how to fish or skip stones.

Her eyes stung again as she experienced another crush of heartache. *Don't cry in front of this stranger! Be strong!*

"You look cold," the man said. "The chill doesn't bother me. Would you like my coat? I really don't need it."

Brianna faced him, astounded by his concern for her. "I'm okay. But thanks."

She fished through the pockets of her sweater in search of the wad of tissues she'd stowed there before leaving for the church, but all she found was her cell phone, still powered off. She hadn't expected any calls, but she also hadn't felt the need to talk to anyone who reached out. She could use a tissue, though.

As if reading her mind, he held out a napkin. "Here. I stuck this in my pocket when I stopped for a snack on my way here. It's clean."

"Thanks." She wiped her eyes and nose, then waited for him to ask what was wrong. But he remained silent, his eyes trained on the lake, and her body relaxed.

The sunset faded and darkness crept in, bringing with it another chilly breeze. Once again she regretted not grabbing her coat. A flashlight would have been good, too, but at least she had a light app on her phone.

"Have you ever seen a sunset on the Outer Banks?"

Brianna startled at his voice. For a moment she'd forgotten he was there. "I have." The gravel in her throat came out in a rasp of words.

"They're spectacular, but I still prefer the sunsets here."

She nodded. She preferred everything here. After all, this was her home.

She angled her body toward him and studied his profile, a silhouette against the lights glowing on the marina's pier behind him. Who was this stranger? And why had he chosen to sit next to her as if he knew what she'd just realized—she didn't need to be alone as much as she just needed some quiet company.

Out of the corner of her eye, she spotted the beam of a flashlight bouncing down the beach. Another silhouette trudged behind it, this one tall and lean. A man's voice called her name.

Taylor had found her.

"Brie!" His voice held a thread of panic. "Are you out here?"

She sighed. Her brief time of solace was over, and she had to go face the crowd at the house for her mother's sake. Then guilt rolled over her. There Taylor was frantically searching for her, and she was hiding out like an immature, selfish child. She needed to be an adult and thank the friends who'd come to express their condolences and emotionally support her family.

But didn't she have the right to be a little selfish when her father, one of the most important people in her life, had been snatched away from her without warning?

With another sigh, she picked up her shoes, then stood. When her unexpected companion looked up at her, she swallowed back another mouthful of sadness. "I have to go."

"I hope . . . everything gets better for you."

"Thanks." Brianna retrieved her cell phone from her pocket, then turned it on and activated the flashlight app before gingerly walking over the rocks toward Taylor. Glancing at her notifications, she found she'd missed several calls from both him and Ava. Now shame rippled through her. They'd been worried about her. Running out when Taylor wasn't looking had been wrong, but she'd known he would insist on going with her when she longed for silence.

She waved her cell phone in the air as she picked up her pace, trying to ignore how the rocks nipped at the bottoms of her feet. "Taylor! I'm over here."

His flashlight beam found her face, blinding her for a moment, and then he raced toward her. "Brie! I was worried about you."

"I just needed a minute."

"A minute? I've been searching for nearly *forty-five* minutes. You don't even have a coat on, and you must be freezing!" He pulled off his suit jacket. "Put this on."

"I'm fine." But she shuddered as he held open the garment for her, then stepped into its warmth. She slipped her phone back into her sweater pocket, and then Taylor threaded the fingers of one hand with hers. She appreciated the feel of his warm skin.

"Why did you turn off your phone?"

"I just never turned it back on after the service."

They walked together up the hill, the din of voices growing louder and louder, and the muscles in Brianna's shoulders coiled with tension as Taylor went on.

"Ava and I searched the house. Then I checked the garage to see if your Mustang was still there. After that, I started looking for you outside. Why didn't you tell me where you were going?"

"I'm sorry. I just needed some time to think."

Gratefully, Taylor didn't press her further. She glanced back toward the beach, wondering if the stranger was still sitting in Mom's chair. It was too dark to tell. If only she could have stayed and enjoyed the tranquility of the lake, stranger or no.

But she had to summon the courage to go back inside. Not just for her mother but for Dad too.

CHAPTER 2

*S*cott gazed down the beach as the woman walked barefoot across the rocks toward the man holding a flashlight. They were both outlined by the lights on the pier, and he could just make out his saying something to her, then holding out his jacket. She stepped into it, and then he took her hand before steering her toward the hill leading to the rest of the Splendid Lake Cabins and Marina resort property.

As the flashlight beam bounced up the hill, he settled into the chair, but his back started to ache. He never understood why so many lakefront and beachfront properties had Adirondack chairs. Although they were pleasant to look at, they were so uncomfortable. He'd contemplated whether his six-foot-two frame was the problem, but one of his former—and petite—girlfriends had agreed with him, confirming his opinion.

He sighed and looked across the lake. He'd discovered this place last summer while meeting a client about a new strip mall a couple of towns over. On a whim, he'd driven here and was intrigued by the small-town feel. Splendid Lake proper had a single stoplight near its charming square, and little shops lined its quaint downtown area. Customers had to drive at least thirty minutes to find a big-box store if they craved more variety than the local stores could provide.

After parking in a public lot, he'd walked out to the lake, where families played in the water, fished, swam, and built sandcastles on the public beach. Beautiful homes surrounded the lake on either side. He'd traveled the world over the years, but nothing was quite as picturesque as Splendid Lake. He'd been taken by the town's simplicity, including its lack of commercialism. No chain hotels or restaurants rimmed the shoreline or cluttered the town. He felt as if he'd stepped back in time. To a simpler time.

He'd also driven out to take a look at the small resort, and later his research revealed it was family owned, a rarity these days. Then an idea hit him. Not only was the resort the only one here, but it was open only in summer and early fall. Those two facts presented a golden opportunity for him and his real estate investment firm.

It had taken him months, but he'd finally convinced Brad, his business partner and best friend, to support him in offering to buy the resort. They had the backing of Phil Young, Brad's wealthy father, as an investor, and after viewing what the property had to offer on the owners' online reservation site, the plan was to modernize the cabins, including installing fireplaces and another source of heat as well. He also wanted to add a year-round retreat center with a spa and exercise facility, which would appeal to a more professional and affluent group of guests and visitors. The property still had plenty of undeveloped acreage behind the main house and cabins.

With these upgrades, he could keep the resort open even in winter and bring in a nice profit for their firm. And of course he would invest in an advertising campaign, plus a better website. Then hopefully he would make their firm a lot more money after he'd flipped the resort and then sold it.

Scott had planned to come back to talk to the owner well before the new year, but his schedule had been packed with meetings and travel obligations until last week. He'd booked a room at the Lakeview Inn next door, which, unlike the resort, was open year-round. Then he'd driven up from Charlotte and planned to talk to the owner of the resort the next morning—a man named Martin Porter. But right after a quick stop at the town's bookstore, Brad had to call him back to Charlotte about another deal before he could even check in. He'd never talked to Martin Porter by phone. Through experience he'd learned that showing up in person to introduce an offer tended to win over potential sellers more easily.

Today he'd finally been free to come back, but thanks to an unexpected phone call and then an accident on Interstate 40, he'd made it to Splendid Lake later than expected. When he arrived at the Lakeview Inn, he found the owners had left him a note on the door, telling him he was their only guest that weekend and they'd be back soon. They also suggested he visit the restaurant in town. He'd considered it, but the snack he'd picked up had been substantial enough that he'd decided to take a walk along the lake instead.

Zipping up his heavier coat, he'd grabbed a flashlight from his car, then sauntered down to the water. Although the crisp breeze threatened to eventually send him somewhere warm, he enjoyed the absence of the city noise he'd become accustomed to—constant traffic, trains, and sirens, as well as planes rumbling overhead.

When he spotted that young woman sitting on a chair, curiosity gripped him. She wore clothes that looked much too light for dropping temperatures. She'd also taken off her shoes, and as she peered out toward the lake, he could see she was crying.

With just enough daylight left, he'd taken in her pained expression, making his insides curl. He was sure he recognized the same all-encompassing bereavement he'd experienced as a child. Waves of sadness could still pull him under and threaten to drown him at times. They appeared in his dreams or when something reminded him of his childhood. But he'd dismissed his own emotions and focused so much on what he was seeing that he'd managed to trip over a downed branch and almost fall.

When he'd approached her, she looked up at him, and he recognized her as the woman at the bookstore. But the agony on her face this time had nearly taken his breath away. He'd also been once again struck by her natural beauty—golden-brown eyes; long, blond hair that hung past her shoulders; an oval-shaped face coupled with high cheekbones. He'd enjoyed their brief encounter, and he'd been intrigued enough to wish he could get to know her. But he'd also noted the small diamond glinting on her ring finger.

At first he'd considered just nodding and continuing his trek, leaving her alone in her sadness, but his feet seemed cemented in place. For some reason he longed to comfort her. He didn't want to appear too bold or forward, though, which was why he hadn't mentioned their earlier meeting. Still, he'd been surprised when she'd agreed to allow him to sit with her.

At one point, he'd been almost certain he saw her shoulders relax, as if his company was a comfort to her. But that seemed like a ridiculous notion. He was a stranger to her. But he hoped his presence had offered her some sort of relief.

When the man on the beach called out, Scott was almost sure he'd said "Brie." He'd been relieved to see the guy give her his jacket before escorting her up the hill. The main house was lit up as if the family who lived there—the Porter family, he assumed—was having a party. Perhaps he'd been wrong about seeing grief on her face. Maybe this Brie was a guest who'd just had a bad day.

Scott looked toward the lake now shrouded in darkness, and he longed for a hot shower and warm bed. Hopefully, the Hernandezes would be back at the inn by now, ready to check him in.

He stood, then switched on his flashlight and strolled back down the beach and up the hill to the large, two-story, red-brick colonial inn with a sweeping, wraparound porch, inviting with its rocking chairs and glider. He made his way to the street side of the house and spotted a gray Toyota 4Runner parked in the long rock driveway next to his pride and joy, his 1971 dark-blue Plymouth Barracuda with a black convertible top. After taking his bag out of the trunk, he headed for the steps.

"Mr. Gibson?"

A woman had stepped out onto the porch. Short with graying black hair, she reminded him of the first office manager he and Brad hired—a lovely soul they hated to lose when she retired. This older woman wore thick glasses with red frames, and a warm smile revealed a gap between her two front teeth.

"You must be Mrs. Hernandez. I'm Scott." He held out his hand, and when she shook it, she cringed a little. "I'm sorry my hand is cold," he told her. "I wasn't hungry, so I went for a walk and wound up sitting by the lake."

"It's no problem. And call me Olivia. Please come inside." She beckoned him to follow her, and they stepped into a comfortable-looking seating area with a desk. After he'd checked in, she invited him to leave his bag by the stairs and then led him into a large kitchen, where he breathed in the distinct scent of apple cobbler or maybe pie.

He took in the beautiful oak cabinets with a matching island in the center of the room, granite countertops, and colorful tile back-splash against one wall. A candle sat burning on a far counter, and Scott surmised that was the source of the delicious aroma.

"Eddie!" Olivia called into a room beyond another doorway.

"Come meet our guest!" She smiled at Scott. "My husband will be right out."

An equally short, rotund man with thinning gray hair and a gray mustache stepped into the kitchen and held out his hand. "Hello. I'm Eddie Hernandez. Welcome to the Lakeview Inn."

Scott shook his hand. "Thank you."

"Are you hungry now?" Oliva asked. "Would you like a snack? Or a drink?"

Scott rubbed his chilled hands together. "Do you have any decaf coffee?"

"Of course. I'll put some on." She fluttered over to another counter and quickly placed a filter in a waiting coffee maker.

Eddie gestured toward a long rectangular table surrounded by eight chairs. "Have a seat. How was your drive from Charlotte?"

"I left the office later than I expected, but that seems to happen pretty often these days. Then there was an accident on I-40, which delayed me even more. But other than that, it was fine." He hung his jacket on the back of a chair, then sat.

Eddie leaned back against the counter with the candle. "I'm so sorry we weren't here when you arrived. We had to attend a funeral today, and then we were invited to spend time with the family after the service. We didn't want to say no since we've known them for years. Then we just lost track of time."

"I'm sorry to hear about your loss."

"Such a shock." Olivia clucked her tongue as the coffee maker began humming and belching to life, sending the scent of its brew across the large room to blend with the apple aroma. "Martin Porter seemed to be in such good shape. He always stayed so busy."

Scott stilled as the name twirled through his mind. "Martin Porter? The owner of—"

"The resort next door? Yes, he owned the place." Eddie pointed toward the wall in the direction of the resort. "We've known him since we bought this inn twenty years ago."

Olivia had been rooting around in the cabinets, and now she brought a container to the table. "Such a nice man, and he was only sixty-three. So close to our age. He dropped dead of a heart attack. He and his wife, Lois, have a lovely family. They've raised three beautiful daughters. Two of them moved away. The oldest is a lawyer in New York City, and the middle daughter works at a publishing house in California." She pointed to the container. "Have a chocolate chip cookie."

Dismay had bolted through Scott, and as Olivia continued to talk about the bereaved family, his mind churned like a cyclone. Martin Porter was dead. His gut twisted as both disappointment and guilt swarmed him. He was disappointed he wouldn't be able to make the offer he'd ironed out with Brad and Phil—at least not right away—but he also felt guilty for even thinking about that as the owner's family mourned his loss.

Olivia set a mug of coffee in front of him, along with a spoon, a stack of sweetener packets, and a small pitcher he assumed contained some sort of creamer. Then she brought mugs for Eddie and herself before sitting beside her husband and facing Scott. "Are you okay, Mr. Gibson?"

"Oh yes." He fastened a bright smile onto his lips. "The coffee smells fantastic, and please call me Scott." He stirred in two packets of sweetener and some creamer before taking a sip.

"What brings you to town?" Eddie asked.

Scott cleared his throat as he tried to think of a viable reason aside from trying to make a deal on a dead man's property. "Business. I'm in commercial real estate, and I'm looking at a property nearby. I just like to stop in Splendid Lake when I come up this way."

Olivia touched her husband's hand. "Oh yes. We just fell in love with it when we visited more than two decades ago. As soon as this place came up for sale, we snatched it up, right, Eddie?" She gazed at her husband, and a look passed between them.

"It's magical." Eddie picked up a cookie and took a bite, a smile on his face as he chewed. Then a frown appeared. "I keep wondering what Lois will do now that Martin is gone. That's a big place for her and her youngest to run on their own."

Olivia shook her head. "It will be tough."

Scott nodded as he lifted a cookie from the container. He took a bite and considered what to do next. He knew one thing for sure. He'd never prey on a grieving family. He'd head back to Charlotte tomorrow and give them at least a couple of weeks of privacy before returning to make his offer. If Porter's death meant his wife and daughter wouldn't be able to run the resort on their own, the deal might even be just what they needed. He also hoped he'd be the first investor with an in, because he still wanted to put his plan into motion.

A new thought occurred to him. What if the sad woman on the beach was the youngest daughter—the one who'd stayed?

CHAPTER 3

*T*ake good care of Mom." Cassie hugged a shivering Brianna as they stood near the departure entrance at Charlotte Douglas International Airport. It was the middle of February now, and the morning air was colder than ever.

"I'll try." Brianna turned toward Jenna. "I wish you could stay longer."

"I do too, but it's been three weeks, and I have to get back to the firm." Jenna pulled Brianna in for a fierce hug. Her oldest sister always seemed determined to squeeze the life out of her. "Call me if you need anything, okay?" she'd whispered into Brianna's ear as if her offer were a secret.

"I will."

Brianna stuck her hands into her coat pockets as her sisters pulled the handles out of their suitcases in unison. "Text me when you get home so I'll know you made it."

"I will." Cassie blew her a kiss.

"Me too. Love you, kid," Jenna called over her shoulder as the two women headed into the terminal side by side.

"Love you too."

Brianna watched them being swept into the throng of passengers, then hopped back into the driver's seat of her father's black 2013 Chevrolet Tahoe. The familiar aroma of leather and the lingering scent of her father's spicy aftershave drifted through the SUV as she eased it into traffic.

Her mind raced as she steered toward the airport exit, then followed the signs for Interstate 85 south. The two weeks following Dad's funeral had blown by in a painful blur. For one thing, she and Mom had been caught up in a whirlwind of paperwork and lawyer visits. As an attorney, Jenna helped, but her expertise didn't have much to do with inheritance.

"Besides," her oldest sister had said, "you'll be the one here with Mom."

Everything had turned out the way the family had expected. Dad left everything to Mom in his will. He'd also had a small life insurance policy that covered the funeral expenses, and they were grateful for that provision. Now all the legal work was done, including a new will for Mom and paperwork giving Brianna power of attorney if it was ever needed. Mom had given her a healthcare power of attorney as well, just in case anything ever happened to her. "We just never know," she'd said with tears in her eyes.

Brianna still had to check out their health insurance. She wasn't sure what bills connected to Dad's death might arrive, but she wanted to be ready.

This new normal was still such a foreign place to navigate. Although she'd managed to get through all that paperwork, Mom had turned into someone Brianna didn't recognize. Gone were her beautiful smile, her contagious laugh, her sunny moods, and her love of cooking elaborate meals nearly every night. Brianna had become accustomed to walking into the kitchen to find chicken cacciatore complete with side dishes, or stuffed peppers, or broiled tilapia parmesan, or lasagna with garlic bread sitting on the table waiting for her and Dad.

Now, however, Mom seemed stuck in a dark, murky fog, refusing to get dressed or eat and walking only as far as the recliner in her bedroom, where she'd stare into space when she wasn't crying. This change in her mother not only crushed Brianna's heart but left her feeling hollowed out. Daily she'd tried to coax Mom into dressing, taking a walk outside, or eating more than half a piece of toast. But nothing worked. Cassie and Jenna had tried, too, with no success.

This morning Mom had refused to ride to the airport with her. She'd dissolved into tears as Jenna and Cassie said good-bye. Her sobs had nearly torn Brianna apart, and both her sisters had left Mom's bedroom wiping their own eyes before walking out to the SUV with their suitcases bumping along behind them on the rock driveway.

She'd understood when her sisters said they had to return to their jobs, and yet she hadn't. Didn't they know how much Mom needed them? How much *she* needed them? But now they were both gone, leaving her to pick up the pieces and carry on while they returned to their normal routines. At least Cassie had helped her thoroughly clean the house while Jenna returned phone calls to clients.

At some point she and her mother had to meet with Dad's accountant. He lived in the next town, but she hoped that visit could wait until Mom was up to it.

She merged onto Interstate 85 south, heading toward 321 north on her way to Interstate 40 west, surprised to see so much traffic this time of day. But she supposed lots of people left the city for the weekend on a Friday, even in winter.

Once she was up to speed, she flipped on the cruise control and powered on the Bluetooth stereo. A playlist with her favorite hard-rock bands serenaded her as she started her nearly three-hour drive back to

Splendid Lake. She tried to relax while singing along, but memories of her father pummeled her like waves after a storm had blown past the coast.

She allowed more tears to flow, hoping a cathartic cry would give her strength before she arrived home to deal with her despondent mother. She had to be strong. She was all Mom had now, and Dad would expect her to take care of the woman he'd loved more than anyone.

Choosing not to stop somewhere for lunch, she arrived home mid-afternoon, then parked the Tahoe in the three-car garage attached to the house. As she walked inside, she took a deep breath.

"Mom, I'm back!" she called as she hung the Tahoe's keys on the pegboard by the back door. The house was completely silent as she walked through the kitchen, where she dropped off her purse before heading down the hallway that led to the master suite and her father's office as well as the laundry room.

When she found the bedroom door closed, she stilled, shutting her eyes and taking another deep, cleansing breath. She knocked softly as she leaned her ear against the door.

"Mom? Are you up?" She held her breath, waiting for a response. When she heard none, she quietly turned the knob and peeked inside. Mom was leaning back in her recliner, softly snoring.

Brianna's shoulders slumped as a strange relief filled her. At least Mom was sleeping instead of staring into space or crying. She closed the door, careful to keep the noise to a minimum, then jogged up the stairs to her bedroom. She stripped out of her clothes and pulled on a favorite work ensemble—a pair of faded, grease-stained jeans; her pink, long-sleeved thermal shirt; her plain gray hooded sweatshirt; and her favorite worn, purple western boots. Then she pulled her hair into a ponytail and stuck it through the back of her pink ball cap that sported a silver Mustang logo.

Last, she pulled off her engagement ring and slipped it onto a gold chain she then fastened around her neck. She never wore her ring when she worked in the shop. Her father had warned her of the risk of losing a finger if her ring ever got caught on a boat motor. In the workshop nearly every day, he'd rarely worn his wedding band at all for the same reason. Her heart squeezed as she recalled the rare special occasions when he did. Her mother would joke, "Oh, so we're married today!"

Brianna jogged down the stairs, then out the back door after grabbing the workshop key. Bucky met her on the porch, meowing and purring as he circled her feet. She clucked her tongue. "Did I forget to feed you this morning?"

The cat responded with a loud yowl.

"Can you find it in your heart to forgive me? It's been kind of crazy around here. I'm sure you've noticed Dad's gone, and we're trying to get used to it." Brianna shook her head as she picked up the cat's water and food bowls. "I'm losing my mind! I'm telling my problems to a cat. If Dad could only see me now . . ."

She slipped back into the kitchen, then wiped out both bowls and filled them before returning outside, where she set them in their usual spot. Bucky responded with more loud purring, then practically began inhaling the food.

"Come see me in the shop when you're done, okay?"

Brianna loped down the steps and then down the hill. Despite a few rays of sunshine, she spotted some lingering dots of snow, evidence of last week's dusting. The air here was even colder than in Charlotte. But she didn't mind. She'd work up a sweat in the shop, clearing her mind and heart of the melancholy that had become a constant companion.

She unlocked the shop door, and the familiar scents of gear oil, grease, and gas wafted over her as she flipped on the lights and heater. This was the first time she'd been here since her father passed away. She glanced around the L-shaped area, taking in the wall with the bay door that led to the driveway, another wall lined with toolboxes and workbenches, the door that led out to the lake, and the pulleys they used to lift the johnboats from the water into the shop.

Tears blurred her vision as she looked at the workbench Dad had used the most. Then her phone rang, and she jumped with a start. Pulling it from her pocket, she read Taylor's name on the display.

"Hey," she answered as she hopped up on a stool.

"How'd it go taking your sisters to the airport?"

She could hear voices in the background and imagined he was greeting customers with a nod as they walked past, his favorite part of the job. Not only had Taylor taken over the business just after his college graduation, but being the overachiever he was, he'd also been elected Splendid Lake's deputy mayor. That meant he knew more locals than even she did.

"Fine."

"From the sound of your voice, though, it's not. What happened?"

"Mom wouldn't go with us. She just burst into tears and refused to even leave her bedroom." Brianna fingered a hole on the thigh of her jeans, making it larger as she fought back another wave of tears. How could she have any left to cry?

"I'm sorry, Brie. What can I do?"

"Convince her to get dressed and eat?"

"I wish I could." He was silent for a beat. "How are you—really?"

Hanging by a thread. Coming apart at the seams. "I'm fine."

"No, you're *not* fine. Stop saying that. I can hear it in your voice. Want me to come over tonight? I can bring some takeout. Maybe your favorite from that Chinese place you love?"

She smiled. "That sounds nice."

"I'll close up right at six and be there by seven."

"Perfect."

"Great. I have a lot to tell you. One of the town council members stopped by, and we talked for a few minutes. We have some exciting plans, and I need you to come to some meetings with me. Oh, wait. Hang on."

She heard muffled voices.

"Hey, I'm sorry, but I have to go," he said after a few moments. "Tammy has a long line at checkout, and I need to help her. I'll see you later."

She disconnected the call and again glanced around the shop. As much as she longed to get her hands dirty and lose herself in a project, she didn't have the emotional or physical strength to do it today. "I'm sorry, Dad," she whispered as she slid off the stool. "I'll try again soon."

She turned off the lights and heater and then locked the door before starting back up the hill. She looked up at the clear azure sky dotted with puffy clouds and breathed in the lake's familiar scent. Then glancing around the property, she tried to imagine springtime, when the grass changed from brown to a lush green. Before she knew it, the maple trees would boast budding leaves and robins would sing from their branches. Perhaps her heart would feel lighter by the time warmer weather descended on Splendid Lake.

Her feet hit the back porch steps just as a loud car engine thundered in the distance. The noise came closer and closer, coupled with the sound of tires crunching on the rock lane that led into the resort.

She'd walked around to the front of the house just as a shiny, dark-blue Plymouth Barracuda with a black convertible top motored up to the house. The engine rumbled loud enough that she could feel the sound thumping in her chest. The gorgeous vehicle came to a stop, and its driver cut the engine.

The Barracuda was a beauty, looking as if it had just left a collector's showroom. Dad would have enjoyed seeing it since he'd been a Mopar fan and loved Dodge and Plymouth vehicles. She closed her eyes for a moment to stop another rush of heartache.

When she opened them, a tall man was climbing out of the driver's seat. Brianna swallowed a gasp as she realized he was the guy from the bookstore, the one who'd also sat with her on the beach the night of the funeral. But he looked different this time—very different.

His hair was perfectly styled, and he'd shaved, revealing a strong jawline and cheekbones that could have been sculpted from fine granite. He also looked like he'd just walked out of a Brooks Brothers ad, wearing an expensive dark-blue suit coupled with a light-blue shirt and a blue tie a shade darker. And she'd never seen such shiny black shoes. The entire ensemble complemented those same baby-blue eyes while accentuating his broad shoulders, wide chest, muscular biceps, and tapered, trim waist.

She froze as she drank in the sight of him, then mentally shook herself. She was an engaged woman.

He smiled. "Hi."

"Hi." Brianna shifted her weight from one foot to the other, suddenly feeling embarrassingly underdressed. She forced her gaze toward the car and pointed to its gleaming hood. "Does that have a four-forty in it?"

He looked surprised, and she clenched her fists, waiting for a typical snarky comment indicating women couldn't possibly know anything about engines. But instead, he grinned, and like nearly all hot guys, he showed her a crooked smile. "Of course. That's the only engine I'd want."

"Nice." She touched the warm hood. "What year is it?"

"Seventy-one."

"Cool." She tilted her head. "We talked on the beach a couple of weeks ago."

"Right. And in the bookstore."

She huffed out a breath. "You remembered."

"I did. I enjoyed the book you recommended too."

"You actually bought it?"

"Of course I did. After all, it came *highly* recommended." He rubbed his jaw and smiled again. "And you were right. The butler didn't do it."

She laughed and then cleared her throat as an awkward silence fell between them. "So how may I help you? The resort isn't open. Not until Memorial Day weekend."

"I was wondering if I could speak to Mrs. Porter."

"She's not available right now." She studied him. "Are you from Mrs. Collins's office? I thought we completed all the paperwork last week."

The skin between his eyes wrinkled as he took a step toward her, his keys jingling as he slipped them into his trouser pocket. "Mrs. Collins?"

"Our lawyer?" Then it dawned on her. "You don't work for her, do you?"

"No, I don't, and I'm not a lawyer. I'm Scott Gibson." He held out his hand, and when she accepted it, he gave her hand a firm shake. Then he reached into his breast pocket, pulled out a business card, and gave it to her. "And your name is . . ."

"Brianna Porter."

"Brianna." He said her name quietly as if answering an unspoken question. "I'm a commercial real estate investor."

Brianna stilled as a black feeling settled in the pit of her stomach.

"I'd like to speak to Mrs. Porter about making an offer to buy this resort. She's your mother?"

"You what?" Brianna's voice was louder than she'd expected, and Gibson took a step back. "You want to *buy* our resort?"

He held up his hands as if to fend off her reaction. "I'm prepared to make a generous offer I'm sure will allow her to live comfortably for the rest of her life."

Brianna began to tremble. She'd joked with this man at the bookstore and then sat with him on the beach the night of the funeral. He'd engaged in playful banter at Bookends, offered her his coat on the beach, handed her a napkin when she cried, and spoke softly to her about the sunset. And now . . .

Suddenly rage seeped into her like water gorging the inside of a sponge. She took a step forward and furiously shook her finger at him. "How *dare* you try to buy my family's property after acting as if you *cared* about my feelings! You were just trying to trick me into trusting you. You were probably already working your plan that day you flirted with me in the bookstore, trying to manipulate me. And that was before my father died!"

"Whoa." He had the nerve to look ashamed. "I didn't even know who—"

"You're despicable! Buttering me up with talk about sunsets, no doubt planning to make an offer on the resort that very night if you could get away with it. You're so shady that you were willing to use my grief against me, believing you could talk me into getting my mother to sell to you. The only problem was my fiancé showed up and foiled your plan."

"Wait a minute." His sheepish expression had to be fake. Oh, he was good! "You've got this all wrong. I honestly didn't know who you were. I was just taking a walk and—"

"Save it!" she snapped as she tossed his business card toward him. It sailed through the air, then hit his chest before fluttering to the ground. "You were a snake in the grass, waiting to strike when my family and I were at our lowest." Angry tears gathered in the corners of her eyes, and she tried to shake them away. "Our resort is *not* for sale, and it never will be."

He swallowed, and his Adam's apple bobbed. "This has been a big misunderstanding. If you'll just give me a minute to explain—"

"There's *nothing* to explain. I've already figured it out." Her finger trembled as this time she pointed toward the road. "Get off our property and never come back!" Then she spun on her heel and marched up the porch steps, her body quaking as she stalked into the house. After she'd slammed the front door and locked it, she leaned against it and tried to calm down as the Plymouth's engine rumbled to life.

She would never again allow Scott Gibson to set foot on her family's property, no matter how many times he tried.

CHAPTER 4

$\mathcal{S}$cott grimaced as he gripped the wheel of his Barracuda and steered it through the town toward Interstate 40 to go home. Disappointment, humiliation, and regret all coursed through him as he recalled Brianna's furious words.

"Great job," he muttered. "You managed to alienate Brianna Porter within five minutes of formally meeting her."

He shook his head as if trying to dislodge the memory of their horrendous conversation. He thought back to the night he saw her on the beach. Then he cringed as he recalled her accusations about his intentions. Of course she would consider him a snake in the grass, waiting to strike her mourning family! He should have kept walking when he saw her crying by the lake. He should have minded his own business.

Scott groaned as he merged onto Interstate 40. Brianna was not only beautiful but knowledgeable about cars, a fact he'd found surprising. But as soon as she'd learned about his intention to buy the resort, storm clouds had overtaken her pretty face. Her voice and tone reminded him of a lioness protecting her precious cub.

He steered his car into the left lane, its engine thundering as it picked up speed. He couldn't allow himself to give up on the resort, though. He still wanted that property, and nothing had stopped a single one of his plans since he and Brad started their firm. Besides, selling really could be best for the two women who'd been left to run it alone. He also knew his ideas for the quaint little resort would bring more business to the town, and why wouldn't they want that?

He was determined to convince the Porter family to sell. He just had to find a way to get Brianna to listen to him—or at least allow him to speak to her mother. He'd get Brad's advice and then try again. Somehow he'd make his dream for the resort come true. Brianna was obviously still grieving, but she'd come around when the time was right. He just had to figure out how soon that would be.

The delicious aroma of Chinese food wafted through the kitchen as Taylor set two takeout bags on a counter.

"You are a lifesaver!" Brianna clapped her hands as her stomach growled. "I haven't eaten much today, and I'm starving. Thank you." She gave him a quick kiss, then pulled two plates from a cabinet and set them beside the bags.

He grinned. "You're welcome. I brought enough for your mom too. How is she now?"

"I'm not sure. She's been sleeping ever since I got home." She retrieved utensils from a drawer.

"I'm sorry to hear that. Oh, I have something for you. I found this on the ground outside."

She spun toward him as he held out a business card. When she saw *Scott Gibson* on it, she couldn't keep her upper lip from curling back in a snarl. "Might as well burn that," she said, but then she grabbed it from his hand and tossed it into their junk drawer.

"Burn it? Why?" His dark eyebrows careened to his hairline.

She looked behind her, making sure her mother wasn't within earshot, then began setting the table. "That guy showed up here today driving the most gorgeous Barracuda I've ever seen and wearing a suit and shoes worth more than my Mustang."

"What did he want?" He wrapped his hands around all three containers of food and carried them to the table.

"He had the gall to say he wanted to buy the resort, and it's not even for sale!" she exclaimed, then peeked out into the hallway, still worried her mother could hear her. She was determined to shield her from this.

She lowered her voice as the anger she'd felt earlier returned. "He was as slippery and slimy as a used car salesman. We chatted about his car, and I figured he worked for my parents' lawyer since he was dressed so nicely. But then he handed me his card and said he wanted to talk to Mom. I told him she wasn't available and introduced myself."

She moved to the cabinet and pulled out two drinking glasses. "Iced tea?"

"Yes, please." Taylor sat down at the table in his usual spot.

She pulled a pitcher from the refrigerator and began pouring. "What really got me is that I spoke to him at Bookends the day my dad passed away and then again the night of the funeral. I never knew who he was."

"He showed up at your father's funeral?"

"No. He was on the beach that night." She set the glasses on the table and then sat down across from him. "Remember when I went outside for some air and you were looking for me?"

He frowned. "Yes, I went to get you a bottle of water and you were gone when I got back."

She waved him off. "I know. I'm sorry I did that. Anyway, I sat down in one of the Adirondack chairs, and he came over and asked to sit with me. He was really nice, as though he were consoling me."

"He *consoled* you?" Taylor leaned forward. "What exactly do you mean by *that*?"

"That didn't come out right. He was just nice to me and quiet. Looking back now, though, I believe he was trying to manipulate me. He must have been watching the house, then lucked out when I went down to the beach." She scooped a pile of fried rice onto her plate and then pushed the container over to Taylor, who was staring at her.

"Is there anything you're not telling me? Did he try something with you?"

"No, no, no. He just showed up and was nice. But I think in reality he was buttering me up. Then he swooped in today and tried to buy my family's resort."

Taylor spooned a small mountain of fried rice onto his plate before covering it with beef and broccoli. "He sounds like a real slimeball."

"That's basically what I told him." She lifted her chin as she found her shrimp and snow peas. "I said worse, actually, and then I threw him off the property. I don't think he'll come back. But if he does, I'll do it again."

Taylor speared some beef with his fork. "I'm sorry your mom had another bad day."

Brianna sighed. "Thanks. That's why I don't want to tell her about this shady real estate investor. I was able to get her to eat a piece of toast and half a scrambled egg this morning, but that's it. I don't see any evidence she ate anything while I was gone. I just don't know what to do for her. I feel like I'm standing on the sidelines, watching her suffer."

"Give her time. My nana was like that when my poppy died. I remember Mom saying she felt helpless too. You just have to be available for her."

"Yeah, I guess so." She ate some more, then ran her fingers through the condensation on her glass as she thought about her sisters.

"What's on your mind?"

"I still can't believe Jenna and Cassie left. Neither of them would even say when they'll be back."

"I'm sure they'll come back as soon as they can. They're reeling from grief, trying to get their brains around what happened. They'll figure out how much they're needed here. Maybe they can take turns coming."

Brianna nodded and lifted her glass. "I hope you're right." She took another bite of shrimp. "This is the best."

He smiled. "I know what makes you happy."

She smiled back. "Thank you. How was the store today?"

"So busy." He rolled his eyes. "Tammy and I could hardly keep up." Then his expression brightened. "I need to tell you about my discussion with Ken Emker. He's wanted a new police station for years, and the mayor told me to handle the project. I'm excited he's giving me more responsibility. So Ken and I started talking, and we're going to bring up the idea at the next council meeting. If it's approved, I can say I'm helping modernize our little police department. Don't you think that will be a great campaign promise when I run for a second term?"

She nodded. "Sure."

"So like I said earlier, I need you to come to some meetings with me. I think people take me more seriously when they see us together."

He talked more about his plans for the town, but Brianna had trouble listening. She had too much on her mind.

After they finished, she carried their plates to the counter while Taylor closed the containers, disposing of the empty ones.

"Would it be all right if I said hello to your mom?"

She set a plate in the dishwasher. "That would be nice."

"Be right back."

Brianna was overwhelmed with appreciation for her fiancé. Taylor was one of the nicest men she knew. In fact, along with his good looks, she'd been drawn to how kind he was even in high school, where they first met and started dating. When Taylor went away to college and she stayed in Lake Splendid to help run the resort, their long-distance relationship hadn't worked and they broke up. But after he graduated, they eventually started dating again.

She'd found herself getting antsy with him when Ava and Dylan married three years ago, when she was twenty-three and Taylor was twenty-five. But soon after their wedding, he'd proposed. Three years later, though, they still hadn't set a date for their own wedding. Whenever anyone asked why, including her family, she told them the truth—they were both too busy.

She looked down at the small, round diamond sparkling up at her from its shiny, yellow-gold band. The ring represented their love and their future. She just wasn't sure when she'd see a gold band sitting behind it, becoming Brianna Reese. And now with her father's death . . .

"She's still asleep."

Brianna jumped with a start.

"Did I scare you?" Taylor smirked when she turned to find him right behind her.

She smacked his shoulder. "I need to put a bell on you."

He laughed, then sobered. "I miss you, Brie. We've hardly had any time together since your dad died. I understand, but . . ." He squeezed her hand. "Want to watch a movie on Netflix?"

"Sure." What she really wanted was to take a long, hot shower and go to bed, but she didn't want to hurt Taylor's feelings. And he'd brought dinner to cheer her up.

She sat down beside him on the sofa and pulled her favorite purple microfiber blanket over her lap as he fiddled with the remote control.

"What are you in the mood for?" he asked.

"A romantic comedy?" She loved to tease him, and he rolled his eyes. "Okay, okay. Action-adventure is fine, but not too much blood."

"Hmm. Let's see. Not too much blood . . ."

As Taylor scrolled through the movie selections, Brianna checked her phone to see if she had any messages from her sisters. Finding her screen clear, she snuggled down and rested her head on Taylor's shoulder. She tried to concentrate on the TV screen, but her thoughts spun with irritation over that nervy real estate investor.

Oh, how she longed for life to return to normal! But without Dad . . .

As the opening credits of the movie began, Taylor wrapped his arm around her.

I'll be all right as long as Taylor's by my side.

The next morning Brianna heard footsteps and turned from the stove toward the kitchen doorway. Mom stood there dressed in jeans and a powder-blue blouse that complemented her eyes. Although the clothes hung on her mother, happiness surged through Brianna's chest and she smiled. She'd decided to make a big breakfast—one of the only meals she was any good at—in hopes of encouraging Mom to get out of bed. Now not only was she up but she was dressed too!

"Good morning, Brianna."

"Good morning! Don't you look bright-eyed and bushy-tailed!"

"Not really, but I did sleep better last night. Those pills the doctor gave me worked." Mom walked over and swiped a piece of bacon from a platter. "Smells delicious."

"I was hoping I could entice you."

"I don't have much of an appetite, but I'll give breakfast a try."

"That's all I can ask for."

"I'll set the table," Mom said as the coffeepot burped, sending the brew's delicious aroma to mix with the smell of bacon, scrambled eggs, and toasted bagels permeating the kitchen.

Brianna scraped the eggs onto a second platter, then carried both to the table before retrieving bagels from the toaster.

"Cass and Jen finally texted me late last night," Brianna told her. "Both of their arrivals were delayed. Apparently there was bad weather in Atlanta."

"I was worried about them last night."

"They promised to call soon."

After a few bites, Mom studied her plate.

"Would you like more bacon?" Brianna pushed the platter toward her.

"No, thank you." She reached for a bagel, then began spreading butter on it. When she took a bite, she chewed slowly, and Brianna wondered what she was thinking about.

"What are your plans for the day?" Brianna worked to keep her voice sunny despite her mother's frown.

Mom gave a half-shrug as she took another bite. At least she was eating!

"What if we went to town together?" Brianna leaned forward, doing her best to sound as if she'd planned their dream vacation to Disney World. "We could stop by the Coffee Bean to see Ava and Brooklyn, and you could get one of their amazing lattes. What do you think?"

Mom pulled off a piece of her bagel, her expression growing grim. "But I might have to talk to people there, and I'm not ready for that."

Brianna snapped her fingers when another idea took hold. "What if I ran in and got the coffee, and then we went to the grocery store and picked up some ingredients for you to make your amazing chicken marsala or your famous chicken enchiladas? We could invite Taylor, Ava, and Dylan to join us—"

Her mother's face crumpled, and the tears streamed down her cheeks.

"Mom?" She reached for her hand.

"Chicken marsala was the last meal I made for your father before he—" She covered her face with a tissue she lifted from a pocket. "I'm sorry, Brianna, but I need to lie down." Pushing her chair back, she stood and hurried out of the room.

Brianna rested her elbows on the table and silently berated herself. The morning had been going so well, and then she'd said the wrong thing.

Great job, Brie!

She glanced at the remaining food on her plate. Her appetite had dissolved as soon as the tears began trailing down her mother's bereft face. With a sigh, she stacked the dishes and utensils before carrying them to the counter, then scraped the remaining food into the garbage disposal.

She picked up her phone from the counter and unlocked it, ready to text Cassie. But then she realized it was only six thirty in California, and her sister was probably sleeping in—if not because of her late arrival then because it was Saturday. She could text Jenna, but she wasn't in the mood for her oldest sister's patronizing advice.

Brianna's fingers found their way to Ava's last text and started a new message, but then she stopped. Her best friend would always listen and offer emotional support, but this wasn't her problem. She had to find a way to help her mother by herself. But how was that possible when her own heart was broken too?

CHAPTER 5

$\int$cott tapped on Brad's office doorframe. "How's it going this morning?"

Brad looked up from his laptop and smiled. "Fine. It's a Friday, right?"

"Last time I checked." Scott stepped into the office and leaned against the wall. "I'm thinking of leaving at lunchtime and heading back to Splendid Lake."

Brad grinned. "Why? Because you haven't been thrown off any properties lately and you're feeling a bit unfulfilled?"

"Not exactly." As Scott dropped into the chair in front of Brad's desk, he glanced at the photo of his partner's wife. He and Brad were the same age, but Brad was the one happily married. He was even expecting his first child soon. "I came on too strong with Brianna Porter, but it's been two weeks since I was last there, and it's already March. I just think if I apologize and explain myself, she might change her mind about me. Also, I'm worried that if I don't try again now, another investor will beat me to the sale."

Brad pointed at him. "There's the truth! You can't stand the idea of someone else buying 'your' property." He made air quotes with his fingers.

Scott shook his head. "You know me better than that."

"I know you're the reason we're here." Brad gestured around the office. "It was *your* vision and drive that got us our first big deal."

"Exactly."

"But I don't understand why you're so obsessed with that resort. If it needs so much work, is it really worth it?"

Scott rested his right ankle on his left knee and drummed his fingers on the side of his shin. "It's a feeling I have, and you just admitted my feelings have been right before."

"Yeah, I can't deny that. You have almost always been spot-on—except for that one condo fiasco in Gastonia."

"We won't discuss that." Scott stood. "All right, then. I'll finish up here and then head for Splendid Lake. Have a good weekend."

"Hey, Scott," Brad called as Scott walked through the doorway. "Just one bit of advice."

Scott pivoted to face him. "Yeah?"

Brad ran a hand through his dark hair. "Don't bug her too much, all right? If you do, she might actually file a restraining order against you."

Scott snorted. "I have a feeling Brianna Porter would do just that."

Brianna pushed open the door to the Coffee Bean, and the bell above her announced her presence. The shop was buzzing with activity as customers sat at the tables or in booths enjoying their coffee and pastries. A few others stood in line at the counter, where Ava and Brooklyn took and filled their orders.

The sisters' dream of establishing this little shop had come true two years ago when their father, a judge in their district, loaned them the money. It had quickly taken off and was known for being one of the most successful coffee shops for miles. A review in the local newspaper comparing the Coffee Bean to one of the chain coffee shops was framed and hung in a prominent place on a wall, and Brianna couldn't have been prouder of her best friend. She often recommended the place to guests at the resort.

Brianna took her place in line behind a group of five teenage girls and then slipped her phone and keys into the pockets of her gray hoodie.

"Hey, Brie!" Brooklyn waved at her.

Brianna waved back, thinking about how Brooklyn compared to Ava, just as she'd compared herself to her sisters the day of Dad's funeral. Brooklyn was twenty-three to Ava's twenty-six, and although they had physical similarities, those were hard to spot at first glance. They shared the same petite frame, warm smile, and sweet personality, yet Brooklyn had her mother's light-brown hair and baby-blue eyes and Ava had her father's wavy dark-brown hair and coffee-brown eyes.

Brianna secretly envied their closeness. If only one of her sisters had chosen to stay in Splendid Lake instead of running off to a big city, maybe they'd have a close relationship as adults too.

"Brie," Ava called from the register. "Want your usual?"

"Yes, please."

Ava nodded toward their favorite table, rather secluded at the back of the shop. It was still empty. "Have a seat. I'll bring it over."

Brianna sat down, and soon Ava appeared with two cups. She smiled as she set one in front of Brianna. "A white chocolate mocha for you and a café mocha for me."

"Thank you." She pulled her wallet from her purse.

Ava waved it off. "Put that away. You know your money isn't any good here. Besides, I've been hoping you'd stop by. I haven't spoken to you since Wednesday, and your texts have been so brief." Her smile faded. "How are things?"

Brianna clutched the cup in her hand. "I'm still struggling with how to help Mom. Some days she won't even leave her room. Other days she sits out on the porch and just stares out toward the lake." She rubbed at her temples as yet another stress headache closed in. "I'm walking on eggshells, afraid I might make her worse by opening my big, fat mouth and saying the wrong thing."

Brianna lifted her cup and took a sip. The coffee was good and hot, filling up the empty parts of her.

Ava covered Brianna's other hand with hers. "You're all grieving, and grief is unpredictable. When Dylan's grandfather died, the slightest thing would set off his grandmother. Dylan once mentioned he was working on Mr. Monroe's old Galaxie at his shop, and Meemaw started to sob because his grandfather had a Galaxie when they were younger. You never know when grief will hit, but you can't blame yourself. I'm sure some things set you off too."

Brianna sighed. She needed to change the subject before she got emotional, even if they were toward the back of the busy shop. "Can we talk about you for a while?"

"Of course." Ava's smile was a little too bright as she lifted her cup and took another sip, and Brianna could see right through her façade.

"Ave, how long have we known each other?"

"Hmm." She tapped her chin. "Good gracious. About twenty years now."

"Right, and I can read you like a book. So what's going on?"

Ava's lips turned down. "I hate to complain when you're dealing with so much."

"Please tell me. We're friends, and we support each other."

"All right." Ava glanced around, then leaned forward and lowered her voice. "I already confided in you that Dylan and I have been try-ing. I thought for sure I was pregnant this month, but I'm not."

Brianna clucked her tongue. "I'm so sorry."

"I just keep getting myself all excited, and then I'm disappointed when I'm wrong."

"It will happen, and you and Dylan will be the best parents."

"Thanks."

The bell above the door chimed as the group of teenage girls left and Cole Spencer walked in. With sandy-colored hair and deep-brown eyes, Brooklyn's boyfriend certainly was handsome. He was also tall, like Dylan and Taylor. He immediately walked to the counter, where Brooklyn greeted him with a warm smile.

"They are too cute together," Brianna quipped before taking another sip.

Ava grinned. "Yeah, they are, and I know a secret."

"Oh really? I love secrets. What is it?"

Ava leaned closer across the table. "Cole went to see Mom and Dad earlier this week and asked for permission to give my baby sister a ring."

"No kidding!"

"I know. They've been together two years now, and he already has a house since he works for his dad's construction company. It's not far from Dylan's and mine."

"Wow." Brianna swirled her coffee and shook her head. "Little Brooklyn is getting engaged. Didn't we have to lock her out of your room during sleepovers just yesterday because she wanted to steal our Barbie dolls and draw makeup on them?"

Ava guffawed. "I'd forgotten about that!"

Brianna grinned. Oh, it felt good to smile. She was so grateful for her best friend.

"So what about you and Taylor?"

"What about us?"

Ava cocked a dark eyebrow. "He gave you a ring three long years ago. When are you going to set a date?"

"I don't know."

"But surely you've discussed it."

Brianna sat back in the seat. "We have . . . in a general way. But we've never talked about a hard date."

"Are you being serious?" Ava tapped the table. "You're telling me you've been wearing that ring all this time and never pulled out a calendar and said, 'So what works for you?'"

Brianna held up her hands. "No, we haven't. Look, drop it, okay? It will happen when it's the right time. All that matters is that we've made a commitment to each other, right?"

"You're twenty-six, and Taylor's twenty-eight. Aren't you ready to settle down and start a family?"

Brianna rubbed her eyes with the heels of her hands. "Can we not have this conversation today? I've hardly slept since Dad died. Right now I'm worried about my mom and getting the resort ready for the season. Planning a wedding is the last thing on my mind."

"You know, if you were married, Taylor would live at the resort and be there to help you and your mom."

Brianna shook her head. "He might be there, but between running the store and serving as deputy mayor, he hardly has time to sleep. I don't see that changing anytime soon, and besides, I need to figure out how to run the resort on my own."

She sighed. "Remember I told you about that Gibson guy? Well, two more real estate investors reached out this week. The vultures must read obituaries to find properties to buy. I hung up on the one who called and slammed the door in the other's face."

"I'm sorry." Ava's mouth pinched. "How *are* you going to handle everything around the resort—especially with your mom so depressed?"

"I'm not sure. I still need to investigate, but I know a few of the cabins need replacement shingles. The pier needs maintenance, and I need to paint the inside of the convenience store and bait shop since we never got around to it last fall. I also have to get the johnboats ready. I'll still have a few teenagers helping during the summer, but we've always needed more help. I was going to talk to Dad about that, but then . . . Anyway, I haven't looked at the books yet, but I'm hoping we can afford to hire someone."

"Sounds like you might have to."

"That's my next task—figuring out how Dad did the books and then talking to his accountant to be sure I understand taxes and all the rest. Mom never did do much with the financial side of the business. Dad always took care of it, and now I wish I'd asked him to teach me. I'm sure the mail has brought some bills I need to pay, but I've just piled it all on Dad's desk."

The bell above the door chimed again, and Brianna's entire body tensed as Scott Gibson stepped inside. This time he was clad in tight jeans, a navy Henley shirt, a black leather jacket, and black boots. She found herself admitting he looked good. Really good.

"Oh no. It's that Gibson guy," she hissed. "You've got to be kidding me."

"What's wrong?"

"That's him. The real estate slimeball with the souped-up Barracuda. What's he doing here?"

Ava's eyes grew wide, and she pointed. "You threw *him* off your property? Are you blind?"

"Quit pointing." Brianna seethed as the man crossed to the counter. "I need to get out of here before he sees me."

"I wouldn't mind him looking at me."

"How would Dylan feel if he heard you say that?"

Ava waved a hand. "Oh, he wouldn't be surprised. You know what I always say. Just because I've ordered from the menu doesn't mean I can't keep looking at all the selections."

Brianna rolled her eyes.

"I'm just kidding." Ava looked toward the counter, then grinned. "He saw you, and here he comes. This should be interesting."

Brianna's hackles raised even higher when Gibson's gaze locked with hers.

He lifted his hand in a half-hearted wave, and with a hesitant smile on his lips, he reached their table. "Miss Porter. Hi."

She glared at him as she pushed back her chair and stood, then looked at Ava as she grabbed her purse. "Thanks for the coffee. I need to get to the grocery store. See you later."

She marched past Scott Gibson and headed toward the exit, depositing her empty coffee cup in the trash can on her way out. Maybe he would get the picture now.

CHAPTER 6

*S*cott's shoulders sagged as Brianna Porter stormed out of the coffee shop with her head held high. He'd been surprised to see her there, but he shouldn't have been. After all, this was a small town.

Perhaps Brad was right. Maybe he should let this property go and keep out of trouble.

"Would you like some coffee?"

The petite brunette was still sitting at the table across from where Brianna had been. She wore a T-shirt and a visor that both read *The Coffee Bean*, along with a name tag declaring she was Ava.

"Yes. I'm Scott Gibson." He held out his hand, and she shook it.

"Ava, and I already know why you're here. What would you like?" She pointed toward the board that explained what blends and flavors the shop offered.

He blew out a puff of air. So many choices. "How about the dark roast?"

"Cream and sugar?" She stood and started toward the counter.

He took a step to follow her. "Sure. Why not?"

She whirled around, causing him to screech to a stop, then pointed back to the table. "You sit, and I'll bring it to you. Then we can have a little chat about Brie."

"Okay." He pulled out his wallet and then took the seat Brianna had before she stomped out on him.

Ava returned after a few minutes and set a coffee in front of him, along with some packs of sugar and creamer and a stirrer.

"Thanks. How much?" He held up his wallet as she sat across from him.

"On the house."

He lifted an eyebrow. "Why?"

"I figure I owe you a cup of coffee and some advice after my best friend snubbed you."

"Your best friend?" He opened the first of two sugar packets and dumped their contents into his cup.

"Yup." She folded her arms and set them on the table. "Look, I'll be honest with you. You're barking up the wrong tree with Brie. She'll never sell that resort. She's as stubborn as her father was."

"How long have you known her?"

"Almost all my life. We met in kindergarten. Splendid Lake Elementary."

"So you're a native."

"Born and bred."

"It's a great little town. I love how it's not commercialized. You don't see that much these days."

"That's true, and the resort is everything to Brie—Brianna to you. She'll never let it go. Her two older sisters tried to talk her into going to college and leaving all this behind like they did, but she refused." Ava bit her lower lip and looked down. "She'd be upset if she heard me share that with you, a total stranger. But there you have it."

"Your secret is safe with me." He added the creamer, stirred, and then took a sip. Ava seemed to be waiting for him to say more. "Delicious coffee, by the way."

"Thanks." She nodded toward the counter. "My little sister and I are pretty proud of this place."

He glanced at the young woman serving coffee to an older couple, then asked the question most on his mind. "Do you have any advice for how to approach Brianna that won't chase her off? I'd still like to talk with her."

Ava laughed. "Her mind is already made up about you. I suggest you head back to wherever you're from and forget about this place." She pushed back her chair and stood. "Have a good day."

"You too."

She took a few steps but then faced him again. "Oh, and, Scott, we never talked, okay?"

"Right." He smiled and lifted his cup as if to toast her. "Thank you."

"You're welcome." Ava slipped behind the counter before walking to the register where a middle-aged woman stood ready to order. "How are you, Mrs. Goffle? Would you like your usual?"

Scott glanced around the coffee shop, taking in the murmur of conversations among the customers of all ages. He sipped more of his coffee and considered Ava's warning as well as Brad's. He supposed they were both right. He should give up and return to Charlotte before he got into more trouble.

But as much as logic told him to do that, his determination wouldn't allow him to walk away from that beautiful resort on Splendid Lake. He had to at least try once more before starting his three-hour journey home. Getting Brianna Porter to listen to him would be a battle, but he was up for the challenge. She'd announced that she planned to go to the grocery store, which meant he had time to kill before he drove up to the resort. He knew better than to seek out her mother on his own. He might as well finish his coffee and take in more of the little town while trying to think of a way to inspire Brianna to listen to him.

He'd give her about an hour and then knock on her door. He just hoped he wouldn't blow yet another opportunity.

"No, no, no! Can this day get any worse?" Brianna let out a guttural scream as she glared at her flattened rear tire on the driver's side. In fact, it was flatter than flat. The rim was nearly touching the ground. Just what she needed!

Earlier she'd hurried through the grocery store, her fury after seeing Gibson fueling her swiftness. Then she'd filled the trunk of the Mustang with her bags before starting for the resort, hoping to spend the rest of the afternoon in her father's office.

While still driving along Main Street, she'd thought she heard a pop. But she continued on and then heard a *flup, flup, flup* as the car pulled to the left along this rural two-lane road. When it was safe, she pulled onto the shoulder, where she jumped out of the car and confirmed her nightmare.

Fuming, she grabbed the keys from the ignition and stomped to the rear of the car, then began loading the bags into the backseat. "Why didn't I just take the Tahoe?" she muttered. "And why did I have to buy so many groceries?"

When she'd finished, she lifted the trunk's liner and yanked out the tire iron and scissor jack. Then she set the iron on an offending lug nut and began pushing. And pulling. And kicking. And yelling. But it wouldn't budge.

Irritation and frustration boiled in her chest. "This can't be happening!" She glanced around but didn't see any cars or even farmhouses on this stretch of the road. She tried again and again, but the pesky lug nut wouldn't move.

Dad, you would be so disappointed in me. With everything you taught me, surely I can remove the lug nuts from my own car!

After trying one more time, she gave in and retrieved her phone from her pocket. She despised having to ask a man to help her, but if she waited much longer, her ice cream would melt, and she couldn't have that. It was Mom's favorite—vanilla.

She found Taylor's cell phone number and called him, glad she still had reception out here. When she immediately got his voice mail, she huffed out an angry breath. She tried his store's number next, but a busy signal filled her ear.

Dylan was her only hope—other than calling for road service, and that would be expensive. She'd never bothered with a membership. She scrolled through her contacts until she found the number for his auto repair shop, but before she tapped it, a loud engine rumbled toward her.

She tented her hand over her eyes and squinted against the sun as a candy-apple red Dodge Challenger rolled toward her. The car slowed and came to a stop a few feet behind her disabled Mustang. From the emblem on the grill, she could tell that it was not only a Challenger but the high-performance model known as the Scat Pack.

She squinted again to get a look at the driver behind the windshield, but the glare blinded her. The driver's door opened, and when Scott Gibson climbed out, she groaned.

"Not again." She narrowed her eyes at him. "Did you manage to stick a tracker in my purse at the coffee shop?" she called to him.

"No, I didn't." He grinned. "But that's a great idea." He leaned on the door and nodded toward her car. "Need some help?"

"No, thanks. Got it all under control."

He came around the door and shut it behind him. "From where I'm standing, you look stranded."

"I'm fine." She held up her phone. "Help is on the way. You can run along back to Charlotte." She gestured toward the road.

He walked over to the flat tire and whistled. "That's a serious flat."

"No kidding, Sherlock."

He snorted. "I like this Mustang. Is it a five-oh?"

"Yup."

"Ninety-two?"

"Ninety-three."

"Pretty." He pointed to the two-tone paint job—bright blue on the top and gray on the bottom. "Love this color scheme."

She glared at him. "Is praising my car your new plan for buttering me up? In case you haven't noticed, this old Mustang looks like a jalopy next to your gorgeous Challenger."

"I appreciate the compliment, but I do like Mustangs."

"So are you going to help me or not?"

He picked up the tire iron, and after slipping it on the first lug nut, he spun it as if it had never been tightened.

"Of course," she grumbled.

He looked up. "What?"

"Nothing." She folded her arms over her chest and tried to ignore the frustration exploding through her.

Gibson loosened the lug nuts and then picked up the jack. "Do you know where you want to take it for service?"

"My best friend's husband has a shop not too far from here."

"I'll follow you and give you a ride home." He began jacking up the car.

"What's the catch?"

"No catch."

"Sure there is." She retrieved the spare from the trunk, then said,

"Do I have to promise to forge my mom's signature? Or will you hold me hostage until she signs the deed of our resort over to you?"

He turned toward her, his expression serene. "There's no catch. I'll just get you home." He dropped the flat tire on the ground and jammed a thumb toward her backseat. "Unless, of course, you're not worried about your groceries."

"I am worried about them." She grimaced. "I have ice cream and fresh meat in there."

He set the spare tire and tightened the lug nuts. After lowering the car and stowing the flat tire and equipment in her trunk, he found a rag and held it up. "Is it okay if I wipe my hands on this?"

"Sure."

"New idea. Why don't we load your groceries into my car? You can get them home, and I'll drive your car to your friend's shop. You can pick me up there." He pulled his keys from his pocket, and they jingled as he held them out to her.

She stared at him. "You're going to trust me with your car. Are you serious?"

He shrugged. "Why not?" Then he jammed his thumb toward her Mustang. "Let's get these groceries loaded up."

They worked together to place all the bags into the trunk of the Challenger, and when they were done he handed her the keys. "Where's the shop?"

She gave him its name and directions, then pulled her own keys from her pocket. "Thank you."

He gave her that crooked smiled. "You're welcome." Then he sauntered to her car and climbed in.

Remembering the ice cream, which surely was starting to melt no matter how well she'd packed it in two paper bags, she shook herself from her shock and hurried over to his Challenger. When she climbed in, the aroma of expensive leather seeped into her senses, and she admired the two-toned black-and-red front seats and matching red and black gauges.

After adjusting the seat and steering wheel to her shorter stature, she looked for where to insert a key. But then she realized it was a push-button start. She examined Gibson's keyring and found a fob for the car along with what looked like house keys. Perhaps they were the keys to Gibson's house. Or his girlfriend's house. Or maybe his office?

Turning her attention back to her melting ice cream, she pushed the button, and when the engine roared to life, she couldn't stop a grin. Oh, how she loved sports cars!

In front of her, the Mustang also came to life with a rumble that wasn't nearly as impressive as the Dodge's, then pulled back onto the road, still void of traffic. Brianna followed, and then as Gibson steered toward Dylan's shop, she headed home.

Brianna's head swam with confusion. While she appreciated the help, she was positive Scott Gibson had an ulterior motive. Certainly he'd come back to Splendid Lake with all intentions of again trying to buy her family's resort. Maybe he'd even been heading toward her house when he stopped. But she'd be strong. She wouldn't allow him to manipulate her, no matter how helpful he was.

When she reached the house, she parked in front of the garage and gathered the two bags with perishables, then hurried up the back steps.

"Mom?" she called as she made her way to the kitchen. "I'm home!"

Her mother appeared from the hallway. "Oh. There you are. I was wondering what took you so long."

"I broke down on the side of the road." She began stowing the ice cream and meat.

"What happened?"

"It's a long story, but"—she didn't want her mother to worry about her being with a complete stranger—"an acquaintance stopped to help me. He's driven the Mustang to Dylan's shop, and he let me use his car to get these perishables home. Now I need to hurry up and go get him."

"Well, bring in the other bags and I'll put the groceries away while you go sort things out with your car."

"Thanks."

After one more trip, she had everything unloaded. "I'll be right back."

"Take your time."

Brianna climbed back into the Challenger and grinned when its engine rumbled to life again. Oh, how her father would have gotten a kick out of this car. The thought sent both amusement and sadness pouring through her.

She enjoyed the glorious feel of the ride as she drove to Burns Auto Repair, where she parked the Challenger next to her Mustang. When she realized Gibson wasn't in her car, she peered through the glass front of the building and spotted him and Dylan talking inside. She could only imagine what Dylan thought of a stranger bringing her car in for a new tire. Actually, she needed four tires, just like Dylan told her she did in December.

When she pulled open the front door, the sweet smell of rubber hit her as she moved past the display of tires and toward where the two men stood.

"There she is," Dylan announced from behind the counter.

"Hey, Dylan." Brianna was aware of her rescuer's presence beside her as she caught a whiff of the woodsy scent of his cologne. "I guess you've already met Scott Gibson."

"I have. And I heard about your flat." Like Taylor, Dylan was tall and had dark hair and eyes, both men the "type" she and Ava had dreamed about since eighth grade. As usual, a bright smile lit his attractive face.

She nodded, and when he opened his mouth again, she cut him off. "I know you warned me about those tires a while ago, but . . ." She swallowed. "I've been a little distracted."

Dylan cringed. "I know. I'm sorry."

"Do you happen to have the tires I need in stock?"

"I do. I already have options pulled up on the screen." He pointed to his computer, and they discussed which tires she wanted and their price. As usual, he offered her the friends and family discount. She wished Gibson wasn't standing right there, but what she really wanted was for him to leave and never come back.

She handed Dylan her Visa. This purchase would take her close to the end of her credit line. Instead of dipping into her checking account, she'd used it to purchase Christmas gifts. But she'd pay it off as soon as she got a handle on Dad's books. He'd always paid her a monthly salary. It just wasn't much since she had room and board as well.

After running the card, Dylan gave her the receipt. "We're a little bit behind today, but I can get to this first thing tomorrow. We open at seven on Saturdays. Do you want to bring the Mustang back then? Or do you want to leave it? If you leave it, I can give you a ride home, and my brother can bring the car to you tomorrow."

"She can leave the car. I'll give her a ride home," Gibson said.

Dylan looked at him and back at her. "Does that sound good?"

She hesitated. If only she'd driven the Tahoe, she wouldn't be in this predicament, depending on someone she didn't even want to know. But then she shrugged. She could survive a short car ride with the man. No matter what he said, she wouldn't let him manipulate her into letting him talk to her mother. "Sure."

"Okay," Dylan said. "I'll just need the keys."

Gibson pulled them out of his pocket and handed them to Dylan. Then he smiled at Brianna. "I liked driving your car. Did you enjoy driving mine?"

"You know your Challenger is way more fun than my Mustang." Her lips defied her resolve and turned up in a smile as she gave him his keyring.

"What kind of Challenger do you have?" Dylan asked him.

Gibson nodded toward the window. "An SRT."

"What year?"

"Twenty eighteen."

"I need to see it."

Brianna followed the men out the front door, and Dylan gave a low whistle. "Wow. I've worked on only a couple of these." He stepped to the Challenger and grinned. "So pretty. Pop the hood."

Brianna stood back while the two men discussed the engine, which was so clean her father would have said they could eat off it.

The men talked a few more minutes, and then Gibson closed the hood and shook Dylan's hand. "Well, it was nice meeting you, Dylan."

"You too, Scott."

They're on first-name terms? Well, she guessed she could call him Scott too. That might actually help put him in his place. And he did help her this afternoon, even though she was still sure his motives were anything but pure.

Scott climbed into the driver's seat, and the car rumbled to life once again.

"I can't wait to hear this story," Dylan muttered to her under his breath.

"Tell Ava I ran into Scott Gibson again, and she'll fill you in on the details."

"This ought to be good."

"You have no idea," she quipped. "See you later." She gave him a wave, then opened the passenger door and joined her escort. But she was no fool.

"Thank you for helping with my car and groceries. But I'm your hostage now, so tell me what the catch is."

As if I didn't know.

CHAPTER 7

$\mathcal{S}$cott frowned as he glanced at Brianna in the passenger seat beside him. "You're not my hostage, and there still isn't a catch. I just wanted to help."

"Right," she snipped. Then she settled back into the leather seat and clicked on her seat belt before folding her arms. Her pretty face clouded with an expression that seemed both impatient and annoyed.

"Look, I came back to apologize, not hassle you."

"Oh really?" Her tone was laced with sarcasm. "So you drove three hours just to apologize? Why didn't you call like another real estate investor did this week? Oh, and by the way, I hung up on him. And I kicked another one off my property like I did with you, so don't feel special."

So his hunch *had* been right! And Brad thought he was losing his head over this property. "Other investors have been contacting you?"

"Yeah. Apparently you people read the obituaries to find your next target."

You people. Those words irritated him, but she had a right to her anger. He just hoped he could find the words to extinguish her rage instead of dousing it with more gasoline.

She ran her fingers over the dashboard. "This car is amazing. How many gorgeous vehicles do you have at your mansion back home? Another dozen? Or more?"

"Just this and the Barracuda, and I don't live in a mansion."

"Well, that's disappointing." She pointed to the steering wheel. "Let's get going. I told my mom I'd be right back."

He put the car in reverse. "Look, I know I came on too strong before, but I'm truly sorry for your loss." He backed out of the parking lot and steered the Challenger toward the exit before easing it into the intersection. "How is your mother?" He gave her a quick sideways glance and found her brow puckered as if confused by the question. "Believe it or not, we people—you know, the shady, despicable, and disgusting human beings real estate folks are—do actually care about others. At least, sometimes we do."

She snorted as if amused by that, and he couldn't stop himself from smiling. "Seriously, how is she?" Out of the corner of his eye, he was almost certain he saw her tense shoulders relax by a fraction, just as they had on the beach that night.

"Well, it's hard to say. She's not the same person." She paused and looked down at her lap. "She used to love to cook. Now I can hardly get to her eat more than half a piece of toast."

The tremor in her voice knotted his insides. "I'm sorry." He turned toward her and found her staring out the window as they whizzed by a farm. He swallowed, not knowing what to say.

"They were married for thirty-five years, so of course she's a mess."

"That long? Wow."

She fingered the door handle.

"How are *you* doing?"

She tilted her head and sighed. "I feel like I'm walking around in a fog. My dad and I did everything together." She suddenly turned toward him, her expression fierce. "Look, we're not friends, okay? Don't think I'm dumb enough to be manipulated by you again."

He ran his tongue over his teeth. "I'm not trying to manipulate you now, and I wasn't trying to when we met in the bookstore or on the beach. I honestly had no idea who you were either time."

"Yeah, right." She nodded toward the next intersection. "Turn left here."

He halted at the stop sign, then flipped on the blinker as he faced her again. "I'm telling you the truth. Yes, I came up here to talk to your father. I'd been planning to talk to him for a while after I stumbled on Splendid Lake last summer, when I was meeting a client in Asheville. I fell in love with the area, and when I saw your resort, I thought it could be . . . well, so much more.

"But then I had to do some traveling, and when I was here the day we met at Bookends, I was called back to Charlotte before I could even check into the inn. Anyway, when I returned the night I saw you on the beach, I had no idea it was the day of your father's funeral. I didn't know he'd passed away. In fact, I'd never met your dad or even talked to him by phone. I was planning to introduce myself in person the following morning."

Her lips twisted as she gave him an icy stare.

"When I got to the inn, the Hernandezes had left a note saying they'd be away for a few hours. So I went for a walk on the beach, and that's when I saw you sitting by yourself. You looked so sad that I decided to ask if I could sit with you. Yes, I recognized you from the bookstore, but I didn't think I should bring that up because I could tell you were upset."

He held up his hand, at the same time glancing in the rearview mirror to make sure a car hadn't pulled up behind them. "That's all.

I didn't understand anything until the Hernandezes told me they'd been to Martin Porter's service and then to his house. And I still didn't know you were his daughter. Not for sure."

A muscle flexed in her jaw as she watched him, her eyes narrowing.

"Do you really think I'm heartless enough not only to pretend to care but to try making an offer on a property the day of the owner's funeral?"

She clucked her tongue. "How could I possibly know the answer to that? I don't know you. I just know you like books and hotrods and obviously have money, which is evidence that you're probably a good businessman. So why would I think your intention was and is anything other than to get me to trust you?"

He felt deflated. Like Ava said, Brianna had made up her mind, and he was wasting his time. He made the turn, then drove up the hill to the resort's entrance before entering the long, winding driveway that led to the main house and cabins beyond.

He parked in front of the three-bay garage next to a black Chevrolet Tahoe.

Brianna turned toward him, still scowling. "I appreciate your help today, but I think it's time for you to go home."

"Brianna!"

Scott looked toward the front door, where an attractive older woman with a kind smile waved as she held open the storm door. "I think your mom is calling you."

She lowered her window. "I'll be there in a second, Mom."

"Is that the friend who helped you?" Mrs. Porter called.

She hesitated, and what looked like panic flickered over her face. "Yes, but he's just leaving."

"I'd like to meet him. Invite him into the kitchen," Mrs. Porter said, then disappeared inside.

Brianna turned toward him and scowled again. She was good at that—and even that glare couldn't dampen her natural beauty.

"So I guess your mom wants to meet me, huh?" He bit back a smile.

Her mouth worked, her glower fading. "Fine. I'll let you meet her, but we need to set some ground rules. Don't you dare say anything to her about buying the resort. She has enough to deal with."

"Absolutely. I understand."

She lifted an eyebrow, and he held up both his hands. "You've got my word. I'll say hello to your mom, and then I'll be on my way."

Brianna gave herself a mental head slap as she took the front porch steps two at a time. If only she'd purchased the tires for her Mustang when Dylan suggested it, this never would have happened.

Stupid, stupid, stupid!

She wrenched open the door, and Scott followed as she led him through the family room and into the kitchen. She stopped short when she found her mother standing at a counter, looking at her favorite cookbook. "Mom? What are you doing?"

Her mother pushed her reading glasses up on her head and smiled past her. "So this is your friend." She split a look between Brianna and Scott. "I don't believe we've met. I'm Lois Porter."

Brianna set her purse on the counter and gestured toward their . . . guest. "This is Scott Gibson."

"Hi, Mrs. Porter. It's a pleasure to meet you." Scott flashed his crooked smile and held out his hand.

Brianna moved behind her mother and shot him a warning look, hoping he'd take the hint and keep his promise not to mention his interest in the resort.

Mom smiled, clearly charmed by the handsome man. "I heard you had to rescue Brianna today. What was wrong with her car?"

Brianna cut him off. She didn't want an actual conversation here. "I had a flat."

Mom looked confused. "You said you broke down, but you just needed help changing a tire? Did you forget how?"

"I couldn't get the lug nuts off." Oh, how she hated saying those words out loud, and Scott's smirk only made it worse.

"Really?"

Scott leaned toward her mother as if he were about to confide in her. "The truth is your daughter *insisted* she had it under control, but it was clear she didn't."

Mom laughed. "She can be a little bit stubborn."

Oh, the betrayal!

"That's what I've heard."

Scott had the nerve to wink at Brianna, but ignoring him, she looked at her mother. "Like I told you earlier, he took my car to Dylan's shop and let me drive his so I could get the groceries home."

"How thoughtful. It's a good thing you came along, Scott."

"I was glad to help." He took a step toward the doorway. "Well, I should be on my way." He nodded at her mom. "It was nice meeting you, Mrs. Porter."

"Oh, you just got here. You have to go already?" Mom actually looked disappointed.

"He has to get back home," Brianna said, giving him a pointed look. "It's a long drive."

"That's a shame. I was just going to cook."

"You were?" Brianna's heart swelled at the news. And then she noticed ingredients spread out across the counter—chicken, tortillas, a can of cream of mushroom soup, garlic powder, a bag of shredded cheddar cheese, butter, and an onion. Pans were already sitting on the stove waiting for Mom to put them to use. She was having a good day after all!

Brianna glanced at Scott, and he smiled. She couldn't stop herself from returning the gesture, but then she shook herself and looked at Mom.

"I'm making your favorite, Brianna. Chicken enchiladas. I've been thinking about them ever since you mentioned them. You brought home chicken and sour cream today, so we have everything we need." Then Mom looked at Scott. "You should stay."

"Oh, no, thank you. I wouldn't want to impose. Maybe next time."

"Nonsense." Mom shook her finger at him.

Oh no. "But he really does have to get going," Brianna said.

"Surely he can spare a little bit of time. The enchiladas take only thirty minutes in the oven. Your friend helped you, and we should invite him to stay."

Irritation twined through her as she looked at Scott, and his eyebrows lifted as he met her gaze as if to ask permission.

"Do you have time to stay?" she asked. If she resisted, her mother would ask too many questions.

He hesitated, then said, "I do, but as I said, I don't want to impose." And to her surprise, he looked as though that was a genuine concern.

Man, this guy is good. And Mom's clearly captive to his spell.

"It's settled, then," her mother said as she flipped the oven dial to bake. Then she turned to Brianna. "Why don't you take our guest's jacket?"

Brianna held out her hand. Once she had his jacket, she hung it along with hers in the foyer closet. When she returned, Scott was leaning back against the counter, just looking at her. She shot him another warning look behind her mother's back.

He pointed to the freezer with another crooked smile on his face. "Did your ice cream make it?"

"Yes."

"Where are you from, Scott?" Mom was shuffling her ingredients around on the counter.

"Charlotte. I drove up for the day."

"That's a long drive for one day."

"I had some business . . . nearby."

Panic clawed at Brianna. She was certain her mother's next question would be *What kind of business?* If Scott betrayed her, if he mentioned his desire to buy the resort, surely Mom's good day would dissolve.

Her eyes snapped to Scott's, and he gave her a quick nod before slipping beside her mother.

"May I see your recipe?"

"Of course." Mom pushed the book toward him. "Do you like to cook?"

"I do, actually." He looked almost embarrassed. "It's sort of a hobby."

"Really? What do you like to make?"

Brianna shook her head as the two fell into an easy conversation about cooking. One thing was clear—Scott was a *professional* manipulator. But even though she suspected he was still determined to buy their resort, she couldn't deny that it warmed her heart to see her mother smiling as she cooked her first meal since Dad died.

And maybe that meant Mom would be okay.

CHAPTER 8

*T*his is absolutely delicious, Mrs. Porter," Scott announced as he set another enchilada on his plate. "I'd love to take a photo of the recipe before I leave."

"Help yourself," Mom said, then patted her mouth with a napkin.

Brianna glanced at Scott, and he smiled at her. She nodded in response, grateful he'd managed to avoid any conversation about his occupation. Instead, he and Mom discussed recipes as they worked side by side, and then while the enchiladas baked, he moved on to telling her about his favorite restaurants in Charlotte and then the best meals he'd had abroad. Apparently he was a world traveler as well as a real estate mogul. Surely, with his good looks, expensive clothes, cool cars, and cooking abilities, he had girlfriends scattered across the globe.

Brianna looked down at her plate and tried not to snicker at the thought. When she glanced up, she found Scott watching her, and she squirmed under his gaze. She was grateful he couldn't read her thoughts.

"I'd love to have that peppered shrimp alfredo recipe you mentioned earlier," Mom said. "Would you please text it to Brianna?"

"I'd be happy to." He looked at Brianna. "I'll get her number before I leave."

Brianna's lips turned down. No way would she give this man her phone number so he could text her every day to ask if her mom was ready to sell the resort. Although she could block him after his first text message. That would solve the problem.

"Sure, Mom." Brianna hoped her tone sounded chipper enough. Then she lifted her glass of sweet tea and took a drink.

"How did you two meet again?" Mom asked.

Brianna choked and started to cough. Mom leaned over and patted her back, and her cheeks blazed with embarrassment as Scott had to gall to look concerned.

"You okay?" her mother asked as Brianna caught her breath and wiped her eyes with a napkin.

"Yeah. The tea just went down the wrong way." Brianna cleared her throat and took another sip.

"So where did you two meet?" Mom asked again.

Brianna glanced at Scott as he took another bite of enchilada, apparently giving her the lead on a response.

"Well, we ran into each other the first time at Bookends."

"Actually, *you* ran into *me*—quite literally." He grinned. "And you stepped on my foot."

"Right. Then we met on the beach later," she continued, speaking at a rapid clip. "And we saw each other again today at the Coffee Bean. When I couldn't get my tire changed, I tried to call Taylor, but he didn't answer and I got a busy signal at the store. Then Scott happened to drive by before I had a chance to call Dylan."

Mom nodded slowly, and then her brow puckered. "You met again on this beach?" She pointed toward the door that led to the part of the porch that overlooked the lake.

"Right." Brianna swallowed. "He was staying at the Lakeview Inn."

"Oh." Mom smiled at Scott. "The Hernandez place is lovely."

"Yes, it is," he said.

"I was sitting on the beach and Scott happened to walk over. We sat on the chairs and watched the sunset together." Brianna froze when she realized what she'd said. Those were her parents' chairs. She held her breath as Mom blinked, and then her mother's face crumpled.

I said the wrong thing again!

"Mom?" Brianna leaned over as Mom dropped her fork on her plate, then said, "Are you okay?"

Her mother shook her head as tears began to fall. "Excuse me," she whispered as she pushed her chair back from the table. "I need a moment." Then she stood and left.

Brianna rushed after her down the hall. "Please don't leave. You made this lovely meal, and you should enjoy it with us. Please, Mom!"

"I need some time."

Her mother shut her bedroom door, and when the lock clicked, Brianna's heart sank. She could hear sobs as she hugged her arms to her chest. How had she managed to ruin her mother's good day?

She reached up to knock, but then she felt a hand on her shoulder.

"Hey." Scott's voice was soft in her ear, sending a strange chill trilling along her spine. "It's okay. Just let her be."

He removed his hand, and Brianna looked up at him, surprised by the warmth in his expression. Maybe his concern had been genuine. "It's my fault. I had to mention those stupid chairs, and that made her think of my dad . . ." She swallowed, afraid she might break down in front of this man she barely knew.

"It's not your fault." He tilted his head. "Didn't you tell me your mom hasn't cooked or even eaten a good meal since your father passed away?"

She nodded and dabbed her eyes with her fingers.

"What was she doing when we walked into the kitchen?"

"Getting ready to cook."

"Exactly. It's a great sign that she felt inspired to make your favorite meal today."

Brianna smiled. "You're right."

"I know." His crooked smile was a little cocky, but she didn't seem to mind. He pointed to the closed door. "Just let her grieve and come out when she's ready."

She took a deep breath and felt herself calm. Then she realized Scott had consoled her just like he had on the beach that night. Could everything he'd said and done been genuine after all?

"Let's go eat," he said. "We can save her some to warm up later. When she feels stronger."

Brianna followed him to the kitchen where they sat down and ate in silence for a few minutes. At one point she glanced at him as he scooped a bite of enchilada into his mouth. Questions swirled in her head as she tried to determine his intentions. She knew he wanted to buy the resort, but he'd also kept his promise. He hadn't told Mom the real reason he was in Splendid Lake. He also went out of his way to be kind to them both.

On one hand, Brianna couldn't wait for Scott to leave and take his offer for the resort with him. And on the other, she was grateful he'd not only rescued her by the side of the road but given her mother someone with whom to discuss an interest—cooking. Other than scrambled eggs, bacon, and maybe baked chicken, she'd never learned to cook herself. Somehow Mom had known better than to try teaching a girl who thrived best in her dad's workshop.

Scott's eyebrows lifted. "Do you have something on your mind?"

"You've been very nice, but I hope you realize I'm still not going to tell my mother why you came here." She scooped salsa onto a tortilla chip. "You should give up that dream."

He reached for the bowl of chips. "Question. Are you a mechanic as well as a sports car enthusiast? You looked like you appreciated the Challenger's engine when Dylan was looking at it."

She blinked at the sudden change in subject—and the fact that he'd noticed. "I'm a boat mechanic." She pointed toward the windows. "My dad and I ran the marina together, along with the rest of the resort."

"That's why your mom teased you about not being able to change the tire."

She popped another chip into her mouth and waited for him to ask another question.

"You have two sisters who moved away, right? Both older than you?"

She swallowed and studied him. "Have you been spying on us?"

He grinned. "Not exactly. The Hernandezes mentioned them. One is a corporate lawyer in New York City and the other is an editor in California, yes? Ava mentioned them too."

"Ava did?"

"Whoops. I don't think I was supposed to tell you that."

"Really?" She leaned forward. "I'll forgive her, but tell me more."

He shrugged. "It wasn't much. After you stomped out on me earlier, Ava gave me a cup of coffee and some advice. She mentioned you're stubborn, and that I should give up trying to buy the resort. Like Mrs. Hernandez, she also said you were the sister who stayed."

"That's all true." She looked down at her plate as she moved a chip through a lake of salsa as if it were one of her boats. "I was the one who decided to follow in Dad's footsteps." She looked over at him. "Do you have siblings?"

"Not that I know of."

She studied him.

"The confused expression on your face is cute." He wiped his hands on a paper napkin. "I never met my father, so I can't be sure I have siblings. Half siblings, I guess."

"Oh." She paused, hoping he would elaborate.

He pushed the basket over to her. "These things are addictive."

"That's the truth." She took a few more.

He gestured back and forth between them. "Look at us. We're having a civil conversation like friends."

"Don't get any ideas, Gibson," she said, choosing to tease him this time rather than shut him down.

He smiled. "Your mom is great, by the way."

More questions about this guy twirled through her mind, but she ignored them. "I ate too much."

"Me too. It was delicious. Please thank your mom for me."

"I will." She stood and gathered their plates while Scott began stacking the platters and bowls. "You can go if you want. You have a three-hour drive ahead of you."

"I'm not going to eat your food and then leave you with a mess. Where do you keep your storage containers?"

Brianna directed him to the correct cabinet, and they worked side by side as she loaded the dishwasher and he stowed the leftovers. Just as she hit the dishwasher's start button, a knock sounded on the front door. Excusing herself, she walked through the family room to find Taylor stepping into the foyer.

"Hi. I wasn't expecting to see you tonight."

"I saw you called me, but I was slammed at work today. Then the fire chief called and started more of his drama about wanting new equipment when he knows we're already over budget for this year."

Taylor jammed his thumb toward the door. "Whose Challenger is that in the driveway?"

"It belongs to—" She spun toward the family room when she heard Scott come in. "Taylor, this is Scott Gibson. Scott, this is my fiancé, Taylor Reese."

"Hi." Scott shook Taylor's hand. "Nice to meet you."

Taylor looked back and forth between the two. "What's going on?"

"I had a flat today on the road between town and here, and Scott helped me. Then Mom invited him to stay for dinner."

Taylor's face clouded with confusion. "Is that why you tried to call me?"

"Yeah. I couldn't get the lug nuts off, but Scott happened to come along and got the job done."

"Why didn't you call Dylan for help?"

"I was going to, but Scott pulled up before I could. He changed the tire and then took the Mustang to Dylan's shop while I used his car to get my groceries home. Dylan's going to put new tires on it and deliver it tomorrow."

Taylor studied Scott, and she could almost hear the thoughts whirling through his brain. She braced herself as a frown creased his brow.

"Scott Gibson." Taylor repeated his name as if trying to make a connection. Then he snapped his fingers. "Aren't you the real estate guy who wants to buy this place?"

Scott nodded. "That's true."

"Well, I found your business card out in the driveway, and when I gave it to Brie, she told me to ignore it. Actually, she said I could burn it."

Scott smirked. "That doesn't surprise me."

Taylor took a step toward Scott, and now storm clouds gathered across his face, grim and foreboding. "Why are you harassing her when she already told you no?"

"That's enough." Brianna stepped between them and placed her hand flat against her fiancé's chest. "Taylor, I know you feel the need to defend me, but it's fine. Scott understands we're not selling. He also kept his promise not to mention anything about that to Mom."

Taylor's lips curled into an ugly sneer. "I think it's time for you to leave, Gibson."

"I agree. I have a long drive home." Scott turned to Brianna. "Would you please get my jacket?"

Brianna retrieved it from the closet. "Thanks for your help today," she told him as he pulled it on. "Be safe driving home."

"You're welcome. And thank you for dinner. Take care." Then he turned toward Taylor. "Nice meeting you."

"Yeah." Taylor grunted as Scott disappeared out the door. "Brie, why was he here?"

"I already told you," she said, her words measured. "He helped me out with my car, and then Mom asked him to stay for dinner."

Outside, the Challenger growled to life. Taylor pointed toward the door, and his mouth writhed before he spoke. "You let that man come into your house after he upset you so much?"

"He *helped* me. And he just happened to come along." Her voice was tight with anger.

"How convenient!" Taylor threw his hands into the air. "Maybe he was following you. You're not going to consider an offer, are you? You can't sell the resort."

"No, of course not. We're never going to sell it." She rubbed her forehead as a headache began throbbing behind her eyes. She couldn't deal with Taylor's usual overprotectiveness. Not tonight.

"Look, I'm exhausted. It's been a long day, and I need to check on my mom." She pointed toward the kitchen. "She made chicken enchiladas. There's a bag of chips on the counter and a jar of salsa in the fridge next to the leftovers in a container. Make yourself a plate and get comfortable. I'll be back."

Outside, the thunder of the Challenger disappeared in the distance, and she imagined Scott steering toward the interstate as she tapped lightly on her mother's door.

When she didn't receive a response, she leaned against the door. "Mom?" she asked softly. "Are you okay?"

She waited for a moment, but only the humming of the microwave in the kitchen filled the hallway. She tried the doorknob. It was unlocked. Perhaps Mom had expected her to come and check on her. She peeked into the room and found her snoring softly in her recliner. She'd changed into pajamas and her new favorite robe, the one Dad gave her for Christmas.

Brianna sighed as a new wave of sadness crashed over her. But then Scott's wise words echoed in her mind. *It's a great sign that she felt inspired to make your favorite meal today.* His encouragement had comforted her, even though she hated to admit it.

She tiptoed around Mom's room, and after covering her with a quilt, she gathered clothes from the hamper in the bathroom and made her way to the laundry room. She started a load, adding her own clothes she'd carried downstairs that morning. Then she gently closed the laundry room door before padding into the family room, where Taylor sat in his usual spot on the sofa, watching an old Adam Sandler movie on Netflix and eating a plate of enchiladas, chips, and salsa.

Taylor looked up and patted the cushion beside him. "Sit. How's your mom?"

"She's sleeping. She had a breakdown earlier." Brianna flopped down next to him and rested her feet on the coffee table.

"I'm sorry. But I promise, it *will* get better."

She rested her head on his shoulder, and while Taylor laughed at the movie, she found herself lost in worry for her mother and curiosity over Scott Gibson.

Then she realized she and Scott hadn't exchanged cell phone numbers so he could text the recipe her mother wanted. Perhaps that was for the best. After all, having made herself clear, she would most likely never see him again. But she found herself wondering why she felt a glimmer of disappointment at that thought.

CHAPTER 9

*S*cott forked a piece of carrot cake into his mouth and enjoyed the sweet taste as he smiled across the table at Brad's wife, Kristi.

"You like it?" Kristi beamed.

With her auburn hair and the smattering of freckles across her petite nose, it was no wonder Brad had fallen for her the moment he'd met her at a real estate conference five years ago. They'd dated for a couple of years and then married, and now they were expecting a son in about a month. His partner had it all.

"No, Kristi, I don't." Scott shook his head. "I love it."

Brad twirled his fork in the air. "You know how all those old movies show pregnant women asking their husbands to get pickles and ice cream for them?"

Scott nodded as he took another bite.

"Well, I'm luckier than those guys. This wonderful lady has been craving cake instead. This week we've had lemon cake, chocolate cake, and now carrot cake—and it's only Tuesday. How awesome is that?"

"So that's why you've been gaining weight too," Scott said.

Kristi snorted at his teasing.

"Hey, that's not nice." But Brad grinned as he touched his middle. "Maybe I should go to the gym."

Scott snickered.

Kristi leaned over and kissed Brad's cheek. "You're perfect the way you are." Then her mouth gaped and she placed her hand on her abdomen. "He's kicking!"

Brad touched her belly, and they shared a laugh and grin.

Scott turned his attention back to his half-eaten cake. He didn't want to intrude on their intimate moment. He'd always envied their loving relationship, but he was happy for his best friend.

From the time he was five, he dreamed of having at least one parent who loved him. But he gave up that dream when he turned twelve and accepted that he was way past the age when anyone would want to adopt him. But then when he was twenty-two and had been out on his own for four years, he'd formed a new dream—a long-lasting relationship that would turn into marriage and the chance to be a father. But now that he was thirty, he understood that dream might not come true either.

Still, as he watched Brad and Kristi plan for their first child's arrival, he felt that familiar tug at his heart. But he ignored the feeling and finished his cake.

"Would you like more?"

Scott found Kristi smiling at him. "Oh, no, thank you. I shouldn't. It was all delicious, though. Thank you for inviting me."

"You know you're always welcome here. You're family."

"Thanks." Scott forced a smile. While he appreciated the sentiment, he wasn't really their family. At least, not in the true sense of the word.

Brad began gathering dishes. "Let me load the dishwasher and then we can sit outside and talk shop. We can have more coffee out there to keep us warm."

"Nonsense." Kristi swatted his hand. "I can handle this. I'm pregnant, not dying."

"I'll at least carry these to the counter for you." Brad lifted the pile of dishes and headed toward the kitchen. Scott followed him with their mugs and set them on the counter before refilling his and Brad's.

"You guys get out of here." Kristi shooed them.

Brad stood over her. "I'll leave only if you promise to put your feet up after you start the dishwasher. No sweeping the floor."

"I promise. Now go."

The two men headed out to the deck, which overlooked Brad's spacious backyard behind his large house in Dilworth, a historic section of Charlotte. Scott shivered in the cool night air as he sat on a deck chair and breathed in the scent of a wood-burning fire from a home nearby. Traffic sounded in the distance.

"Are you ready to be a dad?" Scott sipped some coffee.

Brad grinned. "Absolutely. I can't wait."

Scott held his mug up to toast him. "You'll be a great one."

"I hope so."

Scott peered out toward a large oak tree and imagined a little boy swinging back and forth on a warm spring day as the sun shone in a blue sky above him. His thoughts wandered, and soon he found himself thinking about Brianna and her mother for what felt like the hundredth time since he'd driven home Friday night. He'd tried to get them out of his thoughts for the past four days, but it was impossible. They lingered there, taunting him.

He'd felt a connection to Brianna once she'd let down her guard and talked to him, and he'd longed to get to know her better. But that was completely ridiculous. She was off limits. She had a fiancé—an overprotective fiancé. Not that he blamed Taylor for watching out for Brianna, but he had overreacted a bit. Scott was also concerned about her mother and how she was handling her grief.

If only he and Brianna had exchanged phone numbers, then he

could have used sending the recipe to her as an excuse to check on both women. But once they started talking—really talking—he'd completely forgotten about the recipe. He'd been focused on getting her to open up to him.

But she'd made it clear she wanted him out of her life, if for no other reason than to keep him from asking her mother about buying the resort. If only he could stop thinking about her—and the deal he still thought might be best for everyone.

"I can't believe tomorrow is Wednesday already," Brad said, breaking the silence. "What's on the agenda for the rest of the week?"

"We need to talk about that new shopping center in South Park."

"That's right." Brad angled his body toward him. "Do you think it's a good investment?"

"Of course I do. It's South Park." Scott set his mug on the arm of the chair.

"I do too."

As Brad continued to talk about work, Scott tried to shove Brianna and Splendid Lake completely out of his mind. But his effort wasn't working.

"How's Mom?" Cassie asked through the phone.

"She's in bed already." Brianna sank into Dad's desk chair and dropped another pile of mail onto his desk. "I thought she was better, but then she melted down Friday night." She elected not to mention Scott's presence or that the meltdown had been her fault. "She got up for a while earlier today, but then she retreated to her room around four and fell asleep in her recliner. I woke her up at five and made her eat something. A little oatmeal, but that's it."

Cassie sighed. "I'm sorry to hear it."

"Yeah, it's been tough watching her go through this. I still wish you and Jen had stayed longer."

"I know, but work has been a bear. I'm behind on several projects, and I don't even have time to go to the gym anymore."

Brianna snorted. "Whatever, Cassie. You looked like a professional athlete when you were here. I'm sure you still look great."

"You'd be surprised."

Brianna began thumbing through the stack of advertisements and bills, and she hissed when she found envelopes from two more real estate investors addressed to her mother. Since Mom had told her she didn't care about the mail—not even the many cards her friends had sent—she opened one of them and found a request to talk about a "very generous offer."

"You won't believe this, Cass. I'm going through the mail, and we have two letters from real estate investors. The letter I just opened says the guy wants to come talk about buying the resort, and I'm sure the other one says about the same. I've had calls from others and a few have just stopped by. One actually came here more than once."

"No kidding? What do you tell them?"

"That the resort isn't for sale."

"That's right," Cassie said. "Don't let them bully you."

"Oh, don't worry about that. The last thing Mom needs is to be harassed by someone trying to take advantage of her."

"Call the police if they keep coming. It's trespassing. Tell them you're personal friends with the deputy mayor and the police chief."

"Right. How's work?" While her sister shared details about her current book projects, Brianna flipped through more mail, and her eyes widened when she found an envelope stamped "overdue." She was certain Dad always paid bills on time, but she did have weeks of mail she'd yet to open, and she'd probably missed a payment or two. Worrying about Mom had taken up so much energy.

When her sister finished telling about an author who never seemed to meet deadlines, she said, "Cass, Mom would really love to talk to you. I think hearing your voice would cheer her up."

"I'd love to talk to her too. I have to get going now, but text me when it's a good time?"

"Okay."

"Love you."

"Love you too."

Brianna disconnected the call and set her phone on the desk. Then she began sorting through the rest of the mail. Her stomach twisted when she found not one but three overdue bills. Two were for utilities, but the third one was about some loan. A loan? Dad had never mentioned a loan. She gasped when she saw the amount still owed.

She opened a filing cabinet and began digging. When she located a folder with information from their local bank, she sank back into the chair and began reading. Everything she found matched the loan notice. Then she switched on her father's computer and searched until she found the spreadsheet he used for tracking expenses. When she opened it, her jaw dropped at the column of negative numbers. "This can't be true," she whispered. The resort was in the red. No, it was underwater and drowning in debt.

She leaned her head back on the chair, her lungs constricting as she took in the terrible secret her father had kept from her. He'd fallen behind on property tax bills and used the resort as collateral for a loan to pay them. Then late last year he'd defaulted on that loan. He must have been so distraught. Yet he'd hidden that truth too.

She'd seen the spreadsheet over Dad's shoulder not more than a year ago when she walked into his office without his hearing her. He'd quickly clicked it closed, saying he'd work on the finances later. Did his money troubles go back that far?

Opening another window, she pulled up the bank's website, then pulled out a desk drawer to find the sticky note with her father's passwords. Although she'd warned him not to leave them where someone could find them, now she was grateful he'd never complied.

After logging into his account, she found the grim truth. There wasn't enough money in his checking account to begin to catch up on the loan payments or even the other outstanding bills. And his savings account held only the bare minimum required to keep it open.

She began to tremble as her throat suddenly felt dry and raw. If old Mr. Smith at the bank hadn't died just before Christmas, he would have made sure they knew about this right away and helped them decide what to do. But his replacement had come from Asheville, a younger man who didn't know them.

Mom could lose everything.

Brianna didn't mind emptying her own checking and savings accounts, which should at least cover food and gas for a few months. Dad had cut up every card credit those companies sent to him, preferring to use cash. She had a card for convenience, but her line of credit wasn't large, and she didn't want to go into personal debt anyway.

Dad's retirement account! But when she pulled up those records, she learned he'd emptied that, too, and had paid penalties for early withdrawal as well. Maybe that was the money he'd used to make the loan payments until recently.

"Why, Dad?" she whispered. "Why didn't you tell me?"

Then another thought hit her square in the chest. Mom didn't know about this. If she had, she would have told her. But Brianna couldn't add to her mother's already overwhelming grief. And although their usual Memorial Day weekend guests had booked their cabins the year before, they wouldn't be sending deposits. Now she wished her father had never started that tradition for their regulars, but she couldn't do anything about that now.

Will we have to sell the resort?

"No!" She would never suggest her mother sell the family's legacy, and she wouldn't be party to taking away her mother's home even if it were up to her. But they had no funds to catch up on what they owed, let alone hire the help they needed with Dad gone. It was her burden to get the resort ready for the season, and she had so little time to do it. Yet she didn't have enough cash or credit to even buy supplies. And at what point would the bank just take the resort from them?

Brianna slumped in the chair and looked up at the ceiling as anger and grief swirled in her chest. But she couldn't figure this out tonight. She needed some sleep, and she'd take a fresh look tomorrow. She'd also make an appointment with the new manager at the bank. Maybe they could work something out.

After stowing the bills and powering off the computer, Brianna stepped out of her father's office, and as she walked down the hall toward the kitchen, a heavy silence filled the empty spaces in the large lake house. She needed some company.

She opened the door to the porch. "Bucky," she called. "Do you want to sleep inside tonight?"

The cat appeared at the door and meowed loudly before slipping inside. Brianna shut the door and checked all the locks before heading upstairs. Bucky made himself comfortable, curling up on the foot of her bed while she changed into pajama pants and a worn T-shirt with a Mustang logo on it. As she crawled into bed, panic gripped her. How was she going to keep everything together?

Bucky's soft snores sounded as Brianna stared at the ceiling, worry pulling her down, down, down. She had to find a way to save the resort.

This was her home, the only home she'd ever known. And Mom would never recover if they had to leave.

"Why didn't you tell me, Dad?" she whispered through the dark. "Why did you hide this from me? I thought we shared everything with each other."

Rolling onto her side, she hugged her arms around a pillow, then felt herself sinking into a black hole of despair. Mom needed her to keep the resort afloat. It's what Dad would want her to do. But how was that possible when they were buried in such debt?

The cat snored and rolled over, pushing his little paws against her leg as he stretched.

"If only my life were as carefree as yours, Bucky," she whispered.

She slammed her eyes shut and wished for sleep, but she knew she'd be awake for hours. It would be a long night.

The following evening Brianna walked back into her father's office. After fretting about the debt situation nearly all night, she'd pushed herself through the day, including sneaking away for an appointment with the new bank manager. Thank goodness Dad had signed paperwork saying she could represent her parents if necessary.

The middle-aged man with a balding head was kind as he confirmed she and her mother didn't have much time to catch up on the loan. And he was sorry, but there was nothing he could do. Then he asked if they'd consider selling the resort. She knew he meant well, but she'd told him no and left without saying good-bye.

Then she called the accountant, who confirmed her father had been behind in property taxes. But Dad had assured him he'd taken care of it. Then he asked if she wanted his help with taxes coming due, and she said she'd have to get back to him. He might have to file some sort of extension for them.

She'd done her best to hide her worry the rest of the day, simply saying she missed Dad when Mom asked what was wrong. The truth was her anxiety had hijacked her mind, taunting her with visions of foreclosure if she didn't find a solution. At least she felt certain her sisters would never allow Mom to be homeless.

She sat at her father's desk and spread the bills in front of her before opening the files on his computer and staring at them once again. *There has to be a solution.* Leaning back in the chair, she closed her eyes and tried to open her mind. *Think, Brianna, think!*

Then a thought hit her. What was the property worth? If all those real estate investors wanted it and the bank manager had suggested selling it, perhaps it was worth more than what they owed. Maybe her mother could get another loan to consolidate all the debt and save their home and the resort.

Brianna's heart took on wings as the idea began to form in her mind, but first she needed to find out what the resort was worth. The quickest way was to ask one of the investors.

Scott Gibson's face filled her mind. He was the only investor she'd truly spoken to, and for some crazy reason, she trusted him to give her a straight answer. She glanced at her phone and found it was after nine, but if she didn't call him now, she'd be up another sleepless night worrying.

She hurried to the kitchen, then opened the junk drawer and found Scott's business card right where she'd left it the night Taylor found it on the driveway. She hurried back to the office, sank into the desk chair, and dialed his number, her heart thumping as the phone rang.

He answered after only two rings. "Hello?"

"Scott?"

"Yes."

"This is Brianna Porter."

He was silent for a beat. "Brianna. What a surprise."

"I'm sorry for calling so late. If this isn't a good time, I can call back—"

"It's fine. I was just watching TV. How are you?"

"Fine."

"How's your mom?"

"The same." She settled back in the chair. "Listen, I have a question for you. What is our property worth?"

He paused. "Why are you asking?"

"I need to know."

"Are you putting it up for sale?"

She looked at the letters from other investors. "Several people are interested in it, and I need to know what it's really worth. I'm trusting you to tell me the truth."

"Are you giving me first dibs with your mother?"

"What offer would you make her if I did?"

"Well, it depends." He hesitated. "I need to do some research."

"How soon can you do it?"

"Brianna, what aren't you telling me?"

She rubbed her forehead. "I just need to know what the resort is worth."

"How about this? I'll do the research tonight, then come up there tomorrow and show you what other properties are worth in your area. We can talk about it then."

"Okay, but I'm not making any promises."

"I respect that. So I can come tomorrow?"

"Yes."

"I'll be there."

"Thank you."

"Good night, Brianna."

"Good night." She disconnected the call and blew out a sigh of relief as hope swelled in her chest. If Scott was willing to drop all his plans to come tomorrow, the resort had to be worth a lot of money. And if it was, maybe Mom could get that consolidated loan and fix this.

Maybe, just maybe, they wouldn't lose their home and livelihood.

CHAPTER 10

*M*om?" Brianna knocked lightly on her mother's bedroom door. It was already nine thirty. "Are you awake?"

When she didn't hear a response, she gingerly turned the knob and opened the door. "Mom?" She peered at her parents' king-sized bed, where her mother grumbled and rolled over.

"I'm heading outside to get some work done, but I'll check on you in a bit."

Brianna returned to the kitchen and leaned against the counter, then bit into the bagel she'd smothered in cream cheese as she studied the list she'd made the night before. She'd recorded everything she knew needed to be done before they could open the resort in May. Every one of their dozen cabins needed replacement shingles, several toilets needed repair, the convenience store and bait shop had to be painted, and the pier needed some new boards.

She sighed and started a second list for supplies. She also had to deep-clean each of the cabins, repair some of the stackable washers and dryers in them, and check all the air-conditioning units—to say nothing of getting the johnboats ready.

"How am I going to do this all by myself?" she whispered. "Mom is in no condition to help, and I can't afford to hire anyone until our debt situation is resolved."

But the bigger question loomed at the back of her mind: whether consolidating the debt was possible and would even make enough difference. She'd figure that out once she knew more about the resort's worth. Her heart gave a funny little kick. For some reason she was looking forward to seeing Scott—and not only for information. But that was ridiculous, and she turned her attention back to her list.

After finishing her bagel, Brianna pulled on her favorite gray hoodie and stepped out onto the porch. "Bucky!" she called as she picked up the cat's bowls. She carried them inside, then washed them out and filled them.

Bucky met her on the porch with a loud meow and a shin rub.

"And good morning to you." Brianna set the bowls down and rubbed Bucky's head as he started to eat. When she straightened up, she heard the loud roar of an engine in the distance, then stilled as it grew louder and louder until it sounded as if it were coming up their rock driveway. She walked around to the front part of the porch to see Scott's Challenger. He'd arrived much earlier than she'd expected.

Scott climbed out of the car, wearing the same black leather jacket and a green collared shirt and jeans. His hair was tousled, as if he'd driven with his window open, and the stubble on his chin was gone again, revealing his strong, chiseled jaw. He held a portfolio in his hand, which she assumed contained the precious information that could change her situation.

"Good morning," he said as he jogged up the steps.

"You're earlier than I expected."

"I got an early start." He looked past her toward the porch floor. "Who's this?"

Brianna glanced down as Bucky sauntered over, then flopped beside her feet and began licking his paws. "That's Bucky."

"Hi, Bucky." Scott smiled up at her. "How's your day so far?"

"Okay. I was about to start on some work on the cabins since I wasn't expecting to see you until this afternoon."

He nodded in the direction of the dozen small structures. "Do you need any help?"

"Not unless you know how to roof, fix toilets, and repair piers."

"You bet."

"What?" Surely he was joking.

"I can roof, and I've done some minor plumbing. Maybe I can figure out the pier if I take a look at it."

"Mr. Brooks Brothers knows how to fix things?"

Scott's eyes narrowed as he leveled his gaze with hers. "What does *that* mean?"

Caught off guard, she opened her mouth but then closed it as heat crawled up her neck. "I only meant you looked like you'd just walked out of a Brooks Brothers ad when you came here in that nice suit."

His brow crumpled, and she swallowed against her suddenly dry throat.

"For your information, I wasn't always in real estate. When I turned eighteen, I got a job working construction. I worked that job for five years while I went to school at night and studied real estate. I've built my own shed and my own deck, and I do my own home improvements." He'd ticked off each accomplishment on his fingers. "I'm not a total moron."

She cringed, feeling like a complete jerk. "I'm sorry." She pointed behind her. "Why don't we go inside and see what information you put together for me? We can talk about the chores around here later."

Once in the kitchen, they stood at the counter as he opened his portfolio. She tried to ignore the scent of his cologne with little success.

"Here's what I found about the properties in this area, especially any on a body of water." He selected several printouts. "Of course, you also have the cabins and several other structures. Plus you have the marina and pier and a business built over several decades. Based on the comps and all that, here's what I've determined is the fair value of your entire property."

He pointed to a number at the bottom of one of the documents. She thought it would be enough to move forward with her plan to secure a consolidation loan, but confusion still ran through her mind.

"What do you think?" he asked.

Brianna turned to look out the window.

"Are you open to selling?"

"I-I don't know."

"What aren't you telling me?"

"What makes you think I'm keeping something from you?"

"Well, let's see. When I first tried to make an offer on your resort, you called me names and threw me off your property. You've changed your tune a few times since, but . . . Look, I honestly never expected to hear from you again." His expression seemed to plead with her. "Please tell me what's going on."

She faced him and found he had rested his hip against the counter, and his baby-blue eyes seemed to assess her. "My dad never told me we were in trouble, but he left some serious debt. I don't even know how I can pay for supplies for the repair and maintenance necessary before we open Memorial Day weekend."

He nodded slowly. "I see."

"I haven't figured out what I'm going to do yet. After I tell my mother about this, I need to discuss it with her and probably my sisters as well. But that's why I needed to know what this property is worth. I think it's more than we owe, and I might be able to get a consolidation loan and manage to stay afloat."

"That's a decision you can't make quickly, and I understand." He looked down at his portfolio, then back up at her. "But no matter what, you have to get the resort ready. It can't just sit here. If it stays in disrepair and you can't open on time, the place won't be worth as much—not to sell and not for a loan."

"That's true, but like I said, I don't have money for supplies. I can't buy shingles to replace the ones damaged in a storm we had back in October. I can't buy the lumber to repair the pier. I also don't know how to fix the pier, but I can't afford to hire someone to do it. I'm sort of stuck right now."

He rubbed his chin, and she could almost see a plan forming in his mind. "I'll make a deal with you. I'll personally help with the maintenance and even buy the supplies if you make me one promise."

"What?"

"If you don't sell, or even if you sell to another investor, you'll reimburse me for my time and purchases."

She bit her lip and considered his intentions. Why would Scott Gibson want to hang around here doing physical work when he had better things to do? Was he trying to manipulate her again? Or was he genuinely interested in helping her and her mother?

Who was she kidding? It didn't matter. She was desperate, and if he'd truly worked in construction, he was just the help she needed.

"It's a deal." She held out her hand, and he shook it.

He jammed his thumb toward the door. "I have a bag with more clothes in my car. I was going to see if I could get a room at the inn next door and stay for the weekend if you wanted to keep talking about what my research found. I'll change, and then we can get some of those supplies. I want to be sure I buy the right things."

"Okay." She looked toward the hallway. Mom's bedroom door was still closed. "My mother still isn't up. Let me go check on her again. If she's awake, I need to make her breakfast before we leave."

While Scott headed outside, Brianna hurried down the hallway and knocked on her mother's door. "Mom. It's almost ten. Would you like something to eat?"

No response. She opened the door and found her mother still in bed but staring at the wall. Her heart began to pound. "Mom, are you okay?"

When she reached the bed, her mother looked at her, but her expression was blank—as if she didn't understand what Brianna had said.

"Mom?" Brianna heard the tremble in her voice. "Can you get up?"

Mom blinked but didn't move.

"Mom?" Alarm clenched Brianna's lungs. "Please answer me." She touched her arm, and Brianna's blood went still in her veins as her mother still didn't respond.

"I'm going for help." Brianna rushed down the hallway and into the kitchen, almost bumping into Scott as he came toward her.

"What's wrong?"

"Mom's not responding to me. I-I don't know what to do. She won't get up, and she won't speak."

"Calm down. Breathe." Scott took her hand in his, and the feel of warm skin against hers gave her a tiny spark of hope to hold on to. "Let's go see her together."

She allowed him to steer her down the hallway, and when they reached her mother's bedroom, Scott released her hand. She hugged her arms to her chest as he walked to the bed.

"Mrs. Porter," he began, his words measured. "Can you get out of bed?"

Mom met his gaze but didn't speak.

"Please, Mom." Brianna had to shove the words past her thickening throat. "Tell us what's wrong."

Her mother's eyes closed, and Scott crouched down next to the bed. "Mrs. Porter, Brianna and I are very worried about you. Would you please try to sit up?"

"I-I-I c-c-can't." Mom's words sounded warbled, like water spilling over a creek bed. The right side of her mouth had slacked to one side.

Brianna felt a shock of fear. Something was terribly wrong.

I can't lose Mom too!

"It's okay." Scott's words were calm as he stood. "We're going to get you some help." He turned toward Brianna, then took her hand in his and pulled her away from the bed.

Brianna couldn't stem her tears as they moved to the far corner of the room. She grabbed a tissue from her mother's dresser and wiped her eyes.

Scott's expression was grave. "I think your mother has had a stroke," he whispered.

An icicle formed in Brianna's gut as he pulled his phone from his pocket. "I'm calling nine-one-one. Who can you call to meet you at the hospital?"

She sniffed. "Taylor or Ava, but they're both working."

He held the phone up to his ear. "I need an ambulance right away."

Scott gave the details, and a cold and clammy dread spread over Brianna. She looked over at her mother, who kept her eyes closed. Then she leaned back against the dresser and tried to take deep, calming breaths.

When he ended the call, Scott rested his hands on her forearms.

"Help is on the way. I can go with you, follow the ambulance in my car. I don't mind."

"No, it's okay." Her voice came out in a croak. "One of them will come."

"I have your phone number from when you called me. Do you still have mine?"

She nodded, her thoughts spinning.

He pointed toward the doorway. "I'll stay until the ambulance gets here, but what supplies do you need me to get while you're gone? And then what do you need me to do?"

"There's a list on the counter in the kitchen. On the peg board you'll find the barn keys. Our tools are in there. And any other keys you need should be there as well."

"I noticed an old Dodge pickup truck parked by the barn. Does it run?"

"Yes." She rubbed her forehead. "The keys are on the peg board too." She grabbed the chair from her mother's desk. "I'm going to sit with her." She pulled the chair over to the bed and sat on it, taking her mother's hand in hers. "Mom, you're going to be fine," she whispered, but her mother kept her eyes closed.

When another wave of fear hit her, her lower lip quivered and she looked down at the toes of her purple boots. A warm hand on her shoulder offered a fraction of comfort.

"Hey."

She looked up at Scott and sniffed.

"She'll be okay."

She nodded, grateful he was there, then turned to her mother, ready to face whatever came next.

CHAPTER 11

*B*rianna!" Ava hurried across the surprisingly empty ER waiting area and handed her a coffee and a small paper bag. "I brought your favorite blend and a cinnamon raisin bagel with cream cheese. I didn't know if you'd eaten anything yet today."

"Thank you." Brianna took a sip of the delicious brew. "Perfect."

"My mom came in to help Brooklyn, and I got here as soon as I could. I'm so glad our county hospital is this close to Splendid Lake." Ava frowned. "How is she?"

Brianna took another sip, then shook her head. "I don't know. I haven't talked to a doctor. I'm assuming it's a stroke, but I haven't texted my sisters yet because I don't want to worry them until I know for sure." She felt another wave of fear start to crest in her chest, and she cleared her throat and pulled out the bagel. "Thank you for bringing this. I didn't want to risk missing the doctor just to go to the cafeteria for some lunch."

Ava glanced around the room. "You don't have to thank me. Where's Taylor?"

Brianna swallowed a bite of bagel, then wiped her hands on a napkin. "He's been checking in."

"Checking in?" Ava's eyes narrowed. "You're in crisis. Why isn't he here?" She pointed to the beige tile below them for emphasis.

Brianna set her cup on the little table at one end of a sofa, then sat down. "Apparently he's having his own crisis. Tammy had her baby, so she's out now, which means he's running the store alone. Plus, the fire chief threatened to quit if they don't get the new equipment he wants." She gestured with her arms. "That whole situation has been going on for a while, and it exploded this morning."

"So?" Ava shook her head, and her wavy ponytail swished back and forth as she plopped down beside her. "This is more important than the fire chief getting his shorts twisted over some equipment. Taylor should have asked his father to run the store today. He should be here."

Brianna agreed with Ava, but she didn't have the emotional energy to express it. "I'm just glad you're here."

Ava took Brianna's hand in hers. "You know you can always count on me."

That was the truth. Ava was the first person to arrive at the house after her father died. And she was always there when Brianna needed someone. Brianna did her best to do the same for her.

She'd just opened her mouth to thank her friend when her phone rang. When she saw Scott's name on the screen, her heart flopped like a fish out of water, and that confused her. "Hello?"

"Hey." Scott's voice sounded warm through the phone. "Any updates?"

Brianna cupped her hand to her forehead. "I'm hanging by a thread here. I haven't spoken to a doctor yet. I've only heard they're running tests."

"Okay." He paused. "I can come and sit with you."

Her heart lifted. "I'm fine. Ava is with me." She glanced over at Ava, who looked confused. "How are things there?"

"Good. I like your dad's old Dodge."

She smiled. "The Dodge? It is a good old truck."

"It's fun to drive. I got most of the supplies. I'll have to go back for the rest when we need them."

"Thank you."

"Well, I won't keep you. Text me when you hear something."

"I will. Thanks for calling."

"Of course. Take care."

She disconnected the call and glanced at Ava, who was studying her hard.

"That didn't sound like Taylor."

"It was Scott Gibson."

"Wait a minute." She held up her hand. "Let me get this straight. You told me he rescued you by the side of the road, let you drive his super-cool sports car to save your groceries, and gave you a ride home from Dylan's shop. Then he stayed for dinner, and you figured you wouldn't hear from him again. Now he's calling you?"

"He was with me when I found Mom in trouble. He was the one who called nine-one-one."

"Where is he now?"

"At the house."

Ava held up her hand again. "Whoa. Are you friends now?"

Brianna considered this as she scrunched her nose. "More like frenemies."

She told Ava about her dad's debt, leaving out the full extent of the jeopardy to their home. She didn't want her best friend to worry. Then she told her about her call to Scott and his trip up from Charlotte. "Scott offered to help me with all the preparations I need to make before the resort opens as long as we reimburse him if we sell the resort, even if it's not to him. I gave him the keys to Dad's truck so he could get supplies. He just got back."

"Wow. That's a twist."

Just then a middle-aged woman wearing a white coat walked through the double doors leading to the ER and made her way to Brianna and Ava. Brianna noted her beautiful coloring, short black hair with tight curls peppered with gray, smooth dark skin, and long eyelashes. She also had kind eyes.

"Excuse me. Are you Mrs. Porter's family?"

"I am." Brianna stood. "I'm her daughter, Brianna."

"I'm Dr. Mason." She shook Brianna's hand, then said, "May I please speak with you in private?" She nodded toward a small room with a door off the waiting area.

"Yes." Brianna looked at Ava. "I'll be right back."

Ava nodded. "Of course."

Brianna followed the doctor into the room, then shut the door behind them before they sat at a small table.

The doctor's expression was grave yet caring. "I'm sorry to tell you your mother has indeed suffered a stroke, affecting her right side."

A sob escaped Brianna's throat, and she lost her breath. Mom was right-handed.

"I know this is difficult." The doctor reached across the table and touched Brianna's arm. "The paramedics did a wonderful job, but we're going to run more tests to see how much damage was done. Then when she's able—and I do think she will be—we'll arrange for your mother to enter a rehabilitation facility."

"I . . . I understand."

"Do you have any questions?"

Thoughts passed through her head in a fog. *A stroke! This can't be happening!*

"Will she make a full recovery?"

The doctor blew out a deep sigh. "We're hopeful that she will, but the tests will tell us a lot."

"When can I see her?"

"Soon. We'll formally admit her and settle her in a room shortly."

"Thank you."

The doctor left, and Brianna trudged back to the waiting room, feeling the weight of anxiety and grief pressing on her shoulders as she sank into the lumpy sofa next to Ava.

"What happened?" Ava's words were soft, her pretty dark eyes wide.

"Scott was right. Mom had a stroke. It's affected her right side."

"Oh no." Ava pulled her close for a hug. "I'm so sorry."

Brianna's voice quavered as she shared the information the doctor gave her. Then she settled back on the sofa and stared out the floor-to-ceiling windows. She felt as if her world was spinning completely out of control again, and she was ready for it to stop long enough to catch her breath.

"Talk to me, Brie. Don't hold in your emotions."

Brianna cleared her throat. "I need to contact my sisters."

"Go use one of those private rooms and take all the time you need."

Brianna made her way into the same small room and texted Cassie and Jenna.

Need to talk right away. It's an emergency.

Within a few minutes, she was on a three-way call.

"What's going on?" Jenna said, her tone more demanding than Brianna could take right now.

"It's Mom."

"What's wrong?" Cassie already sounded distraught.

Brianna fought back a rush of sorrow. "She had a stroke. I'm at the hospital with her."

"What?" Cassie cried.

"Oh no," Jenna whispered. "How bad?"

Brianna dropped into a chair. "I don't know yet, but it's affected her right side, and her speech has been affected too. They're still running tests. Then if she's in any condition to do so, they'll transfer her to a rehab facility." She closed her eyes as the reality of the situation stole her breath.

"Do you know which rehab facility?" Jenna asked.

"No, I don't know anything like that yet."

"She needs good care," Jeanna continued. "I'll call around to see which facilities are the best in the area. Maybe we should demand that they send her to Charlotte."

Brianna's nostrils flared as fury boiled in her chest. She had zero patience for her older sister's arrogance. "Jen, I think you're getting ahead of yourself. And me. I'm the one who's here."

"No, I'm not, actually," Jenna snipped. "We all need to think about the quality of Mom's care."

"Uh, Jen," Cassie began, "I think the doctors can decide where Mom needs to go. After all, they're the experts."

Brianna blew out a deep breath. *Thank you, Cassie!*

"That's not true," Jenna said, always countering. "It's our job to take care of Mom."

"As a matter of fact, you're right," Brianna began as some barrier inside her broke apart. She was ready for her sisters to step up. "And that's why I need your help. You two don't even know the half of it! This week I found out Dad left us in serious debt, and I'm still sorting through it all. Meanwhile, I have no idea how I'm going to pay Mom's hospital bills, let alone for rehab. When we got here, I discovered Dad had the most basic health insurance for him and Mom he could find. It won't cover much."

"How much money will you need for the medical bills?" Jenna asked. "I'll send you what I can."

"I don't know yet."

"I'll send you some money as well," Cassie said.

"I have another problem too," Brianna continued. "You know the resort opens Memorial Day weekend, and I have a ton of work to do before then. The cabins need some new shingles, the pier needs replacement boards, I have to get the johnboats ready . . . And that's just the tip of the iceberg. I'm in way over my head without Dad, and now Mom is sick."

"Hire someone to help," Jenna said as if it were the most logical solution—for someone with money.

"I just told you we're steeped in debt," Brianna snapped. "Didn't you hear me?"

"Can't Taylor help?" Cassie chimed. "He always seems to do whatever you say."

Offended, Brianna flinched. "Taylor works two jobs, remember? He's running the farm supply store *and* helping run the town."

"Can't he let his assistant manage the store for a while?" Cassie asked. "Tammy?"

"No. He can't. She's on maternity leave."

"I'll see how much money I can scrounge together," Jenna said. "You know I just moved, and moving in Manhattan isn't cheap. Nothing here is."

"Thanks. But realize this: if you don't come help make decisions about the finances and Mom's care, you don't get to question the decisions I make." Brianna took a deep breath. "You both need to understand that while offering money is helpful, what I really need is your presence and support. I'm feeling completely alone and over-whelmed, and a million dollars wouldn't fix all the problems."

"You always have our support, Brie," Cassie said. "I'm sorry you feel so alone."

Brianna almost smiled. Cassie was a bit selfish, but she could count on her as the sweet and caring one next to Jenna, who was always so quick to judge and condemn.

"I'm slammed at work right now, but I'll do my best to offer you emotional support," Jenna said.

"Thanks," Brianna said, believing Jenna did mean the latter part of her statement. But she'd had enough of her sisters for now. "I need to go. I'll call you both later, after I see Mom."

"Take care," Cassie said. "We love you."

"Give her a kiss for us," Jenna added.

"Sure. Good-bye." Brianna disconnected the call, then gazed down at her phone as her irritation simmered. She'd never understand *why* her sisters were selfish. They'd all been raised by the same wonderful, caring parents. But she loved them, which was probably why she hadn't told them losing the resort was a possibility. Or maybe because they rarely treated her like an adult, especially Jenna.

She returned to the waiting room, and Ava looked up from her phone when Brianna lowered herself back on the sofa.

"How did it go?" Ava asked.

"My sisters haven't changed. They're sending money to help cover the medical bills, I expect, but they didn't offer to come. Not even when I told them about the debt and how much I need them."

Ava rubbed her arm. "Give them time. They'll come."

"I doubt it."

"Did you tell them your mom could lose the resort?"

Brianna's phone buzzed with a text before she could answer. Taylor was asking about her mother.

> The dr said she had a stroke, affecting her right side. She'll have to go to rehab.
>
> *I'm sorry. You okay?*
>
> I'm managing. Ava's here.
>
> *Good. I'll check in soon.*

"He's a man of few words," Ava said, reading over Brianna's shoulder.

"Hey." Brianna pulled her phone away. "It's rude to snoop."

"It's not rude if I'm your best friend." Ava stood and stretched. "I'm hungry. What can I get you from the cafeteria?"

"I'm dying for a Diet Coke and some chips."

"Coming right up. I'll get you a sandwich too."

Brianna opened her purse and reached for her wallet.

"Put your money away. It's on me. Be right back."

As Brianna watched Ava walk toward the hallway to the cafeteria, she smiled. Her sisters had let her down, but her best friend never did.

Scott climbed down the ladder, then stretched and yawned. He'd enjoyed exploring the cabins before spending most of the afternoon fixing toilets in a few of them, noting that all twelve cabins had one bathroom, a galley kitchen, a small living area with a table and chairs, and a small screened-in porch. But half had two bedrooms and half had three.

The cabins were homey and sweet, but he was eager to upgrade them. Some of the furniture was at least twenty years old, and the appliances weren't much newer. He also thought adding a bathroom and bedroom to a few of the cabins was a great idea. They'd be able to charge more rent.

He'd allowed those and other ideas to percolate all afternoon, then after completing what he could inside the cabins, he'd turned to replacing shingles on one of the roofs. Now his back ached, and the muscles in his shoulders were tight. But it felt great to work with his hands again. He'd forgotten how much he enjoyed using tools and seeing the fruits of his labor come to life.

His stomach growled, and he checked the time on his phone. Almost five o'clock. Brianna and her mother had been on his mind all afternoon, and he hadn't received a message from Brianna in more than an hour. Last he'd heard, she'd been in to see Mrs. Porter, but her mother was sleeping.

His heart had splintered for Brianna when he'd realized her mother had probably suffered a stroke. The terror in her beautiful brown eyes had nearly torn him in two, but he'd tried to stay calm and console her. He was grateful she agreed to allow him to work on some projects around the resort. Not only did she need the help, but for her sake and his, he had to be sure the resort was ready to open Memorial Day weekend.

Scott considered his tenuous relationship with Brianna as he walked toward the barn. She didn't even consider him a friend, yet he felt a connection growing between them. That concerned him since he was fully aware she was off limits. She and Taylor were engaged. Maybe they could be friends at some point, though—if she was even interested in that.

He stowed the tools, supplies, and ladder and then headed into the house, where he deposited all the keys he'd used. Then, desperately needing a shower, he collected his duffel bag, glad he always traveled with every toiletry he could possibly need. Once on the second floor, though, he slowly walked down the hallway to look at a line of family photos.

He took in shots of Brianna grinning as a toddler through her graduation from high school. He grinned himself, admiring her school portraits from the days when she had missing teeth to the years she sported braces. One quality had remained constant, though—she'd always been beautiful.

Peering at other family photos, he surmised which sister was Jenna and which one was Cassie based on their relative heights as children. In a photo including all five Porter family members, he took in Martin's smile and decided he'd been a nice man. Brianna had definitely inherited his golden-brown eyes.

He moved on to a photo of Brianna and Martin on a boat together, the lake sparkling around them. Scott took in the happiness in their wide grins, and he could only imagine the depth of Brianna's grief.

Then he peeked into what must be her bedroom, spotting photos of her and Ava, her with Taylor, and then one of all three of them along with Dylan. He wondered what it felt like to be part of Brianna's inner circle.

Her room was just as he'd imagined—obviously a girl's, yet not too girlie. It was a good mix of florals, cars, and boats, which made him smile. Brianna was an interesting puzzle. She was feminine with her purple western boots and long hair, but then she had her mechanical smarts, and Scott appreciated that about her too. He admired everything about Brianna. Maybe more than made sense.

Pulling himself away from her room—her sanctuary—he headed back into the hallway and found a bathroom and a towel. After showering and changing his clothes, he made his way to the kitchen, then checked his phone and found a message from Brianna.

> Should be home in about an hour. Ava's
> bringing me. See you soon.
> *Sounds good. Take your time.*

An idea formed in his head. He was certain Brianna would appreciate coming home to a decent meal after the day she'd had. He just hoped he had enough time to pull one together.

CHAPTER 12

*B*rianna yawned as Ava drove. Neither had much to say. It had been a long day—the longest day—and she was grateful to be on her way home. She craved a shower and a good night's sleep, but first she needed to eat. Perhaps she'd find leftovers in the refrigerator.

Her phone rang, and when she glanced at the screen, she saw Taylor's name. "Hello?"

"Hey. Where are you?"

"On my way home. Ava's driving me." She cupped her hand to her mouth to stifle another yawn.

Taylor hesitated. "I'm sorry for not being there today. The store was busy, and then the fire chief threatened to take a job in Asheville. If he leaves, he could badmouth the mayor and me and ruin our reputations, you know? I felt like a chicken with its head cut off, running around trying to keep up, but you and your mom were on my mind all day. I've been so worried about you."

Brianna sighed. "I understand," she said, working to keep her voice even.

"Why don't I come over?"

"No, it's okay."

"I could bring some food. You've got to be starving, and I know the fare in that place is awful. Why don't I pick up some takeout? Maybe Japanese this time?"

"No, really, Taylor. It's fine. I really just want to shower and go to bed."

"But I want to make it up to you."

"How about another day?"

"Are you sure?"

"Yes, I'm positive. You go rest after your tough day, and I'll do the same."

"Okay." He paused for a beat. "I love you."

"I love you too. Talk to you tomorrow." Then she disconnected the call and gripped the car's door handle with such force that her fingers ached. Thankfully, Ava didn't say a word, but she had to be exhausted too.

She'd wanted Taylor by her side today, not caring whether he was busy. Ava was busy, too, yet she'd found a way to spend the day with her. She considered this as they stopped at a red light. The few times Ava's family had faced an emergency, both Brianna and Dylan were there for her. Brianna had always expected the same from Taylor, but he was constantly overbooked. Maybe that was the burden she had to bear as the fiancée of the town's deputy mayor, but did that make it right?

She contemplated that for the remainder of the ride home.

When they reached her driveway, her heart picked up speed. She'd thought Scott was getting a room at the Lakeview Inn, but his car was still parked beside her Mustang. Why was he still here?

"Will you be okay?" Ava asked, nodding at Scott's car.

"Yes. Don't worry. You need to get home, and I'll let you know about any change with Mom. Thanks again for being there for me today."

"I wouldn't be anywhere else."

Brianna gathered her purse, then exited the car and climbed the steps to the front door as Ava turned her car around and left. Once inside, she moved toward the family room, where Bruce Willis was climbing through air vents in *Die Hard* and Scott softly snored on the sofa.

She shook her head with a smile and tiptoed to the kitchen, where a delicious aroma made her stomach gurgle with delight. She set her purse on a kitchen chair and crossed to the stove to find a covered pot. When she lifted the lid, she sucked in a breath at the sight of beef stroganoff and egg noodles.

Oh, Scott! You read my mind!

She snatched a spoon from a drawer and scooped a bite directly into her mouth. Then she closed her eyes as her taste buds danced with pleasure.

"Too spicy, right?"

She gasped and spun, pressing her hand to her chest to catch her breath.

Scott stood in the doorway, looking blurry-eyed and adorable as his hair stood up at odd angles. "Sorry. I didn't mean to startle you."

"It's delicious, and it's just what I needed. Thank you."

"You're welcome." He walked to the stove and turned on the burner under the pot. "It just needs to warm up a little."

She stared, trying to figure him out. "Where did you learn to cook?"

"I took a cooking class to impress a woman a few years ago." He leaned back on the counter and pushed his hand through his messy hair.

"Did it work?"

He rubbed the chin stubble that had reappeared. "I guess not since the relationship didn't last long."

"Huh." She wondered if he had someone special in his life now.

But if he did, he most likely wouldn't have come to Splendid Lake without her. "Where did you find this recipe?"

He pulled his phone out of his pocket. "Would you think less of me if I told you I have an app for that?"

"Not at all since I'm benefiting from it."

"Good." His crooked grin made its grand entrance. "I assumed you didn't eat, and even if you did, hospital food isn't that great."

"What can't you do?"

"What do you mean?" His brow furrowed as he met her gaze.

She started counting off on her fingers. "You know real estate, you know cars, you can build and fix things, and you're a chef. What don't you know?"

"I'm not a chef, and you probably know more about cars than I do." He stirred the stroganoff with a wooden spoon, then turned toward her with his arms crossed over his chest. "But enough about that. How are you holding up?"

She took a deep breath, and then her lip trembled as all the stress of the day seemed to pool in her eyes.

He dropped his arms to his sides. "Oh, hey. I'm sorry." He started to reach for her but pulled back. At that moment, though, she wished he *would* hold her.

"Don't apologize." She grabbed a handful of paper napkins and mopped her face. "I'm a mess. It's so hard to be strong. How am I supposed to do it all?"

"You don't have to do it all." He retrieved two plates from the nearby cabinet.

"You haven't eaten?"

He scooped some of his creation onto the first plate. "No. I waited for you."

For some reason that made her heart turn over. Why did she so badly want to trust this man? She grabbed utensils and poured two glasses of sweet tea before they sat across from each other at the table.

As she ate, her shoulders relaxed for the first time since they'd found Mom in trouble, and they sat in a comfortable silence for several minutes, metal clinking against their plates.

When she glanced up and found Scott looking at her, a wall of caution inside her crumbled. She lowered her fork. "The doctor told me Mom will have to go into rehab. I'm so stressed. I don't know how I'll ready the resort and manage her care at the same time."

"I told you. You don't have to do it all. I meant it when I said I'll help you."

Brianna rested her elbow on the table and her chin on one palm as she looked at him. "Thank you." Then she looked down at her half-eaten plate of food. "This is delicious."

"I'm glad you like it." He paused. "I worked on the toilets, and then I started replacing shingles on one of the cabin roofs."

"What will I owe you for the supplies?"

"We'll figure that out when you decide what you're going to do. Right now you need to focus on taking care of yourself so you can take care of your mother."

She put her hands over her eyes for a moment. "This has complicated everything. I didn't even know how to broach the subject of this debt with Mom *before* she had a stroke."

Scott opened his mouth to respond, but before he could, the doorbell rang. Brianna pushed her chair back and stood.

Scott stood too. "Are you expecting someone?"

"No."

"I'll come with you." He followed her to the front of the house.

Brianna pulled open the door and found her fiancé glaring. "Taylor, hey. I wasn't expecting you."

Taylor looked past her, his face contorting into a mask of fury. "Well, that's obvious. Is *he* why you didn't want me to come tonight?"

Scott frowned. "I'll clean up the kitchen."

Brianna watched him disappear, and the sound of water running in the sink followed as she turned to face Taylor, trying to keep a surge of anger in check. She pointed to the family room's french doors leading to the porch. "Wait out there for me. I'll be back in a minute."

Taylor stomped outside as Brianna hurried into the kitchen, where Scott stood at the sink rinsing plates. He craned his neck over his shoulder to look at her.

"I'm going to talk to Taylor for a few minutes."

"Take your time."

Brianna found her still-seething fiancé pacing along the porch railing. "Please calm down. It's not what you think. I asked Scott to come evaluate the resort, and he just happened to still be here when Mom had the stroke. Then he stuck around and did a few jobs around the resort. You know I need help."

Taylor's eyes were angry and hard, his lips twisted with resentment. "Can't you see he's using you?" He pointed toward the house. "He wants the resort so much he'll do anything to convince you to sell it to him."

"No, it's not that."

"Of course it is. Didn't you tell me he was nice to you on the beach the night of your dad's funeral just to manipulate you? Are you blind, Brie? That's what he's doing now!"

"No, I'm not blind, and he's not like that." She took a deep breath. "Like I said, I invited him here."

"Why are you asking him to evaluate the resort anyway? I don't understand."

As Brianna filled him in on the discovered debt, Taylor's expression flickered with confusion. "So . . . you're going to advise your mother to sell?"

She held up her hand. "I didn't say that. I just need to know what options my family has."

Taylor looked toward the water, then kicked a post near the porch steps. "Look, I'm sorry I haven't been around. I've been caught up in my own issues."

"It's fine."

"It's not fine, and I hate it when you say that."

She peered at the lake and tried to stop the irritation that bubbled inside her. She was too emotionally exhausted to deal with this tonight. "Why don't you go home? We can discuss this tomorrow."

Something shifted in his expression, and he took a step toward her. "Are you having an affair with Scott?" His voice was cold.

"Are you kidding me?" she snapped. "My mother had a stroke today, and you have the nerve to accuse me of having an affair?" She gave a humorless laugh. "You think I'm blind, but you're deaf. Have you heard anything I've said to you? I need help around here, and Scott offered it—something my own sisters can't even manage to do when I can't possibly take care of my mother and get the resort ready to open by myself all at the same time." Then she snorted. "Even if I wanted to have an affair, I wouldn't have time for one!"

"Why don't I help you around here? Then that guy can go back to Charlotte."

"Really? You didn't even have time to come to the hospital when my mother had a stroke."

He winced, and guilt replaced her fury.

"Look, I'm sorry," she said, her voice calm. "That was a low blow, but I'm stressed out and ready to fall over from exhaustion."

Taylor glared at something behind her, and she pivoted to find

Scott standing in the doorway, holding a duffel bag. "Where are you going?"

"To find a hotel room."

"I thought you were staying at the Lakeview Inn."

Scott shook his head. "I called earlier and learned they're closed this weekend. Apparently they went out of town. I should have checked with them before I left Charlotte this morning, but—"

"You can stay in one of our guest rooms."

"That's probably not the best idea considering the circumstances." Scott's eyebrows lifted as he looked toward Taylor.

Brianna spun to face Taylor and glowered. "Act your age, Taylor. We're all adults, so give me a break."

Then she faced Scott. "You're working here for free until I have the money to reimburse you. The least I can do is give you a place to stay." She turned back toward Taylor again. "You come inside. Let me show Scott upstairs, and then I'll be back."

Ignoring Taylor's scowl, she led Scott upstairs and pointed to the first door on the left. "This is my room." Then she gestured down the hallway. "The other two are my sisters' when they visit. All their personal belongings are gone, but we always keep the rooms made up." She nodded toward the second door on the right. "The bathroom is down there. Just pick a bedroom and make yourself at home."

He gave her an embarrassed expression. "I actually took a shower up here after working in the cabins. I hope that's okay."

"Of course it is." She folded her arms over her chest and lowered her voice. "I'm sorry about Taylor. He's been a bit jealous and over-protective lately. Please don't take it personally."

He cupped his hand to the back of his neck. "I really can't blame him."

"I'm glad you're here." She touched his arm. "Thank you for everything."

"You're welcome. I'm going to turn in. I have a feeling I'll fall asleep the minute my head hits the pillow. Good night." He headed down the hall, disappearing into Cassie's former bedroom.

Taylor met Brianna at the bottom of the stairs and held up his hands as if in surrender. "Look, I'm sorry for overreacting. I know you'd never have an affair. I'm just upset and confused by how you've gone from hating Gibson to inviting him to stay in your house." He pointed up the stairs. "It seems like it happened overnight."

Brianna took his hand in hers. "I promise there's nothing going on between Scott and me. Can we please discuss this tomorrow? I'll call you."

Taylor nodded. "Okay." He brushed his lips over hers, but the gesture felt cold and empty after his accusation. "Get some sleep."

"You too."

Brianna walked him to the door and stood on the porch as he descended the steps before climbing into his dark-blue Hyundai Elantra, starting the engine, and backing down the driveway.

A mixture of frustration, anxiety, and anger buzzed through her, and she suddenly felt wide-awake. She locked the front door and checked all the other doors, landing in the kitchen to finish cleaning up. But Scott had even wiped down the counters and table—and for some reason she wasn't surprised.

Still feeling antsy, she entered the family room, then flipped on the television. She scrolled through the on-demand movie list until she found a film she'd always enjoyed. She hit Play, then tried to relax on the sofa and lose herself in the story. If only for a couple of hours, it would be nice to escape her worries.

CHAPTER 13

Standing in the doorway of the room he'd chosen, Scott had listened to Taylor apologize to Brianna. He'd also rolled his eyes as irritation spread through him like a plague.

Taylor Reese was a piece of work. Not only did he take Brianna for granted, but he had the audacity to accuse her of having an affair! The man didn't deserve her. But that was none of his business. It was up to Brianna to choose whom to love.

As the front door closed, regret washed over him. If he hadn't been here when Taylor came, he wouldn't have caused this extra stress for Brianna on top of her mother's situation. He owed her an apology, but it was too late to burden her with another conversation.

He'd stepped into the bedroom, sure Brianna would be coming up soon, but then he stopped when he heard the television turn on downstairs. He quietly paced the floor for a good twenty minutes, but then he decided she might want some company.

He descended the stairs and found her in the family room watching *The Fugitive*.

She looked up at him and appeared embarrassed. "Did I wake you?"

"No. I've been up." He pointed to the television. "I love this movie."

"It's a classic." She nodded toward the spot beside her. "Want to join me?"

"Sure."

He settled onto the sofa next to her, and she angled her body toward him. Then she hit Pause on the remote control and studied him. "I thought you were tired. Is something on your mind?"

"I'm sorry for causing drama with Taylor tonight. If I'd just left and found a hotel room earlier, you wouldn't have had to deal with that."

She bent her leg and hugged her knee to her chest. "It's not your fault. Taylor is just feeling guilty for not being here for me, and that's his problem."

He scratched his cheek and considered that. "How long have you two been together?"

"Ten years."

Ten years?

"Although we did have a break in there." She leaned her head back on the sofa. "You look surprised."

He looked down at the diamond twinkling on her left hand. "When are you getting married?"

"Sometime soon, I suppose." She gave a sheepish look and bit her lip. "We haven't exactly set a date."

He blinked. What on earth was Taylor waiting for? "Why not?"

She sighed. "We're busy, and it just never seems like the right time. I thought we might get married this year, though. I had this whole romantic plan to bring it up on Valentine's Day. I'd wrap up a calendar and have a date with a heart sticker on it. I'd also get him chocolate hearts and a little bride and groom figurine that sort of looked like us."

She got a faraway look in her pretty brown eyes, but then her expression fell. "Then I lost my dad, and . . ."

"I'm sorry," he whispered.

"Thanks." She picked up a pillow and held it to her chest. "Dad loved Taylor. He's been part of our family since I was in high school. Well, except for those few years when we'd broken up."

"You started dating in high school?"

"Yeah. I was sixteen." She looked down at the pillow and fingered its fringe. "I was a sophomore in high school, and he was a senior. Taylor was best friends with Dylan, which is how Dylan met my best friend, Ava. Ava and Dylan started dating shortly after we did. Then Taylor got a full scholarship to Wilmington, majoring in business."

"Isn't that school about six hours from here?"

"Exactly. We tried the long-distance thing, but it didn't work, and we broke up for a few years. Then after he graduated and settled back in Splendid Lake to take over his parents' farm supply store, we started spending time together. One day he took me to the park and had a whole picnic lunch packed for us. He told me how much he regretted not working harder to make our relationship work while he was away." She smiled. "It was so romantic, and we got back together."

Scott nodded.

"Shortly after Ava and Dylan got married, Taylor proposed." Her smile flattened. "I know our time is coming, but it feels like losing my dad changes everything." Her eyes widened. "I don't mean to sound like it's changed how I feel about Taylor. It's just that . . . Well, I don't know how to explain it." Her shoulders sagged.

"You wanted your dad to give you away at your wedding."

She pointed her finger at him and smiled. "Exactly." She tilted her head. "What about you? Do you have someone special in your life?"

"No." He settled back against the sofa.

Her brow pinched. "Why not?"

"I've dated a lot of women, but they always seemed to want one thing."

She sucked in a breath and hit him on the arm with the pillow. "Scott!"

He laughed. "Not that. Money."

She sat up taller and looked surprised. "Really?"

"Unfortunately, it's true. They see the cars, the suits, and the business and think they've found their ticket. They want material things, not a real relationship."

She frowned. "That's sad."

"I'm okay not dating." He rested his elbow on the armrest beside him.

She looked incredulous. "You don't want a family?"

"I've never had one. I really don't know if I ever will."

Now she looked sad. He glanced at the television, where Harrison Ford was still frozen on the screen. Anxiety churned inside of him. He wasn't ready to share the whole truth about his tumultuous childhood with Brianna. For one thing, he didn't want her pity.

He needed to redirect the conversation.

"I'm getting up early," he said. "I didn't tell you this before, but we need a couple of new toilets for the cabins. Two are cracked and have to be replaced, so I plan to go back to Lowe's for them as soon as I can."

"Don't worry about them. I still don't know when I can pay you."

"I told you not to worry about that. You worry about your mom, and I'll worry about everything here." He stood. "I'm going to get some sleep. You relax, okay?" He started for the stairs.

"Scott."

He turned back. "Yeah?"

"Thank you." Her tender smile sent an unexpected thrill through him.

"You don't have to keep thanking me. Good night."

Scott padded up the stairs, then undressed, climbed into bed, and put out the lamp he'd turned on earlier. He stared at the white ceiling while contemplating Brianna and her decade-long, off-and-on relationship with Taylor. Now he had a better understanding of their history and ties to each other, and he was grateful that Brianna seemed ready to trust him. To even see him as a friend. But what did it matter? He'd never allow himself to disrupt an engagement. And he still didn't know how his agenda and hers would gel when it came to the resort.

Rolling to his side, he closed his eyes and tried to turn off his thoughts.

"Hi," Ava said as she stepped into the hospital room the following morning. Holding a carrier with two cups and a paper bag, she halted after glancing at Brianna's mother in the bed, then grimaced. "I'm sorry. She's sleeping."

Brianna set the *People* magazine she'd been reading on the little table beside the vinyl love seat, then stood. "It's okay. She's been in and out since I've been here. We'll just have to be quiet. Let me help you."

"Thanks." Ava handed her the bag. "I brought a couple of bagels and croissants this time."

"You're the sweetest. What would I do without you?"

Ava shrugged. "Starve, I guess."

Brianna laughed as they sat down beside each other. But when she glanced at her mother, her smile faded. Mom's skin looked ashen, much worse than it had the day of the funeral.

"How's it going?" Ava handed Brianna a cup, and Brianna took a sip of the still-hot coffee.

"When she's awake, she doesn't even try to speak. We tried to FaceTime with Jenna, but Mom could only cry . . ." Her throat thick with sorrow, she took another sip of the hot liquid. "It's hard to take."

"I'm so sorry." Ava rubbed her arm. "My parents send their love. Dylan and his family do too. Everyone is thinking of you and praying your mother makes a full recovery."

"Thank you." Brianna pulled a croissant out of the bag. "Tell me something good. I need some happy news." She took a bite.

"Ooh!" Ava grinned. "I have just the news to brighten your day." She set her coffee on the table beside her, then turned to face Brianna full-on. "Guess who got engaged."

"Brooklyn and Cole?"

"Yes!" Ava clapped her hands, but then her eyes grew wide as she looked toward the bed. Fortunately, Mom didn't stir. "I'm sorry. Again. We're just so excited. My parents are delighted, and we're already planning the engagement party. They want to get married the Saturday before Memorial Day weekend."

"Why so soon?"

"Since they both have jobs and Cole has a house Brooklyn loves, they don't really have a reason to wait. And they just want a small ceremony and reception in my parents' backyard by the lake." Ava beamed. "Oh, we have so much to do. Brooklyn asked me to be her matron of honor. We have to go dress shopping, buy decorations, find a DJ . . . I also need to start planning her shower with her best friend. We told Molly it can be in Mom's garden."

As excited as Brianna wanted to be for Brooklyn and Cole, her heart sank every time her eyes landed on her mother. First Dad's death, and now this. Would she ever be herself again?

"Hey, Brie? I'm sorry. It was thoughtless of me to go on and on about Brooklyn and Cole."

"No, I appreciate the distraction. I like hearing how everyone else is."

Ava pulled a bagel from the bag and took a bite. "Have you talked to Taylor?"

"We texted a little bit earlier." Brianna shrugged. "You know how busy Saturdays are at the store."

"Is Scott working at the resort today or did he go home?"

Brianna swallowed another bite of her croissant and nodded. "He worked on the cabins yesterday, and he's doing more today."

"Where is he staying? At Lakeview Inn?"

"No. The Hernandezes are out of town, so I just let him stay in Cassie's old room."

"Whoa." Ava held up her hand like a traffic cop. "I get that he's helping you, but seriously, how do you go from throwing him off your property to letting him sleep in your house?"

"It turns out he's nice, and we're getting to know each other."

Ava looked unconvinced. "Even serial killers can be nice."

"Serial killers can't cook like he does."

"He cooked for you?" Ava's coffee-colored eyes rounded.

"Yup." Brianna nodded. "Last night he had beef stroganoff ready for me when I got home. And then he made chocolate chip pancakes this morning."

"Oh my goodness!" Ava tapped Brianna's knee. "That settles it. Don't tell Taylor I said this, but you should marry Scott. I can't even get Dylan to wash a dish, let alone make one."

Brianna chuckled and glanced down at her phone, wondering if her fiancé would check in with her again today. "Tell me more about the wedding. I really do want to hear about it."

Ava's face lit up as she talked about Brooklyn's plans for a plywood dance floor and white lights on the trees. Later, she headed back to the Coffee Bean, and then Brianna flipped through the *People* magazine again while the nurses took her mother for more tests.

Before long, the hospital room door clicked open, and Dr. Mason stepped in. Her expression was somber, and Brianna's stomach shrunk into a tight ball as a sick, shaky feeling swept through her.

"Hello, Brianna." Dr. Mason sat down beside her. "Did you get any rest last night?"

"I did my best. How's my mom?"

Dr. Mason pressed her lips together. "The good news is that the damage is much less than we first feared."

Brianna gulped as tears pooled in her eyes. "What's the bad news?"

"Well, it's not really bad. She just still needs the rehab I mentioned yesterday. She needs therapy to walk again, improve her fine motor skills, and regain clarity in her speech. So we'll send her to a rehabilitation center for a while, and if she still needs help after that, the staff there can arrange for therapists to come to your home."

"Does this mean she can make a full recovery?"

The doctor smiled. "That's definitely possible."

Brianna looked down as tears sprinkled onto her purple hoodie. "Oh, I'm so relieved."

"Here you go." Dr. Mason held out a box of tissues she'd lifted from the table beside her.

"So she'll be okay?" Brianna managed to ask while wiping her eyes.

Dr. Mason stood. "Brianna, your mother is a strong woman. I can tell by how frustrated she is, and I think she's going to come out of this. It will just take time."

Brianna nodded as a strange mixture of relief and worry filled her.

"Do you have any more questions for me?"

"When will she go to the rehab center?"

"Early next week. We're working on getting that scheduled."

"Thank you."

"I'll be in touch." Dr. Mason headed out the door.

Brianna took deep breaths as she gazed at a painting on one wall. She had to be strong. She'd get through this. She just had to care for Mom, save the resort, and somehow put off the medical bills until she had the money to pay them—and get better health insurance at some point. But first she had to update her sisters.

Once she had them both on the line, Brianna repeated what the doctor told her about their mother's prognosis. "So that's where we are. And like I said, we'll have both hospital and rehab bills."

"I'm going to send you some money on Monday," Jenna said.

"So am I," Cassie added.

"Thank you, but I've already told you that's not enough," Brianna blurted, her entire body trembling as she realized she had to make a plea for the sake of her own well-being. "I need actual hands-on help. How can I care for Mom and keep the resort going at the same time?"

The line was silent for a moment, and Brianna looked down to see if she'd accidently disconnected the call.

"Maybe I can afford to hire a nurse when she gets home," Jenna said.

"I don't want a nurse, and Mom might not be home for weeks." Brianna nearly spat the words. "I'm talking about now. Don't you get it? I feel completely unsupported by you both."

"You want us to come home?" Cassie sounded genuinely confused.

"This isn't a good time for me," Jenna said. "Work is a nightmare."

"It's not good for me either," Cassie added. "I'm up for a promotion, and if I get it, I can send you more money. But you must understand, Brie. We can't just drop everything and come there. We were gone for three weeks the first time."

Brianna's hands began to shake. "Aren't you listening? I need you."

"Is Mom there?" Jenna asked. "Can we talk to her?"

"No, she's not." Brianna shook her head. "She's not back from her last tests."

"Oh." Cassie sounded disappointed. At least she cared that much. "Will you call us when she's back?"

"I will. And you need to figure out when you can come home. I mean it. I know you have jobs, but get your priorities straight. It's time for you both to step up. Maybe you can take a leave of absence. Or at least work remotely for a while."

"Take care, Brie," Jenna said. "And give Mom our love."

"I'll see what I can do," Cassie said.

Really? Cassie was the only one even willing to consider her suggestions?

With a quick good-bye, Brianna disconnected the call, then dropped the phone into her lap and covered her face with her hands. Reality crashed over her. Even if her sisters decided to come, it wouldn't be anytime soon. Until then, she had to face all this alone.

CHAPTER 14

Scott swung a screen door back and forth before using a screwdriver to adjust the hinges. Then he swiped the back of his hand across his sweaty forehead. After another trip to Lowe's this morning for replacement toilets, he'd not only replaced them but fixed three leaky faucets, poured Drano down a couple of clogged drains, and started assessing screen doors. This had been the last of them.

The shingles he'd bought, however, sat nearby and seemed to watch him. He needed to get back up on the ladder, but he'd been busy with the easier jobs and lost track of time.

He pulled his phone out of his pocket for what seemed like the hundredth time. He'd texted Brianna earlier and received only a brief response:

Spoke to the dr. Will fill you in later. Thanks for checking.

He lowered himself to the cabin's steps, his thumbs poised, ready to reply. But it wasn't his place. He wasn't her fiancé, and he wasn't family. He was just . . . Well, what was he? A friend, he decided. But just barely. He didn't want to push it. It was up to Brianna to offer him information.

After a quick sandwich up at the house, it was time to do the hard work. He ambled over to the stack of shingles, then gathered the tools and supplies he needed and carried them up the ladder. Once on the roof, he sat down and looked at the shimmering lake, taking in the undeveloped land on the Porters' property and imagining what the resort would look like with the improvements he envisioned. A year-round retreat center with a spa and yoga and exercise studios, as well as a large indoor/outdoor pool enclosure with slides. Modernizing the cabins beyond new furniture and appliances, including fireplaces and heat, plus amenities such as Wi-Fi and streaming services.

He smiled and turned his attention to his current task. He'd hold on to that dream until Brianna was ready to hear about it. Right now she was fragile, and her mother's health was the most important concern. Somehow he'd shown up in the middle of a crisis—again.

In the late afternoon Scott heard tires crunching up the main rock driveway, but the engine didn't sound like one of Brianna's vehicles. He climbed down the ladder and headed toward the house. Taylor was walking up the front steps carrying a bag Scott recognized from a Japanese restaurant not far from Splendid Lake. He'd eaten there once.

When Taylor turned at the sound of Scott's footsteps, Scott took in the man's glower.

"Why are you still here?" Taylor snapped.

Scott held up his hammer. "I'm working, just like Brianna told you I would be."

Delighted malice lit up Taylor's dark eyes. "I hope you realize I won't let her sell to you—no matter how hard you try to convince her."

"I think that's the family's decision, not yours."

Taylor huffed and started toward the door. "You act helpful, but I can see through that smoke screen. You have one thing on your mind, and that's getting your hands on this property. Well, I'm the deputy mayor of this little town, and I won't let you do it." He pushed the door open.

"Hey, Reese," Scott called, his body thrumming with irritation. "I have a question."

Taylor spun to face him. "What?"

"Why aren't you at the hospital with Brianna?"

"Why don't you mind your own business? Besides, she's on her way home." With that, Taylor let the storm door slam shut in Scott's face.

Scott shook his head and wondered what Brianna saw in this guy, but he hated the envy coursing through him. He turned and threw the hammer in his hand as far as he could, sending it careening toward the picnic tables. But the act offered no relief. He had to get away before Brianna arrived. The last thing he wanted to witness was her cozying up to Taylor. He was certain it would make his stomach sour. Besides, she was entitled to privacy with her fiancé, even if he was a jerk.

He started back to the cabins. He'd stow the supplies and tools, including the ladder, then go find something to eat in town. Time to clear his mind was just what he needed.

Brianna parked her Mustang beside Taylor's Hyundai and glanced around for Scott's Challenger. Then she pulled her phone from her pocket and checked for new messages. She couldn't recall Scott letting her know he planned to leave for Charlotte this soon. When she saw no texts from him, she wondered where he could be. She hoped he'd say good-bye.

Her mind was still stuck on Scott's whereabouts when she stepped into the kitchen and found Taylor sitting at the table.

"Hi." His smile was wide as he stood, then brought takeout containers from the counter to the table. "I got your favorite—hibachi shrimp and rice."

"Thanks. It smells delicious." She set her purse on the counter, then hung her jacket on the back of a kitchen chair before washing her hands at the sink.

"How's your mom?" Taylor came up behind her and placed his hands on her hips.

"Not that great." She summarized what the doctor told her and looked away when Taylor's expression contorted with worry. "Dr. Mason said she'll go to a rehab center early next week."

"I'm sorry to hear it, but it sounds like she has a great chance for a full recovery."

"That's what I'm holding on to." She walked to the back door and opened it, hoping Scott had just moved his car around back.

"What are you looking for?"

"Where's Scott?" The question leapt from her lips without any forethought. She immediately regretted it when Taylor's face flashed with resentment.

"I don't know. Maybe he left." Taylor's voice was flinty. Sharp.

"I didn't think he'd leave without letting me know."

Taylor's jaw clenched. "I know you aren't cheating on me, but do you have feelings for this guy?"

She took a deep breath. "Taylor, we're just friends. He's been a great support helping me get the resort ready for the season. I know it's probably mostly because he's still hoping there's a chance I'll sell the resort, but I can tell he cares about Mom too. He's just a nice man, and we need all the help we can get."

Taylor watched her, and her skin felt itchy under his intense stare.

"Brie, I want to do better. That's why I asked my father to take over the store this afternoon—so I could be here for you now." His expression softened. "Dad said he'll cover the store tomorrow too. He's glad to give up a Sunday afternoon so I can join you at the hospital."

"I'd like that, and please thank him for me." She pointed to the table. "That delicious food is getting cold."

As they ate, Taylor asked questions about her mom and even her challenges with the resort, but Brianna kept steering the conversation away from her problems. She just wanted to talk about something else, so she asked him about his recent work as deputy mayor, and he seemed glad to fill her in.

After dinner, they cleaned the kitchen and then cuddled on the sofa to watch a movie, but she had a hard time following the plot. She'd set her phone on the end table beside her and kept looking at it for a message from Scott, wondering where he'd gone.

He's a grown man, Brianna. He can take care of himself.

She tried harder to dismiss her concern. After all, Scott's main motive for helping her really was to buy her family's resort. And yet he'd acted like a true friend over the past couple of days. In fact, he'd been such a good friend that she wanted to tell him the latest on her mother in person, not in a text message or over the phone.

A couple of hours later, she and Taylor stood on the front porch. He took her hand in his. "Everything will be fine. You'll see."

When he pulled her in for a hug, she rested her head on his shoulder and recalled the days when his strong arms provided the comfort and promises she needed. But now . . . Her mind wandered back to when she first met him. He was the first guy who paid attention to her, and he'd made her feel smart and pretty. He was her first love. His handsome smile was as radiant as the sun and had brightened her murkiest days. The feel of his arms around her and his lips brushing against hers had always set her heart on fire.

But now, when she desperately needed his love and encouragement, his touch left her feeling cold. What had changed between them?

When Taylor released her from the embrace, he slipped his finger under her chin and lifted her mouth before kissing her. "Good night."

"Be safe going home," she called as he jogged down the steps to his car.

Once back inside the house, Brianna checked her phone, and still finding no messages, she hurried up the stairs. After taking a long, hot shower, she pulled her hair up into a messy bun and put on yoga pants and a sweatshirt.

She suddenly felt as if she needed some air. After slipping on her favorite sneakers, she grabbed her jean jacket downstairs, then pocketed her cell phone and a flashlight and headed out. When she reached the pier, she sank onto the edge of it and let her legs dangle, then breathed in the lake's familiar scent and took in the water sparkling in the moonlight.

She couldn't wait to see colorful sails on boats dotting the lake, water-skiers having fun, and fishermen along the lakeshore. She could almost hear the sounds of laughter as their guests enjoyed picnicking, playing volleyball, tossing horseshoes, and building sandcastles. But now all she heard was the sound of water lapping against the pier and the whir of anxious thoughts.

She tried to put her worries out of her head as she enjoyed the solace and beauty of her beloved lake, but loneliness had settled into her heart. She needed company. Someone she trusted. But it was too late to bother Ava. And if she were honest with herself, she'd have to admit she missed Scott's calm presence. She unlocked her phone, then opened his string of text messages and began to type.

Did you go back to Charlotte without saying good-bye?
Seriously?

Conversation bubbles appeared almost immediately, and her stomach tightened as she awaited his response.

No. Just grabbed a bite. Left my gear at your place.
Oh. Are you coming back soon?
About on my way now.
Okay. I'm sitting on the pier.

In fifteen minutes, the thundering of the Challenger's engine and crunch of its tires on the rock driveway announced Scott's arrival. She bit her thumbnail as she hoped he would join her on the pier.

A few minutes later, she spotted his tall silhouette walking down the hill. Not wanting to appear too eager, she turned to look at the water, then heard the tap of his work boots as he sauntered down the worn and dilapidated boards.

She looked up when he came to a stop and stood above her. His blue eyes sparkled in the pier lights glowing above them, and his thick hair stood at odd angles as if he'd just raked his fingers through it.

"It's nice out here," he said as he lowered himself to sit beside her. "I love being by the lake."

"Me too."

A comfortable silence stretched between them, and she looked up at the clear, dark sky above. The stars seemed to wink down at them as the sparkling water reflected the moonlight.

She took in Scott's profile—his chiseled features, the stubble on his angular jaw, his full lips. "Where did you eat?"

Scott kicked his legs as if he were on a swing. "At that little restaurant in town. Then I walked around the park and window-shopped since the stores are all closed on Saturday nights." He paused. "I wanted to stay out of the way. I also think I should get a hotel room."

"No." She said the word a little too quickly, and his eyebrows shot up. "I can't afford one."

"I don't expect you to pay for it." He rested his hands on the edge of the pier. "I never meant to cause you problems, you know."

"Cause me problems?" She gave a little laugh. "You've done just the opposite. You've helped take my mind off all the work that needs to be done around here. That weighed on me while I was trying to figure out what was happening with Mom."

"I mean with Taylor. We had . . . Well, we exchanged some words earlier."

She blew out an irritated breath. "He's just frustrated with me and jealous of you. It's my fault, not yours."

He opened his mouth but then closed it.

"What?" She leaned toward him. "I can tell you want to say something. Just say it."

He cleared his throat and then stood. "I should go." He started toward the end of the pier.

She popped up. "Wait."

He spun to face her.

"Scott, I want you here. I know that sounds strange, but it's nice to have the company."

He pursed his lips. "Okay. One more night."

She folded her arms. "Besides, I need to talk to you more about my opinions for the resort." As she filled him in on what the doctor said, she barely held back tears. "How am I supposed to take care of this place and my mother at the same time?"

"Hey." He came back.

"I'm sorry." She covered her face with her hands. "I'm a mess."

"No, you're not. You're just human."

She felt the board under her feet shift, and yet another paper napkin was pushed into her hand. Scott's touch made her skin tingle, and the sensation confused her.

"Talk to me," he whispered, his voice husky in her ear.

She wiped her face, then looked up at him. "I'm so overwhelmed, and my sisters just plan to throw money at me. Meanwhile, Taylor's making me feel worse with his jealousy."

Something unreadable darted over his face.

"I just want someone to listen to me."

"I'm listening."

She sniffed. "The doctor said Mom might still need therapy at the house after she's released from rehab. What if the money Jenna and Cass send isn't enough for that, let alone enough to keep our creditors away?"

He tilted his head and looked out over the lake.

"Scott, please just say what you're thinking."

"If you let me buy this place, at least your money problems will disappear."

"I guess so, but I don't know what the right choice is." She made a sweeping gesture toward the resort. "This is our family home and legacy. My father would never understand our selling it. I'm sure he had some solution in mind. I just don't know what it was."

Silence fell between them, and she wished she could read Scott's mind. Finally, she huffed out a breath. "I'm sorry. This really is family business, and I need to figure it out on my own."

"No pressure. You have enough on you. We'll discuss it later. For now, I just want to help." He paused for a beat, then pointed toward the house. "But first, I need to shower."

"And I'm going to bed."

She walked with him up the hill, then they climbed the porch steps and headed into the house through the kitchen. After making sure all the doors were locked, they made their way toward the stairs.

As she moved up the carpeted steps, she puzzled over why Scott was easier to talk to than Taylor and even Ava and her sisters. Something about him inspired her to bare her soul.

They stopped at her bedroom door and faced each other.

"Get some rest, Brianna. You'll feel better in the morning." His words were soft, and the compassion in his eyes sent a current like electricity sizzling through her veins.

She watched him continue toward Cassie's old room. "Thank you."

His crooked smile overtook his handsome face as he turned toward her. "You need to stop thanking me."

But she didn't know how she ever could.

CHAPTER 15

*B*rianna descended the stairs and breathed in the delicious scents of coffee and bacon. When she entered the kitchen, she saw waffles too. "Oh my goodness."

Scott was standing over the waffle iron with a platter of bacon beside him.

"I need to hire you as my personal chef," she quipped as she swiped a piece.

He chuckled as he set a waffle on the platter.

She filled two mugs with coffee, then handed him one. "What time are you leaving for Charlotte?"

"How soon do you want to get rid of me?" he said, teasing her as he poured more batter onto the waffle maker.

How about never?

She tried to ignore that inner voice as she set out a container of creamer, then gathered plates and utensils. Deep down, she knew it would be better for him to go. His being there upset Taylor. That realization had hit her as she lay awake during the night, contemplating her ever-growing to-do list, how to pay the bills, and her fiancé's recent actions. Why had she made that crack about Scott being her personal chef?

She opened the refrigerator and took out butter and syrup, then grabbed a banana from a basket on the counter. "Taylor said he'd join me at the hospital this afternoon."

She noticed Scott's smile wobble just before he said, "That's great." He turned back to the stove. "Hey, I'm thinking I'll come back next weekend. I won't be able to finish those roofs today so—"

"Scott, you've done so much already. I don't expect you to come back again." She peeled the banana, then found a knife to slice it.

He spun to face her, confusion clouding his face. "What do you mean?"

"I'll send what I owe you as soon as I get money from my sisters."

"Oh, that. I told you. You can pay me back after you decide what you're going to do about the resort. You need to take your time and talk to your family." He flipped another waffle onto the platter and poured more batter. "I'll do a few things around the resort today and then head home. On Friday I'll come back and—"

"It's really not necessary. I need time to figure things out on my own, and the rest of the work can wait a couple of weeks."

He studied her. "Do you really mean that?"

"I do." She tried to keep the tremble out of her voice. "The truth is it's better if you go. Taylor is jealous of you, and I have enough stress. I'll send you the money, and then I'll let you know what my family and I decide. We'll definitely consider your offer first if we want to sell. Just leave me the receipts for what you bought this weekend."

He nodded, then without a word, he stacked one more waffle on the platter and turned off the iron before carrying both platters to the table. She divided the banana slices between them.

They made small talk about Splendid Lake while they ate, and Brianna tried to ignore the disappointment that wriggled into her chest whenever she reminded herself this would be their last meal together.

They cleaned the kitchen, and she got ready to leave.

"So this is good-bye, I guess," she said as she pulled on her jacket, then adjusted her purse strap on her shoulder. "You'll lock up when you go?"

"I will."

"Thank you again for everything."

He held out his hand. "I'll still be in touch to check on your mom."

"Thanks." When they shook hands, a flash of heat danced up her arm. "Be safe driving home."

He smiled as he released her hand. "Take good care of yourself."

As Brianna walked to her car, she tried to concentrate on her mother instead of the disappointment she felt saying good-bye to a man she'd come to admire. Even if she couldn't solve all her problems today, maybe she could focus her efforts on the person who needed her most.

Soon after Brianna left for the hospital, Scott took some measurements, then found the keys to Martin's 2001 bright-blue Dodge Ram 1500 pickup truck and drove to Lowe's in Asheville. When he returned to the resort with lumber and the appropriate nails, he set to building a ramp for the front steps in preparation for Lois's return home. Then he'd build another one for the back of the house. He also intended to install the handrails he'd bought for Lois's bathroom.

While he worked, he considered his conversation with Brianna at breakfast. Although he understood her reasoning for asking him not to come back, he'd be lying to himself if he said her request hadn't hurt. He wasn't a fool, nor was he blind. And he had no intention of getting involved with an engaged woman. Still, curiosity had taken root when she'd so quickly told him not to go to a hotel last night.

She might not have admitted it, but he could tell she enjoyed his company. And he enjoyed hers as well. In fact, he felt closer to her than made sense considering they'd met so recently.

When he finished the first ramp, he admired his work. The structure might be simple, but it was solid and serviceable. After grabbing some lunch, he began working on the second ramp in back. He'd hoped to do more of the roofing today, but these projects for Lois took priority. Maybe Brianna would change her mind and ask him to come back, but he doubted it. After all, she was stubborn.

He snickered as he recalled how both Ava and Mrs. Porter had called her stubborn. They knew her well.

When the second ramp was finished, he jogged onto the porch and was greeted by Bucky. The cat meowed and rubbed his shin.

"Hey there. You hungry?"

The cat responded with a louder meow.

"I'll get you some food." He picked up the bowls, and after rinsing and wiping out the water bowl, he refilled it. Then he added dry food he'd seen Brianna grab to the other bowl and placed them both on the porch in their usual spot.

"Enjoy," he told the cat, who'd all but pounced on his meal.

Back inside, Scott installed the handrails in Lois's bathroom, then realized it was almost six o'clock. He had to get on the road. Not only did he have a three-hour drive ahead of him, but he didn't want to be there in case Taylor came home with Brianna. The previous night's confrontation had been enough for him.

He dug the receipts for the supplies he'd bought out of his wallet and placed them on the counter. Then he found a notepad and pen and gazed at a blank sheet of paper while considering what to say. He rolled the pen around in his fingers and then leaned down to write.

Brianna,

I'd planned to finish replacing the shingles before I left, but it occurred to me that something else should take priority. You'll see I built two ramps for your mom, and I hope they'll work well for her even though they're pretty simple. I also installed handrails in her bathroom.

I left the receipts for you, but I'm not in a hurry to be reimbursed. I've been glad to help. Call if you need anything. I'll text to check in on your mom. And on you.

Scott

He loped up the stairs to gather his belongings, then headed to his car after locking the last door behind him. As he climbed into his Challenger, he looked up at the house one last time, hoping he'd have the opportunity to return sooner than later.

Her headlights shining against the garage doors, Brianna nosed her Mustang next to the Tahoe in the driveway, then climbed out. For some reason she'd hardly used the garage lately. Probably because the weather had been so mild.

She yawned as she pocketed her phone and slung her purse strap over her arm.

The morning hours at the hospital hadn't been bad. Mom had been asleep most of the time. But the afternoon had been draining as Taylor sat with her. Her mother had cried most of the time, even when her sisters were on FaceTime with her. It had been painful seeing her so frustrated as she struggled with normally mundane things, like holding a cup in her left hand. She'd lost so much of her strength. But Dr. Mason had said that frustration would serve Mom well in rehab.

Taylor had been supportive and sweet. He even brought her lunch and then bought dinner for them from a nearby deli, but he still seemed a million miles away from where she needed him to be emotionally. They seemed to be drifting apart, like two rafts out to sea with nothing connecting them.

She contemplated whether Taylor was the problem, but then she assumed she was. After all, she'd still been trying to accept her father's death when her mother suffered the stroke. The pain of both was taking its toll, forcing her to reevaluate her whole life. And Taylor was a huge part of her life.

Deep in thought as she walked toward the front door, she froze when she saw the porch steps had been transformed. A ramp, complete with a handrail, sat over them, inviting her to try it.

Brianna felt a surge of gratitude. Scott had built a ramp for her mother. Who else would it be? And she hadn't even thought about how they'd need one. Her heart twisted as she imagined him working hard all day on this . . . gift.

Once again, Scott knew what she needed before she did.

She walked up the ramp to the front door, and after unlocking it, she made her way through the foyer and family room to the kitchen. She set her purse on the counter next to a stack of receipts and a note.

The words Scott wrote sent more gratitude soaking through her. He'd built a second ramp as well, and he'd installed handrails in Mom's bathroom too.

"Scott Gibson, you're amazing," she whispered. She peeked out the back door and took in the second ramp. Then she hurried to her mother's bathroom and found the handrails he'd installed. Warmth curled in her chest. She glanced at the clock next her mother's bed and found it was after nine. Surely Scott was home by now.

She retrieved her phone and sat down on the edge of the bed before texting him.

> Thank you for building the ramps and installing the
> handrails. I hadn't even thought about needing them.

The conversation bubbles appeared almost immediately, as though he'd been waiting to hear from her.

> *You're welcome.*
> How was your trip home?
> *Long and uneventful.*
> That last part is a good thing, right?
> *Yup. How's your mom?*

Brianna held her phone in her hand and considered how to respond. She longed to tell him the truth, but she didn't want to burden him. Yet she also didn't want to lie to him.

> *That bad? I'm sorry.*

She glanced at the screen. He'd known what she was thinking without even seeing her face. How was that possible? She poised her fingers to text again but then stopped.

Scott jumped in again.

*You don't have to talk about it. I understand. Call or text me if
you need anything.*

They're moving Mom to rehab on Tuesday.

Let me know how it goes.

I will.

Sleep well.

You too.

Brianna walked out to the kitchen. Setting her phone on the counter, she began sifting through the stack of receipts. No matter what Scott said, she had to find a way to pay him back, along with settling the overdue bills on her father's desk as well as the upcoming bills for her mother's care. The little money she had plus whatever her sisters sent would cover only so much.

But she was too exhausted to figure all that out tonight. She needed sleep.

CHAPTER 16

*T*aylor steered his Hyundai down Splendid Lake Loop on their way to Brooklyn and Cole's engagement party.

"Did you get any rest last night?" he asked, giving Brianna a sideways glance.

"A little," she managed to say before another yawn overtook her. She cupped her hand to her mouth to stifle it. Strange how she'd slept better with Scott in the house. But he'd been gone for two weeks, and she was exhausted.

As happy as she was to celebrate with her friends, she'd considered texting Ava and telling the truth—she was just too tired to dress up and socialize. But Ava had always gone out of her way for Brianna, which meant she had to at least make a showing. So she'd pulled on her favorite little black dress, a silver sequined sweater, black pumps, jewelry, and then applied makeup before climbing into Taylor's waiting car.

Now she had to find the strength to plaster a smile on her face and try to participate in conversations. Brianna suspected how the evening would go, though. Gossip spread like wildfire in this town, and since everyone pretty much knew everyone else in Splendid Lake, she'd be peppered with questions about her mother's recovery. But she wasn't prepared to respond to those questions.

Yes, her mother had made progress at the rehabilitation center. Her speech had improved, and although her legs were still shaky, she'd also started using a walker. She continued to struggle with her fine motor skills, though. Still, Brianna held on to the hope that Mom would continue to get stronger with the help of the physical therapists.

She stifled another yawn. Worry had become her constant companion as she'd run back and forth between the rehabilitation center and the resort. And when she got home, she worked late into the night trying to get a few projects done. But all she'd managed was replacing a few window screens, repairing some cabinet latches, and checking the stackable washers and dryers in each cabin. She hadn't tackled the big projects, like the remaining cabin shingles, maintenance on the johnboats, or painting the convenience store and bait shop. And she still didn't know how and with whose help she'd be able to replace the rotting boards on the pier.

And now she had only a couple of months to get everything done! At least she'd have her experienced summer teenage helpers when school wound down. Too bad they were all going away with their families over spring break or she might have been able to hire them for the week.

"Did you hear me?"

"What?" Brianna turned to find Taylor staring at her as they waited for another car to park in the Wallers' large field near their house. Ava and Brooklyn's parents had quite a bit of acreage along the lake.

"I said you look beautiful tonight."

"Thank you." She smiled and pointed at him. "And you look handsome." He wore black trousers, a navy-blue button-down shirt, and a black tie and black shoes—an ensemble she'd always loved on him.

"Thanks. By the way, how did your meetings go this week?" Taylor asked as he nosed the car in behind a black Toyota Camry.

"Well, both our lawyer and accountant confirmed my decision to seek a consolidation loan. But they also agreed selling the resort might be for the best."

She'd also called the bank manager to ask if he'd give them another couple of months if she made a partial payment with the money her sisters had scraped together, letting the medical bills go for now. He'd agreed to give her six weeks, which took some pressure off but certainly not all of it.

She'd also come up short when applying for the loan, even though she'd approached several lending institutions.

Taylor placed his hand on hers. "I'm sorry you haven't worked it out yet, but I really do think all this will get better." He traced his finger down her cheek. "But now we're here to have fun with our friends, and you need a break. Can you just relax and enjoy yourself?"

She blinked at him. "At this point I can't remember how to relax."

"I'm worried about you. You look like you're going to come apart at the seams."

"I feel that way too."

He gave her hand a gentle squeeze. "Just put your worries aside tonight, and let's enjoy each other."

She sighed. He was right—they both needed a night of fun.

After gathering her black clutch and the card containing a gift certificate from both Taylor and her, Brianna stepped out of the car, then threaded her fingers with Taylor's and allowed him to steer her into the spacious, brick house where Ava and Brooklyn grew up. Their father's success as a well-respected lawyer before becoming a district judge was evident throughout their extravagant lakefront home.

She smiled and nodded to familiar faces as they made their way through the expansive first floor, passing through the elegant living room, formal dining room, and gourmet kitchen before stepping onto the back deck. It was so huge that she'd once joked it needed its own zip code.

A buzz of conversations floated through the air, along with delectable smells and the familiar comforting sounds of the lake. Brianna hugged her sweater to her body as a light breeze drifted over her. March was still cool, but at least the harsher February cold had gone.

Brianna set the card on a table decorated with baby photos and a formal engagement photo of Brooklyn and Cole, along with a tiered cake piped with silver and periwinkle frosting—Brooklyn's favorite color.

She glanced past the deck to where groups of guests stood talking and eating at high-top tables. Beyond them the lake glittered in all its beautiful glory. Oh, what she would do to be out floating in a boat on her beloved lake right now! That was the solace she craved.

She turned to her left and found Taylor talking animatedly with a group of people she recognized as members of the town council. Leave it to Taylor to lecture her about having fun and then get himself caught up in town business. He wore his "deputy mayor face," with his practiced, polished, electric smile. So much for relaxing.

She spotted a long table laden with hors d'oeuvres and flutes of champagne. As she took in the whole affair, Judge and Mrs. Waller, Brooklyn, Cole, Ava, and Dylan all stepped out onto the deck. Brianna leaned back against the railing and smiled as the newly engaged couple lovingly gazed at each other.

Brooklyn was so beautiful in a short, cream-colored dress with her light-brown hair styled in curls cascading past her slight shoulders. A large, princess-cut diamond glittered on her left ring finger, and her eyes glowed with adoration for her fiancé.

Ava made eye contact with Brianna, and they shared a smile. Ava, too, looked beautiful in a red dress that complemented her dark hair and eyes.

"Everyone!" Judge Waller called over the din. "I'd like to make a toast. Please help yourselves to champagne and join me."

The murmur of the crowd dissolved as everyone turned their attention to the couple standing in the middle of the deck. Someone tapped her arm, and a champagne flute was shoved into her hand. She glanced up at Taylor standing beside her. "Thanks."

"You're welcome."

Judge Waller began his toast. "I'd like to thank you all for joining Gloria and me tonight as we celebrate the engagement of our daughter, Brooklyn, and her fiancé, Cole. Gloria and I weren't surprised when Cole asked our permission to propose to Brooklyn. It's been obvious to all of us how much they care for each other."

Judge Waller held up his glass as he turned toward his younger daughter and future son-in-law. "Brooklyn and Cole, we wish you happiness and prosperity as you plan your life together as husband and wife. We love you. Hear, hear!"

"Hear, hear!" the crowd echoed.

Brianna cheered along with them and took a sip. She turned to say something to Taylor about the nice toast, but he'd already stepped away, yanked into another conversation, this time with the mayor and the fire chief.

"Brie." Ava wound an arm around Brianna's shoulders and gave her a side hug. "You look beautiful tonight."

"So do you." Brianna set her half-full flute on a small table beside her.

"Come with me." Ava glanced around, then took Brianna's arm and led her into the house, through the kitchen, and into a half bathroom. She shut the door. "I see the dark circles under your eyes. Talk to me."

"I just haven't been sleeping much."

Ava slammed a hand onto one of her small hips. "I know you better than that. Fill me in on the latest."

"I didn't come here to complain. I'm just worried all the time. I can't sleep, and I miss my dad. If he were here, we could figure out all this together."

"Hey." Ava pulled her in for a hug. "Look. You can't possibly do it all on your own. I know you have trouble asking for help, but you have to do it. You're not Wonder Woman."

"Who am I going to ask? You and Dylan have your businesses to run, and I can't afford to hire anyone."

"Have you asked Taylor to get some things done at the resort?"

"He doesn't have time. Even at the party he keeps getting pulled into discussions about town business."

Ava handed her a tissue from a nearby box. "Taylor should have offered on his own. You're going to be married someday. That means you're a team and should take care of each other. You need to ask him."

Brianna wiped her nose and then dropped the tissue in the trash can beside her. "You're right. I will."

"Good." Ava pointed to the mirror behind her. "Fix your makeup. Then put a smile on your face and go talk to Taylor. Maybe if you give him some specific things to do, he'll be more likely to make the time for them."

Brianna dabbed her cheeks and refreshed her lipstick, then walked back to the party with Ava, where they found Taylor talking to Dylan.

"There you two are," Dylan announced as they approached. He held out his arm, and Ava snuggled up to him as he looped one arm over her shoulders.

"We were just having some girl talk inside." Ava stood on her tiptoes and kissed her husband's cheek.

"Oh?" Dylan said.

Taylor shot Brianna a concerned look, and she gave him a half shrug.

"Brianna!" someone called.

She sighed. Mrs. Bedford was coming toward them. She was the owner of the mini-golf near the park, and she was also known as the town's most notorious gossip. Her bright-yellow bouffant hairdo, red cat-shaped glasses, bright-red dress, and too much blue eye shadow couldn't hide the fact that she was at least in her mid-sixties—and should know better. "How's your mom?"

"She's getting along. They're working her hard in the rehab center, and she seems to be improving. Thanks for asking." Brianna plastered a smile on her face.

"When will she be home?"

"Hopefully soon." Brianna pushed a thick lock of her hair behind her ear.

"I'm so glad she's doing better. Please give her my regards."

"I will. Thank you."

Then Mrs. Bedford pointed back and forth between Brianna and Taylor. "Haven't you two been engaged a few years now?"

Heat rushed to Brianna's cheeks. *Here we go . . .*

"When are you going to set a date?"

"Oh, you never know." Brianna glanced at Taylor, who looked equally flustered.

Mrs. Bedford smiled, and then, thankfully, she moved on to talk to Ava's parents.

Brianna had almost recovered when another group of well-meaning older ladies grilled her about her mother. Once they left, three of her friends from high school joined them and also asked when she and Taylor were getting married. One even suggested they should elope to save money.

Their questions felt like darts, tearing at her already fragile spirit. She just wanted to be left alone, but she steeled herself for Ava's sake. The last thing she wanted to do was leave too early and disappoint her best friend.

She waited until everyone was engrossed in a conversation about some old friends who'd moved somewhere in the Midwest, and then she sneaked away. She hurried down the deck stairs and out toward the lake, and once she was on the Wallers' dock, she hugged her arms to her chest as another breeze came off the water. She squinted toward the resort and tried to bring her parents' two chairs into focus, but it was too dark. Besides, her mind was swimming with memories of the night she and Scott had sat there together.

Oh, how she wished he'd come back even though she'd told him not to. He texted her just about every other day to check on her and her mother. Their conversations were brief, but they were enough to fill her with the strength to make it through another day. Taylor tried to support her, but his words weren't the same.

She pulled her phone from her purse and scrolled through their last conversation, just yesterday. She'd told Scott the latest version of *She's about the same*. Then he said he was thinking of her, and that was it.

Brianna sighed and locked her phone before tucking it back into her purse. When she heard footsteps, she peeked over her shoulder to see Taylor coming toward her.

"What are you doing out here?" he asked.

"Just getting some air. Are you almost ready to go home?"

"I was hoping to introduce you to some of the council members' spouses you weren't able to meet last week. They're all eager to get to know you."

"Could we do it some other time? I'm not feeling up to it tonight."

His expression warmed. "Sure."

They rejoined the party and searched for their hosts in the sea of faces. They found Brooklyn and Cole first and approached them to say good-bye.

"Congratulations again," Brianna told Brooklyn as she hugged her. "I can't wait to see you as a bride."

"Thank you. Ava will have to show you a photo of my dress."

Once again Brianna took in how Brooklyn radiated with happiness as she glanced at her fiancé, and she found herself wondering when she'd stopped gazing at Taylor with that same look in her eyes. She'd felt that all-consuming excitement of first love at their engagement, but that excitement had fizzled somewhere along the way. What went wrong? And how could she find it again? Didn't she want the same kind of relationship these friends had? The same kind her parents had all those years together?

Brianna left those questions behind as she and Taylor navigated the knot of people to reach Ava and Dylan.

"We're heading out," Brianna told them. "Ava, I'll talk to you soon."

Ava pulled her in for a tight squeeze. "Ask him for help," she whispered.

"I'll try," Brianna whispered back before shaking Dylan's hand.

After saying good night to the Wallers, Brianna and Taylor traipsed to the car and climbed in.

"Taylor, I need to talk to you about something," she began once they were on the road back to her house. "I need your help with the resort. I'm falling behind, and I'm concerned I won't catch up before Mom comes home from the rehab facility. Taking care of her will be nearly a full-time job. Scott Gibson did some of the work, and so have I, but there's still so much to do."

Taylor nodded. "Okay. Have you heard from Gibson?" His lips turned down as he looked at her.

Anger blossomed in the pit of her stomach. "Taylor, I'm asking for your help. Will you help me?"

"Yes, I'll help you. Of course I will. But have you heard from him?"

She huffed out a breath. "He texts me every couple of days to ask how my mom is. That's it. He probably just wants to remind me I owe him money, and he wants to be first to make a bid if we decide to sell."

He was silent for a beat. "Brie, you know I've been investing most of what I make into improving the store, but I have a little saved—"

"Thank you, Taylor, but I'm working on the money part of it."

She didn't want him to know just how far in debt she and her family were. And the truth was she had no idea how she'd get out of this mess without selling her father's precious resort. But she wasn't ready to give up trying to consolidate their debt with a loan so they could somehow go forward.

Taylor halted the car into her driveway and turned toward her. "Let me know what you need help with, and I'll find a way to be here."

"Thank you." She smiled, hopeful Taylor would see that promise through. This would be a chance for him to prove himself—and maybe bring them closer together.

CHAPTER 17

$\mathcal{S}$cott perused the spreadsheets and photos Brad had just handed him.

"I think it's a great investment," Brad said as he took a seat in Scott's office. "It's going to be a brand-new strip mall on Route 74 in Indian Trail."

"By the Walmart?" Scott asked as he looked at Brad across his desk.

"Yes. It's prime property because of the constant traffic there. We can charge whatever we want in rent. You know that area can use some new properties."

Scott opened his mouth to agree, but he was interrupted when their office manager, Allison, burst in from the hallway. "Brad! It's time!" Her eyes were as wide as Scott had ever seen them.

"What?" Brad looked dumbfounded.

Brunette curls bobbed against her shoulders as she nodded with excitement. "Kristi's been trying to call you, but your ringer must be off. It's time!"

Brad gasped and stood as understanding fluttered across his face. "It's time?"

"Yes!" Allison leveled her gaze and spoke to him as if he were a child. "Her water broke. Her mother is taking her to the hospital. And you need to meet them there. Now put on your jacket and find your keys."

"Oh my gosh." Brad looked at Scott. "It's time!" He reached across the desk, knocking over the pile of folders Scott had stacked on one corner, causing a waterfall of papers to spill out across the carpet. "Oh no." He leaned down to get them, and Scott tapped him on the shoulder before waving him off.

"Just go, Brad. I'll get this. You have bigger things to think about now. Take care of Kristi and call when you have news."

"Thank you." Brad shook his hand, then grabbed his jacket and reached for the keys in his pocket. "I'm going to be a dad!" He rushed out of the office, leaving Allison and Scott grinning at each other.

"Do you think he'll remember how to get to the hospital?" Allison said.

"Thank goodness he has GPS."

"Let's hope so for Kristi's sake." Allison squatted and began picking up the mess.

Scott lifted the last piece of paper, then dropped it onto his desk, his eyes focused on the printout with an aerial photo of Splendid Lake.

"Let me know if you need anything," Allison told him as she walked out.

"Uh, thanks," Scott said, his eyes still trained on the photo. An image of Brianna filled his mind, and his heart took note. Although he'd texted her every other day to ask about Lois's recovery, he'd received only short replies with basic information.

But that's not what bothered him. The truth was he missed Brianna. He just knew it was best to keep his distance.

Brianna looked at the YouTube video on her phone once more as she sat on the roof of cabin number eight Friday evening. She glanced up at the sky and glowered. Only a couple more hours before dark, which meant she had to get this done. Taylor had promised to come help with the last of the shingles, but that had been more than two hours ago. She'd texted him once to make sure he was okay, and his answer was Sorry. Can't talk now.

Anger had rushed through her as she began searching YouTube for how-to videos. She didn't have the luxury of waiting for Taylor, and now, taking a deep breath, she stared at a shingle, a nail, and her hammer. She could do this. After all, she rebuilt boat engines for a living, and she'd fixed the radiator on her Mustang too.

Dad's voice rang in her head. *You got this, Brianna. Never let anyone tell you a woman can't do what they consider a man's job.*

"Dad, I'm hoping you're right," she muttered.

She lined up the shingle and nail, then swung the hammer. When it struck her thumb instead of the nail's head, red-hot pain made her cry out. She shook her hand, then sat back on her heels and fought back a scream as her thumb throbbed.

Her phone rang, and she gritted her teeth, expecting to see Taylor's name on the screen. She was surprised to see Jenna's instead. She gave her hand another shake trying to stop the pain, but it didn't work.

"Hello?" Brianna asked, holding the phone with her other hand.

"Brie. Hi. How are things?"

Brianna snorted and sat down on the roof. "It's been one of those days."

"What do you mean?"

"Well, I just hammered my thumb instead of a nail, and that pretty much sums it up."

"I'm sorry. Hang on a second."

Brianna heard the muffled sound of voices, and she imagined Jenna sitting in her fancy office talking to another member of her team.

"I'm back. How's Mom been today?"

Brianna hugged her arms around her knees. "Better. She was in a good mood, and we sat out on the rehab center's patio and enjoyed their pretty potted plants. Then she used her walker the entire length of the hallway outside her room." She rubbed her forehead as renewed anxiety swept through her body. "It's heartbreaking to watch her struggle just to feed herself, but the physical therapist insists she's making great progress."

"That's good to hear."

"I know." Brianna nodded, surprised by the warmth and concern she detected in her older sister's voice. Maybe she hadn't given Jenna enough credit.

"I'm going to send you more money this week."

"Thank you. I got caught up on a few bills with the last money you and Cass sent." She paused. "Jenna, I haven't told either of you how dire this situation is. We're close to losing the resort, our home, everything. I convinced the bank not to foreclose for another few weeks, but I still don't know if I can get the consolidation loan I've been after. Yet I still don't want to sell the resort, and I know none of us do. I'd rather Mom never find out about any of this."

"Why didn't you tell us?"

"I . . . I thought I could work it out on my own." *And I wanted to prove I'm not the little girl you always seem to think I am.*

"You'd really go along with selling the resort?"

"If I have to."

"How much is the loan? And how much is it in arrears?"

She told her, and she heard a soft gasp before Jenna responded.

"Well, I'll see what I can do about sending more money. But I do hope we can keep the resort. It's still home."

"I know. And thanks." Brianna rested her chin on her knee, wondering if Jenna understood they might not have a choice. Surely a corporate lawyer would. But then again, this was so personal.

"So you said you hurt yourself. What were you doing?"

"Trying to replace some shingles on a cabin's roof. I watched a YouTube video and thought I'd give it a try. So far I've just busted my thumb." She examined the red and angry spot as she waited for Jenna to respond.

"Sorry. I'm still thinking about Mom. I know you said you wouldn't want a nurse, but— Hang on." Jenna's voice was muffled again for a few moments. "I'm sorry, Brie, but I have to go. I'll call you soon."

Jenna disconnected the call before Brianna could say good-bye. She set her jaw as she picked up the hammer, then set the shingle in place. Posing the nail for its rightful destiny, she pursed her lips. "All right, nail. This time I'm going to hammer you instead of my thumb."

Sticking her tongue out, she began pounding, and soon she had four shingles done. She smiled as pride expanded her chest. "You were right, Dad. I can do this," she whispered into the breeze.

She'd just aligned a fifth shingle when her phone rang again. She scowled at Taylor's name on the screen, then lowered herself into a sitting position. "Hello."

"Hey, Brie, I'm so sorry." Taylor was talking a mile a minute. "I had all intentions of coming, and I even had Dad lined up to take over the store for me. Anyway, I was getting ready to leave when Ray Andover called to say there's an issue with the permit for the new police station. So I wound up on the phone with him for two hours and then . . ."

Brianna rolled her eyes as Taylor droned on about the town business that occupied much of his time every day. But for once, she wasn't frustrated with him. She was just disappointed, and she was tired. She was weary of his excuses and fatigued by his drama. She had her own problems to worry about, and if Taylor didn't fully understand that by now, he never would.

Brianna interrupted him. "Listen, Taylor, it's fine." She looked over the lake as the sun began to set. "I really have to go. I'm losing daylight here."

"No, wait, Brie." He sounded frantic. "I'll come tomorrow right after work and help with whatever you need."

"Don't worry about it. You do what you have to do. Have a good night."

"But, Brie—"

"Good night, Taylor," she said, then disconnected the call before climbing down the ladder and jogging to the beach, where she dropped into her father's chair and looked at the glorious hues of orange and yellow streaking across the horizon.

Sadness crawled in along with the dusk as Brianna hugged her hoodie against her body. She craved a friendly voice, someone who would listen to her deepest worries. She looked down at her phone and considered calling Ava, but she hated the idea of dumping on her best friend when she was wrapped up in her sister's wedding plans. After all, when she'd spoken to Ava earlier, she'd heard about everything she had to do just to get ready for Brooklyn's bridal shower.

She pocketed her phone, then looked at the sunset again as she settled back in the seat. Her phone dinged. She pulled it out and found a text message from Scott.

What's a good gift for a newborn?

She laughed at the cryptic text, then instead of sending a return text, she found Scott's number. He answered on the first ring.

"Is the response so complicated that you had to call me?"

She could hear the smile behind his words, and it soothed her aching heart. "No, but I need some background. Who's this newborn?"

"My best friend's son."

"Really?" Brianna smiled as she imagined his handsome face. "That's the guy you mentioned is your business partner too?"

"Yes. The baby was born Wednesday night."

"How exciting. Their first?"

"Yes. They named him Cody Patrick Young."

"That's a nice name." She drew invisible circles on the thigh of her worn jeans with her finger.

"Brad and Kristi are excited. But you haven't answered my question. What's a good gift?"

"Well, I haven't had a baby myself, but I assume the parents would appreciate newborn-sized diapers and baby wipes. Lots of diapers and wipes, actually."

"Perfect. I'll have a case of each shipped to their house."

"I'm sure they'll be grateful." She wanted to keep the conversation going. Hearing Scott's voice was just what her soul craved. "Any other news from Charlotte?" She leaned her head back on the chair. Oh, how she'd missed him.

"It's been a typical Friday with meetings, phone calls, and boring things like that. How about in Splendid Lake?"

"The good news is my mom had a good day."

"Is that right? Tell me more." His tone was so warm.

"That's fantastic," he said when she'd finished. "You said that was the good news, though. What's your bad news?"

She frowned. "Well, when Taylor didn't show up to help me finish the roofing, I watched a video on YouTube. But then I hammered my thumb on the first try."

"Ouch."

"You can say that again." She examined her hand. "It's still red."

"You know, I can finish the job for you."

"I appreciate the offer, but I still think it's better if you don't come."

He sighed. "That's the nicest rejection I've ever had from a beautiful woman."

She laughed as her cheeks heated, then quickly decided to change the subject. "You haven't told me all that much about your life in Charlotte. Did you grow up there?"

"Yes and no. I was born in Gastonia and moved here when I was a toddler." He paused for a moment. "I lived in Mecklenburg County after that."

Her mind whirled with questions. Why was he so tightlipped about his childhood? "You once told me you never met your father. Does your mother live close by?"

"She died a long time ago." His tone was somber now.

"Oh, Scott. I'm sorry. And then you were out on your own at eighteen?"

"That's right."

"You told me you went into construction then. You didn't want to go to college?"

"That wasn't an option. What about you? Didn't you even consider following Taylor to Wilmington?"

She picked at a loose sliver of wood on the arm of the chair. "I already knew what I wanted to do, and I didn't need a degree to do it. From the time I was little I'd follow my dad to the workshop and hand him tools while he worked on boat engines. My dream was always to run this resort with him."

"That makes sense."

"How did you get into real estate?"

"I helped build a home addition for a real estate investor, and one day I got to talk to him about his profession. He encouraged me to take classes, and when I met Brad there, we became good friends. When we were ready, we started our firm. I suppose the rest is history."

"That's wonderful how it worked out."

He was silent for a beat. "Are you watching the sunset?"

"Yes. I'm sitting on my dad's chair at the beach."

"I'm on my deck."

"Tell me about your house."

"It's really a townhouse, but I own it. Well, I have a mortgage."

"What's it like?"

"It has three floors and three bedrooms, two and a half bathrooms, a two-car garage, and a small backyard."

She tried to imagine the place. Perhaps she'd get to see it one day. "It sounds amazing."

"It's nice, but not as nice as your family's lake house."

"I doubt that." Her thoughts turned to the receipts he'd left on the counter. "Jenna is going to send me more money. I used my sisters' last contributions to get caught up on some of the bills, but I should have enough to pay you back soon."

"I've told you—"

"I know, but you deserve to be reimbursed as soon as possible. Do you have PayPal or Venmo?"

"If I did, I wouldn't tell you."

"You're incorrigible."

He laughed, and the pleasant, inviting sound took her back to their first meeting at the bookstore.

"I aim to please," he said.

"Tell me more about Brad and his family."

She settled back in her chair and enjoyed the sound of Scott's voice as the sun finished setting and darkness shrouded the lake. The stars above her twinkled as if smiling down at her, and an ensemble of frogs croaked nearby as she breathed in the sweet aroma coming from a wood-burning fireplace somewhere in the distance. She wished Scott had come—again, no matter what she'd told him. If he had, they could be having this conversation in person.

"Have I put you to sleep?" he asked.

"No." She shook her head as if he could see her. "I loved hearing about how Brad and Kristi met."

"It's getting late. You must be getting cold sitting there in the dark. I'm sure you're wearing your favorite purple hoodie instead of something warmer."

"Are you spying on me again?"

"Maybe I am." She could hear the smile in his voice. "But seriously, you should head back to the house."

"I know." She sighed.

"Go inside and get warm."

"I will. Good night, Scott."

"Good night."

She smiled as she disconnected the call. Hearing his voice was just what she'd needed.

Scott smiled down at his phone. He never expected Brianna to call when he sent the text. How glad he was to have sent it.

He scrolled through his phone's photos, admiring the ones he'd taken of Splendid Lake and especially the resort. Knowing the Porters might never decide to sell, he puzzled over his relentless desire to still bring his ideas to fruition.

Then out of the blue, an idea began taking shape. He grabbed a notepad and pen, and as his thoughts fell into place, he realized it might be possible to make both his dream and Brianna's come true.

CHAPTER 18

*I*t feels so good for the four of us to be together again," Ava said as they all sat around a table on Brianna's porch. "It was Dylan's idea to bring dinner over on such a lovely Sunday evening, and I was glad you and Taylor were both available."

"Thank you so much." Brianna glanced around the table and smiled at all three. Ava and Dylan's offer had given her an excuse to relax. Not that the decision she'd thought about all last night wasn't still there at the back of her mind. It was.

She bit into another taco and took a sip of her Diet Coke. When she felt something rub on her leg, she glanced down at her cat, who predictably blinked up at her.

"Hey, Bucky." She tossed him a piece of shredded cheese, and he ate it before meowing for more.

"Are you ready for your mom to come home Thursday?" Dylan asked.

"Yeah, I think so." Brianna nodded, but a wave of apprehension swept through her. Although Mom was doing well, she wasn't sure she was equipped to care for her at home. But she still didn't want a nurse in the house for hours every day, and she needed the money Jenna sent for other things.

"Can I do anything to help you get ready?" Taylor asked.

Brianna turned toward him, surprised. Yet she had to give him credit. On both Thursday and Friday evenings he'd come before dark and helped her finish the cabin roofs. She was grateful he was finally being supportive with his presence.

"Thanks for asking, Taylor. Maybe since she's still using a walker, you and Dylan could rearrange her bedroom so she has a clear pathway to the bathroom."

"Sure," Dylan said as Taylor nodded. "We can do that right after we finish eating."

"Would you like me to come with you to pick her up?" Taylor asked. "That way I can help you get her in and out of the car."

"Yes, I would, thank you." Brianna smiled and felt another rush of appreciation. Taylor was a good man. She'd sold him short lately, and he didn't deserve that. He did have a lot of responsibilities. She turned toward Ava. "How are the wedding plans going?"

Ava grinned. "I'll show you photos of the decorations we found. My parents also ordered a gazebo. It's so gorgeous."

"The wedding will be at your parents' house, then?" Taylor asked.

"Yes. Brooklyn wants to get married by the lake, so Pastor Thomas will come there." She looked at Dylan and swatted his arm. "We should have done that."

"We couldn't have, Ave. You wanted a Christmas wedding, re-member? It would have been too cold—unless you wanted to ice skate during the reception."

Brianna laughed along with her friends, and it felt so good. She needed the distraction.

"The big day will be here before we know it," Ava continued. "I still haven't found my dress, but Brooklyn says I can choose whatever color I want as long as it doesn't clash with all the periwinkle. It's all coming together beautifully, though. And I'm making progress planning the shower as well."

Dylan looked at Taylor. "Hey, man. Don't you think you've made Brie wait long enough? Isn't it about time you two set a date?"

Brianna was sure the blood was draining from her face.

To her horror, Taylor gave an arrogant smile as he shrugged. "Well, maybe something is in the works, but you shouldn't ask questions." He darted a glance at Brianna, but then he popped a last bite of taco into his mouth. Brianna studied him. What was he talking about?

Ava grinned at her. "We might be planning another wedding soon?"

"Ava," Taylor said. "Didn't I just say you shouldn't ask questions?"

Ava gave Brianna a look that said *We'll talk later*, then passed around her peanut butter cookies as Taylor started talking about spring plans for his store. When they'd finished dessert, the men went to her mother's bedroom and she and Ava carried the dishes into the kitchen.

"Well, I do have a question," Ava said as she placed a plate in the dishwasher. "Why was I the only one excited when Taylor hinted he's ready to set a wedding date?"

Brianna busied herself rinsing out the serving containers Ava brought. "What do you mean?"

"You looked terrified."

Brianna shrugged. "I don't know."

"Brie, look at me." Ava glanced toward the hallway, then lowered her voice. "You know you can talk to me. What's going on?"

Brianna turned off the water and faced her. "I've already told you planning a wedding is the last thing on my mind right now, and I don't know what Taylor could be thinking."

"But you guys have been engaged for *three* years. Don't you want to marry Taylor?"

"Of course I do, but I have too much going on right now. I have to take care of Mom, and I have to run the resort. And you know Dad left us with financial issues. I've been working on them, but it takes time. I can't even imagine making wedding plans."

"Okay. Maybe you can get married early next year, then—when all that slows down. You can set a date now but take your time planning the wedding."

"That's still more pressure I don't need." Brianna shook her head as the worry that had trailed her all week bubbled in her chest. "I need to tell you something."

"Okay." Ava looked concerned.

Brianna pointed to the table. Once they were seated, she took a deep breath. "I told you Dad left some debt, but I didn't tell you how bad this is." She quickly disclosed the whole truth.

"Oh no." Ava cupped her hand to her mouth.

"With my sisters' help, I managed to make a payment to the bank, then based on that, I convinced the new manager not to foreclose on the resort quite yet. He gave me six weeks, and I've been trying to get a consolidation loan." Brianna took a napkin from the holder in the center of the table and began folding it over and over. "But so far no lending institution will help us. And if we don't get a loan, we'll lose the resort, either through foreclosure or being forced to sell it."

She paused. "Ava, I thought about this all last night, and I think we need to let Scott Gibson buy the resort. It's worth enough that I can pay off the debt and use what's left to buy a little house for Mom and me. I'll have to get some sort of job too."

"Are you sure that's what you want to do? Sell?"

Brianna kept her eyes focused on the napkin. "I don't think I have a choice. I just have to convince Mom and my sisters. Jenna and Cass know about the debt, but they don't know as much as I've just told you. And Mom still doesn't know about any of it. I almost called Scott to discuss selling with him yesterday, but I chickened out."

"Have you talked to him at all lately?"

Brianna met Ava's gaze. "Yes. I called him on Friday, but not about selling."

"*You* called *him*? Why?" Ava's eyes rounded.

"It was just a fluke. He texted me asking for advice on a baby gift. I called him to learn the backstory, and we talked for a while."

Ava leaned forward and lowered her voice. "Tell me you don't have feelings for this man. I'll agree he's hot, he can cook, and he seems like a nice guy, but he's only after the resort, Brianna. Once you sell it to him, you'll never hear from him again."

"We're just friends, and I don't think he's that callous. Besides, I enjoy talking to him."

Ava glanced behind her. "Taylor would be furious if he knew you'd called him. Dylan says he's made it clear he can't stand Scott."

Brianna rolled her eyes. "He's just jealous and overprotective."

"Again, does he have reason to be?"

She sighed. "Look, I'm going to pay Scott what I owe him, and once Mom's home, I'll have to tell her about the debt. I can't wait any longer. She's the only one who can sell the resort. She owns it, not me."

But what Brianna dreaded the most was telling her mother about the state of Dad's affairs. It was going to break her heart.

"Congratulations," Scott told Brad as the new dad opened his front door.

"Thanks. Come in." Brad nodded for Scott to enter. "How's your Tuesday been?"

"Like most Tuesdays, I guess." Scott followed Brad into the large family room. "How's little Cody?"

Brad pointed to a bassinet in the middle of the room. "He's napping here, and Kristi is resting upstairs."

Scott peeked into the bassinet and took in the tiny baby with his shock of thick, dark hair. He was bundled in a white blanket trimmed in blue. "He's adorable."

"Thanks. I give his mom all the credit. Would you like a soda?"

"Yes, please."

Brad brought him a can of Coke and sat on the sofa. Scott sank into the wingchair across from him, then took a long drink.

"Thank you so much for sending the diapers and wipes," Brad said. "What a useful and kind gesture."

"You're welcome, but I can't take the credit. Brianna gave me the idea."

Brad looked surprised. "You're still talking to her?"

"I text to see how her mother is doing. And a few days ago I texted her to see if she had an opinion about a baby gift. She called me, and we talked for a while."

Brad just watched him.

"She's going to have her hands full when her mother comes home from the rehab center in a couple of days. But she insists she can make it on her own. Both her best friend and mom told me she's stubborn, and she is."

"But she hasn't agreed to sell to you yet?"

Scott shook his head. "No."

"You know how you always think women are using you for your money?"

"Yeah."

Brad waved one hand for emphasis. "Well, it's obvious this one actually is."

"How's that?"

"Has she paid you for the supplies you bought, for the work you did, or for the gas money you spent going up there to help her?"

"No, but I told her not to. At least not yet."

Brad shook his head. "She's using you, buddy."

Scott opened his mouth to say he disagreed just as little Cody began to cry. As Brad gathered his son into his arms, Scott took in the love that glowed on his friend's face and smiled. Brad was a father. He had a family, and although Scott still didn't know if he'd ever experience the same joy, he wasn't jealous. He was happy for him.

Brad moved to the kitchen to prepare a bottle for the hungry baby, and Scott contemplated what he'd said about Brianna. He refused to believe she was using him, but he did plan to offer her a business deal soon, one she might like. If she did, he'd tell Brad all about it later.

Brianna stood in her mother's bedroom and glanced around. She'd spent the day preparing for Mom's arrival tomorrow, and her mind spun with a mix of worry and excitement.

She'd used the little room still on her credit card to pick up a walker and shower chair earlier in the day. Now all she needed was her mother to come home so they could begin adjusting to their latest new normal. Brianna only hoped she could provide the care her mother needed while at the same time struggling with the reality of their finances.

She glanced at the wedding portrait hanging on one wall and took in her father's handsome face. "I wish you were here, Dad. I miss you so much." Then she headed down the hallway and into her father's office. She turned on his computer and pulled up the spreadsheet she'd designed to track their bills. She was grateful for the money Jenna and Cassie had sent this week, and now she had to decide which bills to prioritize.

After spreading the stack of invoices on the desk, she glanced to the far corner and spotted the receipts Scott left. She'd wanted to show her appreciation by reimbursing him, and now was the time.

She pulled up the calculator application on her phone and punched in Scott's expenses, then added an amount to cover gas and his work time. Once she had the final amount, she wrote it on a sticky note. Then she opened the Venmo app and searched for Scott Gibson. When nearly a half-dozen names showed up, she groaned. Why did he have to have such a common name?

Her only option was to write him an old-fashioned check and send it to his office. She retrieved his business card from a desk drawer, then made out the check, attached a note, and stuck both in an envelope. After she'd addressed and stamped it, she decided she'd run by the post office on the way to the rehabilitation center the next morning.

Then she looked back at the spreadsheet, and her mind wandered to the defaulted loan. Though selling the resort to Scott was still on the table, a new idea had hit her yesterday. Maybe her sisters would qualify for a loan. But that left the question of how to make the payments. They both had good jobs, but they also lived in cities with a high cost of living and had no doubt been draining their savings to send her money.

Brianna moaned as yet another headache throbbed behind her eyes. But she had to be strong for Mom—especially tomorrow.

CHAPTER 19

$\mathscr{B}$rianna stepped out the front door and scowled toward the road. Taylor was thirty minutes late, and she didn't like her mother waiting.

"Don't let me down, Taylor," she growled as she walked back inside. "Not today!"

Just as she took her phone out of her purse, it rang. She glared at Taylor's name on the screen.

"Let me guess," she snapped. "You can't make it, and you couldn't let me know a half hour ago."

"I'm so sorry, Brie. Something came up. I can't leave the store, and—"

"Save it," she spat before ending the call. She had no patience for his disappointments today. She paced the foyer as fury and anguish surged through her. Who could she call to help? The staff at the center were so busy, and then she'd be alone when they arrived home . . .

If only Scott were here . . .

She shoved away that thought and dialed Ava's number.

"Hello?" Ava responded breathlessly, voices sounding in the background. "Brie?"

"Hey, I need some help."

"What's going on?" The voices in the background faded, and she imagined Ava slipping into the office at the back of the Coffee Bean.

"Taylor was supposed to go with me to get Mom, but he flaked on me. Now I don't know what to do. What if I can't help her out of the car by myself?"

"No problem. Let me call my mom and ask her to come help Brooklyn. Then I'll pick up Dylan so we can both help you. I'm sure his brother can hold down the fort at the repair shop."

"Perfect." Brianna breathed a sigh of relief. "We'll take the Tahoe."

An hour later Brianna led Ava and Dylan into the rehabilitation center, where they found Mom pouting in a chair in her room.

"Hey, Mom," Brianna said before kissing her cheek. "Are you ready to go?"

"Where have you been?" Her voice was thin, but her words were clear. "You were supposed to be here at ten!"

Brianna glanced at Ava and Dylan, and they all shared an awkward look.

"I'm sorry, Mom. Taylor was supposed to come with me, but something came up. Ava and Dylan hurried over as soon as they could. I thought we could use some help today."

Brianna gathered paperwork from the front desk before an aide helped them out to the SUV. Brianna and Ava loaded Mom's belongings into the back while Dylan helped her into the passenger seat. Soon they were on their way home.

Ava patted Brianna's hand in the backseat. "She'll be fine," she whispered.

When they arrived home, Dylan retrieved the walker from the house and helped Mom get settled with it before walking slowly beside her. Brianna silently thanked Scott again for the ramp as she and

Ava followed them into the house, then into the family room. She'd told Mom about the ramps, and she'd been grateful for Scott's kindness too.

"You're home," Brianna sang. "We're all so glad you're here!"

Mom glanced at the french doors, then looked up at her. "Would it be okay if I sat out on the porch? In back?"

Brianna smiled. "That's a great idea. I bet Bucky will come sit with you."

Dylan helped her get Mom situated on the swing outside the kitchen.

Mom sighed. "Oh, this is perfect. How I've missed my beloved lake!"

Brianna looked out to where a lone boat with a multicolored sail moved past the resort on glistening water, and her shoulders relaxed for the first time since she'd awakened that morning. She turned to her mother. "Would you like something to drink before lunch?"

"Yes, please."

Brianna poured sweet tea into one of the cups with a lid she'd picked up at the drugstore, then added a straw before setting it on the little table to the left of the swing. "Do you need anything else?"

Mom shook her head. "No, thank you." She looked down, and her face lit up. "Bucky! Have you missed me as much as I missed you?"

"Mom, I'm going to say good-bye to Ava and Dylan, then do a chore or two in the house before making our lunch. Call out if you need me. I'll leave the door open a crack."

Brianna found her friends standing in the foyer. She hugged them both before looking up at Dylan. "I don't know what I would have done without your help."

"You know you can call us anytime."

"I'll stay," Ava said.

"No, you have your business to run."

Ava's brown eyes revealed her determination. "I'll stay. At least for a couple of hours." She looked at Dylan. "Would you please pick me up later?"

"Sure." He kissed his wife's cheek and looked at Brianna. "Never hesitate to call if you need me."

"I won't."

After Dylan left, Ava pulled out her phone. "I'll just let Brooklyn know I won't be back for a while." When she'd sent the quick text, she said, "I'll make lunch. You unpack your mom's things."

Brianna removed her light jacket, then carried her mother's bag of clothes to the laundry room. She dumped them into a basket, then started a dark load before returning to the kitchen. Ava had set turkey and cheese sandwiches on three plates, along with some apple slices. One of the sandwiches had been cut into small pieces.

"Do you think your mom will be okay with this?" Ava asked.

"I do. I'll take it to her. She might want to eat out there." Brianna stepped onto the porch, where her mother still looked out over the lake with Bucky sitting at her feet. "Mom, Ava made you a sandwich."

"Thank you." Mom looked up at her. "You look tired. Are you okay?"

Brianna nodded, then sat beside her on the swing, still holding the plate. "I've been worried about you, but I'm glad you're home."

Mom patted her arm. "I'm sorry for putting you through so much, but I promise we'll be okay."

"Right." Brianna's throat dried as worry threaded through her. How could she tell her mother the resort was in trouble?

Mom nodded toward the door. "Go have lunch with Ava. Bucky and I are just fine out here."

"Okay." Brianna put the plate in her mother's lap, then stepped into the kitchen. After she told Ava what Mom said, Ava carried their own lunches to the table.

"Sit. I'll bring you a glass of tea."

"I can get my own—"

"Sit. Let someone take care of you for once."

Brianna sat in her usual spot while Ava poured the drinks, then joined her. They ate in silence for a few minutes.

"Did you talk to Scott about buying the resort?" Ava asked in a low voice.

Brianna shook her head. "I need to talk to Mom first, but I don't think I should tell her today. She already looks so tired."

"Waiting is probably best."

"I just can't wait too long. We have to make a decision soon." Brianna popped a chip into her mouth. "I feel like I'm drowning."

Later, while Ava checked on the laundry, Brianna joined her mother, taking a seat in a rocker next to the swing. She looked at Bucky lounging at the top of the ramp, basking in the afternoon sun.

"Would you like something else to eat or drink?" Brianna asked.

Mom shook her head. "No, thank you. I'm just fine. It's a beautiful day."

"It is." Brianna breathed in the scent of spring. Already, blooming perennials danced in the breeze, and birds sang in the trees as another boat moved through the water in the distance. This one had a beautiful teal and blue sail.

Brianna turned to her mother and found her weary blue eyes still focused on the lake. She worked to keep her voice upbeat and sunny. "What do you think about breakfast for dinner? I could make eggs, toast, and bacon. Does that sound okay? Or would you like grilled cheese instead?"

Mom nodded. "Grilled cheese sounds good."

Silence fell between them once again, and Brianna suddenly missed their time together, not just before the stroke but before they'd lost Dad. What she wouldn't give to hear her mother share excitement about a new recipe or talk about her favorite soap opera. Would their life together always be like this? They used to talk about movies, television shows, and the latest news about Brianna's friends. Mom wouldn't even let her own friends visit her in the hospital or rehab. Emma Lang in particular had been so disappointed when Brianna had to tell her she couldn't come.

And now Mom gazed out toward the lake, not uttering a sound. First Dad's death had changed her, and now this.

Dylan came for Ava, and Brianna again sat with her mother a while before helping her inside for a nap. Later, she made two grilled cheese sandwiches, heated some canned tomato soup, and poured two glasses of iced tea.

Once the table was set, Brianna walked beside her mother and her walker before helping her into her usual kitchen chair.

"*Bon appétit.*" Brianna could hear the phony happiness in her voice, but she had to try.

Mom reached for her glass, and Brianna held her breath as alarm surged through her. She'd forgotten to give her a cup with a lid and straw! As Mom brought the glass to her mouth, unfortunately trying to use her right hand, the tea sloshed. Then she missed her mouth, and the tea spilled on her pink shirt before she yelped and dropped the glass, which shattered on the tile floor. Tears began streaming down her face.

"It's okay!" Brianna rushed to the counter, where she grabbed the roll of paper towels. She gave Mom a few sheets, then fetched their dustpan and broom from the utility closet. After dumping the pieces of glass into the trash can, she crouched and mopped up the spilled tea.

"Are you okay?" Brianna asked her mother as she handed her more paper towels.

"No." Mom moaned. "I'm *not* okay. I should be cooking for you! And your dad should be here."

Brianna's heart twisted. "Mom, I'm so sorry. But we'll get through this. I promise."

She finished cleaning up the mess and then brought her mother more iced tea in a cup with a straw. They ate in silence, and she noticed Mom didn't even try to bring her soup spoon to her lips. Brianna inwardly groaned. What had she been thinking? Her mother wasn't ready for soup, and she'd never tolerate her daughter feeding her.

Before long, Mom used her walker to move to the family room, where she sat down in Dad's recliner. Brianna helped her turn on a Hallmark movie.

Once she was sure her mother was settled, Brianna returned to the kitchen. After loading the dishwasher, she leaned back on the counter, scrubbed one hand down her face, and groaned—out loud this time.

They *would* make it through this. She just didn't know how.

CHAPTER 20

$\mathcal{Y}$ ou've got mail," Allison announced Monday morning as she handed Scott a stack of envelopes.

"Thank you." Scott sifted through the advertisements, then stopped when he found a white envelope with *Splendid Lake Cabins and Marina* printed in the upper left corner. His heart picked up speed as he opened it and a check with a note fell out. He studied the beautiful script.

> Scott,
>
> As promised, here's the money I owe you for the supplies you bought. I'm sorry this is an old-fashioned check, but I couldn't find you on Venmo since your name is pretty common. I added a little extra for your time, work, and the gas you had to buy.
>
> Thank you for helping me. I hope your baby gift was a hit.
>
> Sincerely,
>
> Brianna

Scott imagined her sitting at a desk while writing, and he longed to call her. But he had to be careful not to overstep—now more than ever. He needed her to be as open as possible when he decided it was time to approach her with his latest idea.

"Is that a check for a million dollars?"

He looked up to see Brad leaning against the doorframe. "Don't you have a wife and new baby to take care of?"

"My mother-in-law has insisted on staying with us for a while." Brad dropped into the chair in front of Scott's desk. "And I'm glad she has. She's a wonderful woman, and I truly appreciate the help. Plus, I was happy when she told me I should come into the office for a while. I was ready to get out of the house." He nodded toward the check still in Scott's hand. "What's so interesting about that? You looked like you were memorizing it."

Scott turned it around and showed it to Brad. "It's from Brianna. She paid me back, plus some."

"It's about time."

"I can't accept this."

Brad rolled his eyes. "So she can take advantage of you?"

"No, it's not that. I haven't told you this yet, but I have another offer for her, and I think she'll take it. It works for both her and us."

Brad steepled his fingers. "This should be good."

Scott's pulse trilled as he began telling his partner the plan.

"I think you're all set now." Brianna handed her mother's cell phone to her. "Now this is how you call me." She showed her how to unlock the phone by merely holding it up to her face. "Then click this app, and here's my number."

Mom nodded.

"Want to try it?"

Mom unlocked it but then struggled to hit the button. She looked so frustrated.

"Take your time."

But instead, her mother threw the phone onto the floor. Brianna couldn't recall a time she'd had a short temper. This stroke had truly changed her.

Brianna worked to keep her own frustration in check and her face serene. "Let's try this again."

After four more tries, Mom was able to call her.

"Great! Now just keep the phone next to you." Brianna had set up a folding tray and placed a book, Mom's reading glasses, and a cup of water topped with a cover and straw. "I'll be outside working."

Brianna hurried out the door, breathing a sigh of relief. She was grateful to be on her way out. Too many projects around the resort had been calling her, and it was already Monday afternoon. She had to get going, and as she made her way to pick up the cabin keys she needed, she thought about Taylor.

He'd surprised her Friday morning, arriving at the house with two dozen roses—red ones for her and pink ones for her mother—and an apology. Then he spent the rest of the day finishing the roofing. He'd also brought them dinner that night, as well as on Saturday and yesterday, three evenings in a row.

While Brianna appreciated his help and generosity, she couldn't stop thinking it was all too little, too late. But perhaps she was still expecting too much of Taylor. She was grateful to have more time with her mother over the weekend and that one big project finished. He said he'd do more around the resort this week as well, but she knew better than to count on it.

Meanwhile, she still had plenty of projects on her to-do list. Today she'd start by checking the furniture for any necessary repairs, but what bothered her the most was still not knowing how she was going to fix the pier.

After grabbing the key to the barn in case she needed tools, she stepped out the back door. She smiled as a couple of rabbits hopped by on their way to a nearby bush, and as she took in the bright sunshine and crystal-blue sky, she realized it was the perfect day to paint. She abandoned her initial plan, and in the barn she gathered paint brushes, a drop cloth, and a gallon of the paint Scott bought.

She headed to the picnic area, where a dozen tables sat ready for guests to enjoy. They were in bad shape at the moment.

Brianna recalled how she'd helped her father build the tables a number of years ago, when he'd realized most of the vacationers prepared their own meals and might like to eat outside. Soon she was sanding the first table, then got busy painting it a green just a shade darker than it had been. She was almost done with the first coat when her phone rang. She pulled it from her pocket and saw her mother's name.

"Mom?"

"Would you please help me reach something? I'm in the kitchen."

"Of course. I'm coming."

Brianna popped the lid on the paint can, then set the brush on top of it before wiping her hands on a rag as she made a beeline for the house. Her mom was leaning on her walker near their kitchen pantry—really just a set of shallow shelves behind a door. "What do you need?"

"A snack." She sighed. "I should be getting one for you."

Brianna swallowed her own sigh as she scrubbed her hands at the sink. Then forcing a smile, she turned to her mother. "What would you like me to get?"

"Cookies."

Brianna found a box of fudge-striped bars. Maybe they weren't too old.

"How's this?" She held up the box, and Mom nodded.

Brianna put a few on a plate, then walked next to her mother into the family room. She set the plate on the folding table as Mom lowered herself into her chair. "Do you need anything else? More water? Milk?"

"No." Mom picked up a cookie and bit into it. "I think I'll watch some TV."

Brianna handed her the remote, glad the couple of hours of home therapy she'd had Friday and that morning were already making real-world difference. "I'm going back outside now."

She'd just started sanding another table when her phone rang again. She sucked in a deep breath when she saw who it was. "Yes, Mom?" She tried her best to stay calm.

"Would you mind making me some hot tea? I'm not sure I should be using the stove alone yet."

"Of course. I'll be right there." Brianna's shoulder muscles felt like tight balls as she hurried into the house. At this rate, she doubted she'd finish painting more than one picnic table before sunset.

Brianna stepped out of the shower and yawned. After running back into the house at least two more times that afternoon and then doing her best to cook a decent meal, she was so exhausted her eyes burned. And all her muscles ached. Once in her pajamas and back in her bedroom, she walked to the receiver for the baby monitor she'd set up in her mother's room. She was happy to hear Mom already snoring. Although her mother was capable of getting herself to and from her bathroom, Brianna still worried she might fall or need to call for her in the middle of the night.

Brianna combed out her wet hair and climbed into bed. She

couldn't wait to fall asleep. She settled herself under her comforter and closed her eyes, but then her phone rang.

"Not now," she groaned.

Seeing Cassie's name on the screen, she sighed before answering. "Hey, Cass."

"Hang on one sec," Cassie said. "Let me get Jen on the phone."

Brianna shut her eyes. She was way too tired to deal with her sisters.

After a moment, Cassie was back. "Okay. Jenna is here now. How are things?"

Brianna took a deep breath. "As well as can be expected."

"What do you mean by that?" Jenna asked.

Brianna told them how she had to constantly run into the house to help Mom when she had to get things done around the resort. "She's getting around better than I thought she would, but she still needs my help."

Cassie sighed. "I'm so sorry."

"I was hoping things would be better by now," Jenna said.

"Have either of you checked into taking a leave of absence so you can come help me?"

Cassie spoke first. "Oh. Uh. Well. Remember that promotion I mentioned a few weeks ago?"

Brianna folded one arm behind her head. "Yeah."

"I got it."

"Congratulations! That's fantastic!" Jenna said. "I'm so proud of you."

"That's great," Brianna said. "But I guess that means you can't get away."

"Well, that's the thing. Now I have more responsibility. Be careful what you wish for, right?" She gave an awkward laugh.

"I'm loaded up too," Jenna added.

Of course you are.

Brianna pressed her lips together. She was proud of her sisters' success, but she and Mom still needed them.

"Brie? Are you still there?" Cassie asked.

"Yeah, I'm here." Disappointment swirled through her. "I understand that you both have responsibilities."

"We're supporting you the best we can, but we also know you're working hard and carrying the load." Cassie's tone sounded defensive and apologetic at the same time.

"We appreciate all you're doing for Mom," Jenna added, sounding less apologetic yet genuine.

"Thanks." Brianna rubbed her forehead. She might as well get this over with. "I have to talk to Mom about selling the resort, but first I need to hear from you."

"What?" Cassie said.

"I tried to tell Jenna how dire this is, but I guess she didn't share it with you." She explained about the size of the debt, the ever-growing pile of bills despite their financial help, and her failed effort to take out a consolidation loan.

"There's really nothing we can do to save it?" Jenna asked.

"The bank won't wait to foreclose much longer. We don't have much choice." She sat up and leaned back against her headboard. "I've become friends with one of the real estate investors who want to buy it. If we let him have it, we can pay off the loan, and we'll have just enough left to pay all the bills and buy a little house for Mom and me. Then I'll get a job."

Neither sister said a word for a few moments. "There's no other way?" Cassie finally asked.

"Not unless you and Jen can take out a loan to pay this one and then make the payments." Brianna took a deep breath, mustering all the confidence she could find. "Look, I've looked into every option, and this is the only viable one."

"I understand," Jenna said, and Brianna nearly dropped the phone.

Cassie lingered in silence on the end of the line, then finally said, "It does make sense."

Brianna felt as if a weight had been lifted from her shoulders. Her sisters had heard her. Treated her like the adult she was. "Thank you."

"I'll check into a leave of absence," Cassie added. "Let me talk to my manager and see what options I have."

"Tell Mom we love her and we'll call soon," Jenna said, failing to make the same offer. "I know this will be a blow to her, but she'll be okay. She'll understand."

Brianna wasn't so sure about that, so she just said good night and ended the call. At least Cassie was trying to come home, and she needed to give her other sister a break. Jenna worked hard at her firm, once confiding she hoped to make partner one day.

When her phone dinged, she looked down to find a text from Scott.

How are things at my favorite lake?

She was glad to hear from him, but she was too tired to give an in-depth answer.

Fine.
Liar.

She grinned as she sent him a smiley face.

I don't want your check.

Keep it.

Can we talk?

Too tired. Long day. Later?

Okay. Sleep well.

You too.

She rolled over and melted into the bed. She'd let Scott know they were willing to talk about selling the resort once her mother agreed, but she still wasn't sure how soon she'd be able to bring herself to let her know the jeopardy they were in. Knowing might send her over the edge, and she was already too close.

Still, that's when she might see Scott again, and she had to admit she looked forward to that.

CHAPTER 21

$\mathcal{B}$rianna stepped out of her bedroom Friday morning and heard a crash coming from somewhere downstairs.

"Mom? Are you okay?" She took the steps two at a time as blood pumped in her ears. "Mom!"

She rushed into the kitchen and found her mother leaning on her walker in front of the counter next to the refrigerator, staring down at what had to be a full carton of eggs smashed all over the floor.

"What were you doing?"

"What does it look like?" Mom snapped. "I was trying to make breakfast."

"That's my job."

Mom harrumphed. "No, it's not. And I'm a great cook, but now I can't even make a peanut butter sandwich."

"It's all right," Brianna said as her own nerves frayed. "Why don't you sit down? I'll make some coffee and toast, then we'll decide what else we want."

Mom made her way to the kitchen table, then sat there while Brianna put on the coffee and pulled out bread. When her phone rang, she was relieved to see who it was. "Mom, it's Jenna."

"Oh, good!" She held out her hand.

Brianna handed her mother the phone and then surveyed the mess. Her shoulders sagged. She hadn't even had any caffeine yet.

She grabbed a roll of paper towels, then gazed out the window for a moment, her eyes landing on the workshop. She and Dad had spent hours there, working on the boats, talking and laughing, just enjoying each other's company. Oh, what she would do to get those days back.

Brianna looked at her mother, who was smiling as she listened to Jenna. She hoped Cassie would find a way to come home soon. She really did need help.

She wet several paper towels, then set to work mopping the floor.

Brianna finished the second coat of paint on the last picnic table late afternoon. Thankfully she'd managed to anticipate her mother's needs before heading out, so she'd been able to finish the job. She wiped her hands on a rag as she started walking toward the house. When she felt something soft rub against her leg, she smiled down at Bucky.

"How's it going, buddy? I'll get your food. Just wait one minute, okay?"

She climbed the back porch steps but then stopped when a loud engine boomed in the distance. It sounded like it was coming closer.

"Scott?" she whispered.

The sound came closer and closer, and she quickened her steps as she walked around the porch to the front of the house. Scott's Barracuda steered up the driveway, then came to a stop beside her Mustang. She tried to keep her emotions in check as she fought the urge to run to him, but her heart had taken on wings.

Scott climbed out of the car and waved.

"What are you doing here?" she called, hoping she didn't sound as delighted to see him as she was.

"What's new?" He walked around to the back of the car and popped the trunk.

She met him there. "You didn't answer my question."

He reached in the back pocket of his jeans, then held out her check. "I told you I didn't want this."

She gave a dramatic sigh and rolled her eyes. "This again?"

"I also have another deal to discuss with you. Take the check, and we'll talk about it."

"You know, I threw another real estate agent off this property just yesterday."

He raised an eyebrow. "You're going to throw me off your property again?"

She sobered. "No. But I still have to talk with my mother before I can talk to anyone about a deal, and I'm not sure when she'll be ready to learn the truth. I'm not going to push her."

He pulled a grocery bag out of the trunk. "Of course not. Now, take this, and I'll get the other one."

"Why did you buy groceries?" She took the bag from him.

"I owe your mom some peppered shrimp alfredo." He slammed the trunk closed.

Her heart did a somersault. Scott was either the kindest man in the world or the most manipulative one. But she really did believe he was the former. If she didn't, she'd never consider selling the resort to him.

They ambled up the front ramp, and Scott held the screen door open for her. Then just as they'd walked into the foyer, they heard a crash.

Not again!

They both rushed into the kitchen, where her mother lay sprawled on the floor with shards of glass spread around her like confetti.

"Mom! Are-are you okay?" Brianna's breath came in short bursts as she threw her bag on the counter.

"Mrs. Porter," Scott said as he dropped his own bag on the floor. "Unless you think you've broken any bones, I'm going to pick you up and put you in a chair."

"Nothing's broken," she said.

"Are you sure?"

"Yes."

He picked her up as if she were as light as a child and set her on the closest kitchen chair.

"What happened?" Brianna asked as she took her mother's hand.

"I wanted to get myself a drink. I grabbed that glass, but then one of my pesky slippers came off, and down I went like a klutz!" She gave a little laugh, giving Brianna some relief mixed with concern.

"You shouldn't do that. You need to call me."

"I have to learn to do it myself. You know I can't stand being waited on."

She rubbed her mother's hand and glanced to where Scott had pulled the trash can over and started picking up glass.

"A broom?" he asked.

"In the utility closet." She pointed in the right direction.

Scott disappeared, then returned with the broom and a dustpan. Together they cleaned up the mess, and then Scott stowed the dustpan and broom again.

When he walked past Mom, she patted his arm. "You're a good man."

Brianna was certain Scott blushed.

"Thank you, Mrs. Porter."

"Mom, Scott says he's going to cook for us tonight."

Mom gave her a curious look, and Brianna gulped. *Does Mom think Scott is here because he's interested in me? Of course she would. She doesn't even know the resort is in trouble.*

Her mother pointed toward the porch and said, "I'd like to sit outside for a while. Just give me my walker, and I'll get out there on my own."

"Let us help you, Mom." Brianna moved the walker over to her. "You just fell—"

"No. You can't babysit me all the time." Mom pulled herself up, then walking slow and steady, she reached the door and opened it before setting her walker outside. Then she stepped through the doorway, closed the door behind her, and made her way to a rocker.

Brianna breathed a deep sigh of relief as she watched her mother gingerly lower herself into the chair, then made a mental note to ensure her mother knew Scott was no threat to Taylor. She might not understand right away, but she would when she knew the real reason Scott kept coming.

"She nearly scared me to death," she said.

"Me too."

"So what's this all about? Are you trying to impress my mother with an amazing meal so she'll be open to your schemes?" Brianna couldn't help but tease him as she leaned back against the counter next to him.

"Maybe?" He gave her a sideways glance, then lifted his eyebrows, his striking blue eyes sparkling. "Are you going to let me stay? You already told your mother I plan to cook."

She tapped her lip and pretended to consider her answer, enjoying their easy banter. "You can stay, and you can cook, but you can't eat."

He laughed, and she joined in. Oh, how she'd missed him! Her heart felt lighter when he was with her. But she had to put that into perspective. This was about her mother and the resort.

She set the table, then offered to help. Scott put her in charge of boiling the water and keeping an eye on the pasta.

"How are things really?" he asked when the shrimp was ready for the alfredo sauce to be stirred in.

Brianna glanced toward the porch. "Let's talk later."

He nodded, then they worked in silence for several minutes before he pointed to the boiling pot. "It's time for the pasta."

Brianna drained the noodles and folded them into the sauce with the shrimp and spices. She took in a deep breath. "Scott, you're a *really* good cook."

"Wait until you taste it."

Once the dish was ready, Brianna called her mother, who slowly made her way to her usual spot at the table.

"What's this?" she asked as Brianna scooped some of Scott's creation onto her mother's plate.

"Remember when Scott said he'd send me a recipe for you? This is it. His peppered shrimp alfredo. He made it just for you."

"Oh my goodness! Thank you." Mom grinned. "It smells divine."

"I hope you both enjoy it." Scott graced Brianna with a smile that seemed to be meant only for her, and her heart did a funny little dance.

She took a bite and moaned at the delectable taste. "Scott, this is exquisite!"

"I'm glad you like it."

Mom forked her first bite, and when a piece of pasta dropped into her lap, Brianna braced herself, waiting for her to get upset. But she only laughed.

"See what I mean about being a klutz?"

"Trust me. I can relate." Scott gave her a warm smile. "I've been looking forward to making this for you."

Brianna's heart swelled. Scott Gibson was a special man!

"Where are you from, Scott?" Mom asked him, then glanced at Brianna before taking another bite. Brianna saw a lot of questions in those eyes.

"Mostly Charlotte. I was born in Gastonia, and then my mother and I moved to Charlotte when I was a toddler." He paused. "After she passed away, I grew up with foster families around Mecklenburg County."

Brianna gasped, then set her fork on her plate. "You were in foster care? You told me your mother died, but—"

"She passed away when I was five."

"I'm-I'm so sorry," Brianna stammered as everything he'd told her made sense—that he'd never known his father or knew if he had half siblings, never had a family, and had been on his own since eighteen, with college not an option.

"That had to be difficult," Mom said, her eyes filled with a mother's concern.

He gave a half shrug as he picked up his glass of iced tea. "I survived it."

Brianna's heart tumbled with compassion coupled with a yearning to know more—no, *everything*—about Scott's life. But it would be rude to ask him. She'd have to be patient, waiting for him to feel comfortable enough to tell her of his own accord.

"What are some of your other favorite seafood recipes?" Mom asked, no doubt also sensing he'd rather not say more.

"Oh, let's see . . . I made grilled cilantro salmon one time."

As the two of them talked, Brianna found herself mesmerized. She felt a connection to Scott that seemed to grow stronger every time they spoke, and what frightened her most was the feeling she could trust him more than she could trust Taylor. She was becoming more and more attached to a man who wanted to buy the only home she'd ever known.

Brianna glanced down at her engagement ring, twinkling in the kitchen lights, and guilt nipped at her. How could she allow Scott to become so important to her when she'd made a commitment to Taylor? That was a commitment she intended to keep.

No. She'd be loyal to Taylor just as he'd been loyal to her. She just had to convince her heart to ignore these feelings for Scott. But that seemed more difficult than she cared to admit.

"Sorry I didn't bring any dessert," Scott said as he gathered utensils when they'd finished dinner.

"I have an idea!" Brianna announced.

He turned toward her, curious to see what she had in mind. "I'm listening."

"Why don't we go to the bakery and pick up cupcakes? All the downtown stores are open till seven on Friday nights." Brianna lifted her chin, clearly proud of her idea. "We can clean the kitchen later."

Mrs. Porter rubbed her hands together. "Ooh! Bring me a red velvet one." She pulled herself up with the walker. "Let me get my wallet."

"No, no, Mom. The cupcakes will be my treat." Brianna grinned at Scott. "On one condition, though."

"What's that?" he asked.

Brianna gave him a mischievous grin, and it sent a strange tremor through his veins. "I get to drive your car."

"Oh, so you want to drive the Barracuda?"

She nodded, and her blond braid bounced off her shoulder. "Very much."

"Well, I guess you can drive my 'Cuda if you buy me a chocolate cupcake."

She clapped her hands. "Yay!"

"You two are funny together," Mrs. Porter quipped as she stood and turned toward the family room. "Don't be too long. I'll be waiting."

After he and Brianna stacked dishes in the sink, they headed to the driveway. When they reached his car, he tossed her the keys. "Go easy on her."

"I'll do my best."

They both climbed inside, and he grinned when she started the car and whistled.

"This car is amazing. Did you buy it fully restored?"

"I did."

"Where did you find it?" She backed it up to turn it around.

"At an auction. Hey, stop for one minute." When she did, he stood and pulled down the convertible top before sitting again and refastening his seat belt. "Now we're ready to roll."

"Yes, we are." Her gorgeous brown eyes sparkled.

They talked about the car as she drove to town, then parked on Main Street near Morningside Bakery and cut the engine.

"Whew." He swiped his hand over his brow. "I was worried we wouldn't make it in one piece."

She swatted his arm. "You better not make a crack about women drivers or you'll walk back to the resort!"

When he chuckled, she joined him, then nodded toward the windshield. "Have you ever been in the Christmas Shop?"

"No."

"How about I show you around now?"

"But your mom is expecting her cupcake."

"She'll be fine. Like she said, I have to stop babysitting her, and she carries her cell phone in her pocket now, so she can call me if she needs to. And I don't think she'll be reaching for another glass this evening." She pushed the door open. "Let's go."

Scott followed her inside the store, where several customers milled around more than a dozen Christmas trees, all covered with lights and decorations. Each one seemed to have a theme. One had white lights and all-white ornaments, including snowflakes, snowmen, and stars. Another tree was adorned with blue lights and blue decorations, and a third had multicolored lights and matching glass balls.

Although it was spring, a spirited rendition of "Jingle Bells" rang through the store's speakers, and a suspicious scent of pine filled his nostrils, causing him to wonder if either plug-in air fresheners or powerfully scented candles were hidden around the store.

He couldn't help but ponder if the year-round Christmas theme exasperated the shopkeepers, but the middle-aged woman wearing a Santa hat at the cash register and singing along with the music didn't seem to mind.

"Isn't this place amazing?" Brianna asked, her sweet expression lit with a wide smile as she beckoned him to follow her to a tree decorated with ornaments representing famous cartoon characters.

She held up a Snoopy ornament as excitement flashed across her face. "This reminds me of something fun! When I was a kid, every year we had this wonderful activity day at church called the Advent Workshop. All the kids went to different Sunday school classrooms to make decorations while many of the adults made wreaths. One time Cassie and I made a Snoopy ornament out of coffee creamer cups."

"How do you make Snoopy out of coffee creamer cups?"

"Well, one is for his body, and another one is glued on top of it to make his head. You add a black pom-pom for his nose along with two googly eyes, and then add two black pieces of felt for ears, a little red bow made of string for a scarf, and a red string to use as a hanger." She motioned with her fingers, and when he gave her a confused look, she waved him off and laughed. "It's hard to explain."

"I'll take your word for it."

She swatted his arm again, and he chuckled.

"Just trust me. It's Snoopy! Anyway, we still hang those ornaments on our tree."

"Really?" She was so cute!

When they stopped at a tree with a teddy bear theme, Brianna had another memory to share. "All through our growing-up years, Dad brought my sisters and me here every year the day after Thanksgiving to choose an ornament for our tree. Then we'd drive out to a local tree farm to find just the right tree so we could take it home and decorate it."

"That's cool."

She looked at him, and her face dimmed slightly. It was obvious that she longed to ask him something when her expression grew sheepish. "Did you have a real tree when you were a kid?"

He pursed his lips as Christmas memories, some better than others, tumbled through his mind. "Sometimes I did, but my best Christmas memories are from the last Christmas I spent with my mom."

She stared up at him, and the compassion in her pretty brown eyes was almost too much for him. He nodded toward the exit, still not ready to share about his years in foster care. "Shouldn't we get our cupcakes and head back?"

Brianna swallowed, and what looked like regret settled in her eyes. "I'm sorry. I didn't mean to bring up something so painful."

"It's fine."

Her blond eyebrows lifted.

"I promise that you didn't offend me."

"Okay." Her smile was back, and he was mesmerized by how effortlessly beautiful she looked with wisps of golden hair escaping her thick braid and framing her face. "We'd better get Mom's cupcake before she thinks we ran off to Asheville."

"Good idea."

But he wouldn't have minded more time alone with this woman who so delighted him.

CHAPTER 22

The bell above the door chimed as Scott held it open for Brianna to enter Morningside Bakery. The delicious aroma of baked goods filled the air as he scanned the little shop, finding wood tables and chairs where several customers sat eating their pastries. Photos of all kinds of goodies adorned the walls.

Scott followed Brianna to the counter, where he took in the glass-fronted case filled with delicious-looking treats—a variety of cupcakes, pies, cakes, tarts, and breads that made his stomach gurgle with delight despite the pasta dish he'd so recently consumed.

"What do you recommend?" he asked, overwhelmed by the choices.

Brianna snorted as she looked up at him. "Everything."

"Okay . . ."

"I usually get a carrot cake cupcake."

"I'll have the same."

Brianna ordered their cupcakes and, surprising him, added two coffees, then paid for it all before a young man with curly red hair and an eyebrow ring handed them a bright-blue pastry box and two cups. Scott hurried to the exit and held the door open for Brianna to step back outside.

She walked toward the car but stopped when they came to a bench. "Let's sit for a few minutes."

Scott studied her. "I thought we were in a hurry to get home with your mom's cupcake."

"You said you had a deal to discuss with me, and I was hoping we could talk about it alone. I'll tell Mom we stopped at the Christmas Shop, which we did. She'll understand."

"Okay." They sank onto the wood bench, and Brianna placed the pastry box on her lap. When his thigh brushed hers, a chill danced down his leg. He breathed in the scent of her flowery lotion—maybe it was her shampoo—and his senses spun.

He shook himself. He had no right to think of her this way. He had to fight against this attraction, because nothing good could come of it.

He took in the people walking in and out of the little shops and breathed the wonderful scent that was Splendid Lake. This place seemed even more magical than usual tonight.

He took a sip of his coffee before turning toward his companion. "Now tell me the truth, Brianna. How are you really?"

"I'm hanging on as best I can, but I'd be lying if I told you I was fine."

Scott listened quietly as she told him about her continued problems with the resort and the challenges of caring for her mother, hoping she could see the concern he felt for her in his face.

"I can't help as much as I'd like to with your mom, but when it comes to the resort, what if I had a solution we'll both like?"

She angled her body toward him. "I'm listening."

"What if we became partners?"

She narrowed her eyes at him. "Tell me more."

"What if instead of my firm buying the resort, we invest in it?

Then we can pay off the loan, hire people to help you, and not only get the place in shape but make some renovations."

She shook her head. "Why would you want to invest in the resort instead of buying it?"

Because you love it.

"I like this place. And I have ideas to make it even better."

She looked skeptical.

"Brianna, you might like my ideas. Why don't you listen to them? Then maybe you'll change your mind."

She lifted her chin as if challenging him. "What if I don't? And I can't see letting you take the helm?"

He rested his arm on the back of the bench behind her and grinned. She had no idea how gorgeous she was.

"Why are you laughing at me?"

"Because you used a nautical term. It's cute."

"Cute? Really?" She rolled her eyes. "Next you'll say you don't think I can rebuild a boat engine because I'm a woman."

He was puzzled. "Why would I say that?"

"Never mind. Anyway, I don't know if this can work. You want to change my family's business, and besides, we hardly know you. We can't go into business with someone we don't really know. I can just hear Jenna now."

"Like I said, you might like my ideas, and your family might too. Also, you know I'm not a stranger." He smiled. "Just envision this. First, I said *partners*, so we'll both be at the helm, with your mother involved as much as she wants to be. And we can put this little resort on the map by making it a year-round retreat center, offering a spa and exercise and yoga studios.

"Also, imagine adding a large indoor/outdoor pool to the center, available to all the cabin renters as well as day visitors. And we'll market like crazy. I think these upgrades will attract more people and make more money. What do you think?" He held his breath.

"The retreat center wouldn't have hotel rooms, would it?"

"No. But Lakeview Inn might have increased business from visitors who don't want to rent a cabin."

"I don't know. My grandfather saw this as a place for families, not for rich professionals. So did my father."

"It can be both. We can also upgrade the cabins, adding Wi-Fi and streaming services and a heat source. Just make them more modern and appealing, and maybe adding a second bathroom and a third bedroom to accommodate larger families. Most of all, we can keep the resort open year-round, making it financially stable."

She looked down Main Street, as if trying to square the whole idea with the town he knew she loved. "I need to discuss it with Mom as soon as I tell her how we got here, as well as my sisters. I'll also want to talk to our lawyer and accountant. They've both been advising me."

"I understand." Hope lit in his chest. He was getting through to her!

"Scott, why did you come here when we could have discussed this on the phone?"

"You said we could talk later, but you never got back to me."

She grimaced. "I'm sorry. I've had so much on my mind."

He gave her side a gentle jab with his elbow. "Brianna, I wanted to come. I wanted to see how you and your mom were in person."

Her phone rang, and when she pulled it from her pocket, he peeked over in time to see Taylor's name. He tried to ignore the jealousy surging through him as she answered. But he was almost certain he heard Taylor apologize for not coming to help her today.

So her fiancé still wasn't stepping up. He shook his head.

Brianna sounded unenthused as she conversed with him. Finally she said, "Sure. Good night," then disconnected the call.

Scott had noticed Kristi and Brad always said "I love you" before they hung up, but Brianna and Taylor didn't. Curious.

"Is everything okay?" he asked.

"Yes. It's just that Taylor rarely has time to help me. But I can't make unfair demands. He has two jobs."

He raised an eyebrow. She was making excuses for him again. He hoped she'd see the truth about the guy before it was too late. He took her for granted, and what kind of fiancé wouldn't make time for the woman he intended to marry?

"May I help you this weekend?" he asked. "I came prepared to stay. My duffel bag is in the car."

She gave him a coy smile. "Not if you won't take the check."

"Let's make a deal."

She groaned. "Not another one."

"I'll stay the weekend and help with your remaining projects, and you consider my offer. We'll worry about the check later."

"I guess I can work with that."

She held out her hand, and his heart soared as he shook it. "By any chance is Cassie's room available?"

"For you?" She smiled. "Always."

The delicious aroma of coffee filled Brianna's senses as she jogged down the stairs the following morning. She stopped in the hallway and happily listened to her mother talking. Then she stepped into the kitchen and found Scott at the stove while Mom sat at the table.

She could smell eggs, too, and the table was already set.

"That's what I usually put in my western omelets as well," Mom was saying. "Adding both green and red peppers along with the swiss cheese, onions, ham, and thyme gives them more flavor. Then I salt and pepper to taste, of course."

Scott looked over his shoulder at Brianna and grinned. "There you are, sleepyhead. We were just discussing the best way to make western omelets. I hope you like these." He looked good in a worn pair of Levi's and a faded hard-rock concert T-shirt.

"Everything smells wonderful. Mom and I are getting spoiled by your amazing meals." She tore her gaze away from him. "Let me pour the coffee and make some toast."

Brianna stifled a yawn as she poured the brew into three mugs, then carried them to the table. Two more yawns assailed her as she put bread into the toaster, then gathered creamer, sweetener, and three spoons.

Mom rested her hand on Brianna's when she brought the items to the table. "Didn't you sleep well?"

Brianna was struck by the concern in her mother's eyes. For a moment she was reminded of the woman she'd been before the events of recent months. Brianna held back a rush of emotion and smiled. "I'm fine. Thanks for asking, Mom."

"You need to take care of yourself." She reached up and touched Brianna's cheek.

"I know." Brianna turned and joined Scott, who'd just scooped a large omelet from his pan to a platter. "Are you sure you took only one cooking class? You didn't study under a master chef in Paris?"

He snorted. "You give me too much credit."

"I'll take this one to Mom."

"It looks fantastic," her mother said before forking a piece of the omelet into her mouth. "Oh, and it is. Scott, I think you need to be here permanently. Would your business—"

"That's what I said too! He should be our cook." Brianna wasn't ready for Mom to learn Scott was in the real estate business. She might ask too many questions before Brianna was ready to answer them. She sat down, waiting for the toast to pop up, then watched Scott break more eggs into his pan.

Scott shook his head. "I don't think Taylor would be too thrilled with that."

Mom looked confused. "Why not?"

Scott craned his neck to look at her. "Let's just say I'm not his favorite person."

"That's because you never cooked for him," Mom said. When she laughed at her own joke, Brianna and Scott joined in.

Oh, it was so good to hear her mother laugh! Brianna shared a warm look with Scott, and for a moment, her world seemed nearly perfect.

After Scott brought the last two omelets to the table, he sat down across from her.

"Has Brianna shared the history of our little resort with you?" Mom asked as she reached for her coffee.

"She told me it was passed down from her grandfather."

"That's true. Martin's father bought this place for a song back in the early fifties. His vision was to create an affordable spot for people to vacation. His parents thought he was crazy and said it would never take off. What they actually said was, 'Who would want to come to a lake in North Carolina?' Weren't they shortsighted?" Mom laughed, and Scott and Brianna again joined in.

Brianna silently marveled as her mother shared about when she first visited the resort and quickly fell in love with both the place and

Brianna's father. Although her voice was still a little strained, the slack in her mouth was less noticeable, and she did sound more like her old self. That sent hope singing through Brianna. And yet . . .

Scott was listening to Mom with rapt attention, and soon Brianna found herself lost in thoughts about his offer to partner with her in order to save the resort. After they'd all enjoyed their cupcakes in the kitchen the previous evening, she'd spent hours tossing and turning as she considered his proposal. While she felt the urge to convince her mother to take his deal, so many things could go wrong.

Would changing the resort cause them to lose their regular guests? Or what if their Splendid Lake neighbors despised the changes— especially if they brought a lot more visitors to the lake and community, upsetting their small-town feel? And what if her father's dream gave way to Scott's?

Even worse, realistically, the jury was still out on Scott. What if he wasn't the wonderful guy he seemed to be? She and her mother could still wind up emptyhanded or even homeless if his interests were actually entirely for himself and his firm. After all, how well did she really know him? He seemed determined to help them, but what if that was all a ruse to get her to convince her mother to give him access to the resort? How could she truly know whether his intentions toward her family were pure?

"Brianna?"

"Hm?" She looked up from her empty plate and realized her mother and Scott were both staring at her.

Scott looked curious, if not concerned. "Is something wrong?"

"I'm sorry. Just lost in thought." Heat infused her cheeks as she picked up her mug and took a sip, hoping he'd stop staring at her.

"Did you finish the roofing?" he asked.

"Taylor did."

"Oh." He seemed surprised. "I thought you said he hasn't been able to help much."

"He hasn't."

"Well, what else needs to be done in the cabins?"

"How good are you with a caulking gun?"

He made a production of blowing on the fingernails of his right hand and rubbing them against his chest. "Not to brag, but I've used one a few thousand times."

She grinned at his feigned arrogance. "Would you mind caulking the windows in the cabins and checking the air-conditioning units? You'll probably need to clean out the filters."

"I can handle that. Do I need to get some caulk?" He swiped another piece of toast and then pushed the plate over to her.

"I'm sure whatever we have is old." She took a piece herself, then handed her mother the last one. "While you work on the cabins, I can start getting the boats ready."

Mom divided a smile between the two of them. "Sounds like you two make a great team."

Brianna stilled at her mother's words. Was she talking about more than the resort? Out of the corner of her eye, she spotted Scott looking at her. She swallowed her toast and shrugged. "I'm just grateful to have help."

"And I'm glad to help," he said. "I'll run to Lowe's right away."

Mom stood, then walked out to the porch and her favorite spot on the swing. Brianna closed the door behind her, then turned to Scott. "Don't you feel like we're taking advantage of you?"

"How so?" He leaned back against the counter.

"You cook for us, clean the kitchen for us, shop for supplies and buy them for us, and work on our resort. And all of it without expecting pay. I have a feeling you'll try to turn it down even if we never make a deal. What are you getting out of this? I think you know by now I'd listen to what you have to say even if you didn't do all that."

He rubbed the morning stubble on his chin. "I suppose I get my payment in the form of wonderful company." Then he folded his arms over his wide chest.

Brianna looked out the window and spotted Bucky sitting beside her mother, blinking up at her as she talked to him. Then she joined Scott and lowered her voice. "I was up most of last night thinking about your offer. I'm taking it seriously, but there's still a lot to consider. And again, I want to talk to our lawyer and accountant. But if we do this, we have to first concentrate on opening the resort on time. We can work out renovations later. At least, that's what I plan to recommend to my mother."

"I agree."

"I also have to convince Mom to let you invest in the first place, and I'm not sure how she'll take it after learning why we even have to consider your proposal. You heard how much she loves this place. Change is scary, especially right now. Everything's happened so fast."

"I understand completely, but we can't even begin negotiations without your mother's blessing." He rested his hands on the counter. "What about your sisters?"

"They know we might have to sell, but I need to explain your new offer to them soon so they don't feel blindsided if Mom agrees. After all, they grew up here too."

"Again, I agree." He paused and rubbed the back of his neck. "I need to be honest with you about something."

"Okay . . ."

"When I first planned to buy this place, I was going to flip it."

Her eyes widened. "What? You mean you'd turn around and sell it?"

"Hold on." He held up his hands. "Let me explain. Yes, that was my plan. But that's not what I want now. Being your business partner will be a career shift for me, but I want to help you run this place, not get rid of it—ever. I also want to keep my job at the firm but part-time. Brad and I built it together, and it's still important to me. So I'll do what I can remotely and commute to Charlotte a couple of days each week. I'm also thinking about building a little cabin of my own here."

She mulled all that over and nodded. "Everything you just said makes sense."

"Good."

"So if everyone agrees, especially my mother, I think we have a deal." She held out her hand. "Depending on all the final terms, of course."

He took her hand in his and held on, and she enjoyed the feel of his skin against hers as he went on.

"Talk to your mom, and if she gives the go-ahead, let's discuss all the remaining and upcoming bills as soon as possible. Brad's father, Phil, was willing to back buying the resort, and we're sure he'll back this investment too. But I want to give him all the information up-front. And to your earlier point, it is too soon to renovate. We can start construction on the retreat center after the season is over. We don't want to inconvenience the guests."

"Sounds great."

He shook her hand, and when he released it, her skin tingled where he'd touched it.

He gave her his crooked grin. "May I take your dad's cool pickup truck to Lowe's?"

She grinned back. "So you prefer it to that gorgeous Barracuda?"

He shrugged. "I like it."

"Go right ahead. You know where the keys are."

"Awesome." He rubbed his hands together, then pulled out his phone. "Tell me everything we need so I'll have the list on here. Then I'll head out. And I'll get enough caulk for the sinks and showers in the cabins too."

After she told him what they needed, she smiled. "Don't have too much fun," she said, happy to tease him. But when she looked toward the porch, her stomach filled with what felt like lead. It was time to tell her mother the resort was in trouble.

Scott stood in the cleaning supply aisle and perused what it offered. He picked up a gallon jug of cleaner and read the back, then looked at another one. Finally settling on a third, he set it in his cart next to the tubes of caulk he'd picked up. He started for the next aisle, then stopped when he heard someone call his name.

"Gibson?"

Scott stilled, the muscles in his back tightening. He turned to see Taylor pushing a flatbed cart toward him, a deep frown creasing his face.

"Reese. Fancy meeting you here. How's the deputy mayor of Splendid Lake?" Scott hoped his lips formed a smile instead of the sneer they preferred when it came to Taylor.

Taylor's lip curled. "What are you doing here?"

Scott pointed toward his selections. "Buying supplies. How about you?" From the shelving unit kits stacked on Taylor's cart, it was clear he was also there for supplies. Still Scott couldn't stop the ridiculous question from leaving his lips.

But Taylor just leaned forward on his cart's steering handle and stared daggers at him. "Why are you back in town when Brianna made it clear her family isn't going to sell the resort to you? Are you that dense? Or are you trying to steamroll her anyway?"

Scott gave a bark of laughter as fury boiled in his gut. Oh, what he wanted to say to this guy! Taylor was the one who clearly had no clue how to treat an amazing woman like Brianna.

"Well, Taylor, I think the situation is more complicated than you appear to know. Now, if you'll excuse me, I need to get a few more items and be on my way." He smirked. "You have yourself a great day."

Before Taylor could respond, Scott moved to the next aisle, where he put a case of paper towels, a box of rags, and a pair of work gloves in his cart before heading to the cashier. While standing in line, he pulled his phone out of his pocket, then typed a quick text to Brianna.

Warning—Just ran into Taylor. He wasn't happy to see me. Sorry. Be back soon.

After hitting Send, he placed his elbows on his cart and rubbed his temples. He hoped he hadn't just created a mess, but sooner or later Taylor would learn Scott and Brianna were contemplating a business partnership. The man would have to deal with that whether or not he liked it.

He also couldn't understand how Taylor could take Brianna for granted. Perhaps he didn't realize how blessed he was to have her in his life.

CHAPTER 23

*O*ut on the porch, Brianna took in the beautiful morning and smiled. "It's pretty out, isn't it? The sun is shining, and the sky is so blue. Are you warm enough in that little sweater, Mom?"

"I'm comfortable, thank you." She paused. "Brianna, what's going on between you and Scott?" Her blue eyes sparkled. "Are you planning to break your engagement?"

Ah. She'd been right about her mother's suspicions. But why would Mom seem almost happy thinking she might break up with Taylor? She had to be imagining that.

"No, Mom, I'm not. And Scott is just a friend. But I need to tell you something. I just don't want to upset you." Brianna steeled herself for the discussion ahead. She closed her eyes for a moment, hoping the right words would come to her.

Mom had turned her gaze out toward the lake, where two sailboats floated by boasting their colorful sails. "Your father's gone. What more could upset me?"

Brianna took a deep breath. "You like Scott, right?"

"Yes, very much. He's nice, and he's handsome too."

Brianna smiled at that and then pushed on. "Well, he's not just my friend."

"But you just said—"

"I mean he's more than just a friend." Brianna groaned. "No, I'm not saying that right."

Mom reached over with her left hand and touched Brianna's arm. "Just say what you want to say, Brianna."

"Scott is a real estate investor. He stopped by the resort not long after Dad died because he wanted to buy it, and I turned him away. But then he came back, and that's when you ended up in the hospital. Even though I again told him the resort wasn't for sale, he offered to help me with the work around here as long as I agreed to go to him first if I ever changed my mind. The Lakeview Inn was closed that weekend, and that's the first time I let him stay in Cassie's old room."

Mom waited for her to go on.

"I didn't have anyone else to help me. He's been such a godsend, and now he has some great ideas for the future of the resort."

Mom looked startled. "Are you telling me you want to sell this place? Our home?"

"No. Not exactly." Brianna's hands started to shake. "While you were away, I found out Dad left us with a lot of debt."

"That can't be right. Have you looked at all your father's documents? He kept impeccable records."

"That's true, but he also took out a loan to pay overdue tax bills, using the resort as collateral, and then defaulted on the loan. I've been using what money was still in his checking account, and with my savings and help from Jenna and Cassie, I scraped together enough to make a payment on the loan. But if we don't catch up on all the overdue payments soon, the bank will foreclose on the resort, and we'll lose everything."

Mom looked confused. "What about our savings account? Your dad always saved."

Brianna cringed. "It's empty."

"Our retirement account?"

"Gone. I suspect Dad used it to make the loan payments as long as he could."

"This doesn't make sense." Mom shook her head, her voice rising. "Your dad always took good care of us. He would never let this happen. It can't be true!" Her voice broke as tears flooded her eyes.

Brianna felt a pinch of guilt as she rubbed her mother's arm. "Please, Mom." She jumped up, then rushed into the kitchen and grabbed a box of tissues. Once back, she handed a few to her mother. "I just need you to listen. Dad did the best he could. No one is blaming him, okay?"

Mom sniffed and nodded.

Brianna took a trembling breath. "I've looked into a debt consolidation loan, but I got turned down everywhere I went. We have only two options—sell, or upgrade the resort so we can make it financially stable by earning more profit."

"Upgrade? How would we pay for that?"

"Scott came up with another idea. Instead of selling to him, we can partner with him. He wants his firm to invest in the resort and make some changes to make sure this never happens again." Brianna paused, waiting for her mother to react, but she remained silent. "I think it's a good idea, but Dad left the resort to you. You own this place, so what we do is your decision. I just need you to understand that if we do nothing, we'll lose everything, and we'll have to find a new place to live."

Brianna held her breath as Mom looked down at her lap, tears sprinkling down her pink cheeks. "Why didn't he tell me we were in trouble?"

"I've wondered the same thing." Brianna wiped her mother's tears with a fresh tissue. "He and I worked so closely together, and yet he never mentioned it to me. But now I realize he didn't want us to know."

"You're saying he wanted us to believe we were fine."

"Yes. And I'm sure he thought he was protecting us." Brianna gave Mom's hand a gentle squeeze. "I'm sorry for dumping this on you when you have so much else on your mind."

Mom gave her a sad smile. "You do too. You have to take care of everything now, including me. I'm sorry I'm a burden."

"Stop. You're going to make me cry too." Brianna's eyes stung. "You know I'd do anything for you."

Mom wiped her eyes. "So Scott wants to partner with us?"

"Yes. He and his business partner have a financial backer who will bail us out of the debt, pay up our bills, and fund renovations. He's suggesting a retreat center, a pool, improving the cabins—"

"Do you trust Scott?"

Before she could think twice, an "I do" escaped her lips. "But I need you to be part of this, Mom. It's your decision. I've consulted both your lawyer and accountant about our dilemma, but I want us to consult with them again, this time about accepting Scott's proposal." She felt her lips turn down. "Jenna and Cassie know about everything but this latest offer from Scott. I don't know what they'll say about the changes he wants to make, but I really don't think we have a choice. Anyone else will want to buy the place and make us leave."

"Well, your sisters aren't here to give their opinions, and this is urgent. I say we partner with Scott. We'll work it out with them later." Mom looked out toward the lake. "I trust you to handle this, so long as you consult me on the big decisions."

"Of course. That's fair." Brianna breathed a deep sigh of relief. Now she had to tell Scott they could put their plan into motion. She looked down at her phone and realized she'd missed a text from him. She read the message and groaned.

"What's wrong?" Mom asked.

"Nothing you need to worry about." She stood. "I'm going to see if I can get some work done. Do you need anything?"

"No, thank you. I'm fine here."

Brianna made sure her mother had her cell phone, then turned toward the workshop, her work clothes already on. But then her phone rang. "Oh no," she mumbled at seeing Taylor's name on the screen. She considered going inside the house to talk in private, but then decided to sit back down and face it. After what Mom said earlier, she suspected she knew all was not well between her and Taylor.

"Hi." She hoped she sounded sunny.

"Guess who I just ran into at Lowe's." She could picture Taylor seething. A car engine sounded in the background, and she imagined he was gripping his steering wheel, scowling toward the road ahead of him.

Brianna slouched in the rocker. "Is that a rhetorical suggestion?"

"He already texted you to say I saw him, didn't he? Why am I not surprised? And why is he here? He was buying supplies, and I assume that means he's staying with you again. But you told him you weren't selling, right? I want the truth, Brianna, and I want it now. You're making me look like a chump!"

"Taylor, calm down. I'm not making anyone look like a chump." She spoke slowly, hoping he would listen. "Nothing is going on between Scott and me. Yes, we're friends, but other than that, you're imagining something that isn't there."

Mom turned toward her with eyebrows raised.

"Then why is he back?"

"He came up yesterday to make another offer on the resort, and Mom and I are considering it."

"Wait. You're selling?"

"I said we're considering what he's offering."

"What does that mean?"

"It means we're considering it. I can't go into details right now."

"Why? Because you don't trust me?"

Brianna banged her head against the back of the chair. Why did Taylor have to take things to the extreme? "It's complicated. He wants to invest in the resort. He has a backer, and he wants to make improvements and help market it."

Taylor was silent. "Why are you selling out?"

Anger boiled in her belly. "I'm not selling out. Look, I'm busy. We can discuss this another time."

"I'm sorry." Contrition radiated in his voice. "I'm angry because I was planning to surprise you with a romantic dinner tonight, but it was all ruined when I found out you have . . . company."

She licked her lips. "And I'm sorry I didn't tell you he was here."

He was silent, and the sound of his car's engine and road noise filled the line for a moment. "I'm sorry for getting angry with you," he finally said. "We'll talk after he leaves, okay? When will that be?"

"Sunday."

"Okay. I'll talk to you then."

She disconnected the call and groaned. "Men!"

Mom snorted.

"I'm sorry for raising my voice, Mom. Taylor is upset because he ran into Scott at Lowe's. He says he was planning a romantic dinner for me tonight, but Scott's ruined it."

Mom reached over and patted her hand. "That's not why he's upset. He's upset because Scott's providing what you need right now, and he knows he's not. He feels guilty."

Brianna gaped at her mother, shocked by such clarity. She may had suffered a stroke, but she was still wise. And perceptive.

As Brianna looked out over the lake, she realized how right Mom was. Scott *was* providing what she needed, but her relationship with Taylor was . . . Well, for a long time it hadn't been much more than comfortable, like her favorite purple hoodie. And once again she compared them to other couples in her life—her parents, Ava and Dylan, Brooklyn and Cole . . .

She wasn't ready to give up Taylor, but she could see how faded, out of shape, worn their relationship had become. She just didn't know what to do about it.

Scott parked the pickup truck in the driveway, and leaving the supplies in its bed, he loped up the front ramp and into the house. Then he walked through the kitchen and out to the porch, where Brianna's mom sat looking at the lake.

"Hi, Mrs. Porter."

"Please. It's time you called me Lois." She smiled up at him.

"Okay. Do you need anything?"

"No, thank you. How was your trip to the store?"

"It was . . . interesting." He cupped his hand to the back of his neck as he recalled his strained encounter with Taylor. "I picked up plenty of supplies, and I'm ready to work."

"Wonderful."

"Where's Brianna?"

Lois pointed toward the marina. "She's in the workshop, her favorite place."

"Thank you." He started down the back ramp but then stopped and faced her. "Are you sure you don't need anything?"

"No, thank you."

He gave her a nod and headed down the hill. As he approached the workshop, he heard the sound of hard-rock music. He grinned when he reached the door, and when he opened it, a familiar song sang to him through large speakers. Looking around, he noticed workbenches, the aluminum johnboat sitting on a trailer in the center, and the smell of carburetor cleaner and gas. Brianna stood by one of the workbenches with her back to him, singing while spraying a carburetor with cleaner. Boxes of spark plugs, spark plug wires, and carburetor kits sat nearby.

Scott took in the sight of Brianna's blond ponytail bouncing to the music. She was just as gorgeous in her worn jeans, pink hoodie, and usual purple western boots as she was when he'd seen her dressed up. He longed to stand there and watch her all day long. But she suddenly turned, then gasped before pressing her hand to her chest. He noticed her diamond engagement ring hung from a gold chain around her neck.

She grabbed a little remote control and turned down the music. "How long have you been standing there?"

"Not long." He nodded toward the carburetor. "Having fun?"

"I am. I have to make sure all the boats are ready for rental, but this is my favorite thing to do. Apparently Dad and I forgot to clean this one's carburetor before we stored it. Did you find all the supplies we need?"

"I did." He hung his coat on a peg on the wall, then sat on a nearby stool. "Did Taylor call you?"

"Yes. He was upset, to say the least." She rolled her eyes as she hopped up on the stool beside him. "I'm sure he was a jerk to you. I'm so sorry."

"You need to stop apologizing for him."

"I know." She ran her thumbnail over the edge of the workbench. "He said he was upset because he'd planned what he called a romantic dinner, and then . . ." She grabbed a rag and started cleaning her hands. "I talked to Mom, and despite her shock at what I told her, she's open to partnering with you. Maybe the three of us can talk over dinner. I'll make something tonight. We really shouldn't let you spoil us with your amazing cooking."

"And what would you like to make for me?"

She bit her lip. "How's frozen pizza?"

"Oh. That hurts!" He put his hand over his chest as if she'd shot him in the heart. "You want to follow up peppered shrimp alfredo with frozen pizza?"

"I have one with pepperoni."

He laughed. "I don't mind pulling something together. I'll see what's available when we go inside."

She lifted her chin and crossed her arms over her chest in mock offense. "You're insulting my pizza without even trying it?"

He shrugged. "Actually, I like cooking for you and your mom. I don't get to cook for people very often."

She glanced around the shop and back at him, her mood suddenly somber. "This is the first time I've worked in here since . . . This was where I spent the most time with my dad. He taught me everything I know about engine repair." Her brow creased and her eyes glistened in the fluorescent lights. He had a feeling she wanted to get something off her chest.

"I've never told you about when he passed away."

He shook his head. "No, you haven't."

"It was the day I first met you."

He studied her. "You mean the day we met at Bookends?"

227

She nodded. "Dad and I planned to meet here in the shop that morning. I'd run into town to pick up that book for my mom and get coffee at the Coffee Bean for the three of us. We were all craving one of Ava's cinnamon dolce lattes. But Dad had a massive heart attack before I even got to the coffee shop. In fact, it probably happened right before I talked to you."

"What do you mean?"

A tear trickled down her cheek, and she swiped it away with the back of her hand. "After I paid for the book and left, I started for the Coffee Bean. But then my phone rang, and it was Mom. I told her I was on my way to get our coffees, and then . . ."

The grief on her face made his heart twist. "She told me I needed to come home right away. I found out later she got worried when Dad hadn't come out of the bathroom. She found him collapsed on the floor."

Brianna's lower lip trembled. "He was already gone. I never had a chance to tell him good-bye. I didn't get to tell him I loved him one last time." Her face crumpled as she dissolved into sobs.

Scott couldn't take watching her suffer any longer. He had to do something to console her, and he stood and opened his arms. "Come here."

To his surprise, she launched herself into his arms, burying her face in his chest as her tears dampened his shirt. She held on to him as if her life depended on him. He held her tight and breathed in her scent—one uniquely Brianna.

He closed his eyes for a moment, enjoying the feel of having her in his arms. He had no right to hold her like this, but he abandoned the thought. Right now he had to comfort her. Brianna needed someone—and he was the one she'd trusted.

"I'm sure your dad knows how much you love him," he said softly.

"You're a good daughter. I can see it in the way you are with your mother. And you said it yourself—you're the daughter who stayed."

She rested her cheek on his chest, and he went on. "I know how it feels to lose someone important to you. Grief is unpredictable, and it sneaks up on you sometimes. The wound never heals, but as time goes on, it gets a little easier."

She pulled herself away, then grabbed a tissue from a box nearby and wiped her eyes and nose. "Thank you."

"You're welcome." His mouth dried as he imagined what it would be like to kiss her. He had to change the subject before he did something he'd regret. He could never allow himself to disrespect her and even Taylor by crossing that line. "I'm glad your mom agreed to consider my offer."

"I am too. She took the news better than I imagined." She sniffed. "She says she's in as long as she can be part of the decision making."

"Absolutely. I'll go home tomorrow night and hopefully talk to Brad and his father Monday morning. Then I'll come back and help you until we open. I can keep up with my work at the firm remotely for a while."

"When you work up the deal, will you please send it to our lawyer? I want her to represent Mom." She smiled. "I'm grateful you came back after I threw you off my property."

He snickered. "I'm not that easy to get rid of."

Brianna looked downward, and her long lashes fluttered against her skin. If he didn't know any better, he might've wondered if a blush was coloring her cheeks. He cleared his throat. "Well, I'd better get to work," he said.

"See you later . . . partner." She gave him a little wave before he grabbed his coat and headed out of the shop.

As he walked up the hill to unload the supplies, he was nearly lost in the memory of holding her. But then he chided himself. He'd crossed a dangerous line with a woman who was already spoken for. And now, more than ever, their relationship needed to remain friendly but professional. After all, they were going to be business partners. The resort—and both their futures—depended on them.

CHAPTER 24

*T*he lovely aroma of Scott's braised balsamic chicken still hung in the air as they all sat at the kitchen table, sipping decaffeinated coffee as he detailed his plans for the resort.

"I just don't know," Mom said, shaking her head as she turned to Brianna. "I'm not sure your father would approve of yoga." She wrinkled her nose. "It sounds so . . . hoity-toity!"

Brianna bit her lip, trying to stop a smile as she glanced at Scott, who full-on grinned.

"Mom. It's really not."

"But it is, Brianna. When your grandfather opened this resort, he wanted it to be a place where hardworking families could get away and rest for a week. It was all about them, not people who want to do yoga and things like that. How would those families feel seeing people walking around in yoga outfits?"

When Scott glanced at her with his lips twitching, Brianna looked down at the table, this time biting the inside of her cheek in an attempt to stop her own laughter from escaping.

"And if you add this high-class retreat center with a pool, that means our rates will have to go up. How will our regulars afford to come back?"

"But our rates are one reason the resort is in trouble." Brianna worked to keep her tone gentle. "I checked the books, and Dad hasn't raised the rates in seven years. In that time, our utility bills have increased as well as our tax bills. The latter are what pushed Dad into taking out the loan. I hate to say it, but if we'd stayed competitive all that time, we wouldn't be in this mess."

"Oh dear." Mom shook her head. "I didn't realize that."

"So, Lois, you have guests who come back every year?" Scott asked.

"That's right. The Glenn family has come for many years. Maybe twenty? I watched their children grow up. The Van Dykes have, too, and their grown children come now."

Scott's smile was encouraging. "I believe they'll still come. They should expect the rates to go up, especially if they haven't for several years. That's just how it goes with the rising cost of living, right?"

"Yes, that makes sense." Mom nodded, then pulled her walker close. "I don't mean to be rude, but I'm going to rest in the recliner in my bedroom for a while. It's been a long day." She pulled herself up, then smiled at them. "You two should go do something fun. You've both worked hard. Go enjoy this beautiful spring weather."

Scott flashed his signature crooked grin as soon as her mother left the kitchen. "I know what we can do."

"Oh yeah?"

"I saw a flyer at Lowe's. There's a car show down on Main Street tonight, and all the shops are staying open late. Want to go?"

"I love car shows. Let me get changed."

"I will too."

After pulling on a fresh pair of jeans and a red hoodie with a Mustang logo on it, Brianna pulled her hair into a french braid, slipped on her blue western boots, and then met Scott downstairs. He looked great in his own fresh pair of jeans and a gray Henley shirt.

"You ready?" he asked.

"Absolutely."

He held out his keys. "You want to drive?"

"Really?"

He laughed, a sound she'd come to enjoy. "You haven't wrecked my cars yet, so yes, really."

"Thank you!"

He tossed her the keys, and she hurried out the front door to his Barracuda before he could change his mind. She helped him lower the convertible top before she slid into the driver's seat, then slipped the key into the ignition and turned it. The car roared to life, and she closed her eyes, enjoying the purr of the engine. When she looked at Scott, she found an amused expression on his face.

Her cheeks heated and she gave a nervous laugh. "I'm sorry. I really am something of a motorhead. It's my dad's fault."

"I think it's fantastic. We're kindred spirits."

Soon they were on Main Street, where classic cars had taken most of the parking spaces. Surprisingly, Brianna found an empty spot and nosed the Barracuda between a candy-apple red 1966 Mustang and a bright-yellow 1965 Volkswagen Beetle. They climbed out of the car and met by the hood.

A sea of people crowded the sidewalks, examining the cars, standing in groups talking, and moving in and out of the shops.

"Check out this Mustang," she cooed. "It's gorgeous."

He nodded toward the Volkswagen. "I like the Beetle too. It's fully restored. Someone did a nice job." He gestured toward the row of cars. "Let's walk."

She fell into step beside him, and they stopped to look at several immaculately restored cars as they moved down the line—a 1964 robin's-egg-blue Ford Galaxie, a 1968 purple Plymouth Roadrunner, a 1970 dark-blue Dodge Dart, a cherry-red 1968 Shelby Mustang with white racing stripes, and a bright-orange 1973 Volkswagen Thing.

Brianna felt relaxed. The evening air was cool but comfortable, and the sweet scents coming from the open door of the Flower Shoppe wafted over her as the sun began to set, painting the sky with a brilliant hue of pink.

The streetlights came on, casting their warm, yellow glow over the crowds of people and magnificent cars. When Brianna glanced at Scott and found him smiling at a vintage Mercedes, she longed to know all his secrets. If only she could read his mind. But his secrets were none of her business. They were friends and business partners and nothing more. Still, she felt this invisible magnet pulling her toward him, coaxing her to open up to him, just as she had in the workshop earlier.

When they reached the end of the street, Scott pointed to a food truck. "Would you like anything?"

"Oh, I can never turn down one of those big pretzels."

As they stood in line behind two teenage boys, Scott pulled his wallet from his back pocket. "Salt and cheese?"

"Just salt, please."

"And a drink?"

"Diet Coke."

When it was their turn, he ordered two large pretzels with salt, along with a Coke for him and a Diet Coke for her.

"Thank you," she said when a young woman with bright-purple hair and black lipstick handed them their food.

Scott paid, then he pointed toward an empty bench nearby. "Why don't we sit?"

From the bench, they watched the knot of people admiring cars as they ate. After a few minutes, Scott turned to her, his expression pensive. "I have a serious question for you, Brianna. What's your dream car?"

"My dream car?" She snapped her fingers. "Oh, that's easy. A metallic-purple 1969 Chevy Camaro SS with white racing stripes."

"Huh."

She angled her body toward him. "Why did you say that?"

"I thought sure you'd say a classic Mustang." He broke off a piece of pretzel and popped it into his mouth.

"Well, you already know I love muscle cars, and I've always appreciated the shape of the Camaro. It's just so sleek, classy, and cool." She pointed toward his chest. "What's your dream car?"

He shrugged. "I already own it."

"The Barracuda."

He nodded and sipped his drink.

"When did you buy it?"

"A few years ago, when I closed my first big deal after Brad and I opened our firm." He looked down at the bench and moved his fingers over the wood. "It was a gift to myself to celebrate finally making it. A symbol of how I'd fought my way up from the bottom."

He glanced down the street in the direction of his car. "When I look at it, I remind myself that I'm a survivor, and no matter what I was led to believe about my worth, being tossed around as a child, I'm a success. Success I found through my own hard work and determination."

"That's true, Scott." She nodded slowly. Oh, how she craved to know more about his past.

He finished his pretzel and then met her gaze. "Do you have many car shows here?"

"They pop up often once the weather warms up. How about in Charlotte?"

"The same. I sometimes go out to Oakboro to see them."

"How fun." She studied his face, admiring how the evening light was reflected in his baby-blue eyes.

He met her gaze, and his brow furrowed. "Penny for your thoughts?"

She shook her head. "I was just thinking this is the perfect way to relax tonight. Why don't we go look at more cars?"

They walked down the opposite side of the street, deciding which cars they liked the best. When they reached the Barracuda, they found a group of men admiring it, and Scott popped the hood. One of them was a friend of Taylor's, and she suddenly realized any number of the townspeople she'd seen tonight could mention she was out with another man.

And yet, as she stood by the passenger door while Scott answered questions about the car's engine, she found herself admiring how he was taking the time to chat with people who were strangers to him. She was drawn to his kind and outgoing personality and how he seemed to make friends no matter where he went. Taylor was kind and outgoing, too, and yet the two men seemed so . . . different.

Soon they were on their way home, and as she parked the car by the garage, she realized she was disappointed. Her evening with Scott was about to end.

"That was fun," he said as she locked the back door behind them once they were inside the house.

She smiled. "It was. Thanks for suggesting it."

He gave her a nod but didn't return the smile. Was he disappointed too? But he just said, "Well, I'm heading up to bed."

"I'm going to check on Mom. Good night." As she started down the hallway, she wondered what Taylor would say if he did learn she'd been out with Scott tonight. Well, she'd just tell him about it, again emphasizing that she and Scott were just friends.

But her heart was telling her she better be more careful.

Sunday afternoon Scott pushed the putty knife along a cabin window frame, scraping off the old caulk. When the blade hit a hard spot, it jumped. Before he could react, he'd sliced the side of his left index finger, sending a wave of pain through his hand as he yelped. He looked down to see blood begin to bloom along the cut.

He reached for a clean rag, groaning as he wrapped the wound. He should have known better than to hold his left hand up on the window frame.

He rushed toward the house as the blood began to soak through the rag. When he reached the back door, he yanked it open and stepped into the kitchen, where Brianna was filling the dishwasher with their lunch dishes.

She spun toward him, then gave a sharp intake of breath. "What happened?"

"I'm a moron. That's what happened." He walked to the sink. "I was clearing away old caulk and cut myself."

"Let me see."

He unwrapped the rag, and she sucked in another breath as she took in the blood now covering all his fingers.

"Oh my goodness. Keep pressure on that, and I'll get our first aid kit. We keep it at the front desk."

His eyes stung from the pain as he stood over the sink and rinsed off his hand, then pressed a wad of paper towels against the wound. Brianna returned a few moments later with a bottle of peroxide and a large first aid kit.

"Close your eyes and hold your breath," she said, warning him as she took the lid off the bottle.

He did as he was told and gasped when the liquid hit his finger and then bubbled.

"I'm sorry." Her voice was right next to his ear.

He had to suck in his breath as his senses started to spin at her nearness. The scent of her hair—vanilla maybe?—filled his nostrils, and it was almost too much. He had to keep his distance.

"I'm going to do it again," she said. "I don't want this to get infected."

"Go ahead." He kept his eyes closed and gritted his teeth as she poured more peroxide on the wound.

She placed her hand on his bicep, and the heat from her skin radiated through his sleeve. "Are you okay?"

"Yeah." He opened his eyes and found her watching him. "You must think I'm a big baby."

"No, I'm just wondering if you need stitches."

"The bleeding has slowed. Why don't you bandage it? Let's see if it stops altogether with my finger wrapped up."

She pulled out a stack of individually packaged gauze pads and ripped one open before patting the wound dry. Then she squeezed antibiotic ointment onto the wound before covering it with another gauze pad. Last, she held his hand as she gingerly taped the pad on.

The feel of her touch sent his nerves singing, completely distracting him from the throbbing in his hand.

"How does that feel?"

Great! He cleared his throat. "Stings a little, but it's okay."

She lifted the bloody rag and reached for the paper towels.

"I can get all that."

"No, no, no." She shooed him away. "You go sit and let your hand rest."

He shook his head. "No, I have work to finish before I leave today."

She gave him a frown. "You shouldn't risk getting that infected."

"I'll be careful."

"All right. But let me know if it doesn't stop bleeding, and I'll take you to the closest med center."

"Yes, ma'am."

She shook her head and walked to the trash can. "You're incorrigible."

"Like I've said before, I aim to please."

That evening Scott brought up Brad's number before merging onto Interstate 40.

"Hey." Brad's voice sounded over the Bluetooth when he answered on the second ring. "Do you have good news?"

"I do." Scott moved over one lane and accelerated up to speed. "Brianna and her mother want to partner with us."

"No kidding. Congratulations!"

"Thanks. Could you arrange a meeting with your father? They have that hefty loan to settle up before the bank forecloses, so we need his involvement as soon as possible. Brianna gave me all the paperwork, and I know where to send the payoff."

"I'll call him tonight. Hopefully we can quickly iron out all the details."

"Perfect." Scott's pulse took flight, seeming to move as fast as his Barracuda. He had to tell Brad the rest. "Then I want to come back up here and stay until the resort opens for the season. Brianna needs help getting everything ready. Will that work for you? I know you're not back full time yet."

"We can make it work. As long as you keep your phone on so I can call if I need you."

"Of course."

"Have you considered just hiring someone to help her?"

"I can do the work without having to pay someone."

"Is saving money the real reason you want to do the work yourself?"

"What do you mean?" Scott knew exactly what Brad was asking, but he wanted to make him say it.

"I've already told you I think Brianna Porter is using you—and has from the beginning. Now you're running back up there to help her. You've said you have a feeling about that place, but do you have feelings for *her*?"

"She's engaged, and I haven't forgotten that. I would never disrespect her by doing anything inappropriate."

"I'm not accusing you of doing something inappropriate." Brad huffed a breath. "I'm worried about you getting hurt. Please, just focus on this deal without complicating it. You know what they say about mixing business with pleasure."

Scott frowned. "This isn't my first deal."

"I know, but I think this is the first one with this kind of potential for, like I said, complication. If you get involved with Brianna but then it doesn't work out, we could have a mess on our hands. It's just best for everyone if you keep it professional."

"I know," Scott grumbled. "And I will. You can stop with the lectures now."

"I'm just making sure you hear me. You can be a bit hyper-focused when you see something you want." Brad paused. "Be safe driving home. We'll talk tomorrow."

Scott disconnected the call and stared at the road ahead as Brad's words filtered through his mind. He glanced down at his bandaged finger and recalled the overwhelming attraction he'd felt toward Brianna when she'd tended to his wound. He couldn't deny that he cared for her, but he would keep those feelings to himself.

His best friend was right. He had to keep his relationship with Brianna professional, which meant no more sharing bakery treats or enjoying car shows. He should also stay at the Lakeview Inn, not at the resort.

But he wasn't sure how he could convince his heart to comply.

CHAPTER 25

*Y*our texts were brief this past week," Ava said as she sat across from Brianna in the Coffee Bean. "What's new at your house?"

They sat at their favorite table at the back of the shop as Brianna breathed in the tantalizing aroma of her white chocolate mocha—just what she needed on a Monday morning.

"Well, physical therapy was going well for Mom when I left the house," Brianna said, her chest swelling with happiness. "She's making real progress now."

"That's amazing!" Ava held up her café mocha as if congratulating her mother.

"The therapist had her practicing walking without her walker. I was so proud that I almost cried." Brianna picked up her coffee and took a sip.

"I'm so happy to hear she's doing better. I'd love to come visit her this week."

"I know she'd love to see you. She hasn't wanted any of her friends to visit, but you're like another daughter to her. I couldn't even get Pastor Thomas in." Brianna fingered the warm cup. "I have more news. A viable solution for saving the resort."

Ava leaned forward. "Tell me everything!"

Brianna gripped her cup as she explained Scott's surprise visit and offer to partner with them to save the resort.

Ava's eyes widened as she listened. "He's going to eliminate your debt and upgrade the resort too?"

Brianna nodded as she took another sip. "He has a financial backer. He also plans to upgrade our website and advertise, especially once the retreat center is ready."

"How does your mom feel about all this?"

"She understands we'll lose everything if we do nothing, and she trusts Scott."

"And your sisters?"

"I haven't told them about the partnership yet, but I will soon. It's Mom's decision, though."

"What about Taylor?"

Brianna sighed and studied her cup. "I told him about it last night, and he's not thrilled. You know he's jealous of Scott, but like I've told you both, he has no reason to be. He'd wanted to bring me a romantic dinner over the weekend, but with Scott there . . . He's bringing Chinese for both Mom and me tomorrow night."

Ava nodded slowly. "Interesting. How is Scott?"

"He's great." Brianna looked down at the diamond ring sparkling on her finger, the one she knew Taylor had sacrificed to buy, and swallowed. Her weekend with Scott had been amazing, even magical. She couldn't stop thinking about how safe and protected she'd felt in his arms. And conversation with Scott was easy. She'd also be lying to herself if she thought she hadn't been even more attracted to him.

But these feelings for Scott were wrong when her loyalty belonged to Taylor. She'd made a commitment to him, and when she casually mentioned she and Scott had been at the car show, he hadn't flown off the handle. He'd just asked her about bringing dinner on

Tuesday. She'd been pleased about that. Still, she couldn't deny that she'd missed Scott as soon as he left.

"What's going on with you and this man, Brie?"

"Nothing."

Ava snorted. "You know I can read you like a book, too, right?" She tapped the table. "What are you hiding?"

"I'm not hiding anything. Scott and I had fun this weekend, but friends can have fun together, can't they?" Brianna sipped more coffee as her best friend watched her.

"Had fun how?"

"We went to the car show Saturday night. You know Taylor doesn't care about cars like I do, which I reminded him when I told him about going last night. Scott wanted to go and asked me to join him. That's all. At the same time, we both got some work done around the resort. It was a productive weekend."

Ava tilted her head. "Be honest with me. Do you have feelings for him?"

"We've just become good friends with common interests. That's it." Brianna fingered her cup, ready to change the subject. "I've been meaning to tell you I loved the bridal shower invitation you sent a couple of weeks ago. So pretty."

"I can't believe it's next week!"

Brianna smiled as Ava told her about Brooklyn's shower, relieved Scott was no longer the topic of conversation. Now she just had to get him out of her mind.

"Brie?" Taylor's voice sounded from the foyer.

Brianna hurried down from upstairs and smoothed her hands over her fresh pink blouse and clean jeans. She'd showered and changed after working in the shop all day. "That smells divine." She held her hands out to grasp his takeout bags. "May I help you?"

"No, I got it." He leaned down and kissed her cheek. "It's so good to see you."

"You too."

"Taylor! Aren't you a sight for sore eyes?" Mom appeared in the hallway, leaning on her walker. While she'd practiced moving about without it earlier, she'd said she wasn't confident enough to leave its assistance behind just yet.

Taylor padded over and kissed her cheek as well. "Hi, Lois. You look great."

"Thank you. Is that Chinese?"

"It is. Are you ready for some?"

"I am, but I don't want to interfere with your time together." Mom's blue eyes brightened. "Why don't you eat out on the porch, and I'll eat on a tray in the family room? I want to finish a movie I started anyway."

Realizing she and Taylor did need to talk alone, Brianna led him into the kitchen, where she pulled out dishes and utensils. She served her mother a plate of shrimp with fried rice and two egg rolls, along with iced tea and a few packets of duck sauce. Then Taylor set up their small folding table on the porch, and they carried out their meal before sitting side by side on the porch swing, looking out at the lake.

"This is delicious, Taylor. Thank you."

"You're welcome." He gave her a sideways glance and smiled. "Your mom looks great."

"I know. She's doing better. I'm so relieved."

Bucky trotted over and brushed against Taylor's leg before sitting down and blinking up at him. Taylor gave the cat's ear a rub, then said, "I'm glad I could come tonight. I was afraid I might have to cancel when yet another town issue came up. But I've been dying to tell you about the interesting conversation I had with the mayor last week."

"What did he say?"

"I'll save that for later. First I want to hear more about the business deal you made with Gibson over the weekend." His expression darkened slightly. "Brie, I have to know. Did you ask him to come back?"

"No. I mailed him a reimbursement check for the money he spent on supplies and to pay him for his time and gas. He showed up to tell me he was refusing to take it and had another business proposition."

As Brianna explained Scott's ideas for the resort, Taylor ate, but his expression grew unreadable. When she finished, she took a bite of her own food and waited for his reaction.

"A year-round retreat center with a spa and pool?" he finally said. "You and your mother are really going to allow him to do all that?"

"We don't have much choice. It's either accept his offer as well as his suggestions or lose our home, to say nothing of a job I love."

Taylor nodded, then agreed the town would actually benefit from the business a retreat center would bring. But he also seemed to be pondering something else. "What do you think your dad would say?"

"Well, I don't know. And he's not here to explain why he let the resort go into debt. I wish I could ask him why he didn't tell me. And if he were here, maybe we could find some other way out of this. But he's not, and Mom and I are doing the best we can."

He nodded and forked another bite. She held her breath, waiting for him to say more. But he just peered out at a pontoon boat moving across the sparkling water. She breathed a sigh of relief. This was going much better than she'd imagined.

"So tell me about your conversation with Mayor Fairmount," she asked.

"Oh, right." He took a sip of iced tea and faced her. "I had a meeting with him Friday, and he told me he plans to retire after his next term. He thinks I have a shot at running for mayor then. In fact, he thinks I should set my sights even higher than this little town."

"What do you mean?"

"He thinks I could make a full-time career of politics." Taylor's handsome face seemed to glow.

"A career?"

"Yes! At the state level or even higher." The excitement in his voice was palpable.

"But what about your store?"

He shrugged. "Maybe by then I could pay someone to run it for me. Tammy would be a great manager."

Brianna stared at him. "But our life is here, Taylor."

"We'll figure it out. Let's see if I even win a second term as deputy mayor."

Brianna's head swam. Did Taylor really want to move away from Splendid Lake? He had to be joking. They'd always said this place would be their home, no matter what. Surely he didn't mean he'd expect her to leave her beloved town.

Finished with their meals, Brianna stood and lifted their plates.

"Wait." Taylor placed his hand on her arm. "I want to tell you something else."

She set the plates down and sat.

"I've been doing a lot of thinking lately." He swallowed and looked . . . ashamed? "I know this is long overdue, and I'd planned to say something before now, but then you lost your father."

Her hands began to sweat when he pointed to her ring.

"But it's time I made good on that promise. I've loved you since I was eighteen years old, and I'm ready to get married. Why don't we do it this fall, after the resort closes for the season?"

She looked at her ring and then at him, her body vibrating with apprehension. She tried to swallow, but her throat felt like it was full of sand.

"I know it will be cold, Brie, but we could have the reception inside. Maybe in the church hall or at the firehouse hall. I'm the deputy mayor, so I bet I could get the firehouse hall for free."

"Taylor, I-I don't know what to say."

"You don't know what to say?" He looked pained. "What do you mean?"

She rested her hand on his, guilt replacing her panic. "I'm sorry. This just isn't the right time."

"Why not?" Confusion shone in his eyes. But then she thought she saw a flash of anger there, and she was afraid his suspicion about Scott had reared its ugly head.

"I can't plan a wedding when I'm taking care of Mom and trying to save our home. She needs to recover, and I need to make sure we get back on our feet."

Taylor looked toward the lake. She reached for his arm, but he shifted away, the color leeching from his cheeks. She took a deep breath as regret poured through her.

"Taylor, listen. I'm just saying I need to extend our engagement a little longer. Maybe we can plan something next year, but right now I can't give a wedding the focus and attention it deserves until I get my life back in order."

He shifted back against the swing, and any anger melted away, leaving what looked like anguish. The pain in his eyes punched her like a fist to the body.

"Don't you love me anymore, Brie?"

"Of course I do." She took one of his hands in hers. "I just need you to be patient while I figure out this new normal." She cupped her hand to his cheek. "I can't imagine not having you in my life. You're important to me. I want a future with you, but the future has to wait a little longer. Will you be patient with me?"

He looked relieved. "Of course. I'll give you all the time you need." He brushed his lips over hers, and then she rested her head on his shoulder.

Later, Mom had retreated to her room to read, and she and Taylor snuggled on the sofa to watch a movie. When it was over, she followed Taylor to the front door. "Thank you for dinner."

"You're welcome. We'll talk soon." He kissed her cheek and then jogged down the ramp toward his car.

When she heard her phone ring in the kitchen, she rushed to answer it.

CHAPTER 26

$\mathcal{B}$rianna's heart skipped a beat when she saw Scott's name on her phone's screen. "Hello," she said as she stepped outside to wander down to the pier.

"How are things in Splendid Lake?"

"Interesting."

"Tell me."

"Well, Mom walked unaided during physical therapy yesterday, and she's been practicing."

"Outstanding! That's the best news." She could hear the smile in his voice.

"I agree."

She decided to tell him what Taylor had done, one more step toward solidifying her resolve to keep her friendship with Scott just that—friendship.

"I also had an unexpected evening."

"How so?"

"Taylor came over with dinner, and he asked if I'd marry him this fall."

The line was silent for a moment, and she looked at the screen to see if the call had disconnected.

"Congratulations?" Scott finally asked, his voice soft.

She stepped onto pier and looked out at the lake shimmering in the darkness. "I turned him down."

"Why?"

"I explained I need to take care of Mom and get us back on our feet before I can even think about planning a wedding." She walked to the end of the pier and sat down, her legs dangling over the edge.

"How did he take that?"

"He agreed to give me time, and he was fine the rest of the evening." She looked out to where lights from the houses surrounding the lake glowed. "So what's new in your world?"

"We're all set. We've got our financial backing to settle your loan first thing, and I'm meeting with Brad's dad again tomorrow to firm up all the details."

She blew a relieved breath. "That's great."

"I can come back there on Friday to help you get ready for the season, staying as long as you need me. I'm not sure how soon I can hire more staff, but what's most important now is making sure you can open the resort on time. Meanwhile, the contract between your mom and our firm will be drawn, and I'll send it to her lawyer for her review. I'll have cash soon as well, so we'll pay up your bills."

She smiled, and all the muscles in her back and shoulders relaxed. "I'll be there in a few days, then, and you can put me to work."

"I appreciate that."

He paused. "Brianna, it's all going to work out."

Those words settled over her, and renewed hope took root in her soul. "Thank you so much."

"You're welcome. Now get some rest." His voice was warm and soothing.

"I will. Good night." She disconnected the call and smiled. She was going to help save her home, and she couldn't wait to put the plan into action.

"Thank you, Phil," Scott said as he shook the man's hand the next afternoon. "I'm so glad you want to invest in this project. I think it will be very profitable for all of us."

"I do too. It sounds like a great adventure." Phil pointed at the photos of Splendid Lake Scott had spread out on the conference room table. "I can see why you like it so much. It has charm."

Scott began gathering the photos. "It sure does. I'll be in touch about the rest of the paperwork."

"Sounds good." Phil turned to Brad and shook his hand. "Your mother and I will be by to see Cody again. We can't get enough of him."

"I understand. Why don't I walk you out?" Brad pointed toward the door.

Scott carried his Splendid Lake folder back to his office and sat down at his desk, then opened the folder again and examined one of the photos. He imagined sitting on the beach with Brianna and watching another sunset, holding hands and laughing as they teased each other. How he longed to make that part of his future—having her in his life and loving her every day.

Then he sighed and sank back in his chair. Brianna wasn't his to love. She'd chosen Taylor, and he had to find a way to accept that. Still, his heart fought against his resolve in a continuous battle. Why couldn't his heart let her go?

Pulling out his phone, he sent a quick text to her.

Hi! Quick update. All set with our financial backer. Talking to
our lawyer next. Should have the contract ready soon.

Scott watched the screen, waiting for the conversation bubbles to
start when he heard Brad's voice.

"Hey, I told you my dad would be excited about this new plan."

Scott looked up at his partner standing in the doorway. "I thought
he would be too."

"What were you staring at?"

"Nothing." Scott flipped his phone over and sat it on top of the
Splendid Lake folder. "Now I need to call Gene," he said, referring to
their lawyer. "I'm hoping he'll go with me to Splendid Lake to final-
ize the paperwork. That way Lois won't have to travel. I'll pay him for
his time and expenses, of course."

Brad sat down in the chair across from Scott's desk, and when
he moved his hand over his mouth indicating he was contemplating
something, Scott prepared himself for another lecture.

"Let me point out that you're going way out of your way for this
woman," Brad said.

Scott rolled his eyes. "Here we go again."

Brad held up his hand. "Just let me finish. Are you sure you should
help out until the resort opens? You've mentioned her fiancé isn't too
fond of you."

Scott pushed aside the fact that he'd abandoned the idea of book-
ing a room at Lakeview Inn, telling himself he could be of more help
if he stayed with Lois and Brianna. "I'm keeping a respectful distance."

"Just don't—"

"I know exactly what you're going to say. Don't let her use me.
But I don't believe she is. As her business partner, I'm committed to

helping her get the resort ready for the season until we can hire more staff. You sure you're okay with me leaving?"

"Yes, I can handle things here."

"Thanks."

Scott couldn't wait to get back to Splendid Lake. Keeping a respectful distance from Brianna was better than not being with her at all.

"You make the best coffee," Mom told Ava as she sat on the porch with her and Brianna.

"I'm so glad you like it," Ava said as she looked out toward the lake and sipped her own coffee. "I remembered you once said your favorite is vanilla latte."

Brianna took a bite of coffeecake. "Thanks for bringing us an after-lunch treat as well. It's delicious too."

"You're welcome."

"Anything new with the wedding plans?" Brianna asked.

Ava's smile widened. "I found a dress last night, and Brooklyn loves it." She opened her phone and shared a photo of her modeling a simple, short-sleeved periwinkle dress.

"Beautiful," Brianna said as her mother nodded.

"Thank you. We found flowers too. She wants silk roses the same color as my dress and white daisies. And the gazebo will be delivered tomorrow. Mom is trying to find someone to install the white fairy lights so we don't have to get up on ladders ourselves."

"It all sounds perfect," Mom said.

"Oh!" Ava snapped her fingers. "Don't forget the bridal shower is next Saturday. We'd love for you both to come."

"I'll be there." Brianna glanced at her mother.

Mom gave a hesitant smile. "Ava, you know I love you and your sister, but I think it might be best if I stay home."

Ava frowned. "We'll miss you, Lois. Why don't you want to come?"

"I'm just not ready to face people. I should be by the time the wedding gets here, but right now I don't want to deal with questions about my stroke or comments about Martin." Mom shook her head.

"I understand. You take your time."

Ava's face was full of compassion, and Brianna gave her a grateful smile and mouthed *Thank you*. Then her phone dinged, and when she glanced at it, her pulse ratcheted up.

A text from Scott. She smiled as she read an update he'd forgotten to give her when they'd talked that morning.

"Is that from Taylor?" Ava asked.

"No, it's from Scott."

"I'm going to go inside to get caught up on *Days of Our Lives*," Mom said.

"It was nice seeing you, Lois." Ava touched Mom's hand. "You take care now."

"You too."

Mom left just before Bucky sauntered over and rubbed against Ava's shin.

"Hi there, you handsome guy." Ava leaned down and scratched Bucky's head as he purred—loudly. "What did Scott want?"

"He was just giving me one more piece of information about getting all the paperwork ready for our deal."

"That's great. I've been thinking about the changes he's proposed. A retreat center and spa is a fabulous idea."

"Thank you." Brianna picked up her coffee and sipped it.

Silence fell between them as they both looked at the lake.

"How are things with Taylor?"

Brianna gave Ava a sideways glance. "Fine. Why?"

Ava angled her body toward her. "I know what happened. He told Dylan."

"What do you mean?"

"Please, Brie. Men share as much as we do, at least when it's this important. He told Dylan you turned down getting married this fall." Her brown eyes seemed to search Brianna's. "Do you think you'll be ready next year?"

Brianna nodded. "Yes. Once we're set here and Mom is fully recovered, I can think about a wedding. Taylor said he understood and will give me all the time I need."

Ava was quiet, but Brianna could tell she had more to say. "Just say what you're thinking."

"Are you sure it's not about more than time?" Ava bit her lower lip. "I know it's none of my business, but lately you've seemed sort of distant from each other."

"Maybe. But right now I just want to keep things the way they are. I've been through enough upheaval."

Ava touched her arm. "I understand."

"So tell me more about the bridal shower."

Ava's smile was back. As she talked, Brianna had a hard time paying attention, instead mulling over Ava's comment about her and Taylor seeming distant. In her heart she knew something was off between them, something beyond the worn state of their relationship she'd contemplated the day he'd been so upset about seeing Scott at Lowe's.

But surely they could overcome all that, especially as the rest of her life came together. She couldn't face losing Taylor after losing her father and nearly her mother as well.

CHAPTER 27

*B*rianna's phone buzzed Thursday evening as she cleared the table after dinner. When she picked up her phone and found Cassie on FaceTime, she carried it to her mother. "Would you like to talk to Cassie?"

Mom nodded, and Brianna answered the call before handing the phone to her.

"Hi, Mom!" Cassie's voice sounded more cheerful than usual.

"How are you?" Mom asked.

"Work is hectic, but the days go by quickly when you're busy, right?"

Brianna finished filling the dishwasher and made her way to the laundry room while Mom listened to Cassie talk. She'd forgotten that she'd put in a light load this morning. She'd been so busy trying to get some work done outside that she'd never put it in the dryer.

When she came back to the kitchen, Mom had a bright smile on her face.

"What's up?" Brianna asked.

"Cassie is coming home!"

Brianna sat down and looked at the screen. "You are?"

"Yes. My manager approved a six-week leave of absence." Cassie smiled as she sat in front of a bookshelf. With the time difference, she was probably still in her office. "I'll be there a couple of weeks before Memorial Day."

"That's fantastic!" Brianna exclaimed. "Thank you so much for making that happen."

"I can't wait to see you," Mom said.

"Me too," Brianna added, putting aside any resentment she'd been feeling about her sister's absence.

Mom touched Brianna's arm. "I think I'll go to bed early. You two talk." She faced the phone. "It's so good talking to you, Cassandra. Love you, honey."

"Bye!" Cassie waved. "Love you too."

Mom pulled herself up on the walker and headed toward her bedroom. Once she was gone, Cassie looked curious. "Mom said something about changes to the resort. What was she talking about?"

Brianna stepped out onto the porch, feeling a bit guilty she hadn't called her sisters with this latest news, then gave Cass a brief summary of their plan to partner with Scott. "We're still working out the details, but this means we can pay off the loan, stop a foreclosure, and catch up on our bills. Plus upgrade so we can make more profit and never be in this mess again."

"It sounds like a good plan," Cassie said. "Just keep Dad's spirit alive."

"You know I will. And I'm so glad you're coming. Thank you so much. I know you're rearranging your life to help us."

"You're welcome. I'm excited to see you and Mom again."

Brianna's heart swelled with appreciation as Cassie looked past her, then said, "I need to get going. I have a meeting in ten minutes. You'll tell Jen?"

"Yes. And keep me posted on when you'll arrive."

"I will." Cassie disconnected the call.

Excitement swirled through her as she contemplated Cassie's reaction to the news. She decided she should call Jenna and tell her right away. She just hoped she'd take it as well as Cassie had.

"Hey, kid," Jenna said when she answered.

Brianna rolled her eyes. She would always remain ten years old in Jenna's mind. "Hi."

"How's Mom?"

"She's doing well." Brianna sank into a rocker. "I just spoke to Cassie, and she's taking a leave of absence to come home."

"That's great. I haven't had time to check into taking one. Maybe I can come later this summer."

"I hope so. I also need to tell you something I just told Cassie."

"Sounds serious. I'm sitting down."

Brianna explained the plan for Scott to invest in the resort and eventually make changes.

"Mom is okay with this?"

"Yes. She knows we have little choice."

"Did she know Dad was in financial trouble?"

"No. He didn't tell her either."

"I still don't understand why Dad would risk leaving her in this situation."

"Jenna, he didn't know he was going to die." Brianna tried to clear her throat as emotion swelled there. "Look, this is where we are. Allowing Scott to invest is the best option and really our only option other than selling."

"All right. I understand. This is the best thing. Is Mom close by? I'd like to say hi."

"Hang on." Brianna stepped back inside and took the phone to her mother, who was still up. "Jenna wants to talk to you."

Mom beamed as she dropped into her recliner and took the phone.

"Oh my! I get to talk to both of my big-city girls tonight." She held her phone to her ear. "Jenna! How's the Big Apple?"

Brianna returned to the kitchen where she gazed out the window as relief settled over her. Cassie was coming home, and Jenna had accepted the decision she and Mom made. Maybe, just maybe, their troubles would soon be over.

Scott's headlights bounced off the garage doors as he pulled his Challenger next to Brianna's Mustang. He'd hoped to get on the road earlier, but a last-minute meeting had thwarted that plan. Now it was close to ten. He looked up at the house and spotted lights glowing behind the blinds in Brianna's bedroom. He was grateful she was still awake. He should have called her, but he'd been focused on hitting the road.

As he pulled his duffel bag from the trunk, he heard the front door squeak open and the storm door click shut before footfalls sounded on the ramp.

"I was getting worried," Brianna said as she came around the back of the car. "I almost called you, but I figured you would have phoned me if you wanted me to know where you were."

"When have you ever been afraid to call anyone?" He set his duffel bag on the ground and drank in her appearance. She looked naturally beautiful dressed in purple drawstring pants and a black-and-blue Carolina Panthers T-shirt. And her hair was pulled up in a messy knot on top of her head, with wispy tendrils framing her pretty face. "I was stuck wrapping things up until after six."

She reached into the trunk and grabbed his backpack, and he grabbed a larger bag. "Did you eat?"

"I had a granola bar before I left the office."

"That means you're hungry enough to eat my food."

He grinned. "I guess so." He closed the trunk, and they started up the ramp. Bucky met them there with a loud meow.

"Hello there." Scott rubbed the cat's head before he ran off again. Then Scott followed Brianna into the foyer, where they deposited his bags before they headed into the kitchen, turning on lights as they went. Brianna immediately opened the refrigerator and took out some storage containers.

"I saved you some baked chicken, a roll, and green beans." She smirked as she scooped the food onto a plate. "I have carrot sticks, too, if you want them. It's all really gourmet. Totally beats your stroganoff and peppered shrimp alfredo." She placed the plate in the microwave, then hit a few buttons.

"You've got that right." He moved to the sink and washed his hands. "How are things?"

She leaned against the counter beside him. "Cassie is taking a six-week leave of absence to come home and help. She'll be here a couple of weeks before we open."

"That's fantastic."

"Yes, it is. I'm hoping she'll mostly help Mom, but she won't mind doing whatever we need. She's great at cleaning."

"How is your mom?"

"She's doing well."

"And you?"

"I'm still stressed about the opening."

"But I'm here now."

He reached for her arm, and she stilled, allowing him to touch her. He enjoyed the feel of her warm, soft skin.

"And I'm so glad you are, Scott."

Brianna's expression grew intense, and the air around them electrified. She took a step toward him, her brown eyes glittering in the kitchen lights. His breath paused when something seemed to shift between them. Perhaps she felt it too. Some invisible force was pulling them together.

The microwave beeped, and Brianna jumped with a start before spinning away from him. She removed the plate and set it on the table. Then she poured two glasses of iced tea and brought both butter and utensils to the table before sitting across from him.

Apprehension seemed to flicker across her face. "Mom and I met with our lawyer yesterday, and she told us the contract you emailed her is both fair and sufficient. But Mom still seems a little leery about some of your proposed changes. We'll have to discuss them further."

"Of course."

She rested her elbow on the table and her chin on her hand. The skin between her eyes puckered as she watched him eat, and he could almost hear the wheels in her mind turning.

"Brianna, spill it." He took a sip of tea.

"What was your first car?"

"My first car?" He chuckled. "If I tell you, then you really won't be impressed with me."

She leaned forward, her grin mischievous. "Oh, now you *have* to tell me."

He shook his head as he buttered the roll. "You have to remember I'd just been kicked out on my own, so I could scrape together only enough to buy something semi-reliable to get me to construction sites from the crummy apartment I shared with three other guys."

"I understand. Now tell me, Gibson. What car was that?"

He shook his head and gazed down at his food. "A 1976 AMC Gremlin X."

"A Gremlin!" She threw her arms up in the air. "What color?"

"Black."

"Did it have those hockey stick stripes on it?"

He laughed. "You know more about Gremlins than I expected."

"You forget I was raised by a car nut. What engine did it have?"

He swallowed a mouthful of green beans. "A small V8. The cool thing about it was that the ignition switch was broken, so the key was just for show. All I had to do was turn the switch, and the car would start, which was convenient when I misplaced my keys. Well, on the days it felt like starting."

She laughed, and he relished the sound. "What a great story. What happened to that car?"

"I sold it when I had enough money for something more reliable." He forked more chicken into his mouth.

"Which was . . ."

"Hmm." He rubbed the stubble on his chin. "I believe that was when I bought my first pickup truck. It was a 2002 Chevy Silverado."

"Did the ignition switch work on it?"

"Sadly, it did. So I was out of luck when I lost my keys."

She laughed again. "My first car was my mom's old Honda Accord, which was not as cool as your Gremlin X."

They shared more car memories as he finished eating. Then he checked to make sure all the doors were locked while she cleaned up in the kitchen.

He followed her up the stairs, and she set the bag she was carrying in his room before lingering in the doorway.

"I hope you sleep well, Scott."

"You too."

She disappeared down the hall, and he sat down on the edge of the bed. It was great to be back in Splendid Lake.

CHAPTER 28

*B*rianna sat on a roller chair behind a boat in the workshop the following afternoon. She hummed along with the radio as she worked, and when the door opened, Scott stepped in, then peered at what she was doing.

She wiped her hands on a red rag. "I'm just changing out a propeller that somehow got bent last year. What's up?"

"I'm ready to go buy lumber for the pier. Want to ride with me to Asheville?"

"Only if we stop at Scoops on the way back. I've been craving ice cream for an hour."

"You're on."

After telling her mother where they were going and confirming she wanted her usual vanilla, Brianna followed Scott to her father's pickup truck. The sun shone bright in the azure sky, and the warm air blowing in through the open windows smelled like earth mixed with the fresh aroma of the lake.

She looked at Scott's profile as the truck bumped along toward the main road, and questions that had haunted her since she'd learned he grew up in foster care rushed to the surface of her mind.

He glanced at her and grinned. "Why are you staring at me?"

She fingered the hem of her blue hoodie. "You said you never met your father. Do you know his name?"

He rested his arm on the truck door. "No."

"It's not listed on your birth certificate?"

He shook his head while keeping his eyes focused on the road. "No. All I know is Gibson was my mother's name, not his."

"Have you thought about trying to find him? Maybe doing one of those DNA tests that come in a kit?"

Scott stopped at a red light and turned to face her. "Why all these questions?"

"I'm curious about your life." She hoped he didn't notice the heat overtaking her cheeks.

He blinked at her, and she longed to know what he was thinking. The light turned green, and he steered the truck through the intersection. "I've considered those DNA tests, but sometimes I think it's better not to know. What if he's a convicted serial killer? Or took advantage of my mother? I can't even stomach the idea that I could be the result of violence."

"But what if he's a wonderful man who's never known you existed? What if your mom had a consensual relationship with him, but she kept you a secret?"

"I've considered that, but I guess I'm not ready to face the unknown. Maybe someday."

"How many foster families did you live with?"

He snorted. "I was tossed around like a volleyball for more than a dozen years."

"I'm sorry. What were the families like?"

"Several tried to make me welcome on some level, but others seemed more interested in collecting the subsidy than in nurturing me."

"So how many families did you live with?" she asked again.

"Ten."

"Wow. And from the time you were five until you turned eighteen. Weren't any of them . . . loving?"

He swallowed, and something unreadable flickered across his face. "There was this one family. They treated me like I was one of their own."

"They did?" She shifted toward him. "Tell me about them."

"Their two sons, both just a little older than me, were like my brothers. When they took me in, that was the first time I felt like I belonged to someone and had a real family, like the ones I saw on TV. They took me camping, and actually, that was what I thought of the first time I came to Splendid Lake. It reminded me of those happy times when we laughed around a campfire, roasted marshmallows, made s'mores, shared a tent . . ."

"What happened to them?"

He gave her a quick glance, his lips turning down, before returning his attention to the road. "Mr. Robinson received a work transfer to the West Coast, so I was sent off once more, then passed around again and again for another six years."

"I don't understand why they did that to you," Brianna said, horrified. "How could they just abandon you?"

He shrugged. "I wasn't their biological child. Besides, now I know foster kids in most states can't be moved across state lines, not without a lot of red tape. At least the Robinsons cared about me while I was with them. That's more than I can say about the ones who just seemed interested in the money."

Brianna shook her head, trying to comprehend what Scott had been through.

Silence fell between them, and the sound of the engine filled the cab of the truck.

"I remember a few things about my mom," Scott said.

"Please tell me about her."

"Her name was Carrie, and she was beautiful. She had dark-blond hair and blue eyes, and she was sweet. She always smelled like lavender from a lotion she loved. And I still remember her voice. She'd sing and read to me every night."

"What did she sing?"

A look of longing darted across his face as he gripped the wheel. "'You Are My Sunshine.' And my favorite book was *Goodnight Moon*." He snickered. "I had it memorized. I'd say the words, and she'd turn the pages. She said that was her favorite book when she was little too."

"That's a lovely memory." Brianna was struck by his warm expression. She was certain he was seeing his mother in his mind's eye.

"We went out for sundaes on Fridays. She'd pick me up from kindergarten when she got off the lunch shift at the restaurant where she worked, and we'd go to a local diner and talk about our week."

"I love that." Warmth spread through her as she took in his smile. "I'm so sorry you lost her at such a young age. Was it unexpected?"

His Adam's apple bobbed as he steered the car onto the highway. "She was on her way to pick me up from school, and she never showed up. A guy ran a red light and hit her head-on."

"Oh, Scott. You had to be absolutely devastated."

He gave her a sideways look. "It was on a Friday, our special day."

Brianna's eyes burned. "I'm so sorry." She hesitated for a beat. "And she didn't have any family?"

He shook his head. "Apparently the Department of Child and Family Services searched. But her mom was a single mom, too, and she'd died several years earlier. They couldn't find any other relatives."

"I can't even comprehend what you went through. I know I keep saying that, but my heart is sick for you and what you endured."

They rode silently until Scott pulled into a parking space near the front of the store. Then he turned toward her, smiled, and rested his hands on hers. "It's okay. I found my own way."

She studied his serene expression. "Do you want a family of your own someday?"

He blinked as if stunned by the question and put both hands back on the steering wheel. "Why do you ask?"

"You told me you didn't think it would happen for you, but is that what you really want?"

"Isn't that what we all want? I just don't expect to find it."

"Why not?"

He looked down at the steering wheel and ran his thumb over it. "It's better not to expect something you want so you won't be disappointed when you don't get it."

Brianna tilted her head. She hoped Scott wasn't saying he thought he didn't deserve a family. He'd been so caring, kind, thoughtful, and patient with not only her but her mother. She could imagine him giving that same kind of comfort, patience, and devotion to a wife and children, and a strange tingling filtered through her veins.

He wrenched his door open and glanced at her. "Ready?"

"Yes." She hopped out of the truck, and they walked into the store together.

The aroma of sawdust filled her senses as Scott grabbed a flatbed cart and they weaved through the aisles toward the lumber section. She held the cart steady while Scott loaded the pieces of wood one by one. While she watched him work, her mind buzzed with the stories he'd just shared. She tried to imagine how her life would have been if she'd never known her father, never had siblings, and had lost her mother at such a young age. Being shuffled from home to home, for the most part unloved.

Still, Scott hadn't allowed his tumultuous past to ruin his life. And the way he'd treated her and her mother proved that no matter what trauma he'd suffered as a child, at his core he was a good man.

"Brianna?"

A man calling her name yanked her back to the present. She spun just as Eddie Hernandez pushed a cart toward her. "Hi, Mr. Hernandez."

"Hello." He looked at Scott, then back at her. "Hello, Scott. Haven't seen you in a while."

Scott smiled as he set another piece of lumber on the flatbed, then wiped his palms on his jeans and stuck out his hand. "Hi, Eddie."

"What are you two up to?" Eddie shook Scott's hand, and his expression made it clear he was more than curious.

"Scott is helping me finish some projects around the resort in time for our opening. It's just around the corner, you know."

Scott pointed to the lumber. "I'm tackling the pier."

"How nice of you to help." Mr. Hernandez's expression grew serious as he turned back to Brianna. "How is your mom?"

"She's doing better. Thanks."

"That's good to hear. I'll let Olivia know. She's been wanting to bring a meal over."

"Oh, Mom would love that. Thank you so much."

"Wonderful. I'll tell her." He nodded at Scott, looked back at Brianna. "Have a good day."

"You too," Brianna called as he turned to leave.

"Bye, Eddie," Scott added. Then he grinned at Brianna. "Did you notice how curious he was when he saw us here together?"

"I did." Brianna could only imagine the gossip once Eddie told Olivia he saw them together. She'd have to tell Taylor before he heard a twisted truth.

After Scott paid for the lumber, Brianna helped him load the truck bed. Then they drove to Scoops. The little shop was decorated in a 1950s theme with a black-and-white checkerboard tiled floor, red vinyl booths, chrome high-top tables, and red vinyl stools. Photos of ice cream sundaes, banana splits, and cones dotted the walls.

The shop buzzed with conversations as people enjoyed their sweet treats, and Brianna nodded and waved to acquaintances as she stood in line beside Scott.

"What's good here?" Scott crossed his arms over his wide chest and studied the large tubs of ice cream behind the glass case.

Brianna pointed to the sign on the wall. "Everything."

"Just like at Morningside Bakery, huh? Well, that narrows it down," he said, deadpanning. "What do you normally order?"

"Moose tracks."

"Moose tracks?" Scott's laugh was warm and rich. "Sounds delicious."

"Hi, Chloe," Brianna said, greeting the store manager when it was their turn.

"Brie!" Chloe had been sweet and friendly when she attended high school with Brianna, and she still was. She was dressed in a vintage 1950s pink uniform, including a paper hat covering her brown hair. Chloe's smile faltered. "I was sorry to hear your mom had a stroke. How is she?"

"She's doing better. Thanks."

"Glad to hear it. What can I get you?"

"A vanilla sundae with fudge packed to go and two scoops of moose tracks on a waffle cone."

Scott leaned over Brianna and held out his credit card. "Make that two moose tracks on waffle cones."

Chloe's expression seemed to convey a mix of surprise and admiration as she gave him the total. Brianna pushed his hand back before Chloe could take his card. "This was my idea, Scott. Let me pay."

"No, I've got this."

Brianna pivoted to face him as she removed her wallet from her purse. "But you paid for the lumber."

Scott gave Chloe the card. "Please don't take her money."

Chloe gave a nervous laugh as she looked back and forth between them. "Okay."

Brianna didn't know what else to say, so she kept silent while they waited for their order. When Chloe returned, a helper at her side, they were handed a white paper bag and their two cones. "Here you go. Tell your mom I said hi."

"I will."

Chloe gazed up at Scott. "You have a nice day, and come back to see us."

"I'm sure we will," he told her.

When they arrived home, the three of them sat at the table to enjoy their ice cream. Of course, she and Scott had eaten half of theirs on the way home.

"You were right about moose tracks," Scott told Brianna. "It's spectacular."

Brianna pointed to what was left of her scoops. "The peanut butter cups are what make it so heavenly."

"Exactly." Scott looked at her mother. "How's your sundae?"

"Fabulous." Mom held up her spoon and grinned. "I love the fudge."

Brianna felt a flush of warmth as she and Scott shared a smile. She felt an even deeper connection with him after learning more about his past. He'd become important to her, certainly as more than a business partner. But that scared her. She was still committed to her relationship with Taylor.

Scott interrupted that thought. "Brianna, we've been working hard.

I think we should take a break for the rest of the afternoon. Could we go for a boat ride? Maybe even fish for a little bit?"

"I'd love to."

⟿⟾

After they'd dug up a few worms, Scott helped Brianna gather two life vests, a couple of fishing poles, and a tackle box before they lowered a johnboat into the water and motored out to the deeper waters of the lake. He smiled, enjoying the feel of the wind on his sun-kissed face as he looked toward the beaches and homes that sat beyond them. Then he took in Willard Mountain State Park and Paradise River in the distance.

It was all so beautiful here. This place seemed to be calling him as if it could someday be his home.

Brianna cut the engine, and the boat swayed as the sparkling water lapped its sides. When he looked down, he spotted several fish swimming and shimmering in the water below them.

Soon they were baiting their hooks and casting their lines, and Scott relaxed as he continued to enjoy the scene all around him. He spun around in his seat and faced Brianna, tenting his hand over his eyes. "This is breathtaking."

Brianna nodded as she looked toward the shore with a faraway look in her eyes. "Dad used to take my sisters and me fishing. I was baiting my own hook by the time I was three."

"No kidding."

She shrugged. "He said I was a natural. One time I hooked my hand, though." She laughed.

"Ouch!" He grimaced. "That had to be painful!"

She pointed to her left palm. "It went in here and came out there. I don't remember any pain, though—just being kind of stunned."

"I can only imagine."

"It didn't deter me. I went right back to fishing."

They were silent for a few minutes, and then he felt a tug on his line. "I think I got one."

"Reel it in," she said, excitement filling her face.

He reeled in the line and laughed as a smallmouth bass flopped around in the air.

"Look at you!" Brianna announced. "That's a nice-size fish. You should take a photo."

Scott pulled his phone from his pocket. "Here." Then he held up the line, and she snapped a picture before handing the phone back to him.

"That's bragging rights right there, Scott. Send it to Brad."

He snickered and slipped the phone back into his pocket, then removed the hook and tossed the fish back into the water. "Do your sisters like to fish?" he asked as he baited his hook again.

"Not really. I was the one who never stopped wanting to go out with Dad. Cassie and Jenna got bored with fishing when they were each around twelve or so. But I never tired of spending time with my father any way I could. While Cassie loved to read by herself, Jenna loved cooking with Mom, and I loved being anywhere with Dad." She closed her eyes. "I can read, but you already know I can't cook."

"But those dinner rolls you took out of the package were stupendous."

She opened her eyes and pointed at him. "You know it." She pulled her legs up and sat cross-legged. "I started handing Dad tools in the shop when I was four, and I was helping him rebuild engines by the time I was nine. Mom once joked that I was the son he never had, but Dad always told me I was his girl, and it was okay to like *boy* things. He told me never to let anyone tell me I couldn't do things men traditionally do."

"That's great advice." His admiration for her swelled as he looked at her. "I think you're amazing."

Brianna blushed. "I just want to make sure this resort lives on. It will always have my heart because of my father and how much it meant to him." Her expression grew serious. "Promise me you'll do everything you can to not only save it but also preserve the spirit of what it is right now."

"I promise." He placed his hand on his chest over his heart. "I mean it. It's an honor to be trusted with a place like this." He looked up at the sky, taking in the white, puffy clouds. "I see why you love it here."

"It's enchanting, even to me, someone who's lived here all her life."

But he wasn't talking about only the area. He was talking about her. If only he could have a chance with her. But he had to keep his relationship with Brianna professional, though friendly—no matter what his heart kept telling him.

CHAPTER 29

$\mathcal{S}$cott jogged down the stairs just as Taylor walked by carrying three pizza boxes Sunday evening. The tantalizing smell caused his stomach to growl.

"Hey, Taylor," he said, working to keep his tone pleasant despite the glare he received. Taylor grunted in response as he stalked toward the kitchen as if on a mission. Scott shook his head as he followed him.

"Hi, Lois." Taylor's voice was bright and sunny as he placed the boxes on the counter. "You look great today."

"Thank you. Good to see you." Lois held up her hand so Taylor could give it a gentle squeeze.

Taylor washed his hands at the sink and then made a show of opening the boxes. "I hope you're in the mood for pizza. I picked up a pepperoni, a sausage and mushroom, and a plain cheese."

Scott suppressed the urge to roll his eyes, then grabbed plates from the cabinet.

Brianna stepped into the kitchen from the hallway and smiled at Taylor. "I didn't hear you drive up." She crossed to the pizza boxes. "Smells amazing. Thank you for bringing all this."

"You're welcome. Let's eat." Taylor took a plate from the stack Scott placed next to the boxes and helped himself.

Brianna served her mother a slice as Scott poured four glasses of sweet tea. Soon they were all sitting around the table with Scott at one end, Brianna beside her mother, and Taylor at the other end.

"How's it going?" Taylor asked Brianna.

"Great." She pushed a thick lock of hair behind her ear. "I'm almost finished getting the boats ready, and Scott is making headway on the pier."

Taylor gave him a quick glance, then turned back to Brianna. "No big issues with the boats, then?"

Scott suppressed a grin as he took another bite. Taylor's jealousy was so obvious that it was almost hilarious.

"No. I just had to clean a few carburetors, repair a propeller, and change some spark plugs. Hopefully the last few will be that easy."

"I hope so too. Do you want to work after we eat? I can help you with the boats if you give me instructions."

"Oh, no, thanks. Scott and I are pretty tired." She looked over at Scott. "Right?"

He shrugged as he picked up his glass. "It's up to you."

"I think we need a break." She met Taylor's gaze again. "I appreciate the offer, though."

"Okay." Taylor didn't miss a beat. In fact, he looked relieved. "Did I tell you we have the permit issue for the new police station worked out?" he asked, keeping his eyes fixed on Brianna. "This will be great for my reelection campaign."

Brianna swallowed. "How did you manage that?"

"I had some meetings with the permit office and the construction company. The mayor is really happy with my work, and I've made some great contacts."

Scott fought the temptation to snicker. Now Taylor was bragging.

"Construction will start about a month now."

"Wow!" Brianna said. Was she actually gushing at this? "That's fantastic. Congratulations!"

Scott leaned toward Lois. "Would you like another piece?"

She nodded as she patted her mouth with a napkin.

"Cheese again?"

"Yes, please."

"Hang tight." Scott took her plate and stepped to the counter. When he placed her plate in front of her again, he leaned over and lowered his voice. "I picked the cheesiest one with the best crust."

Lois grinned. "Thank you."

"You're welcome." Scott winked at her, and Lois giggled. How he adored this woman!

When he looked at Brianna, she flashed him a quick smile before turning her attention back to Taylor, who was droning on about town business.

After they finished eating, Scott and Taylor both helped Brianna clean the kitchen before they all went out to the porch. Brianna and Taylor sat on the swing, and Scott took a seat beside Lois, each of them in a rocker.

"Did I tell you I ran into Craig Linwood the other day?" Taylor asked Brianna.

Brianna looked at Scott. "We went to high school with Craig." She turned back to Taylor. "How is his wife? I heard they're expecting."

Scott looked at the lake while Brianna and Taylor talked about their mutual friend. Although he appreciated Brianna's trying to include him in the conversation, he had nothing to contribute, and he was certain Taylor was deliberately leaving him out by bringing up someone he didn't know.

"I'm going to head inside," Lois said after nearly a half hour of Taylor's bringing up one old friend after another. She stood, and Brianna popped up too.

"I'm getting a soda. Do either of you want one?" Brianna asked.

"I'll take one," Taylor said. "Thanks."

"Scott?"

"No, thanks."

Brianna and her mother disappeared inside the house, and Scott watched a catamaran move over the water, then observed a squirrel race across the dirt road before sprinting up a tree. He debated going in to check his email on his laptop. Taylor didn't appreciate his presence, and sitting there just made the evening more awkward for everyone.

After a few minutes, he glanced at Taylor, whose face had crumpled with a frown as he stared at the lake. Scott held his breath, waiting for him to say something sarcastic.

Finally, Taylor rested his arm on the back of the porch swing and sneered at Scott. "Gibson, I'm on to you and your intentions toward my fiancée."

Scott smiled and tilted his head, recalling how it always irritated the mean kids in the foster homes when he killed them with kindness. "Taylor, my friend, if your relationship with Brianna is solid, you shouldn't have anything to worry about."

Taylor blanched as if Scott had hit him, and his expression darkened. He opened his mouth to respond, but then Brianna stepped out holding two sodas. In a flash, Taylor's serene smile was back. Brianna handed him his Coke and took a seat beside him on the swing.

Scott's stomach soured. He couldn't take any more of Taylor's duplicity. It was time for him to retreat to his room.

"I'm going up." Scott stood and stretched. "You two enjoy your evening. Thanks for dinner, Taylor."

Taylor glared at Scott from behind Brianna. "You're welcome."

Scott nodded at Brianna, who for some reason looked disappointed, then he stepped into the house and closed the door.

Brianna stared after Scott, sure he'd grown sick of Taylor. While she was disappointed to see him go, she understood. She hadn't missed her fiancé's nasty expressions whenever Scott looked at him or he thought she wasn't paying attention to what he was saying. Her mind had wandered sometimes.

She pushed the swing into motion.

"Is your mom okay?"

"Yeah. She just gets tired easily."

Silence stretched between them, and she tried to think of something to say. Conversation used to be so easy for her and Taylor. Now it seemed like they spent their time together in silence—unless he was talking about himself.

But conversation was never a strain with Scott. She recalled how much fun she'd had running errands with him earlier. Just a mundane, low-key trip to Lowe's and Scoops had been the highlight of her day. She also considered how kind he'd been to her mother at dinner. While Taylor talked the whole time, Scott had brought Mom more pizza. He was so intuitive when it came to what her mother needed.

"Remember how I told you the mayor thinks I have a real future in politics?" Taylor suddenly asked.

"Yes. But—"

"Well, I've done a lot more thinking, and instead of running for mayor when he retires, I'm considering running for office in Asheville. Then if I win, my next step can be a state office."

"What?"

"I had a long talk with one of the mayor's political consultants a couple of days ago. He thinks I have real potential too." He stretched his arm out on the back of the swing behind her and rubbed her shoulder with his thumb. "I've made some good decisions for this town, and I'm working on improving my rapport with the council, fire chief, and police chief. I believe that will boost my résumé enough to skip running for mayor here and move on."

She blinked. "You're serious?"

"Yes." He sat up straight. "I told you about this last week. I know you were surprised and had a lot of questions, but by now you must realize this is important to me. Are you upset?" He looked confused.

"I'm stunned. I still don't understand why you would want to leave Splendid Lake."

"Because I really do want a career in politics. That life would be good for me." He pointed back and forth between them. "It would be good for both of us. You don't really want to stay here with the resort changing, do you?" He gestured around them.

"But this is our home." She touched her chest. "Splendid Lake is my heart."

"Now, calm down."

He touched her shoulder again, and she pushed his hand away. "Taylor, I don't want to move."

"Let's talk about this later, okay?"

She studied him. He really was serious. Didn't he realize this changed everything?

Taylor stood and held his hand out to her. "I should get going. Would you please walk me out?"

"Brie," he said when they'd walked to his car. "I'll be back to help around here as often as I can."

"I appreciate that."

He leaned down and kissed her cheek. "Good night."

"Good night." She waited until he was in his car before closing and locking the door.

She checked on her mother, and after finding her asleep in her bed, she padded up the stairs. When she reached the hallway, she stopped and looked toward Scott's room. The door was open. She debated whether she should bother him, but surely he wouldn't mind.

Once in his doorway, she spotted him sitting at Cassie's old desk with his laptop open. From what she could see on the screen, he was reading emails.

"Knock, knock," she sang, tapping on the doorframe.

The desk chair squeaked as he spun toward her. "Hi."

"May I come in?"

"Of course." He gestured toward the bed beside him, and she sat down on the corner. He rested his left ankle on his right knee and settled back in the chair. "Taylor left?"

"Yes. Are you okay, Scott?"

"Yeah. Why?" The skin between his eyebrows creased.

"I was surprised when you left so quickly."

"I wanted to give you two some privacy."

She blew out a sigh. "I noticed Taylor giving you nasty looks. I keep hoping he'll grow up."

"He considers me a threat, and it's okay. I'll just stay away." He jammed his thumb toward his laptop. "I also wanted to see if any emergencies had come up at the firm."

"Did you find any?"

He rested his hands on his shin. "No, which is good."

They stared at each other, then she looked down at the carpet before hugging her arms to her chest.

"Are *you* okay? I know it might be a little unnerving to have Brad and his dad as well as our attorney here in the morning." He tilted his head and watched her as if trying to solve an intricate puzzle.

"It's fine. I'm just tired." She stood. "Well, good night." She started toward the door but then stopped and faced him. "Thank you for being so good to my mom. You go out of your way for her, and that means a lot to me."

"I think the world of Lois."

"I appreciate it."

"My pleasure." He gave her a little wave. "Sleep well."

"You too."

Brianna took a long, hot shower, then climbed into bed, her mind once again mulling over the differences between Scott and Taylor. As she snuggled under her sheet and comforter, she came to a conclusion—Scott would be a wonderful husband and father someday. She just hoped he married someone who appreciated him.

CHAPTER 30

$\mathcal{B}$rianna's stomach twisted as she sat on the porch with her mother. Scott was walking around the property with Brad Young, Brad's father, and Gene Clay, their lawyer. Charlene Collins, her mother's lawyer, was touring the resort as well. Brianna couldn't hear what Scott was saying, but from the way he pointed and gestured, she imagined he was sharing his vision for the resort's future.

She glanced at her mother sitting beside her on the swing, and a level of bleakness blossomed inside her. Mom had been emotional all morning, sobbing in her bedroom after breakfast, saying she missed Dad and didn't understand why he had to die so young.

Brianna couldn't stop the fear that her mother would refuse to sign the contract and the day would end in disaster with a foreclosure just around the corner. But she wouldn't give up without a fight. Not that she would fight with her mother, but she would work hard to convince her to make the right choice. If she didn't let Scott invest in the resort, she'd have to let him buy it.

She just hoped she could find the right words to sway Mom in the right direction.

After the tour, Scott led their four guests into the kitchen, where he and Brianna served them coffee and a coffeecake Scott had purchased at Morningside Bakery.

"I think this place is just beautiful," Phil said. "I understand why Scott has fallen in love with it."

Brianna couldn't help but notice Scott and Brad sharing a look, and she puzzled over what that could mean.

"Did you see the downtown area?" Scott asked.

"Yes. It's so quaint and homey," Phil said.

"You need to go to the coffee shop there," Scott said. "Brianna's best friend owns it."

Charlene nodded. "The Coffee Bean has the best coffee in the area. And the ice cream parlor in town is fantastic too."

Brianna glanced at her mother and found her staring down at her coffeecake. "Don't you want any?" she whispered.

Mom shook her head as her lower lip trembled.

The chasm of dread in Brianna's chest opened wider. *Be strong, Mom!*

"Why don't we get down to business?" Brad said. "Today we're going to sign a contract, with our firm making a financial commitment to invest in Splendid Lake Cabins and Marina resort, partnering with Mrs. Lois Porter. Ms. Collins has already reviewed the documents, so this is really just a formality."

As Brianna watched in horror, her mother's face crumpled. Panic wrapped tight around Brianna's chest, squeezing out her breath in a rush. She looked at Scott, and his eyes widened.

"I think these ladies need a moment," Scott said as he stood. "Why don't you all walk down to the pier and take another look at the lake?" He pointed toward the doors leading to the porch, and they all stood and filed out.

"Thank you," Brianna told him as she rested her hand on Mom's arm.

"Take your time." Scott gave her an encouraging look and then headed outside.

"Mom," Brianna began, mustering all the emotional strength she could find, "Brad and Phil seem very nice. Yes, they're investors running a business, but they also have the resort's best interest in mind, and both their attorney and Charlene know what they're doing. I need you to trust us."

Mom shook her head. "I do, but I woke up in the middle of the night and started worrying. I'm not sure your father would approve of this. I know it's our only viable choice other than selling, but something feels wrong. I can't explain it."

"Mom, Dad would want me to take good care of you, and that means keeping our home." She handed her mother a tissue. "Don't you still like Scott?"

"Yes. Very much."

"I do too." She paused. "Remember when he asked me to take him fishing last Saturday?"

Mom nodded.

"While we were out on the water, I told him how much this place means to me. I made him promise he would preserve the spirit of what it is right now. He knows what the resort means to our family, and I don't think he'd do anything to ruin the Porter legacy."

Mom sniffed as more tears trickled down her pink cheeks.

Brianna looked over to where Scott stood outside, watching them through the window with concern on his face. He gestured as if asking to come in. She nodded.

"Lois, may I please talk to you?" he asked after stepping inside.

She nodded.

Scott pulled a chair up next to hers and took her hand in his. "Lois, I promise to always be respectful of your husband's memory.

In fact, I'd like to call our new building the Martin Porter Retreat Center."

"You would do that?"

"Yes. And it would be an honor, ma'am."

Brianna cupped her hand to her mouth as both gratitude and grief rocketed through her. She was so moved that tears stung her eyes. She blotted them with a finger as Scott looked at her, worry filling his expression.

"Oh no. I said the wrong thing."

"No. You didn't." She shook her head. "You said everything right."

Mom sniffed again and squeezed his hand. "If you promise you'll treat this resort like it's your own, then I'll sign. And I expect to see my husband's name on a plaque on that hoity-toity building."

"Yes, ma'am." Scott grinned.

Brianna mouthed *Thank you* before he called the others back.

Scott stood in the driveway and shook each of their guests' hands. "Thank you all for coming so we could sign the paperwork where Lois is most comfortable."

"You're welcome. I'll talk to you soon." Gene gave a wave, then walked to his Cadillac.

Phil followed him. "Wait one moment, Gene. I've been meaning to ask your opinion on something."

Charlene opened the driver's door on her Land Rover. "It was nice to meet you all." She gave a wave before climbing into her SUV, starting it, and backing down the rock driveway.

"I think that went well," Brad said.

"Yes, in the end it did." Scott kicked a stone with his foot. "I was afraid Lois wasn't going to sign, but when I promised we would honor her husband, she agreed. And I will."

Brad looked up toward the house. "Brianna seems like a special woman. It's obvious she cares about you."

Scott's stomach dipped. "You think so?"

Brad patted his shoulder. "Yes. At least as a friend. But remember. You're business partners now."

"I know, Brad. You don't need to remind me."

Scott said good-bye to the three men, then hurried back into the house. After running upstairs to change into work clothes, he found Brianna in the kitchen filling the dishwasher with mugs and plates.

He sidled up to her. "Where's your mom?"

She sighed. "Taking a nap. I was so worried she wasn't going to sign. If you hadn't offered to put Dad's name on the new building, today could have been a disaster. Those men would have come here for nothing, and I'd be packing up our things."

"I came up with the idea yesterday. First I thought about putting his name on the pier, but then I realized it would mean so much more to put it on the retreat center."

"You, Scott Gibson, are a genius." She rested her hand on his shoulder, and when her fingertips brushed the nape of his neck, a chill zinged down his spine.

She stilled, and he took a step toward her, his heart thudding against his rib cage so hard surely she could hear it. Her brown eyes widened, and just as he reached over to touch her face, the doorbell rang.

Brianna sucked in a breath, then rushed toward the front of the house.

Scott brushed his hand over his face and tried to slow his pulse to a normal speed. He'd almost kissed her!

"Oh, hi, Mr. and Mrs. Hernandez," Brianna sang from the front door, her voice radiating with forced excitement. "How nice to see you."

Gathering himself, Scott stepped through the family room to the foyer. Olivia held an aluminum baking pan, the delicious aromas of cumin and garlic filling the area. She looked past Brianna to Scott, her brow pinching for a brief moment. "Scott?"

"Nice to see you." He smiled and hoped he sounded casual.

Olivia glanced at Eddie, and they shared a look.

"We were hoping to visit Lois," Eddie said.

Brianna's smile was a little too bright. "She's resting right now, but I'll tell her you stopped by."

Eddie pointed to the dish. "Olivia made her quesadilla casserole. I remembered how much your mother enjoys it at church potlucks."

"Oh, how nice." Brianna took the pan and handed it to Scott. "She'll love it. Thank you so much."

An awkward moment passed as the couple both looked back and forth between Scott and Brianna.

"I'm sorry Mom's not up for a visit," Brianna said. "Well, she hasn't been up for any visits. But today was an emotional day, so she went in for a nap."

Behind them, Scott was almost certain he heard tires crunching up the resort driveway.

Eddie pointed to him. "I was surprised to see you at Lowe's the other day, and you're still . . . here."

Scott's eyes widened without his permission. Eddie certainly was outspoken.

"Scott is partnering with my mom and me to upgrade the resort," Brianna said.

"You sold it?" Olivia exclaimed. "After all these years?"

"No, we didn't sell it. Scott's firm is investing." Brianna reached over and touched his arm. "He's going to help us add more features to the resort to make it more marketable and increase our business." She gave them a summary of the proposed changes, finishing with the retreat center and pool.

Olivia and Eddie shared another look, this time their expressions full of surprise. Then they both frowned, but before they could respond, Taylor appeared behind them. Scott inwardly groaned. *Could this get any worse?*

"Hi, Mr. and Mrs. Hernandez." Taylor shook their hands, looking every bit the politician as he smiled. "How are you?"

"Fine," Eddie said. "I want to talk to you about that proposal for the new park. I think the location is great. Don't listen to the town council."

Taylor laughed. "Oh, I have to listen to them."

Scott turned to Brianna. "I'm going out to the pier. Lots to do there."

He stalked toward the kitchen and set the large pan on the stove. Then resting his arms on the counter, he ducked his head and sucked in a deep breath, recalling how Brianna had flinched when Olivia and Eddie frowned after hearing the planned changes to the resort, right next to their inn.

Culpability rained down on him. Had he strong-armed Brianna and Lois into risking offending the whole town? What if the community turned against them? He should have checked around, found out what people thought about his ideas before asking Brad and Phil to back him. Yet he knew the resort would never make it without significant improvements. And how else was he going to help Brianna save her home?

He'd have to live with the consequences of his actions, though. Phil invested based on expanding the resort, not just saving it. But Brianna might never forgive him, and if that happened, he'd never forgive himself.

CHAPTER 31

hank you again for the casserole," Brianna called as the Hernandezes walked down the ramp toward the driveway. Then she turned to Taylor. "Why aren't you at the store?"

"I asked my dad to cover for me so I could come help you." He sounded proud of himself.

"Thank you."

"You're welcome."

"I have news," she said as they walked toward the kitchen together. "Mom signed the contract this morning to partner with Scott and his firm. The money will be wired later today to pay off the loan, and soon we'll get all our bills up-to-date."

Taylor's smile dimmed a fraction but then recovered. "That's great, but you still need to get the resort ready, right? So put me to work."

"I'm going to start painting the convenience store and bait shop, but you can help Scott replace the rotten boards on the pier."

He made a face.

"Or you can help me paint."

"That sounds like more fun." His smile returned. "Remember when we painted my bedroom?"

She laughed. "Yes, we got so much paint on the carpet that your parents had to replace it."

"That might have been deliberate. I hated that ugly green carpet." He clasped his hands together. "Let's get to work."

After a quick bite to eat, leaving sandwiches in the fridge for Scott and her mother, they headed to the convenience store and bait shop, where they moved all the shelving units into the center of the room and covered them with drop cloths, then taped around the woodwork.

"Do you remember that time we took one of the boats out in the middle of the lake, and you forgot to make sure it had enough gas?" Taylor asked as he cut in around the front door.

"Yes!" She looked over at him from where she stood on the other side of the shop. "We were stuck out there for hours because we both left our cell phones in our jackets. When Dad found us, he grounded me for a week."

"But I still snuck through your bedroom window to see you, risking my life climbing that tree."

She dipped her brush into the paint can. "Oh, those were the days. We didn't have a care in the world."

"Nope. And we had each other." The love in his eyes made her heart squeeze. This was Taylor—the man who had loved her since she was sixteen years old. She found herself wondering if she should have agreed to set a wedding date.

More memories filled her mind. "Remember when your Celica broke down on the side of the road, and we had to walk three miles to the Burns' auto parts store?"

"Yes! We were afraid to call our parents because we'd snuck out to see that concert on a school night." He chortled.

"And my parents were waiting for me because I didn't realize they had a tracker on my phone." She wiped at her eyes. "We were in so much trouble."

"But we had a lot of fun."

"We sure did."

Both the work and the afternoon flew by faster than she'd expected, and she was grateful Taylor hadn't brought up the idea of moving away from Splendid Lake while they were enjoying each other's company. Maybe he was having second thoughts. She hoped so.

When they finished, she glanced at the time on her phone and frowned. "It's after five. I don't have anything else prepared, so I guess I'll warm up the casserole the Hernandezes brought."

They washed out the paint brushes before walking up to the house, and when they entered the kitchen, they were met by the delicious aroma of Olivia Hernandez's quesadilla casserole. Scott and Mom sat at the table already eating.

"Hi, Lois," Taylor said to Mom, ignoring Scott.

"Hi, Taylor."

"I'm so sorry to be late," Brianna told Scott as she washed her hands at the sink. "We lost track of time. Thank you for warming up the casserole."

"You're welcome. I didn't want to interrupt you."

Brianna looked at Taylor. "Would you like to stay? There's plenty."

"No, thanks." Taylor's expression was frosty as he glanced at Scott. "I'll just head out."

Brianna walked him to the front door. "Thank you for helping today."

"You're welcome." Taylor gave her a quick hug. "I'll be in touch."

As he walked out to his car, Brianna felt more confused than ever. On one hand, she'd enjoyed her time with him. But she still didn't know where their relationship was headed if his dream would take them away from Splendid Lake. They had to talk that out—and soon.

"Come in," Brianna called toward her closed bedroom door as she clicked silver hoop earrings into her ears. She always wore them with the blue sundress she'd pulled from the back of her closet now that it was May and so much warmer.

The door opened, and Scott stood in the doorway, gaping at her.

She grimaced, then glanced at the mirror on her closet door. "You think I look ridiculous, right?"

"No!" He held up his hands as he stepped into the room. "You look fantastic."

"You're just not used to seeing me in a dress." She groaned and walked to the closet.

Time had flown by while she and Scott worked hard around the resort, and tonight was Brooklyn's bridal shower. As much as Brianna longed to support Ava, she dreaded going to the party. Surely she would be questioned about the coming changes to the resort, especially since she was certain the Hernandezes had spread the word about Mom partnering with Scott.

The Hernandezes. When Scott told her he was afraid he'd made a mistake after seeing their reaction to the idea of a retreat center, she'd called them to explain the center wouldn't have hotel rooms. It would bring business to them, not take it away. They were fine then.

"And Taylor didn't raise any red flags," she'd told Scott as well. "If anyone is attuned to the town's interests, it's him."

She turned to her closet. "I don't know what else to wear. I wore my little black dress to the engagement party."

"Brianna." He appeared behind her, and his voice next to her ear made her dizzy. "You look amazing. Don't change."

"Really?"

"Yes, really." He pointed toward the door. "I just wanted to make sure you hadn't changed your mind about going tonight. I promise I'll take good care of your mom."

"I know you will." She looked in the mirror one last time and saw him watching her with an intensity that sent goose bumps chasing each other down her arms. "Too much makeup?"

He shook his head. "You're perfect."

They walked down the stairs and headed to the kitchen, where her mother sat at the table with a cup of tea.

"Oh, Brianna," Mom said. "You look beautiful."

"Thank you." She looked at Scott, and when he nodded, her heart skipped a beat. "I won't be out too late, and I'll have my cell phone."

She grabbed her purse, sweater, and the envelope with Brooklyn's gift inside before she ambled for the front door with Scott in tow. "Thank you again for staying with Mom."

He waved her off. "Go have fun. I plan to cook something she'll love, and we'll be fine." Sincerity etched into the lines around his eyes and mouth. She even saw it in his posture.

She nodded. "See you later, then."

Brianna breathed in the sweet scents coming from the colorful, cheerful flowers in Mrs. Waller's garden. The bridal shower was already in full swing around her on the deck, with half the town's women there, it seemed. Many of them had to be Mrs. Waller's friends, and she saw some of her mother's friends too. But Brooklyn looked like she was having a good time laughing and talking with her own friends at one of the long tables with periwinkle tablecloths and vases of white daisies. Matching periwinkle balloons hovered above them like giant, happy guests there to enjoy the festivities.

"You look incredible," Ava told Brianna as she handed her a cup of punch that somehow perfectly matched all the periwinkle decorations.

"Thank you." Brianna nodded at Ava's kelly-green dress. "So do you."

Ava's smile faded. "I'm sorry your mom didn't make it. I was hoping she would change her mind."

Brianna looked down at her punch. "I know what she told you, but I also think she's embarrassed for people to see her using a walker. She hasn't said so, but it's just a feeling I have."

"I understand, but we all still love her and want to see her."

"I know."

"It must feel good knowing the resort is back in the black now and all the bills are paid."

"It does. And Scott and I have been busy with the remainder of must-do projects all week. He replaced the rotten boards on the pier, and it looks brand-new." Brianna tried to ignore the sadness that nipped at her as she considered how nearly all the work was done. That meant Scott would soon return to Charlotte. Oh, how she dreaded seeing him go.

"I'm making progress with the convenience store and bait shop," she continued. "Taylor helped me paint on Monday. I finished up on Tuesday and then rearranged all the shelves and cleaned them. Our suppliers will have everything to us a week before we open. It will take a while to get it all set up and priced, but Cassie will be here by then, and Taylor offered to help. He's been so helpful lately."

Brianna sipped her punch. "This is delicious."

Ava studied her. "It sounds like things are getting better with Taylor."

"Yeah, they are."

"Does that mean you might reconsider scheduling your wedding for this year? You know I'd help you plan it." Ava looked hopeful.

"And now I'll probably have the money to pay for it. But I don't know." She felt a familiar bewilderment creeping back. "I'm not sure if we—"

"There you are, Brianna!" Mrs. Bedford hurried over, her bouffant never moving, which made Brianna wonder if she'd used an entire can of hairspray. The woman looked around dramatically as if searching for someone, and then her eyes homed in on Brianna again. "Where's your mother?"

"She wasn't feeling up to coming." Brianna set her drink on the table behind her and worked to keep a pleasant expression on her face.

Mrs. Bedford clucked her tongue. "Your family has been through so much. First losing your father and now your mother's stroke. I'm so very sorry."

"Thanks."

"Someone told me you sold the resort, but I told her that couldn't be true. After all, it's been in your family for generations. Why would you do that?"

"My mother didn't sell," Brianna said, working to keep her tone pleasant as well. "She partnered with an investor so we can upgrade the resort and keep it going. When my dad passed away, it not only left a huge hole in our lives but affected our business. We're grateful we're able to move forward."

Mrs. Bedford's eyes widened. "Well, isn't that interesting."

"Yes, and now I'd like to enjoy watching Brooklyn open her gifts." She pointed to where the guest of honor sat. "Have a nice night."

And with that, Brianna picked up her cup and walked to where Brooklyn was surrounded by her friends, who all oohed and aahed as she held up an expensive coffee maker. Brianna tried to stem her ire toward Mrs. Bedford, but it wasn't easy.

"Good for you," Ava whispered as she came to stand beside her.

Brianna shook her head. "I wish that woman would keep her nose out of other people's business."

"I know." Ava looped her arms around Brianna's waist. "But she doesn't have an awesome best friend like I do to keep her occupied at parties."

Brianna smiled. "Love you too, BFF."

CHAPTER 32

$\int$cott scooped a spoonful of buttered pecan from his bowl. "Ice cream is the best dessert."

"Martin always said it fills in the cracks." Lois shoved her spoon into her bowl of cookies and cream. He'd been relieved when she'd said she was okay with one of Brianna's favorites instead of her beloved plain vanilla. That was all he could find in the freezer.

Scott grinned. "I like that. He was a smart man."

He'd cherished his evening with Lois. They'd talked about all sorts of things as he made hamburger steak with onions and gravy. Then over dinner, he'd enjoyed hearing about her cooking fails, and they both laughed as he shared his own.

When he'd served up the ice cream for dessert, she'd smiled. And she'd never once seemed emotional during their time together. He hoped she remained that way, but if not, he'd do his best to calm and console her.

"What else was Martin like?"

Lois lowered her spoon. "He was a good man, a great husband, and a wonderful father. He was funny, caring, and loving. The girls adored him, and he adored them. He encouraged them to follow their dreams, whether to stay here or pursue a career far away, like Cassandra and Jenna did."

"That's wonderful." Scott spooned another bite.

"I loved seeing him work with Brianna in the shop. He never lost his patience with her, even when she made a silly mistake." She gave a little laugh. "One time she forgot to put the drain plug back in one of the boats because she was in a hurry. As soon as she put the boat in the lake, it started taking on water." She hooted. "But Martin kept his cool, and we laughed about it later."

Scott chuckled. "That's funny. I might have to use that piece of information against her sometime."

"Feel free." She dabbed her eyes, and then her smile flattened. "I miss him all the time. I constantly see things that remind me of him. I know Brianna does too. They were so close—inseparable, really. I think she keeps her grief to herself because she's worried about hurting me."

"I think you're right." Scott wouldn't dare betray Brianna's trust, but he also didn't want to upset Lois by telling her how her daughter had broken down that day in the workshop.

"You told us you grew up in foster care."

He nodded as he took another bite.

"That had to be tougher than you let on."

He shrugged. "I survived."

Lois's blue eyes studied him. "That's what you said before, but you seem like the kind of man who holds his emotions inside. I get the feeling you wouldn't tell me the truth if I asked how bad it really was."

"You're a perceptive woman." He wiped his mouth with a paper napkin and considered how much to share. "It was hard being shuffled from family to family, and soon I realized no one would ever love me the way my mother had. But I have to credit the system for making me tough and teaching me I had to work hard for whatever I wanted to achieve. That experience taught me determination and to believe in myself."

Lois looked pensive. "I imagine others in your situation would become bitter, angry, and cold, but you're the opposite. You're kind, thoughtful, and generous." Her expression warmed. "Your mother would be so proud of the man you've become."

He was so surprised by her words that he couldn't speak.

"You're a good man, Scott."

When Lois placed her hand on his, he felt a knot of emotion—a mixture of grief and gratitude—swelling in his chest.

"Thank you," he said, his voice barely above a whisper.

"When do you think you and Brianna will get married?"

Scott's heart thudded as he blinked at Lois.

"Oh my!" She held up her hand. "Listen to me getting all confused. For a moment I thought you were Brianna's fiancé, not Taylor. Forgive me."

"It's-it's okay," he managed to say.

"Sometimes my thoughts still get all jumbled up."

He wondered if that were true. Did he see the hint of a twinkle in her eye?

But as Lois smiled at him, he felt an overwhelming desire to be a part of the Porter family. What would it feel like to have Brianna by his side and call Lois his mother-in-law? For the first time in his life, he felt ready to settle down and start a family—but he wanted that with Brianna. He'd tried to wish the longing for her away, but it had only grown with time.

He couldn't help but wonder what a good man would do in his situation. Certainly not pursue a woman who belonged to someone else.

At least she'd convinced him renovations like the retreat center wouldn't ruin her standing in Splendid Lake's community. If it had . . . He didn't even want to think about it. His friendship with Brianna was too important to him.

When they were finished, Lois headed to her bedroom, saying she wanted to read before turning in early. Scott loaded the dishwasher and hit the Start button. Then he wiped down the counters as the dishwasher hummed.

Looking out the window, he thought about what it would be like to live at Splendid Lake year-round. He was still considering building a cabin for himself—a permanent place to stay whenever he was here. Staying in the house with Brianna and Lois wasn't an option. And sooner or later, Taylor would live there too. Or maybe he'd build a cabin for the two of them. After all, Splendid Lake was the most romantic place he'd ever visited.

Another idea for one of the existing cabins struck him. He didn't expect Brianna home for a few hours. He'd put it all together before then so he could surprise her.

Scott was sitting on the sofa in the family room watching *Beverly Hills Cop* when he heard the front door creak open. "Hey." He paused the movie and smiled as Brianna walked in.

"I'm surprised you're still up."

"How was the shower?"

"It was nice." She sank onto the sofa next to him, dropping her sweater and purse between them. Then she kicked off her high-heeled sandals and stretched out her legs. "Brooklyn seemed really happy, and I enjoyed spending time with Ava. How was your evening?"

"Great. We cooked, we ate, we talked."

"Thank you so much for taking care of her."

"You're welcome. I truly enjoyed it." He flipped off the television.

"You're the best, Scott."

He shrugged. "It really wasn't a big deal. I enjoy spending time with Lois."

"I'll go check on her." She stood, then zipped down the hallway toward her mother's bedroom.

Scott glanced around the room, trying to imagine what the house was like when Brianna was little and her sisters lived at home. He envisioned a loud, happy house filled with laughter and love, an experience he'd had only for that short time with the Robinsons. And he'd mostly put them out of his mind until Brianna asked about his foster care that day.

Now he wondered if he'd ever have a home with a wife and children, maybe even a cat like Bucky and a dog. But for that to happen, he'd have to push past these feelings for Brianna, and that wouldn't happen overnight.

Brianna reappeared. "She's fast asleep."

"Good."

She tilted her head. "Want to go for a walk on the beach?"

"Sure, but I did something I want to show you first. Also outside."

He smiled, then hurried to the check-in desk and pocketed the key he needed. Brianna grabbed a flashlight before pushing her feet into an old pair of Converse high-tops she'd had tucked into a closet.

"Where are we going?" she asked as they stepped onto the porch.

"To cabin twelve." He glanced up at the porch lights, where moths flung themselves against the bulbs, then beckoned her to follow him down the steps. As they walked side by side, Brianna's flashlight beam bounded over the grass, and he enjoyed the quiet.

"What did you do?" she asked with excitement in her voice.

"You'll see." When they reached the cabin, he unlocked the outer door and then turned toward her. "Close your eyes, and don't move."

He pushed opened the screen door, then hurried inside and quickly banished the dark before returning to place his hands on her arms. "Keep your eyes closed and step inside."

As he walked backward, she allowed him to steer her into the cabin, then he gently closed the screen door behind her.

"Okay. Open your eyes."

He took a step back.

Brianna gasped, cupping her hands to her mouth as she spun around and took in the white fairy lights and white lit candles. "Scott, this is so romantic!"

He grinned. "You like it?"

"I love it."

"I thought we could have a honeymoon cabin for newlyweds. I saw those lights stored out in the barn, and then the idea hit me earlier this evening. That's when I also dug into your candle stash. We can add pretty curtains and place rose petals on the bed and vases of flowers throughout the cabin." He shrugged. "It's just an idea."

"I love it! It's brilliant." She touched his arm. "We definitely should add this to the website."

He smiled. "Why don't we take that walk on the beach now?" he asked, eager to spend more time with her.

"That sounds perfect."

He turned off the lights and blew out the candles, then locked the cabin. As they headed down the hill, the air smelled like rain, and the tall maple trees sat still and serene in the darkness. They continued toward the shoreline, moving over the rocks as tiny waves lapped by their feet.

The whole time he had one thought: *If only things were different . . .*

Brianna pointed to the Adirondack chairs where they'd met the night of her father's funeral. "Want to sit for old time's sake?"

"Sure."

When they were seated, she turned toward him, and he could just make out her face in the moonlight barely shining from between the clouds. A fine mist began to fall, but he wasn't ready to leave. Apparently, neither was she.

"I checked our reservation site earlier," Brianna said, "and we're just about booked up through July. I was really surprised. You were right—raising the rates didn't deter any of our annual guests."

"That's great."

"And I'm so glad our teenage hires from last year are coming back. Like I've told you, they help run the convenience store and bait shop and the front desk. I'll be busy maintaining the boats, of course, and Cassie says she'll clean the cabins until we hire more help."

"I've got our office manager, Allison, lining up some people for you to interview. That will save you some time."

"Okay. Thank you."

But her tone sounded almost sad. Then she looked at him, and he held his breath as the overwhelming urge to tell her he cared for her grabbed him by the throat. Instead of speaking, though, he gazed back toward the lake as the fine mist transformed into soft raindrops.

Brianna sighed. "So much for a nice walk on the beach."

"We can try again another night."

They started back to the house as large drops began soaking his T-shirt. Soon they were running and laughing as raindrops fell all around them.

When they reached the porch, Brianna stumbled. She reached for Scott's arm, and he caught her. Holding on to him, she looked up, her eyes rounding as something magnetic passed between them. She flattened one hand against his chest, and his pulse came to life as she reached up and brushed raindrops from his cheek. The feel of her skin on his sent heat and longing tearing through every cell of his body.

Scott placed his palms on her cheeks, then leaned down and brushed his lips across hers, making him lose track of both their surroundings and time. He closed his eyes, savoring the feel of her mouth against his, and a shiver of wanting vibrated through his body.

Brianna leaned in to his kiss, but then she stilled and stepped back, pushing him away, leaving him feeling cold without her touch. Her eyes were wide with something that resembled horror.

"I-I'm sorry," she stammered. "I-I just can't do this. I'm sorry, Scott. I-I just can't."

Then she spun on her heel and raced into the house, the door slamming behind her as she took a piece of his heart with her. Loneliness drenched him like the rain, and he shivered again, this time from the block of ice forming in his chest.

He was a fool, caught up in the moment and the way Brianna had looked at him. But she had wanted him too. He knew it. And she seemed to enjoy it as much as he had—until she realized what she'd allowed herself to do.

Scott looked up at the dark sky and let the rain pelt his face as thunder rumbled in the distance. Brianna's rejection felt like a shard of glass slicing through his heart. But she'd made her choice. He wasn't the man she wanted, and he never would be.

It was time to finish up at the resort and go back to his life in Charlotte. He didn't belong in Splendid Lake. This would never be his home, and he had to cut his losses with the Porter family.

That last realization was the most painful of all.

CHAPTER 33

*W*hat brings you here this morning?" Ava asked Brianna as they sat at their usual secluded table in the Coffee Bean. "It's been four days since the bridal shower, and this is the first I've heard from you."

Brianna wrapped her hands around her cup of cinnamon dolce latte. "I just wanted to check on you before I went to the grocery store. How are things?"

"Oh. They're a little crazy, but okay. The wedding is getting close, and Brooklyn is a bit frantic, but it's all coming together." She sipped her vanilla latte. "How are things at the resort?"

"Good. We have a lot more to do, but I think we'll be ready for the guests. I've been stocking the convenience store, and Scott is painting all the fencing." She shrugged, but a tremor had rolled through her when she said Scott's name.

"Something is up. What aren't you telling me?"

Brianna's shoulders sagged. "That's really why I came here. I have to get something off my chest."

"Oh, this sounds juicy." Ava rested her elbows on the table and her chin on both palms. "I'm ready."

Brianna leaned forward and lowered her voice. "Okay, but I need you to keep this to yourself and not tell anyone, including Dylan. Do you understand?"

Ava gestured as if she were locking her lips and throwing away the key.

Brianna took a deep breath. "I kissed Scott after the bridal shower."

Ava gasped, covering her mouth with her hands.

"Shh!" Brianna looked around, grateful no one had noticed. The last thing she needed was one of the town gossips to overhear them and tell the rest of the population of Splendid Lake.

"How did it happen?"

After Brianna explained, Ava lifted an eyebrow and said, "Is that all?"

"Yes, of course." Brianna cupped her hand to her forehead. "When I realized what I'd done, I pushed away from him and hurried into the house. And now things are so awkward between us. We can hardly look at each other."

Brianna groaned and covered her face with her hands, feeling yet another pang of shame and regret. "I'm a horrible person. How could I do that to Taylor?"

"Because you care about Scott?"

Brianna hesitated, but her heart wanted to scream *Yes! I do!* The truth was she couldn't stop thinking about that kiss. She'd never felt such an explosion of desire in her life. The memory sent a flush of bashful pleasure through her cheeks and made her light-headed. No man had ever wakened her heart the way Scott had—not even Taylor.

Yet she couldn't hurt Taylor. She'd made a commitment to him— a commitment that shown brightly on her ring finger.

She shook her head. "We're too different. He's a businessman who lives in Charlotte, and I'm an engaged boat mechanic who belongs here."

Ava gave her a knowing smile. "You're avoiding my question. Did you kiss Scott because you have feelings for him? Yes or no."

"I can't even think about it." Brianna rubbed her eyes.

"But what does your heart say?"

Brianna swallowed against her dry throat. "I don't know."

"Maybe you should think about that." Ava picked up her cup and sipped.

Brianna finished the last of her coffee. "I need to go. I'll see you later." But Ava's words followed her to the door.

Brianna stowed the groceries before stepping outside, where she sat on a rocking chair beside her mother. Bucky plopped down beside her, making himself comfortable on the porch floor.

"Was the grocery story busy?" Mom asked.

"No. It was fine." Brianna leaned down and gave Bucky's ear a rub, then looked to where Scott was painting the white fence that lined the road leading to the pier and shoreline. At least they hadn't had to repair any of their parking areas. That was a blessing.

Scott looked great in the pair of worn jeans she'd decided were her favorite and a faded gray shirt. He stood and swiped his hand across his forehead, which even from a distance she could tell glistened with sweat in the warm sunshine. The sky above him was bright blue and cloudless. It was a perfect day in May.

Scott glanced toward the porch, and she waved. He nodded, then returned to painting. Sadness swept over her as she recalled the past few days. The coldness and distance between them had nearly sucked the life out of her. She missed their talks and teasing. It had been pure torture to sit at the breakfast table with him and feel as if they were merely acquaintances, making small talk about the weather. It was as if those long, intimate discussions about their lives had never happened.

"Brianna?"

She turned toward her mother. "Yes?"

"You okay?"

"I am." Brianna stood. "I need to get back to work in the store, though. Do you need anything before I go?"

"No. I'm fine."

"I have my cell phone. Call me if you need me."

"Wait. I can't help but notice you and Scott have changed toward each other. What—"

"We're fine, Mom. Just tired."

She jogged down the porch steps, then turned and called the cat. "Hey, Buck. Come with me." He sprinted to join her, and they trudged down the path together.

Before walking inside the store, Brianna looked at Scott one more time. Watching as he crouched to paint the bottom of a fence slat, she felt defeated.

If only things were different . . .

Brianna thought her chest might crack open when Scott walked into the kitchen carrying his bags. He'd told them last night he'd be leaving today, but she thought it would be later—at least after lunch.

"I'm heading out." He set two bags on the floor, then adjusted his backpack on his shoulder.

Mom looked up from her pancakes. "Aren't you going to eat breakfast?"

"No, thank you. I'll just get something on the road." He met

Brianna's gaze, and her stomach dipped. "I finished painting the fence along the road to the beach early this morning, and you already know I painted the one around the perimeter of the resort."

"They look great. Thank you."

"You're welcome."

He hesitated, and they stared at each other. So much was left unsaid between them.

"I'll start talking to architects about our ideas for the retreat center, and I'll let you know when I can come back to show you some plans. I'll stay at the Lakeview Inn or find another place. I won't be here long."

"Okay," she said, but his words cut her to the bone. He'd abandoned his plan to start commuting from here to Charlotte?

She waited a beat, and when he didn't speak, a saturating anguish pulled her down.

"I'll also have Allison set up those interviews for you," he said. Then he looked at Mom. "Good-bye, Lois. Thanks for your hospitality."

"Thanks for all your help, Scott. And for helping us save our home. Good-bye." Mom smiled. "Don't be a stranger."

When he returned her smile, Brianna's pulse zinged. It was the first genuine smile she'd seen on his face for days, and it made her feel warm all over. Oh, how she'd miss him!

He lifted his bags. "Talk to you soon."

His gaze tangled with Brianna's, and she felt breathless, her words stuck in her throat for a moment.

"Thank you, Scott," she managed to say, her ability to say more too tenuous to try.

He nodded, then turned and started for the front door.

Brianna leaned back against the counter and listened as the door opened and then shut. A few moments later, the Challenger roared to life, and the tires crunched down the driveway, away from the resort.

Away from her.

"He won't stay away from you long," Mom said before forking a piece of pancake into her mouth.

Speechless, Brianna studied her mother, then headed for the stairs without a word. If only she could believe Mom's prediction. But Scott was hurt, and she had no reason to believe he'd be back, not even to show her plans. He'd send Brad before he'd put himself through that.

CHAPTER 34

*B*rianna merged the Tahoe onto Interstate 40 the following
Wednesday afternoon and then glanced at her sister in the passenger seat. "Thank you so much for coming. How was your flight
from Atlanta?"

"Not too bad." Cassie covered her mouth with her hand and yawned.
"I just had to get up so early." She looked at Brianna. "How's Mom?"

"She's doing really well. She's been walking a bit without her
walker. She and Ava were sitting on the porch talking about Brooklyn's
wedding when I left."

"That's fantastic. When is the wedding again?"

"Next Saturday. The ceremony will be in the afternoon, and the
reception will go into the evening. Didn't you get your invitation?"

"I did. I just didn't take a close look at it. Wow. It seems like
everyone is getting married except us, huh?" Cassie laughed. "How are
you and Taylor doing?"

Brianna shrugged. "Fine."

"Just fine? Have you set a date yet?"

"No."

Cassie leaned over and examined Brianna's hand. "The ring is still there. What are you waiting for?"

"Now just isn't the right time. I have too much on my plate."

"You've always been busy, Brie, and I doubt that will change. So if it's not the right time to marry Taylor, then why are you still with him?"

Brianna peeked at her sister as those words settled over her. She had to change the subject.

"I'm so glad you're here, Cass. We're fully booked for Memorial Day weekend, and I really need your help. I hired the same teens we had last summer, but my two new hires can't start until the following week."

"Well, put me to work." She tilted her head. "Hey, Mom said her new business partner stayed in my old room. And he cooked for you both and helped around the resort? What's up with that?"

"He was my most reliable help." Brianna kept her eyes on the road and fought to keep her emotions under control. She hadn't heard from Scott since he'd left. She'd picked up her phone at least a dozen times to text him just to say hi or tell him something funny she thought of, but she had no idea if he'd respond. And if she was honest with herself, she'd have to admit what she really wanted was to tell him she was sorry, missed him, and wanted him to come back. But instead, she'd put the phone down with a heavy sadness.

Ava told her to think about her feelings for Scott, and she had. But that didn't change the fact that she'd promised to marry Taylor.

"Mom seems to really like him," Cassie said.

"Who?"

"The guy. What's his name?"

"Scott Gibson."

"She said he's both handsome and friendly."

"He is." Brianna pursed her lips. "So tell me about work. The other day you mentioned a cool book you've been editing."

Cassie settled back into her seat, and Brianna was glad her sister filled the remainder of the long ride with stories about her job, allowing her to at least try to evict Scott from her mind.

When they arrived home, they found Ava and Mom sitting in the family room, watching one of Brianna's favorite romantic comedies, *Fool's Gold*. Ava hit the Pause button and smiled.

"Mom!" Cassie exclaimed as she rushed to the sofa and wrapped her arms around her. "How are you? Is Brie taking good care of you?"

Mom smiled. "I'm doing better, and of course your sister is taking good care of me. Sit down and tell me about your trip."

After Ava and Cassie exchanged greetings, Brianna motioned for Ava to follow her into the kitchen.

"How was Mom while I was gone?" She leaned against the counter beside her best friend.

"Great. After her therapist left, we sat outside and tried to guess where Cole is taking Brooklyn on their honeymoon. He won't say, and my sister seems okay with that." She rolled her eyes. "Then I made us turkey and cheese sandwiches and we started watching that movie. We had fun."

"Thank you so much."

"You're welcome." Ava stared into her eyes. "Are you okay?"

"Yeah. I'm just tired. And we still have so much to do."

"Are you sure that's it?"

"Of course." Brianna opened the freezer. "I need to decide what to make for dinner, but I might just go pick up some takeout." She closed the freezer door and looked at Ava. "Do you want to stay?"

"Oh, no, thanks. Dylan will be home soon, so I need to get going. I'm so glad Cassie is here to help. You know I would if I wasn't involved in all the wedding preparations." She gave Brianna a hug, then Brianna walked with her into the family room, where Ava said good-bye to Cassie and Mom before heading out the door.

Later that evening Brianna sat on the porch with Cassie and Mom, yawning as she moved her rocking chair back and forth. Cassie was talking about Los Angeles and how much she loved it.

Then Cassie's phone alerted her to a FaceTime call. She answered it, and soon she and Mom were talking to Jenna. Brianna leaned over and said hello, but then nodded toward the lake. "I'm going for a walk. Good night."

She felt so miserable as she started down the porch steps. She couldn't stop her mind from wandering to the one person who'd taken up residence there—Scott. Not Taylor. Scott.

Her heart lurched as she made her way to the pier. She stepped onto it and admired Scott's work as she moved along the fresh boards. Mr. Brooks Brothers was a talented carpenter. The pier looked as if it had been professionally renovated.

She walked to the end and sat down with her feet dangling over the beautiful water she loved so much, then pulled her phone from her pocket and checked for messages. Still nothing. Surely he was punishing her for rejecting him that night—or he really was too hurt to even consider being in touch. The pain she'd seen in his eyes when she'd pushed him away had nearly shattered her soul. She'd longed to stay and kiss him until the rain stopped and the sun rose, but she'd made a commitment to Taylor.

Cassie's words echoed in her mind. *If it's not the right time to marry Taylor, then why are you still with him?*

Her sister had made a valid point. Perhaps there never would be a right time to move their relationship forward. And if that was true, maybe she had to face whatever was holding her back from marrying him. Maybe she should be dealing with her feelings for Taylor, not what she felt for Scott.

"It's a beautiful night." Taylor held Brianna's hand as they walked along the shoreline Saturday evening. "It's the perfect time for a stroll on the beach."

"It is."

Brianna looked out over the water sparkling in the moonlight. Cicadas sang their nightly chorus and lightning bugs began making their appearance, announcing the approach of summer. She could almost hear the sounds of their guests who would soon play in the water, lounge on the sand, fish off the pier, eat at the picnic tables, and sail in the boats.

Their season would start in two weeks. This was her favorite time of year, but her heart remained sad. She missed her father. She missed who her mother was before his death and the stroke.

She missed Scott.

"Did you enjoy dinner?" Taylor asked, who seemed oblivious to her grief.

"Yes. It was delicious. Thank you." She gave his hand a gentle squeeze as she looked up at his handsome face. He'd taken her to her favorite Italian restaurant. But while the food had been perfect, the date had been awkward. They'd quickly run out of interesting things to talk about, and then he spent most of the night talking about the store—every mundane thing imaginable.

At least he hadn't brought up his hopes for a political career. Of course, if Taylor wanted to talk about his political dreams, she owed it to him to listen. But did it have to be tonight? She was still struggling with her feelings about their relationship even without that issue.

He stopped at her parents' chairs—the ones where she'd sat with Scott—and nodded. "Should we sit and talk?"

She swallowed, tempted to tell him she was ready to return to the house. But she nodded instead. "Sure."

They sat down, and she dislodged her sweaty palm from his.

"How are things with Cassie?"

She sighed in relief. Maybe they wouldn't have to talk about those political dreams after all, at least not yet. And he'd finally asked about her life. "She's been a tremendous help. We've made great progress deep cleaning the cabins, but we still have to—"

She realized Taylor was looking at his phone. She peeked and found him reading an email from one of the town council members. He'd asked her a question and then failed to listen to her answer? Exasperation tangled with anger.

"Taylor?"

"What?" He looked up. "What were you saying?"

"Nothing."

He gave her a guilty look. "I'm sorry. I'm listening now."

"It wasn't important."

He leaned over, cupped his hand to her cheek, and brushed his lips over hers. She leaned in and waited for the eruption of emotions she'd experienced when kissing Scott, but she felt nothing.

Nothing at all.

It was time to accept the truth she'd known in her heart for weeks. She'd been holding on to Taylor for all the wrong reasons. First, he was the one thing in her life that hadn't changed. He was her past, and she'd tried to cling to him for that reason. Second, she'd truly believed she had to stay true to the commitment she'd made to marry him. But they'd outgrown each other a long time ago, and she had to release him so they could both move on.

When Taylor pulled away, he studied her. "Are you okay?"

"No, I'm not." Her eyes stung. "I've been unfair to you. To both of us."

His eyes searched hers. "What do you mean?"

"When I said I needed more time before setting a wedding date, that wasn't the truth. The truth is I'll never be ready to marry you, Taylor. At some point we stopped moving forward in our relationship, and I think you know we've grown apart. It's time we admitted we're not the same people we used to be, and we're not each other's future." She removed the ring from her finger and held it out to him. "I'm sorry."

Taylor's mouth moved but no sound came out.

She placed the ring in the palm of his hand and closed his fingers around it. "I care about you, and I always will." Her eyes filled with tears. "You were my first love, and I'll always cherish the time we had together. But it's over."

His face clouded. "This is about Scott, isn't it?" His voice was as tight as a rubber band.

"No, it's not. It's about us." She pulled a tissue from her pocket and wiped her eyes.

"I could feel you pulling away, but I hoped I could save our relationship. I still think we can. Just tell me what I've done wrong and I'll fix it. Just give me a chance." He placed the ring in her hand. "I love you, Brianna. Let me fix this."

Her heart twisted. "No, we can't fix this. We're different people now, and you deserve someone who loves you the way you deserve to be loved. That just can't be me."

"But Dylan and Ava are different, and they've made it work."

"We're not Dylan and Ava, and this isn't about them. This is about us." She gestured between them. "We want different things. You love politics, and you dream of a career that will take you away from here. But I don't want to leave Splendid Lake. This is my home."

"But we can hire a staff to run the resort. You can have both." His voice seemed to plead with her.

"No, that's not what I want." She pointed to her chest. "I don't want to be the state senator or governor's wife, holding your arm, smiling as you make speeches. I want to be here." She pointed toward the cabins behind her. "I want to run this resort. I'm not interested in moving away—ever. We can't work this out, and it's time we both face that we want different things."

Taylor took her hand. "Tell me the truth. Are you seeing Scott?"

"No." She released her hand from his grasp. "I'm not seeing anyone. I told you, this is about who we are right now—you and me. I can't see our relationship moving forward."

He eyed her with suspicion. "It was so obvious you and Scott were into each other whenever you were together. He all but admitted to me that he wanted to be with you."

She shook her head. "It was all about a business deal. He got the deal, and then he went back to Charlotte."

"Really?"

"Yes, really. I'm sorry I hurt you. I never meant to. I should have broken our engagement sooner, because we both need to move on. You have a bright future ahead of you, away from Splendid Lake, but my future is here." She held the ring out again.

Taylor swallowed before taking it, and then he slipped it into his trouser pocket. "You're right. I knew it was happening, but I wasn't ready to let you go either."

"Thank you for loving me for so long."

He nodded, his own tears glittering in the moonlight. Then he pulled her in for a hug, and she rested her cheek on his shoulder. "I'll miss you, Brie."

"I'll miss you too."

They walked in silence up to the house porch. After they said good night, Taylor walked away as Brianna lowered herself into a rocking chair and looked at her beloved lake. After a few moments, she heard Taylor's car start, followed by the crunch of tires on the driveway rocks.

Her heart faltered as she recalled the hurt in Taylor's eyes when she told him it was over. But she was grateful he'd finally understood and agreed it was time to move on. Then she felt a calmness settle over her soul. She knew to the depth of her bones that she'd made the right decision.

She felt something soft caress her shin, and she smiled down at Bucky.

"Hi there," she whispered. "Do you think Scott and I could ever work things out between us?"

The cat yawned, then stretched before sauntering to the edge of the porch, where he rolled onto his back, revealing his round, white belly.

Brianna closed her eyes. She'd told Taylor the truth when she said the breakup was about the two of them. But that didn't mean she didn't have feelings for Scott. If only their shared love for Splendid Lake could bring them together again. But now she'd hurt two men, and the one she wanted was far away.

CHAPTER 35

$\mathcal{S}$cott stepped to one of the floor-to-ceiling windows in his office.

As he looked out over the parking lot below, empty on a Friday night, he sighed, his mind swimming with thoughts of Brianna.

Again and again, he'd tried to dismiss her from his thoughts. But she'd lingered there, taunting him no matter how hard he'd tried to forget how he felt about her.

He'd checked with a few architecture firms regarding renovations for the resort, but he hadn't made any progress so he could at least text her with that news. He worried about Lois and hoped she was well, but he didn't want to bother Brianna after she'd been so cold to him the day he left. Of course, he'd been cold as well, trying to protect his heart.

Yet he'd hoped she would at least reach out to say she wanted to remain friends. He'd checked his phone multiple times each day to see if he'd missed a call or text from her, but the line between them remained deafeningly silent, proof she'd already written him out of her life.

A hollow ache radiated throughout his chest. If only he hadn't kissed her . . .

Scott shook his head as he returned to his desk and sank into the swivel chair. He opened his phone, and his thumb accidently hit the app to open his photos. The photo of him grinning while holding up the fish he'd caught filled the screen, and his heart twisted as he recalled that afternoon—that perfect day—he'd spent on the lake with Brianna. He could still smell the water, feel the sun on his face, and see her gorgeous smile as a light breeze blew wisps of her golden hair around her face. Oh, how he missed her! How he longed to be back on the water with her, talking and laughing together.

With a groan, he swiped his screen and the time and date appeared. Tomorrow was Brooklyn's wedding. He imagined Brianna putting on another pretty sundress and attending the wedding with her arm linked with Taylor's.

He scowled as jealousy devoured him from the inside out. He needed to find a way to get Brianna out of his mind before she drove him to the brink of insanity. He couldn't possibly work with her at the resort if he spent all his time wondering what could have been between them. He wasn't even sure he could go back.

Scott leaned back in his chair and studied his blank computer screen. Suddenly he realized the only way he would ever get over her was to tell her the truth. He needed to drive up to Splendid Lake, look her in the eye, and tell her he loved her. Once he got those words off his chest, he'd be able to move on. At least, he hoped so.

He'd drive to Splendid Lake tomorrow and tell Brianna how he felt. He just hoped she'd give him a chance to talk to her alone.

Brianna stood on the Wallers' deck and gazed at the newlyweds swaying together to "Unforgettable" on the plywood dance floor in the middle of the massive backyard.

That afternoon, standing in a beautiful gazebo, Brooklyn and Cole had been married by the pastor of their community church, and now the trees surrounding the deck magically twinkled with what had to be thousands of white fairy lights. Dozens of round tables spread out around the yard, each one covered with a white tablecloth and a small centerpiece with white daisies and the silk periwinkle roses Ava had told her about.

The bride was stunning in her simple, short-sleeved gown, covered with lace and beads, and her light-brown hair was styled in a french twist and adorned with a lovely tiara and veil. She beamed as she looked up at her groom, so handsome in a traditional black tuxedo.

Brianna's eyes filled with tears as she took in the adoration in Brooklyn's and Cole's eyes. She was so happy for her friends, and she wished them a long and wonderful marriage. Then her eyes moved to the fairy lights, and her heart felt crushed as she recalled the romantic honeymoon cabin Scott created. In her mind's eye, she was standing in the cabin as the gorgeous fairy lights and lit candles illuminated his handsome face. Oh, how she missed him.

"Hi." Ava had come to stand beside her, and she was grateful. Now maybe no one would approach her about the broken engagement. She was sure everyone in town knew about it by now.

Brianna smiled. "The ceremony was beautiful. Brooklyn got the perfect spring day for it. It's warm, the birds are singing, and there hasn't been a cloud in the sky. And her big sister looks stunning, as usual."

"Thank you." Ava touched her abdomen and smiled, and Brianna realized she was glowing almost as much as the bride.

Brianna's eyes widened. "Are you . . ."

Ava nodded, then gave a little squeal. "I am!"

"Congratulations!" Brianna hugged her.

"Please don't share with anyone yet. We've told our parents and Brooklyn and Cole, but that's all."

"When are you due?"

"December. It's really early." She touched Brianna's shoulder. "How are *you*?"

"I'm okay." Brianna nodded toward where her mother sat at a table talking to the Hernandezes and Emma Lang. "Mom is having a good day. I was afraid she wouldn't come, but I was wrong. She was in a great mood this morning, and she didn't give Cassie any trouble about putting on a dress and coming out in public."

"I'm glad Cassie is here."

"She's been a wonderful help."

"That's great." Ava's smile flattened. "We haven't talked since you phoned me about the breakup, and I had only a minute. Have you talked to Taylor?"

Brianna glanced to where he stood with Dylan. "We shared an awkward hello earlier, but we haven't really spoken."

"He'll be fine. He'll get over it and move on. He's a big boy." Ava placed her hand on Brianna's arm. "You did the right thing."

"You're not disappointed with me?"

Ava waved her off. "Of course not. I suspected your relationship was coming to an end, especially when you turned down setting a wedding date. You both have the right to be happy." She gave Brianna's shoulder a gentle squeeze. "Have you heard from *him*?"

"Who?"

"Scott, silly."

"No." Brianna looked down at her shoes and acknowledged an achy longing for him. "But I can't stop thinking about him, and I miss him so much. He hasn't even texted me, but I've almost texted him a thousand times." She bit her bottom lip as the truth bubbled up.

"I love him, Ava. But I feel like we missed our chance. I really hurt him."

"But it's never too late to tell him how you feel."

Brianna shook her head. "You didn't see his face when I pushed him away, and he barely said a word to me after that. It was like our relationship was ruined."

"But you were with Taylor at the time. Now it's different."

"I don't know." Brianna looked out to see several couples had joined the newlyweds on the dance floor. "But I do know you need to go dance with your husband."

Ava shook her head. "He can wait a second. Listen. Don't give up on Scott. If it's meant to be, it will work out." She smiled. "We'll talk again soon."

For a few minutes, Brianna watched as couples began to clog the dance floor, then she made herself a plate of food and milled around making small talk with a few friends she thought wouldn't ask her about Taylor. But when one of them did, Brianna started feeling claustrophobic, much like she had the day of Dad's funeral.

She spotted Cassie talking to some of her old school friends, and her mother was still engrossed in a conversation with neighbors, so this was her chance to slip away. She grabbed her purse and hurried down to the beach, then slipped off her shoes to stroll along the shoreline. She enjoyed the comforting feeling of the soft sand as this time she avoided rocks nipping at her toes.

The afternoon faded into twilight as she looked toward the resort and lost herself in thoughts of the new summer season. The first families would arrive on Friday, and then she could preoccupy herself with the resort, which she hoped would help her cope with losing Scott as well as losing her father. But she had a feeling she'd never get over either heartache.

She continued on her way, passing a few more houses before she came to the Lakeview Inn beach. The sun began to set, sending a beautiful rainbow of colors bursting across the sky as she headed toward home. She stopped for a moment to text Cassie. Her sister had driven them to the wedding in the Tahoe, so she had the keys to take Mom home anyway.

She started walking again, but then slowed when she spotted someone sitting in one of her parents' chairs. Her legs felt like cooked noodles when she realized it was Scott.

He'd come back!

She quickened her pace, and when she approached him, he looked up at her. She pointed to the chair beside him. "May I join you?"

"Suit yourself."

She couldn't tell what the expression on Scott's face meant, but as she sat down and dropped her shoes and purse onto the sand, questions rolled through her mind. She angled her body toward him. "You know, the sunsets here at Splendid Lake are the best in all of North Carolina."

"Is that so?"

"Yes. They're even better than the ones in the Outer Banks." She turned back toward the horizon as silence fell between them, stretching out like a great chasm that broke her heart. Maybe she'd lost him forever. But why was he here?

"How was the wedding?" he suddenly asked.

"Beautiful. Brooklyn and Cole are very happy."

"Good."

They were silent again, and her swirling curiosity was excruciating. She looked over and found him watching her. "You're back?"

"I need to tell you something, and I didn't want to text you or say it over the phone."

She leaned forward in the chair as panic rose in her throat. "Are you pulling out of the deal?"

"No." He shook his head. "This has nothing to do with that."

He looked down at his lap, and her shoulders tightened with worry. When he looked up at her, his handsome face had clouded with what looked like sadness.

"What is it, Scott?" she whispered.

"I need to tell you the truth." He licked his lips, looking forlorn. "I'm in love with you, Brianna. I've known it for a while, but I've been in denial, telling myself I could be just your friend. The problem is I can't deny it any longer. You're always lingering at the back of my mind. You're the one I want to talk to at the end of each day. You're the one I want to tell my hopes and dreams to. I miss teasing you. I miss laughing with you. I miss your voice, your laugh, your stubbornness, your courage. I miss everything about you."

He paused and took a deep, shuddering breath. "I know you've chosen another man, but I hope by telling you how I feel I can get over you and move on with my life." He looked at her with an intensity she could hardly take in. "But as I sit here now, looking at your gorgeous eyes, I doubt I'll ever get over you."

Brianna's throat closed, but her heart opened. She had to be dreaming. But Scott was really sitting next to her, telling her he loved her!

"Scott, you're so wrong about everything." Her voice caught. "I've felt something for you ever since I met you at the bookstore. I was drawn to the way you teased me and laughed when we joked about the books. I felt instant chemistry with you. Then when I came down here to sit on the beach the night of Dad's funeral, I felt like I was suffocating. I was suffering through the worst day of my life, and I needed to get out of the house and be by myself. But then you came along."

She took a breath. "You sat beside me, a quiet support. You were *exactly* what I needed. It was as if you knew me better than anyone, and I didn't even know your name. Yet when you came to the house and told me you wanted to buy the resort, I thought you had manipulated me."

He blinked, and she was almost certain she saw tears in his eyes.

"But that's not who you are," she continued, her heart beating fast. "You've always known what I needed, and you've always put my feelings first. And I love how you take care of me and my mother. You're the most caring, giving, and generous man I've ever known. You're my best friend and my greatest confidant, and my heart broke the day you left. I'm lost without you." She fished a tissue out of her purse and wiped her eyes and nose.

His brow crinkled. "What about Taylor?"

"I broke up with him." She held up her naked ring finger. "I realized I was holding on to him for all the wrong reasons. I was determined to fulfill the commitment I'd made to him when he proposed, but really, I was just holding on to the past. Last week I finally realized we'd grown too far apart, and we want different things. I can't live in the past. I need a future, and I believe my future is you."

He shook his head. "You truly believe I can be your future?"

"Yes. This year has taught me so much. When I lost my dad, I lost a part of myself. But over the last few months, I've realized I'm stronger than I thought I was. I managed to take care of Mom, and with your help, I also saved my home. I thought I needed my sisters here, but I was okay. I also realized what's most important—my family and my home. And through it all, I not only found myself, but I found you. You're *everything* to me.

"I almost called you a hundred times a day since you left. I want to share everything with you. You're the first person I think about in the morning and the last person I think about before I fall asleep at night. You're even with me when I sleep because I dream about you."

He hesitated. "Are you saying you're ready to be with me now?"

"Yes. I'm more than ready." Brianna took his hand in hers. "I love you. I love you more than I've ever loved anyone." She smiled. "And that kiss was incredible. I've been dreaming about kissing you again."

He gave her a devious smile. "I can arrange for that dream to come true."

He scooted his chair closer and shifted his body toward her. She leaned over, and her breath hitched in her lungs as his lips met hers. Happiness blossomed in the pit of her belly, and she lost herself in his kiss as she melted against him.

She looped her arms around his neck and pulled him closer. He deepened the kiss, and the contact made her feel as if all the cells in her body were on fire. She closed her eyes and savored the feel of his mouth against hers.

When he pulled away she smiled. "I'm so glad you're back."

"I'm more than back. I want to live here and help run the resort. And like I said before, I'll commute to Charlotte as much as I need to so I can still help Brad run the firm. But I want my life to be here. With you."

"I'd love that." She took Scott's hand in hers again, and as she rested her head on his shoulder, happiness covered her like a warm blanket.

EPILOGUE

*E*njoy your stay," Brianna said as she handed Mr. Van Dyke the key to cabin seven.

"Thank you," he said. "My family and I are excited to be back."

"We're happy you're here too."

After Mr. Van Dyke left, Brianna peeked into the family room and found Mom reading. She was having another great day and had even walked around the house without the help of her walker. Her physical therapist visits continued going well.

The resort had opened the day before without a hitch. This season would be different without Dad to help her with the boats and marina, and Mom wouldn't be up to doing much for some time yet, but Brianna was grateful for all the help she did have. Cassie and their hired teenagers handled the convenience store and bait shop, their two new hires did all the cleaning, and today Scott was walking the property to see if any guests needed help.

Brianna hadn't stopped smiling since she and Scott found each other again. He'd arranged to stay at the Lakeview Inn all summer, saying, "What if we backed up and tried an old-fashioned courtship? I'd love to call for you at the house for dates, woo you for a while. What do you say?"

She'd found that charming.

Scott planned to have the cabin he wanted built once they had the proposals for the renovations, and he'd already told her he wanted her input on its design. The possibility of their living there as husband and wife before too long was real, but for now, she just wanted to enjoy their growing relationship.

Scott slipped into the room and walked to the check-in desk. "Hi there. I heard I can rent a cabin here."

Brianna leaned forward. "I'm sorry, sir, but we're all booked up."

"That's a shame." He rested his elbows on the counter and touched her nose. "I was hoping I could cook a romantic candlelight dinner for you."

"Oh, if you're cooking, then I can definitely arrange for the use of my very own kitchen."

"Well, we don't want to let *you* cook."

"That's not nice!" She swatted his bicep as he laughed.

"How's it going in here?"

"Busy. How about out there?"

"I had to fix the air-conditioning unit in cabin two. I think we'll have to replace it."

She smiled up at him as a sudden rush of joy slid through her.

"Why are you grinning at me?" he asked.

"Because I'm glad you're here."

"I'm glad I'm here too." His expression grew serious. "Brianna, even when I first came here, I felt like I belonged. It was as if the lake had called me. But you're the one who called me back."

He leaned down, and when he brushed his lips across hers, her heart fluttered as though it had the wings of a thousand butterflies. She lost herself in his kiss, feeling as if she were floating on a cloud.

When Scott broke away, he caressed her cheek. "This place isn't just splendid, you know. With you, it's paradise."

DISCUSSION QUESTIONS

1. After Brianna's father dies, Brianna is frustrated when her sisters go back to their lives on opposite coasts. And she's especially irritated with them after her mother's stroke. Do you think her feelings are valid? Why or why not?

2. Throughout the story, what does Scott learn about himself? How does his past inform his desire for love and family?

3. Lois struggles emotionally and physically after suffering her stroke. Do you know someone who has suffered a stroke or another disability? If so, how did that person cope?

4. Brianna is frustrated when the town's gossip pries about her mother, the resort, and her relationship with Taylor. Have you ever had to deal with gossip? If so, how did you handle that?

5. Cassie and especially Jenna question Brianna's decisions about their mother's care and options for saving the resort. Do you think they have the right to criticize their sister?

6. Lois is reluctant to allow Scott and his firm to make changes to the resort because she fears it will tarnish the Porter family legacy. How would you have felt and behaved in her shoes?

7. Taylor never seems to be around when Brianna needs him. Do you think she makes unfair demands on his time? Why or why not?

8. Have you ever visited a place like Splendid Lake? If you could go anywhere for vacation this weekend, where would you choose to go?

9. Brianna knows her relationship with Taylor has deteriorated, but she struggles to end it because of her recent losses. Have you ever experienced an overwhelming change in your life? If so, how did you adapt to that change?

10. Brianna and Ava have been friends nearly all their lives. They're each other's support, especially during tough times. Do you have a special friendship like that? If so, what do you cherish the most about that relationship?

ACKNOWLEDGMENTS

*A*s always, I'm thankful for my loving family, including my mother, Lola Goebelbecker; my husband, Joe; and my sons, Zac and Matt. I'm blessed to have such an awesome and amazing family that puts up with me when I'm stressed out on a book deadline.

Thank you to my mother and my dear friend Maggie Halpin who graciously read the draft of this book to check for typos. And special thanks to my favorite mechanics, Joe and Zac, who patiently answered my nonstop questions about cars, engines, and boats. I appreciate you so much! And, Zac, we need to get a red (or purple!) Dodge Challenger SRT to share. (Kidding, of course!)

To my dear friend DeeDee Vazquetelles—thank you for reading the proposal and the draft of this novel, along with listening to me constantly drone on about Scott and Brie. I don't know what I'd do without your daily texts and endless emotional support. Your friendship is a blessing!

I'm so grateful to my wonderful church family at Morning Star Lutheran in Matthews, North Carolina, for your encouragement, prayers, love, and friendship. You all mean so much to my family and me.

Thank you to Zac Weikal and the fabulous members of my Bakery

Bunch! I'm so thankful for your friendship and your excitement about my books. You all are amazing!

To my agent, Natasha Kern—I can't thank you enough for your guidance, advice, and friendship. You are a tremendous blessing in my life.

Thank you to my amazing editor, Jocelyn Bailey, for your friendship and guidance. I appreciate how you push me to dig deeper with each book and improve my writing. I've learned so much from you, and I look forward to our future projects together.

I'm grateful to editor Jean Bloom, who helped me polish and refine the story. Jean, you are a master at connecting the dots and filling in the gaps. I'm so thankful that we could work together on this book.

Thank you to each and every person at HarperCollins Christian Publishing who helped make this book a reality.

To my readers—thank you for choosing my novels. My books are a blessing in my life for many reasons, including the special friendships I've formed with my readers. Thank you for your email messages, Facebook notes, and letters.

Thank you most of all to God—for giving me the inspiration and the words to glorify You. I'm grateful and humbled You've chosen this path for me.

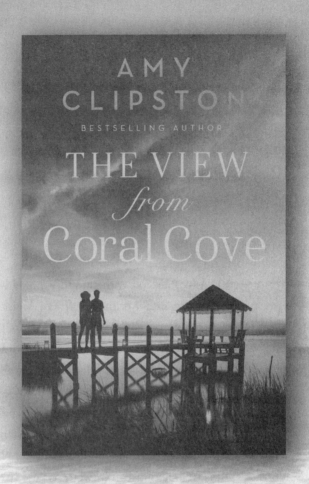

When a jilted romance novelist returns to the small beach town she once loved, she discovers not only inspiration but also a romance to call her own.

Coming May 2022

AVAILABLE IN PRINT, EBOOK, AND AUDIO.

THOMAS NELSON
Since 1798

ABOUT THE AUTHOR

Dan Davis Photography

Amy Clipston is the award-winning and best-selling author of the Kauffman Amish Bakery, Hearts of Lancaster Grand Hotel, Amish Heirloom, Amish Homestead, and Amish Marketplace series. Her novels have hit multiple bestseller lists including CBD, CBA, and ECPA. Amy holds a degree in communication from Virginia Wesleyan University and works full-time for the City of Charlotte, NC. Amy lives in North Carolina with her husband, two sons, and five spoiled rotten cats.

∽৽

Visit her online at AmyClipston.com
Facebook: @AmyClipstonBooks
Twitter: @AmyClipston
Instagram: @amy_clipston
Bookbub: @AmyClipston